The Final Confrontation. . .

Serroi felt her macai stop walking; he shuddered under her, humped his back, fighting the grip on his halter. The bitter orange glow told her it was Charody standing there. She shuddered under her own urge to keep going, the Pull was a torment that never left her; she didn't try fighting it any longer, she wanted this confrontation. She needed it.

"Charody," she said. "I can't stop, I'll take care of the mac, you can camp if you want, come after me later." Her voice came to her ears with so many echoes that she couldn't be sure she was actually saying what she meant. She heard/felt a vibration that might be someone talking at her, shook her head. "Don't say things to me, I can't hear you. There's too much noise in my head."

The macai trembled as the orange light moved away from his head, then resumed his ground shifting long-walk. *Soon,* she thought. *Live or die, this will be finished.*

DANCE DOWN THE STARS

THE DANCER TRILOGY #3

JO CLAYTON

DAW BOOKS, INC.

DONALD A. WOLLHEIM, FOUNDER

375 Hudson Street, New York, NY 10014

ELIZABETH R. WOLLHEIM
SHEILA E. GILBERT
PUBLISHERS

My gratitude to these people for providing information about pregnancy and horses via the SFRT: Dr. Judith Tarr, Deborah Wheeler, Brenda Clough, Jane Yolen, Shiela Finch—and Linda R. Fox for details on weaving.

What Has Gone Before:

THE DANCER'S RISE

Awakened from the tree dream, SERROI finds herself uneasy in the world where she once fit. From the moment she was herself again, the magic force that had faded from the world when she slept uses her as a focus to flow back from wherever it had gone.

And the enemy comes forth. The Fetch troubles her sleep, calling her, calling like a calf to its dam.

As she joins a Company from the Biserica going on Ward to Marnhidda Vos of Cadander, that flow increases, turns to a flood as she heals. She spawns a vast array of new life, nixies for the rivers, dryads for the trees, ariels, fauns, lamias, kamen who are souls of stone, sirens, and many many more. Children are born with new talents. Old forces that had shelled over and lay dormant wake again, arise to walk the earth.

They reach Dander the night that Ansila Vos, Marn of Cadander is killed in a bomb blast. K'VESTMILLY VOS, her daughter, becomes Marn in her turn. With the help of the Company from the Biserica, she takes firm hold of the rule and things seem to be going well enough, but raiders in the hills and an army of attack-ers advancing across the southern plains complicate her life. And the Enemy is busy in the cities. While her forces are busy in the south fighting the invaders, the Cadander Pans (barons with assorted holdings, some economic—as in control of all shipping—some land based) turn on her; PAN NOV (the leader) seizes and imprisons her. She escapes with the help of ADLAYR RYAN-TURRIY (gyes of the Biserica, shape-shifter, mind speaker), ZASYA MYERS (meie of the Biserica, Fire-born chosen, mind speaker), and her consort CAMNOR HESLIN, and rides south to join the army and the General she has chosen, VEDOUCE PEN'S HEIR.

Camnor Heslin is a descendant of Hern Heslin who was Domnor of the Mijloc and Serroi's lover in her first life. This Heslin is a big, clever man with a wonderful, deep voice and an equally deep understanding of the way minds work. K'vestmilly Vos chooses him as her Consort although, at that time, she is in love with Vyzharnos Oram, a poet and rebel against his class who doesn't like her much and has no idea of how she feels. She wants Heslin's intelligence and strength for her daughter; she likes him, but at first he doesn't attract her—it was a choice of the mind, not heart or body.

As K'vestmilly Marnhidda Vos rides from Dander, Vedouce Pen's Heir goes into battle with the invaders, wins a great victory at a cost that would have been higher if Serroi weren't there to heal even the most savagely wounded. As the Marn nears the army, the Enemy strikes at it, Taking over half Vedouce's men; they turn on the others and try to slaughter them. He rallies the remnants of the army, drives the

Taken off in time to get K'vestmilly Vos safe in camp, then the Enemy breaks off the battle and draws the Taken back to Dander.

After consultation, Vedouce Pen's Heir decides to pull back to Oskland in the mountains and rebuild his forces before he marches on Dander.

On the morning of the departure, wearing the Mask of the Marn, K'vestmilly Vos speaks to the weary, angry men, telling them they have fought well and will fight again, not only for her and the life they've known, but also for the future of Cadander since she is carrying a daughter, the next True Marn.

SERPENT WALTZ

Serroi, Hedivy Starab, the gyes Adlayr Ryan-Turriy and HONEYDEW the sprite travel south in a search for the Fetch (Mother Death/the Enemy), the source of the Glory. Hedivy's agents have traced supplies as far as the port city Bokivada on the island Shimzely. Before they can trace the line farther, they are separated and separately captured. Hedivy is taken into a swamp and left with hostages from the Forest. Serroi is carried to the Forest and held, Adlayr and Honeydew escape capture and go hunting for her. Through a series of interlocking events, they meet and start working their way back to the coast.

On the way they meet CHAYA WILLISH, a journeyman weaver, SEKHAYA KAWIN, herbmistress, Chaya's aunt and name-giver, HALISAN WANAYO, harpist and demi-human.

Chaya Willish is betrothed to a journeyman silversmith, LEVAN ISADDO who was close to his master's paper when his master died from a heart attack. Their marriage is on hold until he can find a new master, not an easy thing. The Glory comes into her village, takes over the authorities including the head of her family. To escape being forced into marriage with a Gloryman, she runs. On the way, everything she has is stolen, she is raped, beaten, left for dead in a ditch. On her usual round of visits Sekhaya Kawin has run into trouble with the Glory; in the course of breaking free of this she discovers what has happened to Chaya, collects her and together they head for Hubawern where Lavan was living.

On the way they meet Serroi and her companions, Lavan who's escaping a pack of Glorymen and Halisan the Harper.

Through Halisan, Hedivy learns where the Enemy has her base. He and the others take passage on a ship going to Bagklouss, along with Halisan who has decided to go with them.

TRESHTENY the timeseer is enticed south by a shape-shifting force that takes the form of a dapple gray horse. On the way she encounters Mama Charody and her apprentice Doby. Charody joins her and they all head for Bagklouss and the Enemy/ Mother Death.

Heslin has organized a league of spies called the Web; he has agents watching the Red and Yellow Dans, reporting on the men and supplies delivered to Dander/Calanda; there are even agents in the Pevranamist sending out information on Nov's conferences and other activities. Spider One is a woodworker, GREYGEN LESTAR, who used to be paraplegic and who has been reshaped by Serroi so he can walk, although he has kept that a secret. He collects the reports of the other spiders, passes them on to Heslin. As the Glory tightens her grip on Dander/Calanda, his position becomes increasingly precarious and he plans to escape the cities with his wife SANSILLY and two other families in roughly the same position. K'Vestimily Vos asks Greygen and Sansilly to travel to the Biserica to tell the Prieti Meien NISCHAL TAY what's happening in Cadander and request whatever aid she can give. Having agreed to do this, they leave the city on a stolen barge and some weeks later leave Yallor-on-the-Neck, heading for Southport and the Biserica.

Zavidesht Pan Nov gathers an army and goes marching east, heading for Oskland. Vedouce who is now PAN PEN (his father having been killed) has been training Osklanders to replace as many of the dead and Taken as possible, sends forces west to attack the Nov's reserves and supply lines and to harrass the main force as much as possible. He doesn't have the numbers for a battle in the open, the most he can do is nibble at the fringes of Nov's army and try to slow it down.

One of his snipers shoots into a box on one of the supply wagons. This box contains the Glory's ardors, the bombs that have been devastating Dander and Calanda. There is a huge explosion that kills Nov and most of his officers along with half his army and destroys a good portion of his supplies.

At the moment this happens, back in the Temple in Dander, MOTYLLA NOV, the False Marn, is englobed in a sphere of blue light which rises and darts toward the army, growing larger and more virulent as it flies eastward. The sphere settles over the army and strange things happen. Men shot and killed within the glow get up again and march on, fighting as well as they had when they were alive; some are killed over and over again and still they get up and come on. And any of Vedouce's men who fall into the glow are Taken and turn on their former friends.

Vedouce is forced to retreat.

The sphere rolls on, heading for OskHold.

The Hold is emptied. Vedouce and his men, Pan Osk, his family and as many of his people as are willing to come with him, K'vestmilly Vos the Marn and her people ride out a few hours ahead of the sphere and reach a pass in the Merzzarchars as the blue sphere reaches OskHold.

The minute the blue glow touches the stones of the Hold, there is an explosion that reduces the Hold to rubble. The last thing K'vestmilly Vos sees before she turns to ride into the pass is the small figure of Motylla Nov, the False Marn, standing on the rubble, her head turning as she surveys what she has conquered.

1. Settling In

1

Bagklouss—Tson Kyere

Hedivy Starab was a hunched dark figure in the bow, staring at the houses clustered on the cliffs at the southern arc of the bay, watching them glide closer as the *Ennachul* neared the entrance to the harbor, a narrow gap in the breakwaters marked by an immense stone sculpture of a ship with all sails set. He grunted as Serroi joined him.

She didn't say anything for a while, just watched the sunlight dance off the water and the fishing proas slide in and out of the gap. The voice came into her head again.

MOTHER mother LOOK to your DEFENSES this is MY place MINE

you could have been welcomed with LOVE know now my HATE!

With a deep shuddering sigh, she lifted her eyes to the stone houses on the stone cliffs. This was the Fetch's homeplace, this land. It looked ... ordinary ... so ordinary, it astonished her. She rubbed at her eyespot, turned to Hedivy. "Bagklouss. What I know about the land is two hundred years old and skimpy at best, other than the tongue they speak here. You?"

His hands tightened on the rail. "Not much." After a moment he added, "No reason to."

No reason to. Even at the Biserica. No reason to know

about places so far away. She leaned against the rail and watched the slide of the water as the crew sweated and strained around them, bringing the ship close to the prow of the stone boat, then easing it through a narrow opening in the breakwaters angling from the sides of the bay, their top courses barely breaking the surface.

The *Ennachul* was a broad-bellied merchanter trading out of Tson-Kyere, sole port of Bagklouss, the land where the Fetch had her nest. It would have been better to land somewhere else and smuggle themselves in, but this was the only ship leaving Bokivada on the dawn tide and their need to get away was pressing. She signed. *We'll tweak the truth here and there, pull some moth-eaten dignity about us, try indignation to conceal the holes and hope we get ashore intact. Hope!*

Once the ship was safely through the gap, Shipmaster Yapron Liss climbed to the quarterdeck with a spyglass, stood scanning the wharves and the tracks cut into the stone of the cliffs, tension stiff in his shoulders and belly.

Serroi wrinkled her nose, searched through dim memory for an explanation of that tension; she found none, sighed and went back to scanning the city, following it down curving terraces until it puddled in a hoveltown beside a broad river, scores of naked children running through the gaps between shacks that looked as if a breath would blow them over. Beyond the river there was a swamp thick with graybearded trees and flocks of black-furred birds that rose and settled, rose and settled like smoke on a rainy day. She contemplated the swamp and the myriad water channels running back under the trees. *If we find trouble coming at us, we could go to ground there.*

The sails furled except for the minimum of canvas to give them steering way, the ship crept along among small boats skittering about like water beetles. A square scow with a sweep oar came edging out from behind one of a number of other merchanters already tied up at the wharves. Liss turned his glass on it, smiled and relaxed; he folded the glass and handed it to his aide, a boy who followed him about like a shadow.

The barge slid ponderously across the chop, a man standing in the center, wearing a robe so thickly embroidered it looked as if he stood it in a corner when he took it off, his head encased in a complicated structure of gilded straw, a horned staff in one gloved hand, the other clutching a silvergilt crescent bolted to a pole rising from the middle of the flat bottomed boat.

Liss raised his hand, his lips moved as if he were counting, then he brought the hand sharply down.

The anchor dropped.

A sailor atop the mainmast loosed a weighted line, unfurling a large pennant with the ship's sigil appliquéd in the center of both sides, a second pennant with a sun's rayed face on a black ground snapping out above it.

A sailor blew a loud, flat fanfare of a sort on a complicated horn, a rolling minor wail that went on and on.

Sailors brought Halisan the Harper and Adlayr Ryan-Turriy up from below, escorted them to a cleared space before the mainmast, and dropped the Company's gear beside them.

Two more of the crew appeared beside Hedivy and

Serroi, took their arms and led them to join the others.

Serroi glanced at Adlayr, caught a glint from Honeydew's eye as the sprite peeked through the buttonhole in his shirt pocket. She smiled, then turned to watch Liss and his scurrying aide move to the main deck as sailors from the crew hoisted the man in the robe onboard, paying him the kind of sweaty deference that shouted his importance. Two acolytes followed, thin dour men in knee-length black gowns, their skinny legs marked with scars, their feet bare, the thick horn on the soles scraping on the wood.

The deck tilted very slightly back and forth with the play of the chop. The fanfare stopped, the horn-player tucked his battered instrument under his arm and stared straight ahead. Aside from the background of the noise from the bay, and the ordinary creaks from the rigging, the ship was eerily silent. Waiting.

The weight of the Fetch's presence increased. *Something's about to happen,* she thought. *And we aren't going to like it. I wish I knew . . .*

The newcomer's face was so immobile it might have been made of polished bronze. He raised the horned staff, pounded it on the deck, drawing muffled booms from the planks, intoned, "Barta bar'a'ta barta." His voice was determinedly deep and resonant, as if he'd practiced shouting down holes until he got it right. Before the echoes died, he turned an umber gaze on the Shipmaster and said more sedately, "Yapron Liss."

"Yubbal Canpyan."

These two know each other, Serroi thought. *It's a dance they've practiced a long time.*

"So what do you bring us?"

The Shipmaster reached round and the boy slid a clipboard into his hand. Two crewmen came forward with lidded bowls, clay fired rough, unglazed and heavy. "The manifest and offerings from the cargo, Ó Yubbal." At a gesture from the Yubbal, he passed the clipboard to the tall thin acolyte standing at Canpyan's elbow. "Four passengers only," he finished. "Their papers are with the lists." A sweep of his hand. "They stand there."

The Yubbal gestured at one of the bowls. The Shipmaster took the lid off and stepped aside to let Canpyan unfold the linen cloth and examine the contents. Serroi couldn't see what was in the bowl, had a notion that Liss had herded them where they were for that very reason.

As soon as the Yubbal's polished bronze hands had refolded the linen, Yapron Liss replaced that lid, lifted the second.

When he finished the inspection, the Yubbal stretched out his hands and a second acolyte wiped them with a cloth moistened with rosewater (the scent strong enough to wrinkle Serroi's nose as the wind brought it to her), patted them dry with another. "The Offerings are acceptable. Tie up at the Go Bazip, the doya Baskur will be there to check your manifests and provide hand carts to transfer your cargo to the appointed merchants. Now—the passengers. Doya Tasab, the papers." Hands slipped inside his wide sleeves, he paced toward the small group with a dignity as ponderous as the barge that brought him.

"A motley lot." He spoke over his shoulder to the acolyte. "Read me the first."

"Adlayr Ryan-Turriy, gyes, on Ward to Marnhidda

Vos of Cadander. That's the pale one with the long hair."

The Yubbal lifted a finger. "Cadander?"

"Northland. Glass and leather."

"Interesting. Go on."

"Hedivy Starab, Cadandri, bodyguard. He's the one standing next to the woman with the green skin. That woman is one Serroi, no cognomen, healer, Biserica certified. The other's a Harper, one Halison Wanayo of Shimzely."

"Which is the leader of the group?"

"There is no indication in the papers."

"Ask the Cadandri who he's bodyguard for."

The doya sidled a few steps from his master to stand in front of Hedivy. "Hedivy Starab, Cadandri, bodyguard, whose body do you guard?"

Hedivy was wearing his sullen, stupid look. "Her," he said. "Healer."

The doya made a note on the papers, sidled back and repeated Hedivy's words as if foreign speech could not be allowed to soil the hallowed ears of the Yubbal.

The interrogation continued in that fashion with a deeply absurd seriousness; Serroi chewed on her lower lip and stared intently at the planks.

Line by line the story they'd thrown together was unreeled for the Yubbal, sickness in Cadander, the healer sent to Bagklouss to confer with the herb-women and healers whose fame had reached all the way north, the bodyguard and the gyes were sent as escorts to protect the healer in this long journey and negotiate the way through the various lands they had to cross. Halison traveling because that's what she did, harping her way about the world. It wasn't much of a story, but told in snippets that way its weaknesses were masked.

The doya prodded at the gearsacs, walked round behind Adlayr to inspect his longgun. He didn't quite finger the gyes' weaponbelt, but he eyed it speculatively, then walked back to murmur to the Yubbal.

When the interrogation was finished, Doya Tasab eased the top sheaf of papers loose and tucked them into a pocket of his gown, gave the clipboard to the Shipmaster's aide. A moment later the crew was bustling around the Yubbal, lowering him to his barge, helping his acolytes scramble after him. As soon as the barge was free, the anchor came up and the ship started creeping toward the designated wharf.

Once Shipmaster Liss got his ship tied up, he went overside and began talking with the squat man waiting for him, the Master's aide making industrious notes on the top sheet clipped to the board as he listened to the two men.

Serroi looked up at Hedivy. "Ei vai, what do you think?"

He glanced round the busy harbor. "Don't trust 'em. Should grab a boat . . ." He waved a hand at the small sailboats darting back and forth across the bay, then at the swamp that had caught Serroi's attention. "Head in there and get lost." He scowled as he saw a line of men winding down a cliff path, the sun glinting off the metal molded round their bodies. "Now."

With Honeydew perched on her shoulder, a tiny warm patch trembling against her neck, Serroi watched Adlayr flip over the rail and slice into the water; briefly he was a sleek gray shadow in the green, then gone as he swam for the boat they'd chosen, a small speedy proa. She shifted the strap of her gearsac because it was cutting into her, then glanced quickly around. There were no sailors aloft and none of those hauling cargo about seemed in the least interested in them. Her mouth tightened; it was as if the passengers' fate was so determined that crew and master alike had put them out of mind. Through the spaces between Halisan and Hedivy, who were standing close together to block view of Adlayr going overboard, she could see boxes and bales being hoisted from the hold, loaded onto trucks and wheeled down the gangplank. Shipmaster Liss was calling items in a low voice as they appeared, his aide checking them on the manifest.

Out in the bay a form surged from the water, shifted in mid leap and landed on the deck of the proa. The three men sailing the boat were overside before they recovered from their astonishment. A few breaths later Adlayr had ropes and tiller in hand and was bringing the proa about.

When he reached the *Ennachul*, Hedivy lifted rope coils off a hook, dropped them overside, picked up Serroi and swung her over the rail so she could catch hold and slide down the rope.

Serroi hit the deck and danced out of the way as Hedivy landed behind her. Halisan thumped down, got her harp and herself over to Serroi as Adlayr helped Hedivy push the proa away from the *Ennachul*.

A roar from the ship, then Liss was leaning over the rail. "Get back here, you want to get killed? Kakky, get the Guards."

Hedivy snorted, glanced at Adlayr, raised his

thumb. Adlayr grinned at him. A brisk wind blew across the bay; the proa's sail filled and she picked up speed.

A loud crack, a splinter jumped from the rail. More shots. Serroi dropped flat on the deck, heard the others go down, then Adlayr was shooting. More shouts, sense of confusion behind, boats coming at them, but they'd got too good a start and were gliding into the shadow under the trees before the chasers got close enough to interfere.

YOU think you can ESCAPE me MOTHER you can't escape YOU'RE MINE, I'll have you. I WILL HAVE YOU.

2

ON THE COAST OF THE STATHVOREEN

A candle flickering beside her, night winds howling round the eaves and sliding through cracks in the scraped jelen hide that took the place of glass, stirring the hair on her neck and prickling her skin, K'vestmilly Vos sat at a table in the loft of the Longhouse at Riba Arenqué, writing an account of the past weeks in the journal she was keeping for her daughter, and listening to Heslin, Pan Osk and Vedouce talking round the hearth on the floor below.

Reports were still coming in from Calanda and Dander, dribs and drabs of bad news. The Enemy's hold tightening down. Schools open again, taught by parsonas, children chanting songs no one had heard of before, hymns to Glory. Charnel houses multiplying. Long lines of flagellants. Knife-dancers making the streets lethal while they whirled in their deadly trances. The glasseries and mills shut down, the leatheries slowing their output, boots and saddles and all the rest down to a trickle while hides rotted in the vats because the mixes were wrong, most of the master tanners dead or fled. The river Nixies meaner than before, upsetting any boat or barge that moved away from the wharves or tried to come up the Red Dan. Strange rats running through the warrens, attacking children, sometimes sleeping adults.

The loft floor extended about a third of the building's length, the end closed not with a wall but a low rail. Zasya Myers stood on guard in the shadows near the wall while the Fireborn was a flicker K'vestmilly saw now and then as he rambled about the angled space.

Voices and other sounds came clearly from below.

"Winter will close the passes." Pan Osk's bootheels beat an irritable tattoo on the planks as he walked out his impatience. "First snows will be here before the month's out. We sit on our behinds and that Spros sinks its claws deeper in Dander, Maiden knows how we're going to pry them out, Berkwast sends his spies sniffing around, the minute he scents a weak spot, he's going to be all over us. Heslin, the Mijloc. . . ."

"Will extend its sympathies and do all it can to close its borders tight." Heslin's voice was weary.

K'vestmilly smiled, shook her head; he'd said it before more than once, but Osk wasn't much good at hearing what he didn't want to hear—and every time he thought of all those traitor Pans stripping away his wealth, she could almost see steam come out his ears.

Heslin cleared his throat, tapped his fingers on the table beside his chair. "It isn't getting into Dander that's bothering me now, it's what's coming out. Four

Sleykyn running loose somewhere. And what else? Vedouce, what do your men tell you?"

Vedouce shifted in his chair, the legs squeaking across the floor. His laugh was a humorless rumble. "Farewell. Nothing to keep anyone here. Stathvors in the hills staring down at you, hating you for taking their land and their houses. Fish for breakfast, fish for dinner, fog in your ears and stink in your nose. Sitting around watching the tide come in and go out. Every day more of 'em head for home. Hard to blame 'em." He shifted again. "We're starting to get recruits from the Harozh. Ank's being pushed to his Hold and he can't feed them so he's sending them across. If we can get resupplied with weapons, come spring we can use AnkHold as a base and strike south into Dander, retake the Cities and start prying Cadander loose from the traitors and the False Marn." He coughed as a sputter of smoke blew from the hearth across his face, pulled a handkerchief from his sleeve and wiped his mouth. "If Hedivy and those can locate the Enemy and remove her, or at least fidget her enough so she takes her eye off, we could have a better than even chance. Heslin, if the Mijloc won't send men, what about weapons?"

"Nik. A number of reasons. Defense. Keep the neighbors from getting hold of our best weapons— with Sankoy, Kryland, Assurtilas and Minarka as neighbors, you can see why. And except for a few traders that agitate for it, the Council dislikes the thought of being death merchants. As long as we're prosperous enough without that line, it won't happen." Clink of glass against glass as Heslin poured more wine. "The Neck's where you'll resupply, there are gun shops on half the hills from Shinka to Yallor." Silence while he drank. "Ungh! Miserable vinegar. The Marn thought of that when she sent the messengers to the Biserica. If the Prieti Meien agrees to her terms, the Biserica will do the bargaining and send enough meien and gyes to make sure the goods are delivered, even past the Skafarees. If Nischal Tay agrees. We should know by midwinter."

3

SHIMZELY—BOKIVADA

"Alo, zinya, where you going, so bright and pretty you are?"

Chaya pulled her mouth to a straight line and kept walking, trying to count the turns and ignore the man.

"Snooty are you? You gonna have to learn better, jakaz." He grabbed her shoulder, started to jerk her around to face him.

Terror blinding her, she broke away, pounded along the pavements, turning and turning until she was thoroughly lost. The silence finally brought her out of her panic; she leaned against the nearest wall, gasping and shuddering. The street was empty, the houses around her silent, shut against her but not threatening. *Stupid . . . stupid . . . stupid. Halisan warned me about them, why did I wait so late? Go in the morning, she said, end of the first daywatch is the best, they'll be sleeping then. Get your marketing done, your errands, be home before noon. If your luck's bad one day, run hard around a couple corners, that should do it. There's easier prey in plenty here in Freetown.*

The trouble was, when the snaska grabbed her, the bad time came flooding back, the thieves who beat and raped her, the horrible trip across the wasteland, all the nightmares she still had. . . . "I'll have the dreams again tonight. Poor Lavan. . . ."

Still shaky she pushed away from the wall and looked for the sun. "Ahwu, west is that way. Find the bay, find the Trade Hall."

"We don't exactly have guilds in Freetown, so this doesn't count for much." Freewoman Shisell looked down at the torn, stained certificate Chaya had sewed into her blouse before she left home, the one thing she hadn't lost to the thieves. "Now this . . ." She smoothed her hand across the Harper's note. "This is worth more. Halisan says you've a fair touch and a true eye. She has friends here and respect. T' t' t', I know a person with a loom he's not using. Would you be willing to give him one bolt in three? Just tradecloth, nothing fancy, you could probably do it in your sleep, and it would help establish a market."

"And the yarn? I'll go the bolt if he pays for his yarn. I'll do the buying for my own work."

"Mmm. As long as you stay off brocades and damasks; he won't want to wait forever for his bolts."

"Without Guild certification, there's no point to investing that much time and work."

"Oh, there is a market, Freewoman, but you'd best learn our ways before you try it." She folded the certificate inside the note and gave it back. "You're young and pretty enough. Are you open to liaisons?"

"I am wed and he shares the Harper's house with me. No liaisons. That should be made clear to your friend."

"Too bad; it could have smoothed the way, but things are as they are. I'll inform him of conditions and send a note round by sundown, letting you know if he accepts or not." She got to her feet, a tall thin woman with a shock of coarse gray hair and brown eyes almost lost in the gulleys of her laughlines. "We've got a lodge of sorts here, some other women and I. There's a lunch tomorrow, you might want to come. Freewoman Nyama lives out your way, she's an herbwoman . . ." She chuckled. "Among other things. Useful to know in case you get pregnant. Take the lane three houses in from yours and head wallside, two houses down, hephamin tree peeking over the garden wall, on a hot day you can smell it clear to the bay. That's her. If you want to come, let her know. She's got a guard half the size of a maremar and no one bothers her." She stepped into the hall, looked around, called, "Yane, come here a minute."

Yane was a skinny one-eyed boy with a rakish black patch and a grin wide enough to endanger his ears. "Yee?"

"Escort the Freewoman home. She's new here and didn't know this is a bad time to be out alone."

"Woshi, I'll do that." He caught Chaya's hand and started tugging her along, chattering as he moved. "Once you get sponsored, Freewoman, you'll have a badge and the snaskas'll stay away, 'cause the sponsor he'll have their legs broke they bother one of his."

Chaya smiled, amused by his exuberance, comforted by the warm wiry feel of his hand. "Sponsored?"

"I expect Freewoman Shisell's taking care of that right now. She'll get y' a good 'n and 'splain all 'bout it. You mind me asking where you come from?"

Chaya thought about that for a while, letting him lead her through the halls and down the stairs to the sidewalk. "No," she said finally, "but you wouldn't know the village, it's a pimple on the land's face called Hallafam."

He slapped his side and gobbled laughter. "Pimple. Land's face. I like that. I like it. Mind 'f I tell me friend? He makes songs, joke songs a lot."

"It's yours, Yane. Why not?"

As they moved through increasingly crowded streets, she was nervous at first. He was only a boy, what could he do? She soon saw that who and what he was didn't matter; the simple fact that he was with her made people look at her differently. She relaxed and began to enjoy a brisk, odor-filled, noisy afternoon.

"Do you know Freewoman Nyama?"

"Yee, sure."

"Take me by her place on the way, hm?"

"Can do."

The prickly mint smell of the hephamin tree filled the narrow lane; a featherduster of pale leaves with batches of the large red hephaberries peeped about the dun wall, adding a touch of color to the dull face with which buildings fronted the world here in Freetown.

"You see the bell pull?" Yane pointed at a large bronze berry dangling at the end of the pull-chain. "One yank means you sick, two a problem you got to talk about, three you jus' visitin'."

"I have it." The weariness flooding back into her sounded in her voice. "Thank you."

He was quick to hear what she didn't say and took her at a trot to the Harper's house, left her with a grin, running off before she had a chance to say anything or pass him a coin for his efforts.

* * *

Chaya leaned against the door a moment, eyes closed, fatigue like weights strung about her body. She knew a little more now about what her life might be for the next few months. Beyond that . . . She drew in a long breath, pushed away from the door. Beyond that she didn't have to look right now. "Sekhaya," she called. "Thazi, you home?"

No answer. The house felt empty. Se climbed the stairs to their bedroom, changed into working clothes and went down to the kitchen garden she was putting in beside the back door.

It was good to dig in the earth again, turning it over, loosening it, working in dung from the stables, bringing it back to life and fertility. Her own kitchen garden was the result of generations of putting back and fertilizing and working and working until there was a bed of black soil deep enough to drown in; the tubers, greens and other food that came out of it had a flavor she missed in food she bought in Freetown markets. And everything was so expensive. The money the Harper had left with her was melting fast enough to frighten her.

There was nothing planted in the garden yet, though she was almost ready for the first settings. Some onions, of course, wefi and homboes for salads; this was farther south than Hallafam and sheltered, she might be able to get in a crop of yams and other tubers by first frost. There was honey in the market. Lavan liked honeyed yams. *I hope he's all right. And Sekhaya. Feels good to be by myself for a while. So many people here. . . . Lavan is excited, he likes the chop and change here. I don't know what I think. No choice now. Not while the Glory's out there. Halisan said the Forest was still free and she didn't think the Glory would get*

much of a hold here. If it does, what are we going to do?
What can we do . . .?

4

SOUTHPORT—ON THE WAY TO THE BISERICA

As the *Wanda Kojamy* turned into the Degelea Gulf, the deep incurve of the western ocean that led to Southport, Sansilly leaned over the rail and waved to the silkar girl who'd crossed the Sinadeen with them, riding the bow wave of the *Wanda Kojamy*. The slim creature leapt from the water in a shimmering emerald arch, flipped over and came up again, waving a last time before she followed the others back to the open water.

"You'd best go below, Wana Lestin."

She turned to see Shipmaster Am'litho standing behind her, arms folded across his burly chest. "It's such a lovely day."

"But an unlovely coast, Wana. The Krymen will be watchin' and thinkin'. If there's a fight, you leave it to me 'n my men, eh?"

Sansilly slipped into the tiny cabin, trying not to wake Greygen. The crossing had been hard on him. The first few days of the voyage, he alternated between nausea and astonishment; he'd been fine on the river, even while Biddiya's boat crabbed down the coast to Yallor, but as soon as he couldn't see land any longer, the long waves of the open sea and what they did to the *Wanda Kojamy*'s movement proved more than he could take.

"Sansy?"

"Zhalazhala, Greg, I thought you were asleep. 'Twon't be long now. Am'litho says we'll reach Southport about three days on, barring trouble."

A long wavering sigh, then Greygen said, "Sansy, I don't know if I can face this again. Maybe we could stay here. Bring the boys out when this is over."

"Hm. I don' like jumpin' 'fore I see where m' feet'll go. Ask me again after we been here a while."

The *Wanda Kojamy* sped along the Degelea Gulf, her motion exaggerated by her haste. Greygen groaned and spewed, Sansilly held his head and wiped his face, too busy and too worried to bother with what might be happening on deck. Now and then she heard a flurry of yells, several thumps, felt shudders running through the ship, but the *Wanda* didn't stop and each time the noises settled to the routine creaks and groans.

On the third day, the motion eased, and Greygen sighed, stretched out and went to sleep. Sansilly grimaced at the noisome bucket, picked it up and left the cabin.

There was a relaxed feeling on deck, the sun was low and land was a blue line on the horizon ahead of the ship. A sailor grinned at Sansilly, took the bucket, tied a rope to the bail, dunked it a few times and brought it up clean.

"Thanks, Jy. How long now?"

"Two, three hours."

"Doesn't look like you took any hits."

"Nope, worked the bow catter a couple times, chased 'em off." He scratched at his stubbly beard. "Easy run, this'n."

"How often do you do this?"

"We gen'rally make a turn-round ev'ry three months or so. D'pends on cargo and how many stops we got."

"Zdra zdra, thanks, Jy." She patted his arm, smiled and went below.

Southport was a tiny place with huge warehouses and bigger wharves than Yallor. It was a transfer port, a funnel where goods poured in from all over the world and flowed out again with new owners, a safe port, watched over by the Biserica and its meien and gyes—and a huge rammed earth wall to keep out the raiding Krymen.

Leaning heavily on Sansilly's shoulder, Greygen emerged into a cool, pleasant twilight. His knees wanted to fold on him, but he set his teeth and kept walking, his eyes on the planks slanting onto the wharf, solid and unmoving.

Am'litho took a minute from his unloading and came over to them. "Your gear's piled over there, pick it up when you're ready. No worry, whenever you come, it'll be all right. You'll be wanting the Varou, that's what the Biserica calls its office, pass between those two warehouses. There's a lane behind them, go 'long it till you reach the main street. Turn north along that till you see a big stone building with the Maiden carved over the door. That's what you're lookin' for."

"Thanks. Appreciate the help."

They moved on, slowly, Sansilly not complaining though he knew his grip on her plump shoulder must be paining her.

One of the Fenek sailors strolled over. "Ha'ya, Wana. Like I said. Southport."

Sansilly grinned at him. "Like you said, Jy. Time to give me a hand here?"

"Better'n a hand." His teeth glinted in the lanternlight. " 'Nother leg, eh?" He brought his hand around, flourished an intricately carved cane. "Lean on this, Wano, no ground's gonna hit you in face."

"All that work, Jy. How can we . . .?"

"No problem, pass the time, better nor braidin' rope. Play pretty, Wana. Din't y' mama teach you to thank a man for a present?"

Sansilly thrust the cane into Greygen's hand, grabbed Jy, gave him a hug and a kiss that sent his eyelids fluttering. "And that's a thank you won't forget." Chuckling at the young sailor's embarrassment, she took Greygen's arm and helped him down the ramp.

Greygen closed his hand tight about the cane's handle and thumped along, weak tears stinging his eyes. He was angry at Sansilly for the exuberance and effusiveness that men were always misreading, angry at his body for letting him down; he knew how stupid it was, but he couldn't help it. His hands were useless things, weak and trembling, he couldn't protect himself, let alone his wife. He thought he'd come to terms with that after the accident, but getting his legs back had changed things, he was a whole man now, he should . . . He ground his teeth and chased his thoughts back to the practical. *Between those two warehouses and down the lane. . . .*

The Maiden figure was carved in deep relief, serene and smiling. They stood on the sidewalk and looked at her a moment; it was like coming home, to see her like that. Sansilly sighed and pressed close to Greygen, her warmth and her energy giving him strength, pushing aside his angers. He hugged her against him for a moment, then shifted more of his weight onto the cane. "Time, Sansy. Let's go."

5

IATSON PASS IN THE ASHTOPS—ON THE WAY TO BAGKLOUSS

Centuries of foot traffic had beaten the unpaved trade road half a foot below the level of the slopes of the Kirojens; Treshteny and her companions toiled up to the pass called Iatson, the snow-streaked peaks rising high above them, the summits mostly lost to sterile clouds. Up and around, higher and higher they went, walking now because the fodder was so scarce and the last of the corncakes they'd packed were being saved for emergencies.

Horse had shrunk to half his original size and taken the shape of a mountain rarga; his curly horns glinted like obsidian in the pale, hot sun, his split black hooves clicked and clacked on the pounded earth of the track. Fascinated by this new shape, Yela'o the baby faun trotted beside him, his own tiny hooves clicking and clacking in double time.

Mama Charody was smaller and denser also; she made Doby keep hold of her hand as she stumped upward, feeding into him trickles from the force she drew from the earth. In her other hand she held the lead rope of the string of packhorses; it was a conduit also, feeding more trickles of that force along the braided leather and into the four beasts trailing behind her.

Following close behind them, hardened by the trek

south, moving with the measured, minimal stride that long walk had taught her, Treshteny looked into the earth and saw that force branching out, green as baby Yela'o, an inverted tree spreading deep into the mountain, gliding along beneath Charody. The mountains' time was long and slow beneath the unregarded flit of vegetable life across their slopes, soothing and comfortable. Resting on this tick-tock of centuries, she moved through the hours without thinking about them.

Toward evening the track flattened and began a sinuous dance between the peaks.

Iatson Pass.

The entrance to Bagklouss.

Bagklouss, the Land of Mother Death.

Treshteny blinked, lifted her head and stared anxiously about. "Go," she cried, and began stumbling forward, hands groping before her, eyes blind with panic.

Mama Charody dropped the rope and caught her wrist as she ran past, pulled her around so she could grab the timeseer's other hand and hold her still. "What is it, Teny, what do you see?"

"The mountains," Treshteny whispered. "Moving ... explosions, hot, so hot, so hot ..."

"Zdra zdra, we hear you. Quiet now. We'll go as fast as we can. If we wear ourselves out, what good will that do? Horse, get back in shape so you can carry her." She swung the boy onto the first of the packhorses, handed him the rope. "Doby, don't let them run themselves out. I'll be coming 'long behind, nik, lad, don't worry, we'll be all right, now get going." The mountain rumbled. "Zdra zdra, old heap, we're getting off you fast as we can."

2. Tserama Spirit Reader

Tserama strode along the Sacred Road, enjoying the late Spring sunshine, the feel of the stone setts beneath her bare feet, the touch of the errant breeze against her face, the tickle of the small hairs escaping from the high twist into which she'd coaxed the longer strands.

She was a lean woman of forty some years, short in the waist with long wiry legs that scissored off the miles at a pace that looked more leisurely than it was. Her travel clothing was worn and old, but comfortable and easy to move in, loose black trousers cut off at the knees, a sleeveless black blouse made from two squares of cloth sewed up the sides and across the shoulders, leaving a hole for the head. Over that she wore a tsadar, which was a heavily embroidered length of coarse woolen cloth with a slit for the head in the middle and a hood of the same cloth, also embroidered, attached to the slit. The embroidery was separated into bands, each representing a year in her life; starting with her birth at the hem on the front side, the bands marched upward, year by year, moving over her shoulders and partway down the back, marking her first visions, the Signdreams at puberty, her apprenticing to the old Spirit Reader Maraban and each of the yearly Sacred Journeys they made to-

gether, her induction in her fifteenth year as Spirit
Wife to Danoulcha, the village that became hers
when Maraban fetched her from the Ytama Round,
her children as they came one a year for the next ten
years, the passing of the Wedding Bracelet to the
next Spirit Wife, her first Journey alone when
Maraban's legs would no longer carry her on the
Round, and all the years since then. The hood's images were different, they were her totems and the sig-
ils that marked her as a Speaker to Spirits.

Because the tsadar was lined with suppa cloth
which shed rain like a waterfowl's fur, it made a better than average shelter for those nights when she
had to sleep rough. This afternoon was hot, but it
was easier wearing the tsadar than carrying it, so she
ignored the sweat that crept down her temples, slid
down her neck, pooled in the hollows of her
shoulderbones and oozed beneath her arms. She sang
as she swung along, her staff thumping on the stone
beside her, a two-note walking song more sound than
words, without much sense to it, but a carrying
rhythm. "Long road," she sang, a wildness in her
hoarse alto that matched the solitude around her.

Long road ode ta ray   rum tum   caaaann dle time
Thong toed ode da day   rum tum   saaaan dal time
Prong load ode pa hay   rum tum   haaaann dle time
Strong goad. . . . .

On and on, stump and sing along the Sacred
Road—a band of stone that rambled about the hills
of the Lakelands, wide enough for Tserama's feet and
the beat of her staff, but not an inch wider. It had
carried her from Danoulcha to the hill called Briada
Ri, then Yontan Ri and Doskran Ri.

When the day was nearly gone, she could see the posts and lintel of the shrine on Skyoga Ri standing dark against the sky a few miles on. She stopped the song, pulled a blade of grass from the verge and walked on, chewing it to take the edge off her thirst.

Her value to the Hill Spirits was her Talent for sorting what the Sem Ris said into coherent signs and images in a way that they could not. They were like a flesh man who could gather flour and honey and fruits and wood and fire, but had to find someone else to make the tarts he loved. And there were resentments that had to be healed or the Hill Spirits would grow too hot and too dangerous. She had to understand and see that those injuries were made right. It was what she did, her place in the rhythm of life.

"Sem Ri Skyog," she called, bowed, straightened, knocked the butt of her staff against the Road. "Sem Ri, Tserama Spirit Reader greets you. Open the Way. Let me come to you."

The air stilled. A moment later a swath of grass on the hillside turned over to show the silver side and flattened in a path that led up the slope. The Sem Ris were tricksy beings, vain and malicious, but they had their little ways and held to them more rigidly than any man would do; after two score years of this she knew them well enough to step onto the path without fear and climb to the summit without hurry or fuss.

She could feel the Sem Ri tickling at her, tasting her, could feel the layers and flows of it, the growing strength. The first three Sem Ris had been lazy and half dormant, but Skyog had lots to say and was impatient to get started. She ignored the prods. It never paid to let them think they could push you.

Skyoga Ri was one of the tallest and craggiest of the Spirit Hills in the circle round Danoulcha and the path was long, with places where she had to tuck the staff under her arm and climb up notches cut into a rock face or slide along a narrow ledge. There were easier paths to the top, but Skyog always made her take this one, it was just one of his ways.

When she reached the summit she settled herself between the stone uprights, legs crossed, hands on her knees, the staff angled out past her left foot. "Speak, Sem Ri Skyog."

She felt it nestling around her like a kaya scratching around, planting its furry butt against her leg, its tail flicking back and forth across her face. There was a fluttery sigh inside her head, then Skyog began unreeling its tale.

feel/taste of a bird ... land running beneath ... a swatch of molten gold shifting and flowing ... a drench of blue ... screaming, broken bits of flesh folk figures swirling tumbling ... pain as jagged forms of red and black ... smell of bread baking ... rotten fruit fermenting ... a man's face twisted in anger ... a woman with legs raised, head of a baby showing ... point of a stick jabbing and jabbing at the earth, feet beside it, a blur above them ... need need need ... water eddying and bubbling, gliding along, flowing over in a fall that seemed about knee high ... anger anger anger ... twisted, distorted shapes filled with energy and anger and other things as powerful for which there were no words in any language she knew ... desire desire desire ... the world gone black and white, rushing along, smells exploding in the head ...

The flow of sensory impression and otherness went on and on, raining into her head. Her tongue rasped across dry lips and thirst was sandpaper rubbing her throat, but she pushed the discomfort away and listened/read.

On and on the Sem Ri went—until she was a waterskin plumped to overflowing, until she could take not another drop.

Skyog burped, then pushed at her and prickled at her to give the tale shape and coherence.

"Garos," she said. "I will have garos. I must have garos."

A burnt feather smell, a tingle of a storm gathering force, a grumbling rumble like the Gopar Stengi's belly the morning after a feast.

She tilted her head back as far as she could, opened her mouth and waited.

Amber drops squeezed from the air, falling onto her leather tongue, the drops merging quickly into a delicately flavored liquid that took away the pain, the thirst, the weariness, as it slid down her throat.

When the flow stopped, she closed her eyes and began reshaping and rearranging the polysensual data the Sem Ri had poured into her, building fragments into wholes and chaos into an ordered tale.

Jeylza the Lionness, the largest of the moons, was full of face and directly overhead when she began what Spirit Readers called The Chastening of Story.

Jeylza the Lionness was sliding behind the Ashtops when she spread out her hands, placed each palm flat against the cold stone of the Gate and reeled the Tale out again for the pleasure of the Sem Ri Skyog. When she finished, she curled into her tsadar, pulled the hood over her face and went to sleep.

* * *

Irritable and still bloated from the feeding, the Sem Ri Skyog pinched and poked Tserama awake as soon as the sun peeked up over the horizon in the east; it was finished with her and wanted to see her off its ground as soon as possible.

She sat up, yawned, moved to a cistern built beside the Gate, used the tin cup chained to the rim to scoop up the rain water trapped in the basin. She drank deeply, scooped up more water and splashed it over her face, emptied the rest on the Sitting Stone; humming a ragged tune she filled the cup and emptied it again and again, darkening the stone uprights and the ground around the seat as well as the Stone itself. When the basin was empty, she bowed to the sun, caught up her staff and started down the trail she'd climbed the night before.

Before she stepped onto the Sacred Road, she turned. "Sem Ri Skyog, may your wrongs be righted and your year be filled with goodness."

She cocked her head to one side, listening. There was a grumble and a rumble, a feel of a large hairy beast turning over, then something like a snore.

Chuckling to herself, she started off along the road, singing her rumtum song again. There was a farmer's house a little way on, she'd beg breakfast there, then it was back on the Road again, heading for Modmor Ri. Then there was Drundil Ri, Parbya Ri, Satchu Ri and last of all Drinby Ri. The nine Spirit Hills of the Danoulcha Round.

The house had a more prosperous look than the last time she passed here, instead of thatch there were pantiles on the roof, their orange-red glistening with the water the farmwife had thrown on them in her morning clean. And two small rooms had been added like ears sprouting from the househead. A small naked boy was playing in the puddles from the roof washing, plastered with mud with his wispy hair standing in peaks. He was just born last year when she came by, a sickly mite, the first boy after five girls.

She tapped her staff against the door jamb. "Spirit Reader Tserama, kye Kyada. Come to beg a meal of you."

Silence from the house. Tserama wrinkled her nose. Kyada was in there, she could feel her. Feel fear and anger and doubt. She shrugged and turned to smile down at the baby in the mud. "Nobody home, Karan-nini. Your mama gone to the fields?"

There was a flurry of steps, Kyada came rushing past her, snatched up the baby and ran back into the house, slamming the door and barring it.

Tserama raised her brows. Tsan pyya, there was still a need to do her duty. "House of Dustog, hear me," she called out, making her voice loud enough to reach through the wall and the planks of the door. "The Sem Ri Skyoga has complaints against this house. The goats of Dustog are eating its grass and messing on its earth. This will stop or by its sworn word, the next goat dies, the second after carries the jiji plague to this House and those who live here."

Still no answer. Tserama shrugged and moved to the well. She raised the bucket, filled the clay cup left on the well coping and drank. With a glance at the house and another shrug, she broke the cup against the stone, let the shards drop and walked away, doing it herself this time, rather than leaving it to the farmwife.

The maize in the field nearest the Sacred Road was

high enough to have ears plumping out. She chose half a dozen, dropped them into an inside pocket, wrenched loose another and made her way back to the road, shucking the ear, chewing the tender green kernels from the cob.

As the sun rose higher and higher and the last of the cobs was behind her, Tserama went to chewing Skyog's Tale. There were things in it that meshed with the tales of the other Sem Ris. Things connected to the Tale of Pangya's Sacrifice and the Transformation of the Prudjin. These new bits were twists on what she knew, a pushing beyond, a presentiment of pain to come combined with the coldness from several of the farm families, though Kyada was the first to refuse even to talk to her. It was unsettling. She didn't know how to deal with this.

Pangya's Sacrifice

The Dread Nyin of Dropai Cave came to the woman in the straw where she slept and whispered to her, Please me, Pangya, and all that you wish will be yours.

It was true that there was a man in her village who turned away when he saw her looking at him, Agisov the Gopar's son, beautiful as morning, whose flute could charm a demon's breath into a lover's kiss.

It was true that she had rags for her back and dust for her shoes.

It was true that the Riya-riyon had cursed her father so he drank his life from a jug in the Pothouse and left his land to do as it chose and it chose to walk away.

It was true the Riya-riyon had cursed her with her father's thirst, not for beer, but for all the things that others had and she did not.

She walked the long way, the hard way to the Ashtops in the Kirojen Mountains where the Caves were found, the Breathing Holes of the World's Heart. They are dangerous to the body and to the soul, yet Pangya followed a trail that many had walked before her.

She lay in the dreadful dark and did this and that and all that the Nyin wished of her and when the sun rose, she walked home again.

Agisov the Gopar's son smiled on her and sent his uncle to call upon her kin.

Her father slept in a ditch and died of a brul bite, but the brul was heavy with young and grew drunk on the blood she drank and slept beside her kill. Pangya sold the snake and her unborn brood to a healwitch for a sack of gold.

When her time came, Pangya the Wife of Agisov bore a daughter. Though Agisov frowned on her for not giving him a son, she was pleased. She dug the afterbirth from the hole beneath the doorstep, wrapped it with the child in the skin of a baya and walked the long way, the hard way to the Dropai Cave, laid the bundle in the dark and came away again.

This is whispered in all the villages of the Ston Gassen, the Land of a Thousand Lakes, but who could do anything against Pangya the wealthy? The Nyin of Dropai Cave protects her and Agisov the Gopar's son who is Gopar now will hear no evil spoken of her. Wealth is hers and seven sons and followers who drink from her cups and eat at her board. It was only a daughter, of course, nothing all that bad had happened to the child. That too was known, because the girl was seen at the Dropai Cave. Nyin-fed and Nyin-reared she grew up wild as a drugger pag.

The Transformation of the Prudjin

The Child without a Name watched a pag sow walk past with her paglets trotting single file behind her.

She grunted like the paglets and tried to follow. The Dark said to her, That is not your way. Do not do that.

She watched a brulsnake open her mouth and swallow her young to protect them from threat, watched them come wiggling forth when danger was gone.

She lay upon the ground and wriggled after the brul. The Dark said to her, That is not your way. Do not do that.

She watched wild bayas mate and tend their pups, feeding them from mouth and dug.

She crawled to the baya dam, whining and begging as the pups had done. The Dark said to her, That is not your way. Do not do that.

The Child without a Name watched men and women come furtively to the Cave to seek the Nyin's Favor. She followed one of them as he left, like the paglets had followed their dam, but he screamed when he saw her and ran too fast for her to catch him. The Dark said to her, Listen and learn from these. They are your kind.

The Child without a Name watched the others come and go. She crept close as she could without driving them off and listened to the sounds that came from their mouths and when they were

gone, cried those sounds into the Dark. And the
Dark was pleased with her.

And year turned on year and the pile of bones
from the meat that the Dark brought to her grew
larger. And the blood flower bloomed. And the
Dark nuzzled at her.

In her fifteenth year, the Dark shuddered and
closed around her, air burned her, rivers of force
drove up through her body. It was the ReBirth. It
was the Mother ReEntering the world.

The Nameless No-More Child stretched and
twisted, screamed in a pain beyond anything her
mind could hold. She took the Dark into herself,
she took all the Darks from all the Caves into herself, she reached her hands into Earth's Soul and
ripped a great dripping piece of Earth's Soul free
as she ripped the flesh from the beasts the Dark
had given her, ripped it loose and drew it into herself.

AND KNEW

AND HAD A NAME—THE PRUDJIN

AND CRIED OUT, MOTHER! I AM HERE.
WHERE ARE YOU? COME TO ME.

And heard the silence.

And wailed her need and her sorrow.

And reached beyond the Caves into the Land
and the Lands beyond.

And thus it was that the Prudjin came unto the
Land, Speaker of the Goddess and Fount of all
Good—so said the Goppal Li, highest priest of
all the priests in chapel and shrine—blessed by
the Prudjin with Power and Right—so said the
Goppal Li.

Tserama wasn't much interested in what games the
Prudjin played with the priests and their like or with

folk in other lands, her duties lay with the land in the
Ston Gassen, keeping the Balance for Danoulcha, but
there were hints in this round of Tales that The Dark
Hunger was turning her eyes on the Covenant of
Women, the healwitches, the midwives, the diviners,
the spirit and earth readers and all women's rites
joined to fertility and the Sacred Round of birth and
death. That She meant to devour the powers and di-
vert the rites.

Even so little as a year ago Tserama would have
brushed that aside as nonsense, a Sem Ri with a spir-
itual bellyache, but she'd seen things beginning to
happen, the tiny green shoots of strange plants that
had already taken root in her village and in the farm
houses around it. Twice this time as she Paced the
Round, she had been denied all but a grudging drink
of water and in one case she looked back to see the
scowling woman break the cup she'd used into shards
and cast it away. And then there was Kyada, whose
fear was an astonishment.

New things. New ways. Tserama wasn't used to
seeing things around her change like this and it made
her nervous. 'Twas true that people died or ran away
or lost their money or their land, took wives from
strange villages. Houses burned, storms knocked
them down, or they rotted, new ones were built.
Readers were born in one Round, apprenticed in another. But that was the Great Round, that was a
rhythm that had been there from before the beasts
forgot to speak.

She could remember sitting on the floor of Maraban's house, listening to her teacher's grandmother tell
of her grandmother's time when the spirits seemed to
grow pale and sleepy as if the Wasting Disease had
got them like it did some children. It was a bad time,

she said, the seasons were all wrong, the rain came at harvest and it was dry for the planting and the bayas turned wild and attacked their masters and the paya packs came down from the Kirojens and savaged the flocks and the grapes withered before they plumped and many people stared and some went wild as the payas and killed their own kind. And the priests blamed the Covenant of Women and there were burnings. But in the end the Balance came back and the rhythms were right again and people were ashamed of what they had done and never spoke of it.

The Spirit Readers remembered because the Sem Ris wouldn't let them forget. Tserama flicked a fly off her nose. That was something else to chew over. No sly jabs about the Wild Time in this Round's Tales. It could mean there was another Wild Time coming . . . mmm . . . could mean a lot of things. She walked on, thinking sometimes, sometimes just walking and singing, raiding fields for food when the sun was sitting on the Ashtops, wrapping herself in the tsadar to sleep the night away.

Late on the fifth day after Skyoga Ri, when the posts and lintels of the shrine atop Modmor Ri were black against the setting sun, the Road jerked like a twitched rope and nearly threw her off her feet. A moment later the sky was filled with dragons and ariels and the shy shapsa who lived in the trees and rocks.

At the edge of her mind's ear she heard the high, singing words. *SHE COMES. THE MOTHER COMES.*

3. Stalkings

1

BAGKLOUSS

Hedivy swore as the proa's float snagged on a submerged stump, the sails shuddered, the masts groaned. Adlayr snatched the boathook cleated below the rail, shoved the hook under the float, dug at the rotten wood of the stump, popped the float free, dropped to his knees as the boat slued under him, then surged forward.

Serroi knelt in the bow, steadying herself with her hands on the rail, frowning at the waterway ahead. The trees grew taller, thicker, closer together. They couldn't stay on this boat much longer; already the canopy was beginning to close in, stealing the wind from the sail. They were moving slower and slower and before long they'd be lucky to creep ahead as they pushed against the sluggish current. She could hear yells behind them, muffled and anechoic— which told her the shouters weren't out on the bay, not any more. She wrinkled her nose. "This might not have been the best idea."

The Harper got to her feet. "Any choice?"

"I suppose not."

Halisan kicked at the long skirt, untied the placket laces and slid it over her hips. Beneath, she wore hightop boots and knee pants, linen dyed a dark blue. At Serroi's quizzical look, she laughed. "Traveling clothes, Healer; you never know what's going to dump you on your ass, so I like it well covered." She rolled up the skirt, slipped it into her knapsack. "You want that skirt shortened? If you have to run . . ."

"Ei vai, if you will, but what about that?" She pointed at the harp case sitting on the deck.

"Ahwu, harp first, then the skirt." Halisan closed her eyes, a vertical crease appearing between her brows as she lifted the case by its shoulder strap, swung it shoulder high. The case vanished in slices as if it slid between two curtains onto a shelf that only she could see. Without comment, she knelt and used her belt knife to cut Serroi's skirt to a length just below the knees.

The proa was starting to struggle as the sail fluttered despite all that Hedivy could do to chase the elusive airs. Adlayr glanced back, reached for his shirt buttons.

Serroi kicked away the circle of cloth. "Nay," she called. "Save for that later, Adlayr. If we need it. Where's Honey?"

The sprite swooped from the top of the tallest mast to hover in front of Serroi. Honeydew come to you, poet poet poet, eeee, Serreee.

Honey, could you go up and take a look? We want a place to walk if we have to leave the boat.

Honeydew can do. The sprite worked her wings and powered up, riding the wind gusts aloft. A glimmer hovering above the treetops, she looked back along the curving bayou. Honeydew see long skinny boats coming, lots and lots of paddlers, fast, Serree, faaaaast. And lots of guns too. She fluttered higher, zipped ahead of the laboring proa. Baaaad news, Serree, this water pinch off round a couple bends. Goooood news, I see tree roots 'n some grass and maybe something you could walk on . . . wait, something else . . . ahh, tell Hev to go round second bend, push the nose in mud and all you take off . . . Honeydew thinks help it's coming . . . Her mosquito voice broke off and she darted out of sight past the tops of the taller trees.

Serroi jumped up, swayed as the proa slid round the first bend, yelled, "Hev, Honey says we've hounds on our tail and getting close and no water ahead. We'll have to ditch the boat."

He grunted. "Where?"

"Next bend, there's land and roots we can run on."

He scowled at the sail. "If we can make the next bend. . . ."

Serroi grabbed for the rail as Hedivy drove the bow into the mud, then went over the rail after Halisan, landing in ankle-deep water and sucking mud. Feet squelching in the black ooze, she ran a few steps onto the interwoven roots of the trees, stopped beside Halisan as Adlayr and Hedivy shoved the proa from the mud and sent it out into the middle of the bayou where the current began inching it downstream. Where it would finish she couldn't tell, just hoped it would be misleading. Adlayr ran past her, longgun in his hand, Halisan loped after him, moving easily over the roots and mud. Serroi trotted behind Halisan, while Hedivy followed, on guard behind them.

They moved deeper into the swamp, running blind, sloshing through mud and water, running over strips of sand, tough sawgrass twisting about their ankles.

Honeydew came swooping down, followed by a flier with wide leathery wings, a male with a crest of orange-red hair, dressed in feathers and bits of leather. Serroi blinked; the memory he evoked was so

strong that for a moment she was transported back to
the Plateau, the trek with Hern . . .

*The odd little creature hovered above her, a tiny
man with long thin arms, talons instead of feet, leathery wings covered with fine gray-brown fur. Longer
fur was tufted over his ears and along the outside of his
limbs, gray-brown fringes that rippled in the breeze
stirred up by the sweep of his wings. Having gathered
his courage, he spilled some air and swooped closer, his
round dark eyes lively, bright with curiosity and intelligence. His small mouth pursed and he uttered a few
high humming sounds.*

*Moving very carefully, Serroi pushed off from
Hern's shoulder until she was sitting upright.
"Friend," she said, singing the word. At the same time
she projected as warm a friendliness as she could dredge
up out of herself, friendliness and reassurance.*

*The flier retreated to the far side of the wash, wings
beating furiously for a few seconds, then he was gliding
again, riding the current of air flowing along the
wash. Bright eyes watched her as he glided back and
forth, back and forth, then she heard a modulated
squeak; after a few more repetitions she resolved the
squeak into words. "Kreechnii asiee," he was saying.*

*"Kreechnii asiee," Serroi repeated, talking from
the top of her throat, trying to match the lilt he gave
the phrase.*

*The flier tumbled into laughter. Wings beating,
soaring and curling into seried loops he pantomimed his
joy. Then he was back in front of her, slapping at his
chest. "Pa'psa."*

Serroi tapped her own chest. "Serroi."

*Once again the tiny male went into aerial giggles.
His antics woke an answering lightness in Serroi.
Hern's hand was warm at the small of her back, his*

fingers moving in a soft slow caress. His laughter mixed with hers and made a kind of muted music for the airborne dance in front of them. . . .

She stood staring at the newcomer without really seeing him, tears gathering, an emptiness cold inside her. Her 'children' . . . they were something . . . like cuddling smoke, though . . . Hern . . . memory brought her that other, harsher love, prickly and difficult, but ah . . . so strong. . . . She closed her eyes. *What am I now . . . what am I going to do . . . where. . . .*

Serree?

Serroi shook herself out of the malaise that had claimed her for the past few seconds. *Honey?*

This is Lyef, Serree. He's Shapsa, you know, Honeydew told you 'bout the Shapsa. Lyef don't like them from the city, Serree, Lyef says he lead you where they can't follow. Ei vai?

All right, Honey, I'll tell the others.

Serroi heard the shouts as the guards . . . youmbards, that's the word . . . the youmbards found the boat. They were uncomfortably close. She breathed a prayer that they didn't have trackers capable of tracing anyone over this muck, then concentrated on her footing as the shapsa Lyef flew ahead of them, Honeydew at his shoulder, guiding them deeper and deeper into the swamp.

Silence thick and heavy as the waterladen air settled about them; mud sucked at them and splashed over legs and clothing, sticky stinking black ooze that wouldn't dry. Black biters smaller than pinheads rose in swarms each time one of them brushed against some foliage, crawled on faces, arms, any bit of bare skin, lapping at the sweat beading there. Out in the opaque water of the bayou, bubbles popped, eyes rose above the surface and sank again, now and then a snake undulated along, only its head showing. Other shapsa darted from the treetops, flew a while beside Lyef and vanished again after a short exchange of rapid, high-pitched speech. Honeydew didn't bother reporting what they said, so Serroi didn't bother worrying.

Late in the afternoon, Lyef brought them to one of the larger islands and showed them a spring bubbling out near a pile of mossy rocks, and a heap of fruit for their supper. He whispered a moment to Honeydew, then flew away.

Honeydew sipped from Serroi's cup, then settled on a branch beside her, sighing as she worked her shoulders, fluttered her wings then let them fall. Honeydew is tiiiiired.

What about the youmbards, Honey? What are they doing?

Lyef's cousins they come to tell him what's happening. The boat jammed into 'tother side the bayou, so them from the city they all nosing 'bout over there, didn't find anything so they give up a couple hours ago and head out. So we pretty well loose right now.

Has Lyef left us then?

His territory ends here. He went to talk to anyone, see 'f he can find us another guide. We know tonight, maybe tomorrow morning.

When the sun rose, another shapsa showed up at the island, hovered there while Honeydew rose to meet him. Pelsin was smaller and darker than Lyef and less outgoing. He led them deeper and deeper into the swamp, carefully choosing ways where the footing was best. At the end of the day, he left them on a sandy island with a small, clear stream running through the middle, lots of flying biters and land bugs, but dry earth under them. Even the water in the deeper stream alongside the island was clear, almost clean. And like Lyef's kin, his cousins left a pile of tubers and fruit for them to eat.

Hedivy and Adlayr went hunting with slings and pits from last night's fruit because there weren't many pebbles in the muck and sand; they brought back several birds which they roasted on improvised spits.

Hedivy sat scowling at the fire, a pile of bird bones by his knee. He looked up. "We're here. We're loose. What now?"

Adlayr was stretched out on the ground, fingers laced over his chest, his gearsac beneath his head. Honeydew was curled up against his hands, drowsing after the long day's flight. She yawned, lifted her head.

Halisan stared at the fire, withdrawn—as if to say whatever you decide, I'll follow along.

Serroi scratched at her nose. "On my shoulders, hm? We head for the Ashtops, look for Mount Santak and stay as quiet as we can while we're doing it. Other than that . . ." She shrugged and took a bite from a plum she'd saved for dessert.

By the tenth day in the swamp no one was speaking more than a word or two to any of the others; they were filthy, hungry, bad tempered and tired—mostly because they spent the hot, steamy nights scratching bug bites rather than sleeping. The shapsa guides kept appearing, a new one each morning, and each night the shapsa clan in that territory left its tribute of fruit and yams; sometimes they added fish, sometimes birds.

The dank, drowned land showed no sign of ending. Serroi was beginning to feel as if they could spend years in here wading through mud and slapping at bugs and getting nowhere. Each time she looked at Hedivy she worried even more; he was increasingly morose, eying the shapsa guides with suspicion and fingering his longgun. Adlayr was watching him too, staying close enough to grab him if he had to.

She watched Honeydew flying beside the shapsa, talking a streak as she usually did. The sprite was enjoying herself enormously, tired each night, reviving the next morning because she had a new audience. *Honey! Could you come here a moment, please?*

Honeydew touched the shapsa's arm, then curved around and swooped down to land on Serroi's shoulder. *Serree?*

"*Honey, Hev's getting spooky, do you see? Press your friend a little, how much more swamp do we have to cross? Doesn't have to know for sure, but a fair guess would be useful.*

Serree, Honeydew ask already, he don't know. Didn't ask if he could guess. Honeydew can do. She glanced at Hedivy, wrinkled her tiny nose. *Hev always spooky, hunh.*

Honeydew came fluttering back, settled on Serroi's shoulder. *Vyetli say he seen big people coming down bayous in skinny boats, trappers going for zuppig hides, those the long toothy things in the water. He say they don't stay the night, just set their traps and go way, so he 'spects they don't have a long way t' come. He say there's none of 'em now, they don't come this time the year. All he know is swamp, so he can't say more.*

That's something. Another day or two, sounds like.

Serree, Vyetli says his wife is real sick, she's about to have a baby and they 'fraid it going to be bad time and maybe the baby dies and maybe his wife too.

And you told him about me.

Ohhhhh, not him exactly.

Honey, you know what happens when I heal. Along with everything else, it'd be like announcing here I am.

I know, Serree, but he's soooo afraid and his last baby has a twisted leg and her wings aren't growing right and his cousins want to throw her from the nest and. . . .

Serroi sighed. *Ei vai, Honey, tell him I'll stay behind and as soon as the rest of you are clear, I'll see about his wife and daughter. Tell him I can straighten the child's leg and fix her wings But not before the rest of you are out of the swamp. And that means you too, Honey. Do you understand?*

SERREEEE!

I mean it, Honey.

As the sprite fluttered off, Adlayr moved up to walk beside her, silent for several strides. "Not a good idea," he muttered finally.

"I know." She moved away from the branches of a bush that was mostly shoots with tiny green leaves at nodes along them; there were drops of nectar at the base of each of the leaves, and if you brushed against the shoots you got black biters in the face and a stench that made the mud seem like perfume.

"Then why . . ." He jumped lightly from one root to the next, while she sloshed along in the shallow water.

"It's something I can't not do."

Halisan looked back, nodded. "I know," she said.

"Adlayr, remember what the waterform was like. Is that a call you'll deny the next time you hear it?"

He didn't look at the Harper. "I'll stay with you," he said.

"Nay, Adlayr, you and Honeydew are the best defense against the Enemy."

"All the more reason . . ."

"I have my hands, gyes." Out in the deeper water, a ripple caught her eye. Hastily she jumped onto the roots ahead of Adlayr. A few experiences with the zuppigs had taught her caution; the dozens of tiny crooked legs moved a lot faster than one would think and those rows of yellow teeth looked capable of cutting through a tree bole. Splitting her attention between her footing and the man behind her, she said, "Would you want me touching you if I had reason to be annoyed?" She caught hold of a branch and used it to swing across a stretch of water, then stepped out of Adlayr's way as he jumped across behind her. "I'll catch up if I can. If the hunters find me, I'll go along with them until I can break away and meet the rest of you in the Ashtops."

With Vyetli perched in the tree over her head, Serroi watched the new shapsa lead the others away. When she couldn't see them any longer, she looked up at Vyetli. "You'd best go be with your wife, friend. If things start going bad, come get me immediately, otherwise in two days, all right?"

"All right," he squeaked at her, then went flying off, trailing waves of anxiety.

Shaking her head, Serroi went to the high point on the island and curled up to sleep.

As she drifted off, she felt the Fetch looking for her, casting about like a highborn angler too proud to be called fisherman manipulating his flies. Casting blindly, thwarted rage like smoke blowing over the tops of the trees. *It's the shapsa*, she thought, *I don't know how, but they're keeping that Thing out.* She smiled drowsily and relaxed into sleep.

In the morning Vyetli was back, hovering over her, squeaking at her till she splashed water on her face. Myel his wife was whimpering with pain and hot to the touch. He wanted Serroi to come NOW.

"All right, I hear you." She lifted her knapsack, pushed her arms through the straps, found the staff Adlayr had cut for her before he left. "Calm down, I'm coming. You go ahead and lead me the fastest way you know. Remember, I can't fight zuppigs or walk on water."

Without speaking again, he darted off.

Moving as quickly as she could, she followed him through the morning murk and the increasing heat to a hill higher than most, crowned with a flowering tree she hadn't seen before, a slim, pale gold trunk with intricately branching limbs. There were nests dangling everywhere like teardrops of grass and fiber. Away from the nests, a platform of twigs and grass had been woven and tied with grass cords to a tangle of branches. On this a small, golden female was writhing and groaning, others gathered around her, trying to hold her still and keep her wings from being bruised.

Serroi looked from Vyetli to the platform high over her head to the bark that looked slippery as deepwinter ice. "You'll have to bring her down to me. If you could ease her into my lap, that would be good. Tell your kin that I have a healer's touch and will need nothing but that."

* * *

With Myel screaming all the way, four of the larger shapsa males caught hold of her arms and legs and lowered her to the cloth pulled tight across the hollow between Serroi's thighs, then they hovered, watching, blowpipes in their hands. There was no spoken threat and no need for one; she knew and they knew if she hurt either mother or child, she'd have so many darts in her, she'd look like an outsize pincushion.

She bent over the shapsa and the need to heal erased all else. She slipped one hand beneath Myel's body, laid the other above the swollen belly, closed her eyes and let the earth force flow through her righting what was wrong between her hands.

She held the tiny mother through a quick, easy birthing. When the glow faded, she took her hands away and let the shapsa women lift the infant to the mother's breast and clean them both, darting about, ignoring her as the earth replenished what she'd expended.

She waited for something to happen, but the heavy damp air blew past her, the sweet perfume of the tree dropped about her along with the happy chirruping of the shapsa, the day moved on without change or disruption. She sighed. "Vyetli, if you could bring your daughter down. . . ."

"There, Pili, it's all fixed now, does that feel better?" She tickled the soft vermillion fluff on the child's head, smiled as the shapsa girl no bigger than her thumb kicked repeatedly, laughing as the no-longer withered leg functioned without pain or awkwardness. The little girl flexed her fledgling's wings and managed to lift herself a full inch off Serroi's lap.

"You'll be flying like your papa in fewer years than you think."

There was a loud whistle, two older shapsa girls darted down, caught hold of Pili and carried her off, mothers and fathers were emptying their nests and darting away. Two males came racing from the swamp, shouting in tones so high Serroi couldn't make out the words.

Vyetli and several of the other males rushed to meet them, hovered in midair talking excitedly.

The newborn clinging like a burr to her chestfur, Myel fluttered above the platform, calling to Vyetli, panic in her voice.

He broke away from the scouts, darted to Serroi. "Youmbards coming," he shouted to her, "they have a sabak. It sniffs magic, it'll be here soon. Come, we have a place."

"Nay, Vyetli, if the sniffer has me, they'll just track me to you." She stroked her fingers across the ferns growing beside her knee, smiled as the frond tips curled tight at her touch. "I'll be fine, but I don't want you around for hostages. You go with your family, I'll wait here."

The sabak was a snaky looking quadruped with short, sleek, black hair and half a dozen crooked legs. If it had eyes, they were no larger than pinheads, lost in the hair that drooped from its crest, and its ears were rounded nubbins, but the black glistening nose was huge. It tugged against its leash, scratching up divots of grass and sprays of sand.

There were two men with the sabak, one holding the leash, the other swinging a longgun about, looking for a target. Youmbards. Short squat figures in dull black, black leather hoods pulled over their heads, the front part cut away to leave their mouths visible. After a slow intense scan of the deserted island, they turned glinting eyeholes on Serroi.

The lead Youmbard jabbed the barrel of his longgun at her. "Where the others?"

She frowned at him, not understanding what he wanted, her mind set on the fleeing shapsas.

With an iron patience, the hooded man repeated the question. "Where the ones who came in here with you?"

"Gone," she said. "All gone."

They looked at each other, then the sabak handler shifted the leash to his left hand and stepped toward her.

She pulled a fern loose, got to her feet holding it out. "Do you see this?"

"So?"

She crumpled the lacy plant and closed her hand about it, opened her fingers to show it blackened and dead. "Do not touch me. I will go with you, but do not touch me."

2

BOKIVADA

Chaya Willish Isaddo-na looked up from her notes as her Name-aunt came storming into the kitchen. "Thaz?"

"Bunch of stinking bli'djers!" Sekhaya Kawin slapped the roll of papers on the table, poured herself a cup of bitter, lukewarm cha from the pot by Chaya's elbow.

"What did they say to get you so upset?"

"I don't know town ways, I'd give wrong advice

and upset things, it's a delicate balance here, so many
different kinds all crowded together. Mixes with special needs. On and on like that." Sekaya gulped at the
cha, scowled at the dregs and banged the cup down.
"How can you drink acid like that? Eat the throat
right out of you." She sighed. "Trouble is, they're
right. I don't belong here." She pushed the hair off
her face, stood staring out the window over the sink,
seeing nothing but the images inside her head. "Kazi,
I'm going north. It's what I meant to do before all
this came up. They say Fundasendle is clean of the
Glory. I can live with that."

"It's a long way off."

"At least I'll be moving and away from all these
walls."

Chaya watched the herbwoman's van slide in behind a goods train from the wharves. It was one more
loss she owed to the Glory. There was a cold knot
under her ribs because she was sure she'd never see
her Thaz again.

Yane was leaning against a wall a short distance off;
he straightened, strolled over and touched her arm.
"You wanna go someplace?"

"You know the Turtle's House?"

As he wrinkled his long nose, the patch over his
missing eye tilted and seemed to wink at her as the
shiny black leather caught the morning sun. "Ahwu
ahwu, everyone knows the Turtle. You just follow."
He took off along the walkway.

He'd hung around a lot the past few days, seemed
drawn to her, maybe too much, though he was only
a boy. Lavan didn't like him, but Lavan was too busy
these days to take much notice of what happened
outside the shop where he worked. Or even listen to

her when she talked about her plans. *Ahwu, Lavan's Lavan and not about to change. I went into this eyes open, I knew it's me who's going to have to make the running. Naka naka, he's a good man and he loves me, just needs a little reminding.* She sighed. *Sometimes though, I get so tired. I wish ...* She shook her head, not finding words for what it was she wanted, unwilling to look for them because that might stir up more than she could bear thinking about.

Since Yane had brought her the chain and the bronze medal with her patron's turtle sign stamped into it, the snaskas had left her alone and going to market in the morning no longer brought terror and knots in her stomach, but she was just as glad the boy was willing to walk about with her. Not as protection but as a kind of living sign to let other people know she wasn't alone. She'd put off going to look over the loom, too busy helping Sekaya get ready to leave. Now it was something to distract her from her loss.

The Turtle's house was invisible behind walls higher than those around Freetown, only the red tiles of the roof peaks showing; a guard tower rose above the gate, narrow slits opening on the street and overlooking the heavy doors. The Turtle. She'd never met the man. Shisell had handled negotiations from the Trade Hall, sent witnesses to his House for signing and sealing, saying that's the way he was, he used agents to do his business and never came from behind his walls.

The Turtle was the only name Chaya had for him; she still found it difficult to believe anyone would welcome such a name, no matter what reason he had for sinking the one he was born with, but Freewoman Shisell assured her that was how he expected to be addressed if Chaya ever met him—something not at all that likely.

Yane fidgeted as she reached for the bell pull. "You gonna be in there all day?"

"Probably, though I should be home to get Lavan's dinner." She examined the knob at the end of the chain and was surprised, then amused, to see it was a small bronze turtle. She tugged on it, heard the clang of a loud bell somewhere inside.

As the heavy door started to open, Yane shifted from foot to foot a moment longer, then went scooting off. "See y' later," he called over his shoulder, then vanished around a corner.

In the narrow gap a tall, thin man scowled down at her. He was dressed in metal and worn leather, a longgun slung by its strap over his shoulder; gray-streaked black hair hung loose to his shoulders, his face was seamed and scarred, his mouth enclosed in a thin black mustache and close cropped beard. "You want?"

She drew in a breath, straightened her shoulders. "I am the Weaver Chaya Willish Isaddo-na. I am contracted to use the loom." She held the medal where he could see it.

He peered at it, then looked at something on the other side of the door. "Yes, your name is on the list. Come in." His voice was harsh, rusty, as if he seldom spoke.

After swinging the massive bars into their clamps, he strode off without a word.

Chaya followed, oscillating between amused relief and irritation; she'd been replaying the Freewoman's comments about liaisons and wondering what she might expect in here, but it looked like seduction wasn't on the list.

The guard led her round the back of the main house, to a neglected weed-choked garden with a small, square building near the back wall. The structure had a tile roof with a high peak and dozens of shuttered windows. He scowled at the shutters. "Should be open already."

"No matter," she said. "I can't do much more than get things started today."

He shrugged, handed her a heavy iron key. "The door. Keep it." Without another word, he swung round and marched off.

Chaya swallowed a giggle, dropped the key into a pocket in her skirt and started opening the shutters.

The air was filled with dust that danced in golden motes in the sunlight pouring into the eastern windows; the single room was empty except for the loom, warping creel and bench—a big, old, eight-harness loom, covered in dust. Chaya wrinkled her nose, checked the action and the leather parts, found them in better condition than she expected. Hands on hips, she looked round. *No spools in sight, no . . . ah! Closets. Or something.*

She opened the first door. Broom closet. Mop, bucket, broom, dust rags, a wide-mouthed jar filled with gray-green soft soap, a tap with a dusty sink under it. "That's useful. Maybe." She turned the tap, listened to a rumble gurgle bang from the pipes, then a thin stream of brownish water came out, trickled into the drain after soaking through the web of dust demons matting the bottom of the sink. She forced the tap open as far as it would go, watched the thread of rusty water strengthen while the howling and clanking of the pipes reached the level of tortured pig. "That has to be fixed."

She turned the water off and shut that door, opened the next.

This closet was filled with paper boxes. She tore a hole in one, saw the thread cone, unbleached something; she thrust her fingers through the hole. "Feels like hala thread. Must be what he means for his share. Ahwu, at least there's that."

The third door opened into a lavatory with a shower, tap and basin, a comfort chamber behind a halfdoor—holes in a tile floor and a hose to wash the floor down. She tried the water here; it flowed more strongly, not so brown and gummy. Someone had made an attempt at cleaning the place up, had thrown a couple of threadbare towels across a wooden bar screwed to the wall beside the shower. There was a barred window high up in the wall above the basin, the panes in it smeared with dust and cobwebs. The cleaner hadn't touched that.

She took one of the towels, tied it around her head and went out to set the place to order. She was a weaver, not a cleaning woman, but she'd been trained far too well to foul her work with dust and grit.

At noon a maidservant brought her a tray with sandwiches and a pot of hot cha.

Chaya looked around from the window she was wiping down, smiled wearily at the girl. "Thanks. What's your name?"

"Hawina, Kos." She was a slight, dark girl, very young, with huge brown eyes and a sudden smile that turned her plain face almost pretty.

"Name me Weaver Chaya, Hawina. And do you think you could bring me more dry rags, a pen, some ink and paper?" She glanced at the floor, wrinkled her nose. "And a polishing stone?"

"I'll ask, Weaver Chaya. If they ask me why?"

"The room must be clean as a kitchen should be,

Hawina. Else the cloth gets spoiled. Hm. Nearly forgot, I have to get the dust down from those rafters, so I'll need a ladder." She looked at her hands. "And more towels. Ask if they want me to bring my own. Once I start threading the loom, I have to keep my hands clean too. Loom. I'll need polishing oil, wax and rags for that." She smiled. "Too much to remember. Just bring me the ink and paper and I'll make a list."

Hawina curtseyed and turned to go, turned back. "Does that take a long time to learn, Weaver Chaya? Is it hard?"

"I was a little younger than you, Hawina, when my Family apprenticed me to the Weavers Guild. The more you learn, the more complicated it gets, but the beginning is more wearying than hard."

The girl's dark eyes slid toward the loom, then she curtseyed again and left.

When she finished the meal, Chaya set the tray outside the door, got the broom and began sweeping the floor.

While she worked on floor and walls, she felt eyes on her, though each time she turned, there was no one visible at the windows. *Probably more servants coming to look me over. I've a feeling Hawina's a chatterer.* She finished the sweeping, brushed the debris out the door, filled the bucket and began the first mopping.

Brought to life by the soapy water, the floor turned out to be beautiful, chips of different woods set in a leaf and vine pattern like a wooden brocade. A shame to neglect it like this. If they brought enough of the wax, she could use what was left over and polish the floor.

By the time she was satisfied with her mopping, the room was beginning to darken. There were no lamps, the only light was what came through the windows. That was another thing to add to her list. She dumped the last of the dirty water into the sink in the broom closet, stretched her aching body, yawned and groaned. She was exhausted, but she felt good; it was as if the world had tilted crazily for several months and now was settling back into the old comfortable ways. She crossed to the loom, ran her hand along the frame; the wood seemed to arch against her palm, almost like a cat responding to a caress. "Soon," she said, her voice echoing in the empty room. "We'll do, oh yes we will."

Yane joined her the minute she turned the corner and was out of sight of the watchtower. "Go good?"

She smiled at him. "No problems. Your day?"

"Same's all the days. This'n that. You see the Turtle?"

"No, only a guard and the servant who brought lunch."

"Good. He mixed up in bad things."

"Oh?"

"Word is, his shipmasters they climb other ships if things 're right, strip 'em and sink 'em. And there 're them that 're slavers."

"But here, in Bokivada?"

Yane shrugged. "Keeps his nose clean here. Far as most know. There are things . . ."

"There always are, Yane. People talk. What they don't know, they invent. Ahwu, I'm not going to worry." She touched his arm. "I'm weaving, Yane. Nothing else."

"If you're let."

"I doubt he's fool enough to mess with me and

foul his homeplace. I'm Guild, not some backstreet drab. Don't fuss, Yane."

His face gone sullen, red patches over his cheekbones, Yane scraped his feet over the planks of the walkway, slapping his hand on the wall as he walked beside her. A moment later he went trotting off, vanishing down a sidestreet, melting into the crowds down near the Market.

Chaya glanced after him, shook her head and sighed. *Looks like something's there I don't know about. Ahwu, just as well, he was getting a bit possessive, no telling where that might have gone. Duokhmi, I can certainly do without more complications in my life.*

Freewoman Nyama turned into the street the same time as Chaya, caught at the fluttering ends of the green headcloth that marked her profession, hesitated, then crossed to walk beside her. She was fair enough to be a Forest exile, though the tilt and intensity of her green eyes said she had other blood in her. "I heard that your Thaz left this morning. I hope you don't hold hard against us for that."

Chaya shook her head. "No problem, Freewoman. She was getting fratchety as a cat with fleas. All these walls, you see."

They walked in silence after that until they reached Nyama's turn. The herbwoman touched Chaya's arm. "There's a dinner and dance at the Trade Hall on Titchly Eve. The Banye folk . . ." She waved her arm in a short arc. "We're meeting by my house; it's safer to go together."

"I have to see what Lavan wants. How soon do I need to let you know?"

"No need. Just show up at my corner an hour before sundown." Nyama chuckled. "Follow the noise, you can't miss it. Maiden Bless." With a wave of her hand, she walked away, the ends of the green scarf fluttering wildly, the whole thing threatening to come off her head.

Halfway through dinner Lavan broke off what he was saying and frowned at her. "What's wrong, Chay?"

"Nothing, just tired. Go on, Lav, what did Hanzo say after that?"

He pushed his plate aside. "Don't go playing Henny Perfect on me, something's bothering you. I want to know what."

She speared a bit of tuber with her fork, pushed it around in the gravy. "I'm really just tired. Makes me imagine things, you know that, Lav." She glanced at him, sighed. "It's the patron Freewoman Shisell found me. It's a good loom, he leaves me alone, so there's nothing to worry about there, but Yane says he's a pirate and a slaver, then he got mad at me, Yane did, when he saw I wasn't going to stop going there and he took off."

"Yane. You want to be careful of that kid, Chay. He could turn on you. . . ." He folded his arms, leaned on them, looked past her into memory. "A couple years ago, before Sekhaya found Casil, I was way up north beyond Lake Hiliz. A town called Qubulafam. Near the pass into Fundasendle. Reason I was there, they'd put up a Guild Fair, the Qubulans had, metal smiths from Fundasendle and Jamafund. I talked to as many masters as I could get to listen to me, no takers. Then a man came up to me. He seemed friendly and interested. Bought lunch for me, was all over me, like he thought I was the best thing since honeycream. Then he showed me his work. I never saw such junk. I was polite, but he didn't want courtesy, he wanted praise. A gush of praise. One minute I was going to be his son in all but name, the next he turned on me, called me things I wouldn't want to repeat, don't even want to remember. The next three days he went around spreading lies, filth, about me. One of the masters took me aside after a while and said not to worry, he'd done this kind of thing before, everyone knew about him, a few years back he was good enough to get his papers, but something happened to him, turned him crazier'n a rabid bat." He sighed. "Chay, that Yane's got the same shine to his eye. If he's gone off you, he could turn really mean. I think you should go see the Freewoman soon as you can and tell her about what happened. Do you want me to walk you to the Turtle's House?"

"No. That's all right. I don't think Yane's as bad as that, though I will keep him at a distance if he comes by again. He was getting too . . . mm . . . I guess possessive. Tell me about Hanzo. What DID he say when Merric challenged him?"

Careful not to wake Lavan, Chaya eased out of bed and went to sit in the window. The garden below was full of shadow and silvery glints where the moonlight touched wind-turned grass and leaves. The Banye District was always quiet at night, the wharves and the taverns of the waterfront were far enough off that the sounds from there didn't reach them. She thought about Lavan's story. It explained a lot of things she hadn't understood. Those years had been worse for him than he'd let her know, some of it out of pride, some of it to keep her from worrying. It explained why he was digging in so deep here in Freetown; he still hadn't got over the humiliations of that time, the fear. *I think I'm going to like it here*, she thought. *Spite of everything. I can*

*breathe here. Now that I've got a loom . . . a good loom
it is, too . . . I don't really want to go home . . . ahwu,
home is here.*

She leaned her head against the wall, pulled her
legs up onto the seat. *It's an uneasy thing, living in
someone else's house. What we'll do when the Harper
comes back? I'd better start looking about, there's no telling how long we've got here . . . see what's available . . .
we need to know the people round us . . . can't tell what's
going to happen . . . markets . . . once I get the loom
set up and finish the Turtle's cloth, I can start my own
projects . . . Shisell says the Turtle could help me sell the
cloth, if he takes a notion . . . she's not worried about him
. . . ahwu, I'm going to weave and let the rest go hang . . .
wonder if Yane IS dangerous? Lavan's right, I should to
go see Shisell .. ask her about him . . . he's about the same
age as Belitha's son who shot that spy like he'd shoot roost-
ing ingana for a gana pie. . . .*

She shivered, suddenly cold. After a last glance at
the garden, she left the windowseat and slipped back
into bed.

Shisell frowned. "I'll see he doesn't bother you.
He's had a terrible time since the day he was born,
Chay." Her face twisted with distaste. "You don't
want to know, it's enough to make a pig sick. Ahwu,
don't worry, we know what to do. This isn't the first
time he's tried to move in on someone; before you
there was Bucik the Woodcarver. How's the loom
look? Do you think it's going to work out?"

"It's a good machine. How long since it's been
used?"

"Ten, fifteen years. One of Turtle's women used to
weave, but she died."

"Oh?"

"Far as I know he's not looking and I made it clear you're not available." Shisell tapped her nails on the table. "If you want to cancel. . . ."

"No." Chaya laughed. "I've already spent a day dusting and mopping, I don't want to waste my work."

"Mopping!"

"A decade leaves a lot of dust." Chaya got to her feet. "Ease Yane away and calm him down, that's all I want."

Chaya pushed the door open and stopped, surprised.

The floor glowed with wax and oil, the loom was a golden shimmer in the light pouring through the windows, light with almost none of the dancing motes that had been there the day before. The room smelled like the Weave Hall after Spring cleaning; memories flooded back, bringing tears and a weakness in her knees. She clutched at the doorjamb, drew a deep breath and scrubbed the back of her hand across her eyes.

When she got herself together and went in, she found a table set in one corner with a tin of cha, another of crisp wafers, a strainer, a pot with matching cup and saucer, an enamel kettle with the lid placed beside it, a small brazier with a kettle rod above it, a pad of lined paper, a bottle of ink and a pen. She touched the paper, opened the cha tin, sniffed at the leaves. "Ahwu, somebody has nice ideas."

Once the cha water was heating, she pulled a box of thread cones from the closet and began working on the warping creel.

Hawina brought the lunch tray, set it on the table and went to stand beside Chaya, watching her turn the crank on the roller. She stood carefully silent while Chaya finished counting the turns, secured the threads and cut them. "It takes a lot of time to get ready, doesn't it?"

"Anything worth doing . . ." Chaya stretched and groaned. "Thanks for carrying the message."

"The Turtle got on the housekeeper and made the dust fly." She clasped her hands behind her and ambled about to inspect the creel. "I asked him if you could teach me. I'm one a his bastards and he likes to get us settled in trades, so he said I could ask." She bent down, fingered the thread coming from one of the cones, tilted her head, slanted a look at Chaya. "Will you?"

"If . . ." Chaya moved away, thinking furiously. *One of his . . . she's so calm about it . . . he likes to get them settled, huh? . . . maybe that's why . . . I can live with that. . . .* She looked at the neat slices of cold meat, the bowl of fruit sections, the fresh-baked bread, poured herself a cup of cha and settled in the chair. "Sit down, Hawina. The bench. I have to think about that."

"If there's a problem. . . ."

"What I started to say was, if this wasn't Freetown, I couldn't do it. I'm only a journeyman and you're not articled to the Guild." She rolled up some of the meat in a slice of bread. "Ahwu, if you're willing to put in a lot of hard, dull work, I'll do what I can. Have you had your lunch?"

"Oh yes."

"Ahwu, while I eat, I'll talk, then we'll see what you remember, then you can help me start the threading."

Lavan was waiting for her when she came out.

She laughed, clicked her tongue, but took his hand and strolled along with him.

"I talked with your Freewoman . . . Shisell, wasn't it? She says Yane stayed away from the Trade Hall, he's never done that before and she's worried. If he doesn't show tomorrow, she's going to see what she can find out. She said you shouldn't blame yourself, Chay, he's nudging puberty and that can take boys like him strange."

Chaya lifted his hand, rubbed it against her face. "I don't want to think about him now. I've had a lovely day, Lav. I actually have a student. Take me to the wharves, I want to watch the ships go in and out. I've never seen ocean sailors."

"Why not?" He tapped a knuckle against her chin. "A student?"

She giggled. "Mm hm. The little maid I told you about. She comes in, tells me without a blink of those huge brown eyes she's one of the Turtle's bastards and he likes to get them into trades and would I teach her how to weave."

"Whooeee, Chay."

They sat on the end of a deserted wharf, watching a ship glide across the bay.

Chaya leaned against Lavan, her head on his shoulder, his arm warm about her. "You ever wonder what's happening with the Healer and the rest?"

"No." He kissed the top of her head, his breath warm against her hair. "Can't do anything, so why bother?"

"Mmmm. Me too." After a minute she tilted her head back, looked up at him. "Do you miss being able to move around outside Bokivada?"

"Nay, Chay love. I like it here. It's too . . . I don't know . . . yes I do know . . . too narrow back home. Maybe we can go back to the house in Hubawern when this business is finished. Do you? Miss home, I mean."

"I'll be sorry not to see the Weave Hall again and them in it. That said, I like it here. Look at that ship, Lav, how beautiful the sails are with the sun like copper shining through them."

3

IN THE ASHTOPS

Ash dropped like gray snow, a silent fall without end. The land shifted and bumped under them, even Horse stumbled now and again, but there was a bubble of clean air about them so breathing wasn't a problem. Yela'o was the one doing that, Mama Charody said.

A blob of molten rock flew through the ash, hit a boulder beside the trail and splashed; Horse jumped aside, squealing as the lava just missed his leg.

"Brothers of stone, come." Charody's shout was hoarse but loud, ringing in Treshteny's ears.

The Kamen came, faster this time than they had in the Neck. Four of them. Without speaking, they took their places, one walked before them, one behind, one on each side. The missiles turned away after that.

They kept moving all night, down and down the mountain, struggling through ash ankle high, then knee high and piling higher with each moment that passed. Down and down, the air leaching moisture from mouth and nose until thirst was a scream. The water had to be kept for the packhorses, though Mama Charody moistened a rag for Doby to suck on.

Down and down, sounds coming eerie and muffled

through the ash curtain, screams from rargas and other beasts as the mountain's spittle seared through fur and skin, groans from the stone that heaved and split, roar of avalanches, crashes as trees tore loose.

Down and down in a darkness where Yela'o shone like a green lamp and Horse glowed with witchfire.

Down and down in their bubble of precarious safety with death all round them.

Morning brought a faint glow filtering through the ash that still fell without any sign of abating.

They reached a flat that had been a meadow before the smother. Mama Charody raised a hand. "We stop here a while, let the horses eat and rest."

Treshteny slid off Horse, grimaced as the fluffy gray-white grit puffed up around her. As Doby broke up the last of the corncakes and fed them to the packhorses, then filled their leather buckets from the waterskins, she coughed, rubbed at her eyes, turned to Mama Charody. "How long is this with us?"

Charody laughed. "You ask me, Timeseer?"

"I can't see anything, it's all gray." She moved her foot, gloomed at the pouf of fine ash. "Smoke. Like that."

"Zdra, I'll ask." Charody waded over to one of the kamen who squatted at the rim of Yela'o's shield, ash settling over him, turning him to a shapeless mound. She bent over, rested her hand on his shoulder, stood like that for several minutes, then came back.

"He says probably three days. Till we're off the mountain."

Treshteny moved her head, looking at the ashfall, at the ash underfoot. "We need water."

"They know."

* * *

Down and down, the horses weakening, Doby
stumbling in a weary daze, Yela'o's green glow steadily paling, the rim of the shield closing in until it was
half the size it'd been. Claustrophobic . . . choking
. . . even though the air was still clear.

Down and down, rest an hour or two, press on—
because if they stopped, settled, they might never get
up again. . . .

Midmorning on the third day the ash began to thin
and the ground to level out.

By late afternoon, though there were dark threads
blowing across it, the sky was blue again, the sun visible enough to stretch long, thin shadows ahead of
them. As they moved out onto a shallow slope,
Treshteny opened her eyes wide. For a moment she
saw the land as *now* instead of a blur of maybe, was
and will be. A lush savannah spread before her, a tri-
angle of grass, lakes and scattered trees that widened
as it went south; to the east and west were heavy dark
lines that marked the thicker forest. A mile away,
half-a-mile down from the broad cliff they rode
along, one of those lakes was a round blue disk, glittering where the wind blew the water into chop.

Abruptly, the oneness was gone.

Treshteny smiled and moved her shoulders, set
herself to watching for would-be hazards on the trail
ahead.

In the grove beside the lake there was a tangle of
berryvine, a scatter of white flowers on the canes,
their overly sweet perfume drifting among the trees,
and with the flowers clusters of ripe fruit. Treshteny
blinked when her fingers told her both were *now*.

Mama Charody stepped away from the Kamen,

watched a moment as they sank back into the earth. "Doby, go see what wood you can find, will you? Down wood. Mm . . . let me fix this. . . ." She shook out a scarf and tied it over his face. "Careful of the ash, boy."

She watched him disappear under the trees, then went to the horses and began stripping away the gear. They stood hipshot and head down, too used up even to go for water until she slapped them lightly on sunken haunches. She caught up the rope straps on the water skins and took those to the lake to wash them out and refill them.

Treshteny began gathering the berries, filling one of the cooking pots, grimacing as ash covered the dark succulent fruit, so ripe it left purple stains on her fingers. She was tempted to eat some of them, but didn't, since she didn't know them. Safer to wait for Charody's approval. Or Yela'o's. He was out in the lake, splashing and swimming, getting his color back. She glanced over her shoulder, smiled at the antics of the little faun.

"Tena, leave that a minute, will you? And help me get the tarp stretched. I've had more than enough of this ash falling on my head."

Treshteny crunched the tail of the fried fish, licking salt and fragments from her lips with a sigh of pleasure. She reached for the cup of berries. One furry leg crossed over the other, his head on her thigh, Yela'o was eating fistfuls of the berry flowers. She spooned up a berry, bit into it. The sweet, tart juice burst over her tongue. "Mmmmm."

Charody laughed, jabbed at the tarpaulin stretched overhead, keeping the ash away from them. "After that trek, a sour brosk would taste good." She looked

at Doby, curled up asleep on the far side of the fire.
"Too tired to enjoy hot food. Ahwu, come morning
he'll be hungry again." She yawned. "About another
minute and I'm joining him."

A thin cry from Doby wrenched Treshteny from
the heaviest sleep she'd known in days.

Mama Charody was on her feet, glaring at a man
hooded in black leather who held Doby by the neck,
the barrel of a shortgun pressed against his temple.
Beside him stood a squat figure in the same sort of
hood with a bronze chain about his neck, a medallion
hanging from it. This one was the leader; he wore
authority like a cloak.

There were other men out in the darkness, Treshteny could hear them, though she couldn't see them.

The squat one spoke, his voice grating. "You'll
come with us. If you make trouble, the boy's the first
to die. The next will be one of you."

4. Confrontations and Contrasts

1

ON THE SHORES OF THE STATHVOREEN

A shot. Another.

A roar of fury and pain.

"Hold! Next in your head."

Wrenched from sleep, K'vestmilly Vos had the shortgun from under her pillow and was sitting up, holding it in front of her before she was awake enough to realize what was happening.

"Kimi, hold it." Heslin's voice, a thread of sound, then his hand warm on her arm.

In the faint light coming through a window denuded of its parchment panes, she saw Zasya standing braced, shortgun steady on a dark figure crouching below the window, Ildas a golden shimmer on the sill above him. The croucher sprang for the window, screamed again. The Fireborn was a burning membrane across the opening, blocking him, charring the black armor until the stench of burning velater hide filled the room. The figure hit the floor and sprang up again, still deadly, terrifyingly fast and driven by an urgency to survive so strong K'vestmilly could smell it over the stink of the hide.

Zasya shot again, bullets slamming into the intruder, staggering but not stopping him.

She dropped the empty gun as she leaped aside, her saber flashed up and around, slicing through a

weak point of the armor where Ildas had burned it
thin. Blood spurted in a leaping arc, spattered over
the end of the bed.

The Sleykyn howled, his hand caught hold of the
quilt, pulled at it, then he shuddered and lay still.
There was a pounding at the iron door, voices shouting.

Ildas leaped from the windowsill, flowed through a
wall lamp, flaring the wick, danced around from lamp
to lamp until the room was filled with light, then he
trotted across to nuzzle against Zasya Myers. She
clicked her tongue at him, muscled the Sleykyn over.
His eyes were open and staring, but he wasn't seeing
anything. "Dead." She got to her feet, wiped her
hands on her tunic.

Heslin pulled on a robe and slid from the bed.
"Good work, meie. We can dump him out the window ... mm, I'd better stop that fuss. Think you
should send Ildas out, see if he's got brothers hanging
about?"

"They don't usually hunt in packs, but these aren't
usual times." Zasya moved across the room, stood to
one side of the window and took a quick look out.
"With those clouds, it'd be hard to see a snowbear.
Ildas, search."

K'vestmilly set her gun down. "You'd better let me
do the talking, Hes. Hearing me will calm them
faster."

He cupped his hand under her chin, chuckled
softly. "My finest student."

K'vestmilly unlatched the cover of the small round
peephole, let it fall, yelled, "Quiet all of you. Listen."
In the resulting stillness she said more calmly, "Everything's all right here. A Sleykyn got through, the
meie took him out before he could do anything. Get

back on guard, see that another one doesn't get past you."

Ildas wriggled in through the window, dropped to the floor and went to sniff at the dead Sleykyn.

Zasya pushed the hair off her face. "Ei vai, that's all right. He's the only one round."

K'vestmilly watched Heslin and Zasya muscle the corpse through the window and contrive a cover for the opening from a spare blanket—and wondered about the next time someone would try to kill her, when it'd be and how close they'd come.

2

BISERICA

The thing whined and vibrated, a black metal beetle hitched to a trailer piled high with bales and crates with a tarpaulin roped tight across the load. Greygen watched uneasily and with some annoyance as Sansilly danced around the thing, opened hatches in the sides under the amused eyes of the meie who was checking the ropes a last time. Synggal, she said her name was, when she agreed to take them to the Prieti Meien. Synggal Kryderri, meie of the Biserica. She was a tall, lean woman with hair like a straw thatch and pale blue eyes. One leg was stiff, with a deep scar visible beneath the hem of the divided skirt she wore; there was another scar on her left arm just above the elbow, a puncture wound that had healed badly.

"Ready to go," she said, and opened one of the rearward hatches. "If you'll get in, we can make the Complex before the whole day's gone. Om Lestar, if you haven't room for your legs, I can move the front seat up a hair."

Greygen took Sansilly's arm to help her in.

"Nik nik you go first, Greg. I want to watch the meie and see what she does."

He sighed. "All right, Sansy." He eased his head past the rim of the hatch, folded up and slid across the padded bench; it was cramped back there, but comfortable enough, though he found the vibration that came through the pads disturbing in a way he couldn't describe.

The bench bounced a little as Sansilly straightened her skirts and wriggled about until she was comfortable; she winked at Greygen, then tugged on the inside latch to make sure that it had caught and they were safely enclosed.

The meie called a farewell to the others standing on the loading dock at the back of the Varou, slid onto the front seat with the ease of long practice. She pulled the front hatch shut and turned her head. "You all right back there?"

Sansilly glanced at Greygen. He spread his hands, dropped them to rest on his thighs. "Fine," she said. "What's that sound? What makes this go?"

The meie chuckled. "The sound's the motor and how that works, don't ask me. What I know is, if I push these buttons like this . . ." Her thin tanned fingers danced across a square surface, depressing parts of it, parts that sprang back the moment she took the pressure away.

Greygen sat up, interested for the first time. It was like one of his puzzle locks.

The sound deepened and steadied, the vibration smoothed out. "And if I trip this switch . . ." She turned a lever that was like a smaller version of the door latches. "And ease up on this pedal . . ."

The black beetle moved smoothly forward despite a slight jerk as the trailer dragged on the hitch.

She touched another switch and a bell began ringing, clang clang clang clang clang clang clang. Raising her voice to be heard over the noise, she said, "That's to warn walkers, carters, whatever, that I'm coming. Ei vai, Omma Lestar, these streets are narrow and a bit tricky and with the bells going it'll be hard to hear, so if you don't mind we'll save more talk until we're out of the town. Hm?"

The beetle crawled along, twisting and turning through the streets of the town, the trailer rattling behind it, the bell clanging, the motor's hum lost in the noise. Other beetles crouched in side streets, walkers ducked into doorways; there were a few riders, they turned aside or waited for the meie to pass. It wasn't a big place or a crowded one, nothing like Calanda or Dander; in less than twenty minutes she'd passed the gate in the town wall and turned off the bell.

The meie moved her shoulders, drew the beetle to the side of the road. She swung round, leaned on the back of the seat. "Ei vai, it would be useful if you'd watch out the back and sides for blue faces. Krymen hang about the Dike; most of them are more pathetic than dangerous, but one never knows."

Sansilly blinked. "Blue?"

"Kind of a slaty blue, darker blue hair in a crest top of their heads. They usually wear it in a braid with leather thongs wrapped round it. You see something like that, let me know, especially when we get close to the hills ahead. This time of year there are a lot of young ones about, trying for their manhood coups; getting through the Valley Gate and up into the watchtower is one of the things those itchers dream about." She grinned, slapped the top of the seat and swung around. "Hang on, we're taking this bit fast."

The land on both sides of the road was dry scrub with patches of dead grass and low scabby dunes; a short distance off the Dike cut off the view to the left, a sand-colored wall thirty yards high. No sign of farms or any life at all, nothing but this dark road that stretched like a knifecut across the waste.

The acceleration was gradual; Greygen didn't notice it at first since he was focused on the distance looking for signs of Krymen. Then he glanced down and saw a patch of brush whip past.

He gulped. Even racing down the swiftwater of the Chasm hadn't felt so fast. He glanced at the meie. She was leaning back, one hand on the steering bar, her other arm stretched out along the top of the front seat. Sansilly's eyes were sparkling. He remembered her singing in the bow of the boat as they took that last long slide out of the canyon; if it weren't for the meie she'd be singing again. She was loving this. She winked at him, reached for his hand. Hers was hot and sweaty, the life and vigor in it flowing into him, warming away the doubt that was ice-heavy in his belly.

The mountains that in the beginning were washes of blue against the paler blue of the sky swept toward them, pushing higher and higher until he couldn't see the sky at all, only the steep, barren angles of stone. The road began climbing, swinging back and forth around the shoulders of the mountains, up and up until he could see the massive wall built across the pass.

Meie Synggal started the bell clanging again and by the time they reached the wall the first gate was already open for them.

As they started through it into a kind of pen, another gate before them, still closed, there was a sudden thump, then another, on the roof of the car.

Synggal swore, brought the beetle to a sluing stop.

Scrabbling sounds. Sharp cracks, thumps, whingging squeals.

A young kry tumbled down to lie in a heap against the wall.

Shouts.

The second kry jumped from the roof and stood with his hands raised.

A crisp order. Greygen didn't know the words, but understood when the boy scooped up his companion, muscled him over his shoulder and stalked off.

Synggal started forward again; the gate slammed shut behind them, the second gate opened. She drove through it and kept on going, picking up speed again, moving along a level, winding road between two cliffs.

The Valley astonished Greygen. Near the road it was more like a garden than a collection of farms; each patch of ground was growing at least three crops, trees, vines and groundplants, watered through flexible pipes that looped from pole to pole, dripping on the roots through small holes. Plants were so green and lush they looked painted, the fruit was the biggest and juiciest he'd ever seen, the wind through the open window brought the smells of rich black earth, of fruit, leaves, fertilizer—the air was so thick with them that each breath was a meal.

He leaned back and closed his eyes, the body that for days had been stretched like a sail with a bellyful of wind went limp; he was so tired that even the noise and vibration of the beetle couldn't hold back the waves of sleep.

Sansilly shook him awake. "Greg, we're here."

Head throbbing, eyes grainy, he sat up. They were stopped beside a brick wall, another wall visible a short distance off on the other side. That said city to him. Alley. He felt more at home than he had in weeks.

The front hatch was open and the meie was gone. "Where?"

"Synggal went to get us a room in the Hostel. That there." Sansilly nodded at the wall beside him. "She has to deliver the supplies she picked up, then she'll see the Prieti Meien for us, get us an appointment." She caught his hand, squeezed it. "This place, Greg, this *place*."

"You like it, hm?" He smiled at her.

"Oh yes. I . . ."

"Meie's coming back."

"Zdra zdra, here we go."

The Meie Synggal set Sansilly's pack down, straightened and brushed her hands. "Right. The room is yours free of cost for three days. Supper and breakfast is provided, there are plenty of cookshops and taverns about where you can get a good and inexpensive lunch, the hosta Skarat will give you a list if you ask her; she speaks Trade and Cadandril. You don't have to worry much about understanding people, you can find lots around who can talk to you, ancient ties between the Marnhiddas and the meien mean it's one of the languages we teach our students." She pursed her lips, looked past Greygen as she went through her head for what else she should say. "Um . . . three days . . . after that, unless Nischal Tay makes special arrangements, you'll have to find other housing. You should hear from the Biserica Varou before the Guest Days are over. Um . . . the Hosta can change your coin for you to the tokens we use here in the Valley."

Sansilly looked down at herself, wrinkled her nose. "Is there a place where I can wash our clothes? I haven't had anything really clean for months it feels like."

"Oh. Right. Go see the Hosta, give her the things you want washed and she'll get them back to you by morning. You might as well hand over everything. If you want to go out, she'll give you visitors' robes; you can wear those anywhere, you'll see plenty of others dressed like that and it'll let folks know you're new. I think that's all. Probably won't see you again. 'Twas a pleasure. Maiden Bless." She left.

Sansilly looked at Greygen and giggled. He didn't blame her for that. The robes were black and somewhat skimpy, with a braided leather rope for a belt. His hit him above the ankle and made his long thin feet look silly. Hers snugged against her curves as if it loved her. He gave her a hug. "Let's go see what's here."

There were lights all over the huge pile that was the Biserica with its attached outbuildings, but the shades were pulled across the windows and the doors were firmly shut, the lamps above them extinguished. Farther on, though, the street lamps turned night to day in front of the taverns, cha houses and cookshops that peaceful years had brought to cluster about the Old Buildings; these were what part Synggal had called the Complex. It was a happy, noisy, busy place, as crowded with all sorts of people as Dander was on a High Market day.

Greygen felt his body and his mind expanding; he hadn't realized how clenched he'd been since the Glory came. He rested his arm on Sansilly's shoulder, rubbing gently at the muscle under the coarse cloth. She looked up at him, eyes laughing.

It was one of those autumn nights when the breeze is just cool enough to feel like silk along the skin. They walked through a very young crowd, most of them still in their teens, all colors, sizes and shapes, many from peoples he'd never seen before even with all the traders visiting Dander/Calanda, the mix spiced with a few merchants, meien and gyes, all of them ambling about the Complex, some laughing and shouting, some quieter, a few solitaries sitting at tables or holding up walls.

After awhile, Sansilly leaned against him and groaned. "Greg . . ."

"Mm?"

"A while ago I was feeling young as them, but my feet are telling my years. Let's sit a while. And I want a cup of cha."

"What about that place there?" He pointed.

"As long as there's a table with chairs."

The cha house's tables spread out into the street, thick, short candles with glass shields burning in the middle of each. There wasn't room for a skinny snake outside, but when Greygen eased past the crowded walk and under the roof, he found a small table for two tucked into a corner.

He got Sansilly seated, slid into his own chair and had a chance finally to take note of what was happening around him.

Girls in aprons carried trays from a door at the far end of the room, moving with a peculiar gliding gait that was almost a dance as they went between the tables, emptied their trays and sped back for refills.

Near that door there was a small raised stage. A young woman sat on a stool with an instrument whose like Greygen had not seen before, five or six strings, metal from the sound of them, a triangular sound box. At the moment she was tuning it, plucking the strings, turning the keys. When she finished, she called out something in mijlocker, laughed at the answers she got, then took up an ivory pick and settled to her playing. It was a joyous noise she made, fast and furious, a sound to set the foot tapping and the blood racing in the veins.

"Kak' trevah?"

Greygen twisted round. "What?"

"Ei vai, Dandri?"

"Yes."

"Um . . . what . . . um . . . want?"

"Ah. Cha. A pot of cha. How much?"

"Um . . . nik, no pay." She pinched the cloth of his robe between thumb and forefinger. "Visit. Biserica . . . um . . . gift." She moved her smile from him to Sansilly, then went gliding off.

Sansilly watched her a moment, turned back to him. "Zdra, isn't that a friendly thing. I like that music, don't you, Greg?"

"Mm."

"Makes me want to dance. Remember when we were just wed, how we used to dance holes in our shoes?"

"Mm."

"You!" She reached across the table to him.

He took her hand, closed his fingers tight around it.

* * *

The young woman finished her piece, bowed and stepped down from the stage. A tall, narrow woman brown as bitter chocolate came running up the stairs, long black hair flowing like water over her shoulders. A blond girl as tall and thin, so pale she was almost albino, followed her, waving a flute. In the explosion of applause, the blonde settled herself on the stool, the dark woman began pacing back and forth along the stage, her eyes lifted to the smoky rafters.

"Kitun and Arenquey." The girl giggled as she set the pot on the table with practiced ease, then the mugs and a plate of wafers, a jar of honey and tiny pitcher of milk. "Poet 'n ... um ... music writer." She clicked her tongue with annoyance as someone outside began whistling for service, then went trotting off.

On the stage Kitun clapped her hands together, intoned a string of words. Arenquey began drawing a soft flow of sound from the flute. The talking at the tables hushed, faces turned toward the stage.

Greygen guessed at a few of the words, but he didn't really need to know what she was saying to take pleasure in the twining of the flute around the strong supple voice of the poet. He sipped at the tea, watched Sansilly enjoying the night and felt a deep and abiding sorrow that Calanda and Dander no longer had such peace and pleasure.

3

ON THE SHORE OF THE STATHVOREEN

With the cloak draped about her to conceal her pregnancy, her hair a fall of polished gold, Tingajil sang one of the Poet's songs, an invocation of happier times with that touch of sentimentality that cursed all his work, but made him enormously popular. The Agentura's Cadandril was imperfect, but she could see that he was catching enough of the sense to be impressed. *What more can you ask of a Marn's Poet? And this is how we spend our substance to keep Skafaree's Berkwast from scenting our weakness and scooping us up to sell to that child who calls herself Marn.*

She glanced along the board with its load of food and wines, though most of the bottles held water or cold tea. Osk gloomy in his finery, that was all right, it was his nature, even the Agentura knew that. The Panya Valiva regal in a velvet robe with jewels glittering in the candlelight. They were real, though as temporary as all this fare if Osk decided he'd rather have guns than crystal history. Vedouce, massive and smiling. *I am blessed to have him with me. The mind behind that dull face, I think it never stops. Him and Heslin. They aren't all that fond of each other, too alike, I suspect, and Vedouce only tolerates foreigners, but they're too practical, both of them, to let antipathy wreck what they're trying to do.*

The rest were Osk's officials and Vedouce's trivuds, wives and daughters scattered among them, putting on a brave show. She let her eyes drift over them, blessing the Mask for hiding her face and shift of her gaze. *Brave show—and the best part is, it doesn't look a show. He's disappointed, this Agentura. He expected a rag-tag chaos. That's good; when we bargain tonight for supplies, he won't have the edge he'd thought would be his. I won't pay famine prices. If I have to, I'll deal with Karpan aNor or the Sharr. Maiden Bless, I miss Oram. Mother was right, I need someone who'll do my spying and won't be bought. If Hedivy escapes whatever happens with*

*the Enemy . . . Nik, think of that later. Watch the man.
This is no time to let your mind wander.*

As Tingajil finished her song, the Agentura
snapped his fingers in the island way of applause.
"Splendid songbird, O Marn. As lovely in face as in
voice. Should you ever grow tired of her piping, my
Master would have a place for her; perhaps we could
arrange something, ah ah?"

"I think her husband would have a thing or two to
say about that, O Agentura."

"Husband, ah yes, well husbands have taken the
belibot before this and turned their heads away."

"Our customs are different, Man of the Skafarees.
But to each, of course, his homeways are most dear.
How goes your master? I've heard he is coming from
his mourning time and ready to wed again."

4

BISERICA

The Prieti Meien Nischal Tay was a harried woman
with gray hair drawn tightly into a braided bun. Her
face was square, heavy in the jaw, her nose long and
thin; her voice was remarkable, deep, almost a bari-
tone. "It is difficult," she said. "We're an educational
institution these days, a place of research and a
manufactury of interesting trifles, not so much a
renter out of guards. Still . . . hm . . . we have strong
reason to be grateful to every Marnhidda Vos since
the first and your Marn has an unanswerable argument, though not one I'd try on the Mijloc Council."
She dipped a pen into a bottle of ink, wrote on a
small square of paper, talking as the nib danced

along. "They've forgotten a great deal with these past two centuries of peace. If the Glory had put roots in Oras it might be different. Ei vai." She waved the paper to dry the ink, then folded it over and reached for a stick of sealing wax. "I have the will, if not the latitude of action my predecessors enjoyed." She melted a pool of red wax, slipped a ring from her finger. "While I'm doing my consultations and my cajoling, you needn't worry about expenses or living quarters." She pressed the seal into the cooling wax, slipped it back on her finger. "Take this note to the hosta Skarat and she'll provide what tokens you need." She pushed the note across the desk, smiled as Sansilly collected it. "You'll find a young woman waiting for you, a meie trainee, she's from Yallor-on-the-Neck and speaks Cadandril as well as a number of other languages and she's been told to make herself useful."

"My name is Zayura." She was taller than Sansilly but extravagantly thin, as if she'd grown a third again the past year and hadn't had time to catch up with herself. Her dark hair was cut short, bits swinging into points at ear level, her eyes were strange, very pale gray with a black rim round the iris. Those eyes widened when she looked at Greygen. "I see we have a friend in common, the little Healer, I mean. One leg on me, two on you. Ei vai, we can talk about that later. It's past noon. Have you eaten yet? Or would you like to freshen up a bit first?" She held up a book, eyes twinkling. "I've got studying I can do."

Sansilly sopped a washrag into the basin, scooped a fingerful of the soft soap from a glass bowl beside the tap, then began patting at her face. "What do you think of her, Greg?"

"Smart. Acts older'n she looks."

She ran the washrag over her arms and hands. "You think she's a runner or did her folks send her?"

He rubbed at his nose. "Runner."

She rinsed out the rag, splashed water where the soap had been, took the towel he handed her. He watched her rubbing briskly at her face, then her arms. She hung the towel with that neatness she always showed in other people's places, began dragging a comb through her tangled hair. "Prieti Meien, she's going to do it, isn't she?" She didn't wait for an answer. "She's a lot like Jasny was before her troubles, stubborn and clever. Marn'll get all she can give. I hope it'll be enough. Zdra zdra, we won't talk about that." She wrinkled her nose at the mirror. "Skin's peeling worse'n when I was a tadling chasin' my brothers about. Let's play today, Greg, do you mind? I'm so tired of fighting."

"Look at things and just fool about?"

"Mh, wear ourselves numb so we don't think about you know. And find out if that girl is playing that music again, maybe somewhere we can dance. And you get that look off your face, Greg. It's been a long time since we stepped together, but it's not a thing you forget."

Greygen chuckled, let her pull him to his feet. "We'll see."

"The Son's War finished here." They were standing on the top of the wall looking down at the weeds and grass on the outside. Zayura went on, "I've been reading about it. Weeks of fighting right here, the first longguns and other things, a terrible time. The

Healer and Hern Heslin were in that tower for a while. You see where it's all black and crumbling? Heslin was burnt near dead with vuurvis fire, but she brought him back. And it was just after that when the glass dragons came and the Healer rode one of them up there." Zayura pointed at the rugged granite wall rising more than a hundred yards from the Valley floor. "See that tall ragged looking tree? That's Ser Noris, he's still prisoned there, angry enough to chew nails if he had a mouth. The Healer was up there for two hundred years, a lacewood tree growing beside him, but a stranger came from nowhere, touched her and woke her." Zayura made a face. "Sad, in a way, because she leaves one war and the minute she wakes she's facing another. Um ... Omma Lestar, better not lean on that merlon, the Wall hasn't been maintained much. Pieces of it break off every day. Where would you like to go next?"

Sansilly glanced at Greygen, her dark blue eyes twinkling as she said, "Do you have woodworkers here?"

5

ON THE SHORE OF THE STATHVOREEN

The wind whipping the Stathvoreen into white peaks caught at K'vestmilly's cloak, ran in icy rills down her back and legs as she walked the Agentura to the pier and the boat that waited to take him to the Skafar galley waiting dark and sleek out beyond the shallows. The Osklanders and the Marn's Own lined the walkway, cheering and snapping their fingers, lifting children to see the Marn in her Mask. They were dressed in their best clothes and making a goodly show, only half pretense. They knew what Skafars were like and what cargo many of those galleys carried south.

"Your people look healthy and in good heart."

"As good as one could expect," she murmured, "when their hearts yearn for home. We will be back, you know. There are things happening beyond our sight, be assured of that."

He glanced behind her at the blank-faced meie. "Oh I am, Marn, I am. And I will convey my thoughts to the Berkwast."

She smiled with her hands the way her mother had; behind the Mask her mouth was twisted with disgust and anger. It would be easy to let him know what she thought of him and his slave-taking master, but she needed the food shipments and she couldn't face another war, not with winter coming and enemies who could hit and be across the sea again before she could reach them.

K'vestmilly Vos stood at the end of the pier, watching the galley slide toward the horizon, the meie behind her, blocking the view if there were snipers in the hills. Heslin said Sleykyn seldom used the longgun, they liked their kills up close and personal, but there was at least one who didn't fit that mold, the one who'd nearly skewered her with a crossbow bolt a few months ago. That was why she'd ordered Heslin, Vedouce and Osk to stay inside. Don't give them that much of a target, she'd said. Don't tempt the notneys. I have to go. You know that. Not you. Not any of you. Osk didn't matter, but she couldn't let him know that. Heslin and Vedouce were vital.

She straightened her shoulders, swung around. "Time to go back."

Zasya's face was impassive, her eyes darting from side to side, watching the Fireborn, watching the crowd, her longgun ready, the holster flap undone to free the shortgun if she needed it.

Lifting her hands to acknowledge the cheers from her people, who had little enough to celebrate but took a grim pleasure in sending the Agentura off with a bug in his ear, K'vestmilly could see them loosening up, the pretense turning real. *I have to think up more things like this, Hes might have some ideas. Got to keep morale up, or they'll melt away, cross the Sharr and go to ground till the war's over. Mother was right. They need myth as well as reason, maybe more. The Healer ... something to do with her ... celebrate ...* She laid her hand on the mound of her child, stopped, startled. "She kicked me." She caught the eye of a woman in the front row, saw her grinning through tears. She turned to the woman, she didn't know her name, but that didn't matter, she took the woman's hand and pressed it against the child and, as the baby kicked again, thought *This one, she's Marn in the womb.*

"She moved. The little one moved."

Then, somehow, Tingajil was standing in the door of the Longhouse, picking a quick joyful tune from her lute and between one breath and the next the crowd was dancing. An Osklander, a miner, ran to his lodgings and was back a moment later with a fiddle, more players joined him and the gathering turned from a show of force to a spontaneous celebration of whatever they thought to celebrate.

K'vestmilly Vos made her way to the Longhouse, slipped in behind Tingajil. She gave Osk and Vedouce a hand-smile, beckoned to Heslin and let him escort her up the stairs to the loft.

* * *

"That was well done, Kimi."

She slipped the Mask off, looked at it a moment, then set it on the table beside her chair. "Yes," she said, "I think so. And there'll have to be more of this."

"But carefully done. Too much and you lose what you've gained."

"I know. If things go well, the baby and Spring will come together. We could build toward that." She closed her eyes, the strain of the past days pressing down again. "At least we got food out of that notney and at a fair price. We need bullets, powder, more guns. If I don't hear from Greygen fairly soon, I'll have to send someone to the Neck . . . I'm afraid it'll have to be you, Hes . . . I can't see anyone else coping with those land zarks . . . even Mother was wary of them . . . we'll need spring steel . . . I want someone making crossbows . . . we could have contests . . . that might be one way of building good feeling . . . not invented, they all know how much we need . . . Maiden Bless, what I'm doing to my people, Hes . . . tell me I have to do it . . . make me believe it. . . ."

"I won't waste my breath telling you what you already know, Kimi." He moved around behind her, began kneading the stiff muscles of her shoulders and neck. His hands were warm and soothing, she leaned into them and let herself relax.

6

BISERICA

Greygen took a long pull at the beer, sat smiling at nothing much as he thought about wood and working with it. That old woman who ran the wood shop was a master carver and joiner. When Greygen lifted the toy table and ran his hands over the joins, his pleasure was almost as great as when he made love to Sansy. The grain perfect, not a nail in the whole thing and so sweetly glued that there was no smell, not a trace visible. He rolled the taste of the brew on his tongue, enjoying it, enjoying even more the invitation he'd got to come and work with them. The war and all its horrors was suddenly so far away in distance and time, he almost didn't believe in it any longer. He drank again and listened to Sansy exercise her curiosity.

Sansilly sipped at her cha, then set the cup down, fixed bright curious eyes on Zayura. "You know a lot about us."

"My father's the Galyeuk of Yallor. He let me stay around to hear the reports his spies brought him." She twisted her face into a sad scowl. "And Treshteny the Timeseer went by there on her way south. She read me three futures and I liked none of them, so I came away here."

"Mad Treshteny?"

"If she's crazy, it's only in spots. She knows a thing or two. The Enemy will find that out, one hopes when it's too late to counter her."

5. Hunting the Balance

With the sun breaking the horizon in the east, Tserama put Drinby Ri at her back and took the Sacred Way as it curved from the Hill Circle and headed toward Danoulcha through the richest of the farms and vineyards. In the northwest, the sky was still black with smoke and ash. Drifts of ash were settling on grapevines and maize rows, dropping silently onto the yam plants and the grain sprouts, but the ground had stopped trembling and Sem Ri Drinby had turned sluggish as It always did once excitements were over, so she knew the mountain's cough was done and the sky would start clearing in a day or two.

As she swung the staff and strode along the Sacred Way, she was heavy with portent, weighted down with message, tired of her walking and tired of her smell. That was as it always had been, but there was more this time, an unfocused uneasiness that was a lump in her stomach as if she'd eaten bad meat.

She passed into Kyin Chagcan's farm with its neat row of bren houses, naked bren children playing in the dirt with bayas, paglets and goats, coughing from the ash, round dark eyes opening wide as they watched her stump past on the stone road they were spanked for touching. Yearlings and tads they were, too young to know who she was, the older ones were already in the

Chagcan's fields with their parents. No tug here, so there were no messages for Kyin Chagcan. There seldom were. He was a man the Gan Khora had touched at birth, happy and friendly, so he almost never had quarrels that needed patching; he did his duties well, tending the spirit in the kingpost of his house with rite and food, providing for his bren so they could tend theirs. He had the grass pulled from the Sacred Road, sent his daughters each day to sweep the dust off the stones and wet them down down so the heat wouldn't crack them. The spirits on his land were fat and happy, the air was full of ariels (even today, bright glimmers in the ash, translucent flowerforms with tendrils like roots trailing beneath them), tame brus kept his fields clear of pests (she caught the flicker of their low-to-the-ground spirit forms playing tag among the maize stalks, heard their high-pitched mind-laughter mixing with the milder gabble of his roof-hibbils), wild brus lived in his woods and chased away lightning in the rainy season, the cuchimi in his wells kept his water pure, his maize was the tallest in Danoulcha Round, his rasba pods burst with the burden of their silky fibers, his bales brought the highest prices at the Pya Fair at the End of Dry, his beasts threw twins almost every time and both gets grew strong and healthy.

Walking this arc of the Sacred Way was like resting in a hammock on a warm day; it was a thing she tasted on her tongue at the beginning of the Reading Round and it helped her endure the last days. She sighed and smiled and swung along.

That changed the moment her foot crossed the boundary onto Kyin Progsan's farm.

!Anger! !Hunger! !Fear!

Progsan's spirits screamed at her in voices muffled

as if they were sealed in bags and buried deep. And so
few of them. No brus. No ariels. And if there were
cuchimi in his wells, they were silent and withdrawn.
A chill went down her spine when she thought of
how few were left. Eaten? Driven away? What happened to the others?

The fields were nearly as rich and green as
Chagcan's, the maize almost as tall. Why? If the brus
were banished, what took their places? The goats in
their pen were fat and sassy, their fine white hair so
long it brushed the ground. Yet the spirits were gone.
Why?

She walked past a row of neat bren houses with
bren children playing in the mud. The houses were
dead, the hibbils gone from the thatch, the house
spirits driven out of the kingposts. Driven somewhere, she couldn't tell where. The children stopped
their playing when they saw her, scuttled into the
houses.

There were strange poles set up by the door of the
farm house, black and shiny with a rayed face painted
gold. She didn't recognize that sign, it wasn't the Gan
Khora, not the Maid-Who-Blesses, that was sure.
Hard and shiny. Gold. Odd. Gold in any of its forms
belonged to the Jeboh off in far Ragyal. Why would
Progsan do that? He must have been given the right,
the Jeboh's youmbards would have his head off in a
minute without it. Why? The Jeboh left the Lakelands alone except for taxtime and that wasn't for
what . . . two months? three? Why? The Sem Ris
hadn't given her any of this. Why? What did it
mean?

She thumped the butt of the staff on the thick
hairy leaves of mugsa weeds growing in the cracks of
the Way stones, wrinkled her nose at the musty

smell. *Progsan and his poles. Braying to the world the Jeboh's Favor. Gold. It has to be that. Here in Danoulcha. We don't want the Jeboh looking at us.* She crossed her fingers in an avert sign. *Oh Gan Khora, O Maid-Who-Rules, turn the Jeboh's eyes away from us.*

With the fearful weeping of the spirits rasping at her mind, she plodded along, the tonk of the staff a count of paces steadier than her breathing. Grit fell from the air, tiny tinklings on the stone, grit rasped beneath the soles of her feet and tumbled down the heavy folds of her tsadar. The wind was hot and erratic, teasing the short hairs loose to tickle her face, squeezing beads of sweat from her pores, turning ash to mud on her skin.

Even when she crossed the boundary into Kyin Chidril's farm, she could feel/hear the wailing of Progsan's spirits.

Danoulcha sprawled beside the Danu, one of the Five Lakes of the Ston Gassen, a northwestern Province of Bagklouss. It was a village of one hundred families, with a leatherworker's shop, a tailory, cobblery, smithy, and dozens of other small establishments that made whatever the Danoulchans needed. In the Mita Jri, the square at the center of the village, there was the fountain called Te-Ba or Navel and beside the fountain a wide stone bench known as the Reader's Bench. The Gan Khora's GodHouse was built on the east side of the square, the other sides were lined with cookshops and chahouses with round tables scattered out across the paving where their customers ate and drank.

Looking neither right nor left, Tserama walked along the ashy cobbles of the main street, disturbed again by the weary sad whispers of evicted house

spirits and the sense of dark, dead houses like patches
of rot on the living fabric of the village. A month ago
when she left on her Reading Round it wasn't like
this. Such a short time. So many changes. As if the
explosion in the north had its cousin here.

The people in the streets, gossipers, men and
women both, women and men hurrying along, they
left a wide space about her. That was as it always had
been. The Reading built an aura about her that kept
people off until she was ready for them. But there
were others that stared at her, then turned their
backs. Like the houses, they were dark to her.

Shopkeepers were out sweeping off the flags in
front of their doors, wiping down their windows.
Half a dozen Priestboys were on the roof of the
GodHouse washing down the tiles. More were out in
front, cleaning the incense altars and washing the
carved relief on the front of the GodHouse that
showed the Gan Khora bending down to give her
hand to a child. They scowled when they saw her,
but that too was nothing unusual. They belonged to
the Covenant of Men and found the Woman's Side
an intrusion on what they considered their ground.

The water in the Te-Ba's catch basin was black
with ash, thick and sluggish, and the jet that usually
shot from the frog's mouth was reduced to a trickle,
the fountain's pipes being clogged with grit. She
turned her back on the choking frog, settled crosslegged on the Readers Bench, her hands resting on
her knees, the tsadar bunched up, its stiff folds angular about her body.

"Tserama."

"Munyel."

The old woman pulled her shawls about her narrow shoulders and eased a bony hip onto the bench. "Changes."

"Mm."

"The Sem Ris tell you what it's about?"

"They're agitated. Something's going to happen, but they won't talk about it, not even to me."

"Ah."

Tserama closed her eyes and waited for Munyel's message to come swimming up. Colors swirled behind her lids, exploded out, coalesced again to show a girl lying by a stream, her clothing torn half-off her, blood on her thighs, her eyes wide and staring.

"Mechana . . ."

"You know the father? You know who did that to my grandchild?"

Once again Tserama closed her eyes, letting the scene play out before her mind's gaze. "Piwann's second son Chagu was with those who caught Mechana as she went to bring in the wash; he helped them trap her but he's not the father. Chagu stood watch while the other three used Mechana then frightened her worse than they hurt her. They told her if she said anything, they would see her whole family taken in chains and sold to the Fahláhin across the mountains. I didn't understand who they were before, but I do now after I saw Kyin Progsam's Farm—the Jeboh's youmbards are come north to greet that sour man. I don't know why."

Drawing in a long breath, she lifted her head and squinted her eyes at the Priestboys who'd stopped their work to stare at her. "Progsan is dark. He will not believe my Reading. He has the Jeboh's sign at his House. Silence is best. Take Mechana to the Healwitch Bayacan, she needs to mend the torn places in the child's soul." She set her hand on the old woman's arm. "Gan Khora bless you and yours. And watch where you put your feet, old friend."

"Tserama."

"Piwann."

The cobbler was a short, stocky man, his fingers thin and knotted from the years bootmaking. He couldn't wait for her to bring up the dream, burst out, "Is there news of my son?"

Tserama closed her eyes and saw the one youmbard who stood aside. Short and broad, clad in leather and metal straps, a knee-length tunic dyed a dark red, he was armed with knife, gun, longgun slung across his back, stood with feet apart, hands clasped behind him, as he kept his eyes on the trail along the stream. A black leather hood covered the top half of his face with holes cut for his eyes. She began to know things about him, it was as if these things were written on the air around him.

He wasn't standing aside from reluctance but because he'd lost his chance when the four of them diced for the girl. He was irritated and hot, shifting from foot to foot as he stood outside the grove, grinding his teeth as he listened to the sounds behind him while he kept an eye out for their gyaman who'd string them from their ligpas if he caught them messing with a local virgin. He kicked at a clod, sucked his teeth as it exploded into dust. He was thinking about his father, wondering about his chances of sneaking off to see him without the Headman finding out he was back; he scratched at his crotch, ground his teeth some more at the whimpers, grunts and other noises coming from the grove.

Tserama sighed and opened her eyes. "He's alive and well enough, he was thinking about you not so long ago."

"Where?"

She hesitated, then shrugged. "With the youmbards."

"Ssst. I would rather not have heard that." He got to his feet, his face sagging, bobbed his head in farewell and stumped off, all the lines of his body drooping.

Though many stared and turned away, a slow trickle of people came to sit beside her. She could feel a kind of relief in them as they listened to the stories and messages she had for them, as if they'd seen too many changes they neither understood nor wanted and were holding onto her as a pole of stability in the midst of this confusion. She was a sign of the old times, the days when they knew what life was and how to deal with it.

By mid afternoon she knew no one else was coming and she was still weighted with messages she couldn't release until she faced the person each message was meant for. Those who hadn't approached her wouldn't listen whatever she did, but she had the need to tell; after that, the consequences of ignoring what she said would rest on their shoulders, not hers.

She got to her feet, shook out the tsadar, looked round at the tables and the people sitting there, eating handfood and drinking cha. None of them pulled at her. She turned slowly, felt the strongest tug and marched to the saddlery.

"Matsoï."

"Go away, woman, I want nothing from you."

"Matsoï . . ." Her eyes went up and words came out of her in a rush, words she hadn't arranged before, saying things she hadn't known before. "You have taken the Widow Karum's coin with false promises and mocked the spirits of her house."

"Pah." The gob of spittle bounced off the cobble by her foot, missing her more by chance than intent. "Old bitch got her money's worth." He ran his tongue over his lips, his eyes mocking her. "You should know."

She turned away, disgust sour on her tongue, her step a fraction lighter with that message peeled away. She followed the next tug, then the next and the next, looking into Danoulchan faces, the accumulated messages emerging when a presence triggered them. Up and down the streets she went. In and out of the shops. Emptying out what the Sem Ris had poured into her.

The afternoon wore on, the sun sank lower until it was a blurry glow behind the thickest layer of ash.

She passed a kerchief across her sweaty face, grimaced at the smears of grit on the worn white cloth. "It is done," she said aloud. "The Word is given. Gan Khora hold the rest of it."

The Spirit Reader's House was apart from Danoulcha, built on a rise that looked straight down to the lake, the soil rocky and thin, a place no one else wanted. It was a small house with a tile roof, one large room with a sleeping-loft where her children had spent their nights, a wallbed for the Reader, a second for her apprentice when she chose one, a kitchen and a pantry. Out behind there was a hoist for raising water from the lake, a washfloor with a brick stove for heating the water, drying lines, an earth closet and the kitchen garden.

Tserama could see smoke rising from behind the house, spreading out over the roof. *Ammeny must be doing the wash. Again.* She sighed. Her daughter was a problem no Sem Ri or God dream could help her with.

She set her marketing inside the door and walked around the house to the washfloor.

A fire was burning brisky under the vat of boiling water; the lines were full of dripping clothes. Tserama wiped her hand across her brow and wondered if she had anything clean left to change to.

Ammeny was a small dark figure bent over the washtub, scrubbing vigorously at a mass of dark clothing. Her hair was pulled into a tight knot atop her head, her face, arms, hands were red with heat and the rasp of the harsh soap. She didn't look up as Tserama came round the tub.

"Where's Brajid?"

Ammeny scrubbed at the clothes, arms going up and down at a steady rhythm, body swaying. After a few minutes, she said, "He went off day before yesterday with Brussal and Chouse."

"And he hasn't been back?"

"Don't know." She twisted a skirt into a long roll, squeezed out the water and tossed it into the basket beside her, reached into the gray, soapy water and pulled up a dishwipe, began rubbing it over the washboard.

"He didn't come back for meals?"

"No." Ammeny's body dipped and rose, dipped and rose. Sometimes, even when she wasn't doing the wash, she would sit in her chair and rock like that, Tserama didn't know why.

"Do I have any dry clothes?"

"Skirt and blouse. Washed them yesterday. Brought them in this morning."

Stiff with grit and ash, I suppose. Ah, Ammeny, I wish I understood the why of you. "Menny, you'll have to stop now. I need the tub for my bath."

"I've got to finish. I've got to finish."

"Hang up what you've got there, Menny love. You can start getting things ready for supper. I brought some meat and greens from town, we'll have a stew. If you'll get carrots from the garden . . ."

Ammeny went still for a minute, then she got to her feet and lurched off. Her right leg was shorter than her left; it was strong and didn't hurt her, but it gave her an ugly walk. When she was little, she was angry all the time because the other children mocked that walk, called her three-legs, dead bird, flop fish and worse; crying and screaming, she fought them and Tserama spent half her days soothing down the parents of bruised and bitten children. When Ammeny got older, she was sad because no one wanted to be around her, as if her lameness and her difference would rub off on them. As her older brothers and sisters married and moved out, then the younger ones began courting, she started doing odd things like the rocking and washing, washing, washing the clothes and things until they were worn almost transparent.

Tserama had always been detached from her children, though she was fond enough of them when they were babies; she was too busy at other times to pay much attention to how they turned out. Since she was a Spirit Wife, the village itself was their titular father, the names of their actual fathers never spoken. So she was the only parent they had. Hard luck for them, she sometimes thought.

Danoulcha dowered the girls and gave the boys landrights in farms out beyond the Ris where most folk were afraid to go, so she didn't have to worry about that. Chuskya, her oldest daughter, was the only one who'd inherited any talent, but it was a different sort, not the Reader kind. She was apprenticed to the Healwitch Bayacan.

One a year the others had gone, to farms or to marry, but never Ammeny.

Tserama wrung out the last of the clothes, tipped the soapy water into the run-off channel, cleared out the coals from the heater fire, smothered the unburnt sticks of wood and set them aside. There was enough water for her bath already hot in the boiler. Wood cost and the headman had been complaining for several years now about the amount she used. She looked at the basket of wet wash and sighed once more. If she left it sitting, it would sour and have to be washed again, if she hung the things up, the ash would do the job on them and they'd have to be washed again. *Still, better that than mildew.* Clicking her tongue, she shook out the skirt, pinned it to the line, reached for the next piece.

Brajid slid in as Tserama brought the stewbowl from the kitchen. She stood holding it and looking at him.

A muscle twitched beside his eye, then he smiled, that wide glowing grin that meant he was buying time to think up a good lie. "Yabba, ma, have a good Read?"

"Mm hm. Ammeny says you haven't been home since day before yesterday."

"Oh, her, she wouldn't know. I just came in after she went to bed."

"Mm hm. Anything I should know?"

"Ma aah." The sound was pure innocence, but his eyes flickered in the lamplight and slid off hers; he was very like Matsoï the saddler, who'd fathered him eighteen years ago when he was hardly older than this son of his.

"What I don't know, I can't cure. Thieving again?"

"Ma aaah."

"I see." She set the bowl down, turned to the chest for plates and spoons. "I'll tell you a thing, Brajji," she said over her shoulder, "a warning if you'll have it so." She straightened. "Here, take these, I assume since you're here, you'll be eating with us. There's a bad time coming." She lifted mugs from the chest, brought them to the table. "Listen to me for once, will you? The Woman's Covenant is going to be rubbed away for a while. I don't know if I can save myself, I certainly can't do anything for you. So be careful what you get yourself into."

"I'm not into anything, Ma."

"We won't talk about it any more."

He was looking hurt because she didn't believe him, but she didn't believe that either. He was the youngest, the wild one, the spoiled one, and he'd tried to lie his way out of trouble from the minute he'd lisped his first words. It was too bad he'd been born into this family with her as his mother. He needed a stronger hand and a warmer love than she could give him.

She nodded at his chair, then went into the kitchen.

The cha was brewed, the greens dished up, waiting to be taken to the other room. And Ammeny was washing her hands again. Tserama reached for her, then let her arm drop. Ammeny didn't like being touched. She picked up the pot and the greens platter, cleared her throat. "Menny, Brajid's back. Come on in and eat with us."

Tserama woke with a thundery feel in her head, lay staring into darkness thick and still above her. *Has to be way after midnight.*

The hibbils and House Spirit were unhappy because in her weariness and worry about her children, she hadn't noticed their agitation ... no ... call it anger, and it was their fratchetting that waked her. She pushed the quilt off her and sat up, rubbing at her eyes. "Tsan pyya, I'm coming. Hush now. Give me time."

She pushed the slide back and struggled out of the wallbed, a whole month's tiredness like weights on her shoulders and knees. In the sleeping loft above her, she could hear Ammeny's hoarse breathing, nothing from Brajid. He was gone again. She sighed, shook out her sleeping shift and stumbled through the shuddering dark toward the kitchen and the banked fire so she could light a lamp and see what was going on.

A nightshade on the lamp so she wouldn't wake Ammeny, she settled beside the kingpost, tapped it with the nail of her forefinger. "So, what is it?" She whispered, but the words sounded loud in her ears.

The House Spirit in the kingpost, the other spirits that dwelt in roof and wall, even the water spirits that visited from the lake—all of them yammered at her at once, pouring their complaints into her head.

"Enough," she whispered. "Be quiet and let me sort this out."

Because Ammeny refused to have anything to do with spirits, Brajid was supposed to keep the kingpost polished and the spirit dishes filled with oil and maize flour. He'd promised to do it, sworn he wouldn't forget. He kept it up for three days after she'd left, then got distracted or just didn't care.

"I have to find someone with the Gift," she murmured, speaking more to herself than them. "I have to put the word out I'm ready to apprentice. I let it go because Ammeny might try to hurt her. I can't wait any longer. It's a bad time, but I can't wait."

Strong agreement from the spirits, the spirit in the kingpost loudest of all.

"Tsan pyya, no one has spoken to me. What's the nearest round with a Reader coming on?"

Spirit talk was a buzz in her head that she didn't bother sorting out. She sat with her eyes closed, waiting.

Sense of flow and fluctuation, of immensity, image of yellow sunlight splashing, rippling, rings going out and out . . .

No one?

Sense of frustration . . . thistle leaves across her skin . . . fear . . . tiny buds of fear, tight and new. . . . *Not yet*, they told her, *we will look and find. The times are hard and strange, but we will find.*

Tserama got to her feet and groped her way to the kitchen; she found the cruse of oil and dipped up some maize flour, took these back to the living room. Walking as quietly as she could over the grass mats she herself had woven on rain-drenched nights between the Reading Rounds, she filled the oil dishes and poured a cone of flour in each.

"While you're at it, you might have a look and see what my son's up to." She poured a dollop of oil on a polish rag and began working it into the wood of the kingpost, smiling as she felt the spirit turn in the wood, pressing into her hand like a stropping cat. "I'm home a while, so there's no hurry on the girl." She yawned. "When I'm finished this, I'm going back to bed, hoping you'll let me sleep through this time."

A frantic banging dragged her awake again.

She undid the latch and pushed the slide back. "Wha . . . Brajji?"

"Ma, you gotta come."

She pulled her hand across her mouth, shut her eyes a moment. "What'd you do?" she said, eighteen years of weariness in her voice.

"Nothing!" The word was crisp, angry; she blinked, startled into believing him. "Headman caught holda me, said to get you'n Menny to the Mita Jri fast, Priestboys running everywhere, banging on doors saying the same thing. Youmbards all over the place."

The tables and chairs were pushed back, the portable stage from the GodHouse was set up in front of the fountain, and the Mita Jri was jammed with people by the time they reached the square. The crowd was clotted into muttering groups with serpentine paths between them; Brajid used these to wriggle his way to the front, but Tserama was content to stand in the shadow of Drepor's cookshop awning, the lump in her belly colder and harder as she waited to know what this was about; she could hear well enough and she didn't need to see, didn't want to be seen. Arms folded across her breasts, her eyes blank, Ammeny stood beside her, head bobbing as she moved in that back-and-forth rocking that disturbed the others around them so much that they left an arms length between her and them.

The muttering in the crowd grew louder, almost drowning the scrape of sandals on the flags and the throat clears—then quieted as the two doyas came from the GodHouse and climbed onto the stage. They looked around, whispered to each other, clumped down the stairs and went back inside.

Tserama rubbed at her arms, ran her tongue over her teeth. The cookshop's House Spirit was silent, hunkered down; its fear was a stench around her. The shop's roof hibbils were crouched in the openings under the round tiles, their eyes tiny yellow glows in the shadow there. Brus ran hither, thither, leaping from thatch to thatch. Ariels drifted overhead, so pale with dread that they were barely visible. Chabbil and cuchimi, the water and well spirits, wriggled up the fountain's spout and fell back with the droplets. The invisible inhabitants of Danoulcha were gathered thick around the Mita Jri. It was not a good sign.

A drumbeat started inside the GodHouse. A line of Priestboys came out, climbed the stairs and sat on the stage, the double drums on their knees, their quiet rattle going on and on.

A youmbard stumped up the stairs with his hand on a boy's neck; he took his place at the back of the stage, held a shortgun pressed to the boy's temple.

A second youmbard followed holding onto a thin youngish woman with a vague, wandering gaze, a third prodded ahead of him a much older woman, stocky and fierce. Tserama blinked as she saw a small creature trotting beside the thin woman, a spirit boy with short curly horns and the hind legs and hooves of a goat, green as newly unfolded leaves, translucent as glass. He saw her watching, stopped to stare at her, then rushed to catch up with the thin woman.

A fourth youmbard marched onto the stage with Yubbal Paggoh of the GodHouse following him.

Tserama sniffed. Paggoh and she'd gone round and round in past years, messages from the Sem Ris he didn't want to accept, niggling at the village council meetings when he tried to get her allotment reduced. He was peering out at the crowd as he moved, looking for her, she thought, and stepped deeper into the shadow under the awning.

The elbows of the drumming boys flew and the noise they made increased—then stopped as the sticks dropped and hands stilled the drumheads.

The youmbard's voice growled out at them. "See these women. They've come to steal and tear down, to turn your peace into bloody war. They come disguised with harmless looks, but don't be fooled. They are spies and killers, only the first to invade our land. No, they are not alone. Others are loose in the land. Don't listen to them when they come whispering treason to you. They carry disease in their bodies and murder in their hearts." He lifted a hand. The boys drummed again, a crescendo of noise that broke off as abruptly as before.

"There is a reward. If any of you see strangers about, report them to the GodHouse. For each confirmed sighting, the reporter will be excused all taxes for this year. If that sighting means the stranger is captured, the one who reports and those who capture him or her will be exempt from taxes for seven years. Anyone who reports falsely will have his tongue cut out."

He lifted his hand again.

The drums sounded, went silent. "A squad of youmbards will be housed in each Round of the Ston Gassen. They are to be obeyed in all things. The gyaman of each squad has full authority to levy fines for insolence and insubordination or give orders for the defiant one to be flogged." He paused, turned his hooded face slowly from side to side; when he spoke again, his voice had deepened. It was a basso roar that came at them. "THIS IS BY ORDER OF THE GRAND JEBOH OF BAGKLOUSS, ONKYON BASSOD OF THE HOUSE OF BASK."

He swung round, marched off the stage and into the GodHouse.

Tserama climbed the hill to her house, pondering what she'd heard, the chill moving from her stomach to the rest of her. *That's what the posts meant. Youmbards living here. More girls like Munyel's grand-daughter. Brajid . . . he'll get himself flogged, the young idiot . . . or worse. I wish I knew what he was up to.* She glanced at Ammeny trudging beside and wondered what this meant for her. Not good. Not good. Not. Good.

6. Deeper and Deeper

1

BAGKLOUSS

"Come up here." Standing on the wharf and looking down at her, the leather-masked youmbard with the gyaman's chain and medallion round his neck jerked his thumb up and over. "Your mouth shut, your hands where I can see them."

Serroi gathered her skirt, tucked it into the waistband and caught hold of the ladder. She went up without speaking, maintaining the silence she'd kept from the moment she'd let the blackened fronds fall; her captors had been equally silent, orders given by gesture and grunt, so she wasn't that surprised at this brusque greeting.

When her head cleared the planks, the youmbards waiting for her backed off, their guns lifted and ready. If she hadn't been so tired, so grungy from the days of travel in those canoes, she'd have been amused at their fear. She stepped onto the wharf and let her skirt fall, the frayed ends where Halisan had cut it off tickling her legs. *I must stink like swamp water. Maiden Bless, what I wouldn't give for a bath. . . .*

"Stop." The gyaman held up one hand, waved the other to send his men back another two steps. "Stand there and do nothing. If I catch a smell of trouble . . ." He didn't bother finishing the threat.

She sighed, folded her arms and stood looking past

them out across the estuary, wondering where they meant to take her next. Hedivy and the others were away clean, the disgruntled mien of her captors made that clear, so it was time to start thinking about how she was going to get out of this mess.

Just stay quiet, let them see how small and helpless I am . . . maybe that bit with the fern was a mistake . . . still, this is a new lot, they haven't seen me do anything . . . telling doesn't have the same force as seeing . . . time is what I need . . . let them relax a little . . . or put me on land . . . call on the kamen now . . . nixies? She glanced at the bay where the effluents from the river set a brown stain into the blue; no sign of nixies here. The healing must have spawned something, but she had no sense of what her children were this time. She sighed.

There were drums going up on the cliff, an odd double beat she'd never heard before. And columns of greenish black smoke. *Like they're fumigating the place. Figures.* She pinched her lips tight, fixed her eyes on the planks. *What's this waiting about? Why are we standing here staring at each other?*

The youmbard circle broke apart and a cage sitting on a dolly with four large wheels came trundling down the planks, pushed along by two gnarled old men in loose white shirts and pants, their heads shaved, their ears cropped; they moved clumsily, their ankles cuffed, the long chains between the cuffs clanking along the wood. The cage was almost a metal box, its sides, ceiling and floor a lattice of wide steel straps, the spaces between them about two inches square, barely wide enough to squeeze her hand through.

One of the old men threw a friction brake and stopped the dolly in front of Serroi. The other peered at her from rheumy eyes, fumbled with the padlock on the cage door until he got it open and freed of the staple, then both of them backed away.

The gyaman banged the barrel of his gun against the lattice. "Get in."

Serroi hesitated, glanced quickly around. The half dozen youmbards who'd fetched her from the swamp had rowed their proas into the bay and were sitting out there with their guns on her. The youmbards on the wharf were tense, fear coming off them like fog off ice. And the drums kept going.

With a grimace that acknowledged her lack of choice, she pulled herself onto the dolly and yanked the door open, stepped over the sill and into the cage. It was barely big enough to hold her; if she'd been any taller, she couldn't have stood upright.

There was a clunk and shudder as the old men slammed the door shut and replaced the padlock, then leaned their shoulders against the push bar. The smell that came off them smothered the ghostly odors of the cage, and her own. She scratched at the back of her neck, swore under her breath as she felt something scurrying away from her fingers.

The gyaman stalked beside the cage as it bumped along the wharf and onto the concrete road that ran between the landings and the row of warehouses chiselled from the stone of the cliff. An empty road. Nothing like the busy scene there when the *Ennachul* tied up and all this started.

Definitely don't want me contaminating the commons. This is getting strange. She wrinkled her nose, then shifted her feet to regain her balance as the cage rocked and twisted.

Not the first time this has been used . . . lots of practice shifting prisoners . . . should have realized that from the

*way they kept hold of me coming here . . . ei vai, Serroi,
you might as well relax till we get where we're going . . .
I need someone who can DO something, not just take orders . . . if I can't get away before the talking starts.*

The old men pushed the cage around a curve in
the cliff, then down the cracked and potholed road
past the shacks and garbage of the slum (as empty as
the port, even the children gone elsewhere), till they
reached landings on the bank of the river that emptied into Tson Kyere bay; they maneuvered along
these and stopped by the single riverboat tied up
there.

The cage and its dolly were winched on board, tied
down in the bow, then the leg chains of the two old
men were snaplocked to one of the wheels. Beyond
them the boat's crew moved about, busy getting it
ready to sail, ignoring her and the youmbards with an
intensity almost tangible although, from the look of
things, she was the principal cargo this trip.

The gyaman came round so he could see her face.
"There will be someone watching you every minute.
Do you see that jug?"

It was a large earthenware demijohn, salt glazed
over ugly yellow and brown horizontal stripes, a
waxed roll of leather stopping the neck; it was set
into a spring clip on the foremast, its neck handle
turned outward for quick grasping.

She nodded.

"Good. It's filled with drohma oil. If you try anything, you'll be doused with that and set on fire. Do
you understand?"

She nodded.

"Good. The journey to Ragyal will take about three
days. You will be provided with one towel a day to keep

yourself and the cage clean. The gog bucket will be set beneath the hole in the cage. The porgs . . ." He flicked a finger at the old men. "They'll empty it for you. Do you understand?"

She nodded.

"Good. You'll be given food once a day, in the morning. Water three times a day, one cupful each time. If you complain, you'll be given none. Do you understand?"

She nodded.

"Good." He swung round and marched off.

As they worked, the crew kept circling carefully around the cage and the two porgs chained to it. Not one of them looked directly at her. The sounds they made mixed with the noises of the city on the cliffs, noises muffled by distance, stone and a tangle of brush on a hillside whose slant was too steep to build on. At this point the river was a broad sweep of water separating into several channels that ran between long narrow sandbars fringed with dark wiry reeds. The swamp smell from the great fen on the north side of the bay and the stench from the mudbanks and the slum fought with the wind rushing down the river from the heart of Bagklouss, carrying ash from the pall that obscured half of the northern sky and sent black fingers groping south.

Serroi eased herself down until she was sitting in the cramped space, her back to the mast and the jug of oil. *Ei vai, let's see what else we can finesse.* She leaned against the side of the cage, looked at the old man closest to her. "What's your name?"

He opened his mouth, showed the stub of his tongue and made a harsh grating noise.

Serroi blinked. She cleared her throat, swallowed.

"Would you want to speak again? I'm a healer, I can do that. I can grow your tongue back, and your ears if you want."

He stared at her a moment, then shook his head, resettled himself and turned to his companion, his fingers flickering in a fluid gesture speech.

She found that interesting. The movements were small, so inconspicuous that the two men could carry on a conversation under the noses of their captors with little to betray what they were saying or that they were talking at all. How many years had it taken to develop that skill? How long they been prisoners? And why? What had they done? Likely she'd never know. *Too many years. No fire left in them. Not about to risk what they've got just to help a stranger. Hm.* As the boat left the landing and headed upstream, she eased herself into a corner of the cage, leaned her head against the lattice and dropped into an uneasy doze.

By the time the sun rose on the fourth day the riverboat had left behind the placid river villages, the lush fields, and nosed into a huge lake, blue spreading suddenly from horizon to horizon. The wind freshened, raising chop like horripilation on the water's surface.

Their white sails shining in the sunlight that struggled through the drifts of ash overhead, dozens of proas danced through the chop, the men on them bare except for a twist of cloth about the loins, brown bodies glistening in the cool morning light as they dropped nets into the water and hauled them back shortly afterward heavy with glinting silversides.

Falling grit filtered through the top and sides of the cage and mixed with three days' accumulation of sweat and oil. Serroi scratched at her wrist, where a rash was spreading across her skin. She looked at the redness and thought of healing it, but decided it wasn't enough of a problem for her to attract attention she didn't want.

They didn't bring her the usual bowl of porridge and hunk of hard bread. They didn't bring her water. They didn't come near her.

Frowning at the rim of the padlock visible at the edge of one of the open squares, she stroked her fingers along the waistband of her skirt, feeling the small hard spots where the picklocks were sewn into it. She could reach that lock any time she wanted, have it open in a breath and a half—but there was always someone watching her. She could feel the eyes, smell the spicy bite of fear. She glanced at the demijohn with the oil and knew she hadn't the courage to face burning, knew it wouldn't even kill her, knew that she'd heal and burn again and heal again, her body drawing force from water and earth no matter what her mind desired, and the pain would not stop, it'd just go on and on. . . .

She sighed and once more looked out across the water, missing the nixies, missing their glub-glub laughter and their mocking comments. Come to that, she missed Honeydew's exuberance, Halisan's music, Adlayr's complexes, even Hedivy's dour competence. *Since Ser Noris threw me away that time, I've never been alone. There was Tayyan and the meien, then Dinafar, then Hern . . . ayyy, Maiden, will I ache for him till I'm finally dead?*

The shores of the lake dropped out of sight as the ship plowed on. For a while there was only water and the distant etching of the mountains and the ash cloud that thickened with every hour that passed, then smudges appeared against the horizon, smudges that grew more solid as the hours passed.

Two islands. The largest had buildings in white marble with extravagant flourishes of colored stone, an abundance of green trees and vines, masses of red and yellow blossoms, paths that glittered from the white marble chips laid down on them, people like bright flowers walking on them.

The second was dark and forbidding. It was much smaller, the only green on it smears of moss and a few ropes of weed cast up on narrow pebbly beach. She sighed as the boat turned toward the dark one. *Figures.*

The youmbards supervised her unloading with the same fingertip care, the gyaman shouting orders at the two porgs who steadied the cage until it was on the meager landing; they stopped the dolly beside the jug of oil, set the brakes, then dropped to the squat with the cage between them and the oil, hands chatting sporadically as they waited.

A circle of youmbards formed around her, one of them with a lighted brand held ready, while the gyaman climbed the steep path up to a door recessed into a stone wall.

Serroi could hear his voice going on for several minutes and the low rumble of the answer, though she couldn't hear what was being said. She was impatient for him to be done with all this nattering. Once she was inside, someone would probably tell her the why of all this, give her some idea of what was going to happen to her. At least ask some questions. Questions could give more information than the questioner got.

* * *

The gyaman came striding back. He snapped his fingers, pointed up the path.

Ankle chains clanking, the old men rose, set their shoulders to the push bar and started the cage up the path, wheels creaking, their bare feet slipping on the stone, their breathing harsh as they struggled upward. Serroi sat tense, willing them to make it. If they slipped and let her go, the cage would scoot back down the path, fly across the landing and drop into the water; the thought of drowning was minutely more appealing than perpetual roasting, but it wasn't something she wanted to experience.

The slope eased off, the cage rumbled under a portcullis and into a corridor with a pierced ceiling. She felt eyes following her through those watchholes and above the creak, squeal and rumble of the dolly she could hear the clank of metal and the shuffle of feet. This lot was even warier than the others. As if she were a bomb the slightest wrong touch could set off.

Accompanied by the unseen escort, the old men pushed her deep into the fortress, stopping the cage at last in the middle of an empty room. They dropped to a squat behind the cage and waited.

It was an odd room. The strip where the cage sat was bare and dully gray as the hallway they'd pushed her through, the other section had a line of glass-filled doors on the north wall, sunlight streaming in through the panes, white marble walls and white tiles on the floor, jewel-bright rugs scattered across the floor, piled on top of each other, tapestry hangings on the walls, dozens of huge tubs glazed in green or blue or red, filled with lush green plants and ferns, a throne of sorts on a dais in the middle. The throne was a broad squat construction of ebony inlaid with ivory and gold, a gold silk cushion with silver fringes tossed onto the seat. Gilded cages hung from the high ceiling on gilded chains, yellow birds in them. In that deeply silent room, the only sound was their warbling.

Between the two sections there was a screen of black iron, beautifully wrought but as effective as bars at blocking access to the other side.

One of the doors opened, showing the balcony outside. Two young girls came through it, dropped to their knees, heads bowed, hands pressed palm to palm, raised before their faces. They were lovely creatures, with huge black eyes, black hair falling loose, the ends brushing the floor, slim bodies wound in gold tissue elaborately tucked and folded.

In her cage Serroi pressed her lips together. In the early days of the Mijloc there were scenes like this in the Domnitor's palace, and it was a girl like one of those who ran and took others with her to plant the seeds of the Biserica.

A woman wrapped in folds of white tissue came through the door, a woman of extraordinary beauty, moving with a sensuous grace. She crossed the room, went to her knees on the first broad step of the dais. "The Grand Jeboh of Bagklouss," she chanted, "Onkyon Bassod of the House of Bask."

The man who came through the door when she finished was a disappointment at first. His black robe seemed more important than he was, stiff with golden embroidery and glittering with spray on spray of diamonds clamped into gold claws; he was short and plump, with insignificant features set in a turnip shaped head, a wispy mustache framing a pink pouty mouth.

The two girls followed him across the room, took

his hands and walked him up the stairs, lowered him onto the golden cushion, then knelt by his knees.

He stared at her a moment, then turned his head and murmured something to the woman in white.

She lifted her hands, held them vertically, palms toward Serroi. "The Jeboh says: We know why you are here, Witch. We wanted you to see us, to know your death before it greets you, to know you need not die if only you surrender to the will of the One. We are the Compassion of the Glory. Accept the touch of Our Hands, accept the Gift of the Glory and you will go free. Your friends who are in Our Hands will go free."

Hedivy and the others? I don't think so. Go free? Ei vai, go free as long as I let you tie your strings to my mind.

Her lack of response was answer enough to bring the yellow shine to his eyes.

Taken, she thought.

He leaned toward the woman again, muttered at her.

"You have chosen. So let it be," she chanted.

The girl at his left hand rose with liquid grace, plucked a square of gold tissue from inside the folds at her waist and dropped it over his head, obscuring his face.

The woman in white rose to her feet and walked to the screen.

"Take it away," she said. "You know where."

The old men tugged the cage out the door and into the corridor; they pushed it deeper into the pile, then through another door. After setting the brake, they shuffled out. In the doorway, one of the porgs dug into a shirt pocket, tossed the key to the padlock onto the dolly. They slammed the door shut; two bars thunked home, then Serroi heard the mute old men trudging off.

She folded her hand, eased it through the straps and managed to get hold of the key. A moment later she had the door open and was on the floor looking around.

It was an iron room, walls, floor and ceiling studded with rows of rivets holding the plates in place, with slits up near the ceiling that let in narrow slants of murky light and a trickle of air. *Behold your death, that woman said.* She stood on tiptoes, tried to reach one of the slits, though they were too small to crawl through, even for her. She hooked her fingers over the bottom of one, pulled herself up and looked out into a littered court. She dropped to the floor, brushed the hair off her face. "I wonder what they're going to try. And when." She crossed to the door, grimaced when she saw there was neither latch nor lockhole on the inside. "So we wait. Hm. Ei vai, . . . when they come for me . . ." She looked at her hands. "I'm going to make someone very unhappy."

For the next half hour or so, the silence around her was profound, not even the scuttle of a bug on the wall. Serroi sat with her back against a wheel, watching a bar of light from one of the slits creep across the floor.

A clang. Several thuds, dragging noises.

She sat up. "Who is it? What's happening?"

No answer.

The noises went on, muffled, irregular, bursts of louder clunks and rasps, stretches of time with only a few pops and crackles to break the silence.

A wisp of smoke drifted in through one of the slits;

the floor where she was sitting and the air around her began to heat.

"They're roasting me." She sprang up, looked frantically about the room, but nothing had changed; there was no way out. The iron floor began to burn through her bootsoles. "I won't let this happen. I won't." She pushed the cage against the wall, climbed up on it so she was close to one of the slits. "Children," she cried. "Help me. Kamen, come to me. Nixies. Lamia. All of you. Come to me. HELP ME!"

2

Honeydew circled in a last farewell with the shapsa Sfirin, then darted away to catch up with the company. She settled on Adlayr's shoulder, sighing and silent for once, too lost in old memories and new to talk about them.

The mire was only fingers of stagnant water out here, except for a silt-laden stream that wandered through the thinning trees. They followed that stream into rolling grassland with a range of low brushy mountains to the east and a pall of black that covered the sky in the northwest. A few high-flying raptors made angular hieroglyphs across the patches of sky visible between poufs of cloud, and on the horizon in the west a dark blot oozed slowly along, a herd of grazers with riders like bright dots moving with them.

Hedivy stopped beside one of the last trees, a low gnarled thing with pointed, pale leaves and clusters of small, star-shaped flowers yellow as egg yolks with an over-sweet, rotten smell. He stood scowling at the distant herd, then turned his head. "Riding macs," he said. "We need those."

Honeydew stirred, the sound of his voice breaking through her doze. After fluttering up to sit on one of the crooked branches, she stretched, yawned. Glanced around. Blinked. Halisan was gone.

She went spiralling up above the tree and hovered there, looking back along the stream. A few birds, a furtive shadow or two scurrying from bush to bush. Nothing larger anywhere in sight.

Below her the two men were talking, but this disappearance was far more intriguing than what they were saying. She circled higher, zipped back along the stream a short way and looked again. Nothing.

She fluttered down, flew along the stream bank, scanning the tracks they'd left. Men's tracks. None of the smaller, narrower prints from Halisan's boots.

Honeydew hovered a moment, then started back, more puzzled than ever. It was as if the Harper had climbed into that *place* where she'd put her harp, and left not a smell of herself behind. Was she gone to help Serroi? Or . . . Honeydew shook her head and flew faster so Adlayr and the others wouldn't vanish on her as Halisan had.

She saw Hedivy and Adlayr where she'd left them and fluttered wearily toward them, picking up the discussion that had started up before she went off and hadn't got very far the whole time she'd been gone.

". . . how long it'd take. After dark, maybe." Adlayr was seated on one of the roots, his legs drawn up, his eyes on the grass. "See how many remounts they've got and what the watch is like. And we've got to get a lot closer before I try it."

Hedivy scratched at the beard that was long enough now to be a mat of wiry curls like his head hair, though it was a faded red instead of a faded brown and looked like a bad fake. "Mm. Guards're no problem. You just wait till that herd's well settled then go sicamar upwind. If those beasts are like the ones m'da had, they'll hit for the horizon soon's they get a whiff of you. Just be sure you drive them my way."

"Look, it's not as easy as that. Flying takes a lot out of me. And too much shifting too fast, I can get lost in there."

Honeydew heard the panic Adlayr tried to push down deep and hurried to hover by his shoulder, breaking into the tension growing between the two men. Hallee's gone, look round, Adlee, she's nowhere 'bout. You see her go? Honeydew didn't. She was there when Sfirin left, next time Honeydew look round, no Harper. Honeydew went back along the stream, no tracks, Adlee. You think something got her? Or did she just go?

Adlayr got to his feet, looked around. "You're right." He wiped his hand across his face. "It's like I couldn't remember she was supposed to be here until you said something, Honey. Hev, Halisan's gone. Honeydew says she came out of the swamp with us, disappeared after that. You see her go? Because I sure didn't."

Hedivy looked round, confusion then annoyance putting a momentary touch of color in his cold gray eyes. "Her business," he said. "She can take care of herself. Let's get moving. Be a couple days anyway before we get close enough to that herd."

Honeydew nestled on Adlayr's shoulder as he strode along, keeping on Hedivy's heels; he was tense and unhappy, nerving himself for the shifts to come. Though he kept up a good face for the others, she could feel his fears in the tightness of his shoulder muscles. Since that time in the Forest he was never sure he could come back once he shifted. He'd gone quietly berserk in the days afterward, forcing himself through shift after shift . . . well, he'd needed to, the way things were . . . but he did more than he needed to prove he could . . . and it didn't prove anything, the doubt was always there . . . and when he went in the water, it was a bad one . . . he was almost late because he was so close to getting lost . . . he didn't say anything to the others, but he told Honeydew about it a few nights ago . . . when nightmares wouldn't let him sleep . . . I wanted to stay there, he said, I wanted it so bad . . . if I'd had a hair more space, a hair less pressure, I don't think I could have come out of it . . . water pulls me now . . . even this muck . . .

He nodded his head at the muddy water of the stream.

. . . though not so much as the sea . . . I have to be careful, Honey. Very very careful.

Serroi had fixed Hedivy's leg so his limp was gone, which was just as well because when the stream turned east and they plunged into the grass, walking was difficult. The land was uneven, with washes and shallow ravines, rocky hummocks, some of them smallish hills, while the grass that concealed much of this grew on several levels; there was a short curly sort, another kind rather like very thin, very short bamboo and tough as wire, that whipped about their knees and was a trap to ankles and a third kind, scattered more sparsely, with sword-blade leaves and a central column whose feathered head was nearly shoulder high; fine yellow pollen flew about with the lightest brush against those long stalks.

Honeydew sneezed so hard she nearly fell off Adlayr's shoulder.

He tucked her into his shirt pocket, found a handkerchief and pushed it in with her so she could wrap it about her and breathe through the cloth, keeping most of the pollen away from her.

They stopped late in the afternoon to eat the last of the shapsas' fruit and worry down some trailbars They didn't talk.

Hedivy finished quickly, went to stand on a pile of rocks atop one of the faint blue mountains beyond; there were too many stades to go yet before he'd be able to lay his hands on a guide to lead them to Mount Santak, but it was somewhere in that range.

Adlayr set out fruit and water for Honeydew, moistened the end of the handkerchief and put her down on a tuft of grass so she could wash herself off and eat, then sat chewing at the trailbars, brooding over what waited for him.

Honeydew sipped at the capful of water and tore the section of fruit into bite-sized pieces. She wiped at her face with the damp cloth as she ate and drank, then curled up, the handkerchief wrapped around her, dozing until Hedivy came stalking down the slope to stop in front of Adlayr.

"They've turned, coming this way."

Adlayr lifted his head. "Ah?"

"We keep going, come night herd'll be maybe fifteen stades off. That close enough for you?"

Adlayr caught the straps of his pack, swung it up as he got to his feet. "Not yet. Another day. So let's get moving." He scooped up Honeydew, slid her into his pocket with the remoistened handkerchief and went striding off.

* * *

Three hours after sundown on their third day in the grass, Honeydew blew her nose, wiped her hand on the black fur at the base of the trax's long leathery neck. Her eyes were still burning from the assaults of the pollen while the grit and ash from the sky were irritating her skin, but she'd insisted on coming along; she'd heard the touch of desperation in his voice and how it steadied when she refused to stay behind.

The wind up near the clouds was tricky, blowing little gales then collapsing. Sometimes Adlayr dropped several yards before his wings caught and powered them up again. Though the wash where Hedivy waited was only a short distance off, he was getting tired. Gliding was difficult with the air the way it was and he was fighting himself, afraid of settling into the trax form and letting it do the flying. Honeydew was silent; she wanted to help him relax but she didn't know what to say.

The herdsmen's fireboxes were pinpricks of red in a darkness that was near total because of the clouds and the ash pall. Now and then a shadow blotted one of them out as one of the drovers walked past. She counted three nightguards from the noises they made with their rattling gear and their droning songs. One of them even had a flute he played at now and then. Badly. She made a face. *Hoosh, Adlee, were it Honeydew down there trying to sleep with that screech in her ears, Honeydew swear she'd tromp him flat.*

The trax coughed as Adlayr's mind laughed; more of the tension washed out of him, his body softened, his wings shifted angle and seemed to relax into the wind. *Honey, if my ears could grow flaps . . .*

Honeydew dug into the neck fur and pinched him,

heard the mindlaughter again. Good, she thought, get him laughing, doesn't matter how feeble the joke. Take his mind off and keep it off.

The herd was restless; about half of them were down, the others on their feet, wandering about, butting into each other. She saw a fight start between two of the younger beasts, then an adult moved between them, snorted and made annoyance sounds. The juveniles pulled in on themselves, went docile and wandered off. There were more of these brushes, some getting farther along than the others. There were blatting complaints at all the restless movement. They're really itchy, Adlee, maybe this muck in the sky's doing it. Shouldn't take much to get them running.

An absent mindgrunt from Adlayr, then he was flying above the camp. There were two men there, lying wrapped in blankets beside a boxed chip-fire, a third moving about, doing something at the back of a wagon. A bit farther on there was a rope corral with half a dozen macain dozing inside the ring.

Adlayr dipped low to judge the direction of the wind near the ground, then went swooping over a few hummocks and landed with more than his usual maladroitness, his feet and wings catching in the grass.

He shifted and rubbed at his sore nose.

Honeydew giggled. Adlee funnn eee. Adlayr grimaced, prodded at his nose a last time and got to his feet, muttering as he rose, "It's those zhaggin gas sacs, they throw my balance off. If my wings could carry my weight I'd be as adept as you, Honey, so shut your mouth about it, huh?"

A herd beast blatted and more of the herd rocked onto its feet as Adlayr knelt atop the tallest of the

nearby hummocks looking out across the camp.
"Smelling me already. Honey, go find you a mac and
stay with it. I'll give you ten minutes before I go
sicamar and start screaming. You be careful now."

She fluttered to him and patted his cheek. Honeydew do.

The camp was silent, the fireboxes faint red glows.
Out with the herd the man with the flute was trying
again. After a few minutes of this his companions
yelled the flute into silence; he started to sing then
and it was a measure of the awfulness of his playing
that his singing was preferable.

Honeydew chose her macai, settled in the spongy
growths along his neck; she put her mouth against
his skin, blew a warm buzzing song into his spine. He
quieted, stood groaning softly with pleasure as she
kept up her tease.

The sicamar's wild scream rode the gust of wind
that brought his scent to the herd.

Between one breath and the next the grazers were
on their feet; a second scream and they were off.

Two hours later, Hedivy and Adlayr were mounted,
each with an extra macai on lead. They pushed the
macs into a long lope and headed west, hoping to be
out of reach before the herders recovered their herd
and took a count of their spare riding stock.

7. The Winter That Didn't Come

The breeze off the Stathvoreen stirring the curtains was the only thing that made the loft bearable; in the living quarters at the back of the Longhouse, the smaller rooms were like ovens. K'vestmilly Vos sat slumped on a stool, watching the healwoman Olmena Oumelic pour water in a basin and wash her hands.

Zasya Myers stood on guard in one corner; Ildas lay beside the rail across the open end of the loft, his eyes fixed on the stairway. The meie was silent, so much a shadow that half the time K'vestmilly forgot she was there.

Olmena was a plump, smiling woman from Calanda, head healer in the clinic attached to Pan Pen's steel mills. She'd come away with Vedouce's wife in the frantic scramble when Pan Nov made his move to take the Pevranamist and Mask. She dried her hands with brisk efficiency, turned to face K'vestmilly.

"Haven't been doing your exercises, mp?"

K'vestmilly groaned. "I haven't had time. Too much to do, then I'm too tired." It was true enough, as an excuse. She'd moved constantly among the fighters and the Oskland refugees, showing the Mask, letting the women feel her daughter kick, using the vigor of her unborn child to rekindle hope and give them the strength to endure the uncertainty and the boredom. She'd spent hours with Heslin, listening to the reports from the spy web in the cities and outlands, still more hours with Vedouce working out strategy for retaking Dander/Calanda. Before she was Marn, she'd ridden and hunted, filled her days with activity and been rail-thin with the energy she'd expended. All that wasn't possible now. *Exercise, phah!* She hated those *things* Olmena wanted her to do. *Boring.*

"You're healthy enough and so's the child, but you're soft as butter, Marn." A twitch of Olmena's long nose, a minatory gleam in her dark blue eyes. "The longer you put off building strength, the tireder you're going to be. Works that way. And you know it, K'vestmilly Vos. So. On your feet. We'll make a start today. Set a time for tomorrow and tomorrow." Her eyes twinkled. "And I'll be here to see you do what you should."

"It's too hot to move."

"Bath after. Up."

As she stretched and clenched under Olmena's critical gaze, K'vestmilly listened again to the rumble of voices drifting up from beneath the mat she lay on, Heslin and Vedouce going over last night's spy reports.

"... doesn't dare go inside, but Spider One says the Temple glows like it's burning." Heslin's voice was clear and carrying though he was trying to speak low enough to keep her from hearing the uglier parts. She smiled as she sucked in as deep a breath as she could, tensed her abdominal muscles. *Speechmaker. Habit had got away from him again.*

"... pyre in the court that's kept going, lots of

black smoke coming from it. Rumors. Unconfirmed. That the new Preörchmat is sacrificing a dozen women a day on that fire. Only women. No children, no men. Spider One says she doesn't know why."

Vedouce grunted, said something, but K'vestmilly couldn't catch the sense.

Heslin's chair creaked as he shifted. She smiled again, visualizing him shuffling through page after page of his scrawled script.

"Arms still coming in, but only a trickle. Again rumor, the treasury's about empty. Almost no trade, your mills shut down, fires out."

Vedouce clumped away from the table, raised his voice. "Heard that before. Naught I can do about it. Get to the army. How big, how well armed and how soon's it coming through?"

Olmena Oumelic touched K'vestmilly's shoulder. "Right. That's enough for now. Put this round you." She helped K'vestmilly get to her feet, wrapped a knitted coverlet around her shoulders, clicking her tongue at her feeble attempt to push it away. "Nik, nik, I know it's hot, but you've been sweating and I don't want you catching cold."

After she got K'vestmilly Vos seated in the armchair, the elbow table beside it laden with a pot of cha, a plate of crisp wafers and fruit slices, she moved to the door into the living quarters, stopped and turned. "Marn. Marazi'll be up here in one minute with a glass of my tonic. Now don't scrinch up like that, you'll get stuck that way. You drink it or I'll come 'n pour it down your face, huh?"

K'vestmilly watched the healer bustle out. "Bad as Bozhka Sekan used to be with Mother." She pushed the coverlet aside, pried herself from the armchair and walked heavily toward the window, mouth twisting at the ache in her knees.

Zasya was suddenly there, between her and the casement. "Marn, best not."

She looked at the meie for a long minute, then at the fluttering curtains. "Chert!" she said finally, her anger packed in that ugly word.

Zasya said nothing.

"Zdra zdra, you've made your point. Now go where I don't have to look at you and remember why I can't even lean out my own window." She swung round with something of her old impetuousness and marched back to the chair, pulling it over so she could catch the breeze, turning it so her back was to the meie.

The air coming through the windows was as hot as any midsummer wind, though this was supposed to be winter. It'd started to be winter, frost on the trees, heavy black clouds threatening snow—then the sun came up double its usual size and burned away the clouds, the frost. And the cold winds turned hot. And the passes stayed open. And an army was forming by the ruins of OskHold, free to come at them as long as the passes were open. Heslin was worried. There was no way they could stand up to an attack, not here.

A while later, as she was drinking her cha, she heard the door slam down below and a man's voice. Osk. Stumping in, complaining with every step he took as he settled his wife at a table where she could take up her embroidery and efface herself as usual.

". . . this stinking pimple. The longer we sit here, the feebler we get."

K'vestmilly swallowed the thick gummy drink her

maid had brought and thought about going down to sooth him back to reason, but her body ached, her mind felt like rammed cardboard and the smell of her sweat was thick in her nose. She set the glass down, wiped her mouth, let her eyelids droop and went on listening.

His raspy growl moved back and forth under her as he paced restlessly about the long room on the ground floor. "I tell you, we should get the Marn across to the Sharr where she'll be safe, leave some men to guard her and go looking for some real help. The Skafarees, they'll sell anything. Karpan aNor. Fenka. Tell the Fenekel they'd better get moving or they'll be eaten alive the minute we go down, and if we don't, we will remember who our friends were."

Vedouce gave a short barking laugh. "Sell! Cash and cutthroat, all that lot. What're you going to pay them with?"

Unseen in the loft, K'vestmilly Vos stiffened, her mouth clamped tight, her hands squeezing the chair arms. *I smell ambition, little man. Shunt me off, park me somewhere? Hah! And wrap your sticky fingers about everything you can get hold of.* She sighed and levered herself onto her feet, sniffed at her arm pit, grimaced and crossed to the washstand.

As she was sponging off the sweat, she could hear Vedouce and Osk shouting at each other, both Pans, both with inborn arrogance, grind wheels turning against each other and shooting off sparks.

". . . saving their asses and you know it," Osk roared, "our blood, our substance, our wealth."

Give it a rest, Osk. We KNOW how you feel. You've TOLD us how you feel.

"Without us," he shouted, rolling over Vedouce's

attempts to answer him, "they'll have to fight their own battles. You tell me the Galyeuk in Yallor doesn't know what's heading this way? Hah! The Berkwast, you think he sent his Agentura out of good will? The Malkiate in Tuku-kul, you know what they're like, trying to smarm their way clear." He was calming a little, his pleasure at the gathering force of his argument softening the thunder of that argument. "That works while we're here, keeping the False Marn busy. We go, she looks south the next breath. They know it. You know it."

"We leave here, we've got nothing to sell."

"Chert! What have we got if we don't leave?"

"The Biserica." Holding tightly to the rail, K'vestmilly Vos came down the stairs with the meie a step behind her and the Fireborn running ahead. She crossed to stand beside Heslin's table. "We heard from them last night."

Heslin watched her, his face expressionless. He didn't approve, but she knew she was right this time.

Osk opened his mouth, shut it again, stood stroking his beard, a big burly man thrown off his verbal stride. The Panya Valiva put her embroidery down and leaned forward, her thin face lightly flushed, her eyes opened wide.

"Synggal Kryderri, the meie in charge, she reached us by com last night." K'vestmilly Vos took Heslin's arm let him lower her onto the backless chair he'd fetched for her; he stayed standing behind her, his hand on her shoulder. "Late last night. Around midnight."

Ildas was a firestreak seen from the corner of the eye, trotting busily about the long room, nosing into corners and moving behind the drapes. Zasya crossed the room, pulled the door open, stepped into the vestibule. K'vestmilly could hear her talking to the guards lounging there, then she came back in and stood by Heslin's table, her hand resting lightly on the grip of the shortgun, her eyes flicking from the Fireborn to the windows to the Marn and round the circle again.

Osk and Vedouce glanced at the meie, the angry red receding from their faces. Vedouce pulled a chair around, straddled it with his arms crossed on the back, prepared to listen. Osk planted himself in front of K'vestmilly Vos, hands clasped behind him, eyes opaque, body rigid. "So?"

K'vestmilly Vos readjusted the Mask. "The meie Synggal Kryderri reports she and the rest of the Biserica force are on board ship now, heading north with a hold full of munitions and other supplies. They'll be here before the month ends." She drew a long breath, let it trickle out, the warmth of it creeping upward behind the Mask. "No numbers were given. The meie was being cautious because she couldn't be sure who was listening. Osk, you're right, we can't sit here. Not with the passes open and an army gathering at OskHold."

His face relaxed, but before he could speak, she went on.

"However, a begging round is useless. Vedouce is also right, I spent what capital we had when I sent the messengers to the Biserica. The Berkwast, the Galyeuk, the Malkiate, they won't lift a finger for us. You could talk all day and all night about them being next, but they won't see it. They'd rather sit back and watch, thinking they can finesse the Enemy some way should she turn on them. Mother knew them and she taught me." Another breath. "Prak, this is what I've decided. As soon as the supply ship gets here, we march north, cross the mountains into Ank, turn south the way we planned before. We'll just be doing it sooner."

"We?" Osk swept his eyes across the bulge in her robes. "Nonsense."

"We," K'vestmilly Vos said quietly. "I'm Marn, not a brood mare. The child will take her chances with me and the rest of you."

Vedouce stirred. "Marn, if we lose you, we lose our center."

"If I'm dead, I won't be caring, will I? I know what you're saying, Pan Pen, but where would I be as safe? If I'm not there, I lose no matter what the outcome and I won't have that." She spread her hands in the Marn's smile. "Two thousand generations of Marn-hidda Vos clamor in me and will be heard."

The Panya Valiva stood suddenly, came with her usual grace to stand beside her husband, her hand on his arm. "Yes," she said, "the Marn's right. She has to be there." She lifted her head. "As do I and the other women. I've talked to Panya Jonosa, Vedouce, and the wives of your men. This is live or die. We all have to be there." She patted Osk's arm, smiled her charming smile. "I'm as good a shot as you, my love. You should know. You taught me." With a bob of her head in a sketched curtsey, she glided round and went back to her sewing.

"Whatever it takes," K'vestmilly said, her words falling heavily into the silence. "Osk. How many of yours will march when the time comes?"

For a moment she thought he was going to flare at her, but his ambition was stronger than his anger. "Leave the women and children here, Marn. We don't want our men distracted."

K'vestmilly shook her head. "How many would

stay if I tried that? They're not fools, Osk." She ignored his growl, glanced past him at Valiva, saw the
Panya's mouth twitch. *I've been blind, haven't I. Dis-*
missed you as a shadow of this bear in front of me. "Nor
am I a fool. Or careless with my people. It would be
inviting slaughter to leave them unprotected—which
we would have to do because for every man we leave,
the False Marn has three or four. The women will
come with us, those that want to, the others, zdra,
we'll follow your thought and send them into the
Sharr. That means boats." She twisted her head
round, looked up at the man behind her. "Heslin,
how many will we need, and how many can we get?"

His hand moved a little on her shoulder; when he
spoke his voice was deliberate and colorless, meant to
take the heat from the conversation. "To the first, I
don't know. Perhaps Valiva Panya Osk can tell you.
As to the second, depends on what we can pay. The
only boats available beyond the few we already have
would be those of smugglers and they won't go for
tin."

"We've got a month, get us a list of those who . . ."

A crash, snap of breaking slats.

A curtain billowed, a small dark form hit the floor,
sprang up, ran at the Marn.

Heslin whipped round the chair to put his body
between K'vestmilly and the intruder, his eyes traveling urgently about, looking for other dangers.

Zasya brought her shortgun up and shot. Once.
Twice.

The intruder grunted and kept coming, the meie
shot a third time and he folded.

As the door slapped open and the guards from the
vestibule came rushing in, Ildas squealed, went red-
hot and fully visible and leaped at a movement at the

back of the room. Heslin shifted position the minute he saw the Fireborn, Vedouce shouted, lunged after the little beast.

A shot. Heslin touched the top of his ear, brought his fingers away with a smear of blood on them, a lock of his hair fluttered to the floor.

Ildas squealed again and lunged for the intruder's face, plastering his immaterial body across eyes and mouth, the man's cloth mask charring under the Fireborn's body. He screamed as Ildas' heat seared through his eyelids.

With Osk a tardy second, Vedouce reached him, wrenched away the shortgun, hauled him to his feet. Two of the guards reached them a moment later and took charge of the prisoner.

Ildas dropped off the hood, trotted over to Zasya, his glow fading and his form melting into the air as he moved, but not before K'vestmilly got a sense of smug pride from the creature.

As she struggled onto her feet, Heslin stepped back. "Stay where you are, Milly," he murmured, "there's no need . . ."

"Nik, Hes," she said, her own voice held low for privacy's sake. "Stop thinking with your blood." She touched her tongue to her lips, closed her eyes a moment. "Husenkil told me that. Before Nov had him shot. I need your head in good working order, love."

She smoothed her sleeves and shook out her skirt, then straightened to face Vedouce and the writhing, screaming man the guards were hauling toward her. When they reached her, one guard tightened his grip on the captive's arms, the other grabbed the hair at the back of his head and yanked his head up. His eyes were reddened and leaking blood, his charred beard reeked and smoked.

"Who are you?" she said. "You're not Sleykyn. I can see that."

The intruder was a meager little man, ravaged eyes set deep in nests of wrinkles; one of his front teeth was broken to a snag, his lip swollen where the snag had cut into it. He was blinking and wriggling, whining, "My eyes, my eyes, I can't see, my eyes . . ."

Vedouce snorted. "Chovan." He glanced at the dead man. "Him too, I suppose." He walked around the captive, inspecting him thoughtfully, then swung his arm in an open-handed slap that nearly took the chovan's head off his shoulders. "So. What gave you the nerve to try this?"

The blinded chovan spat toward the sound of Vedouce's voice, the gob of spittle landing on the Pan's shoulder.

Vedouce pulled a handkerchief from his sleeve, wiped the mess away, then he stepped back and waited, not bothering to repeat the question.

The chovan drew together as much as he could. "What's in it for me?" His voice was a whine that conceded defeat.

"Die fast or die slow."

"Price," the man muttered. Eyes narrowed to pulsing, oozing slits, he smiled. Not a nice smile. "One thousand gold on her head." He pointed at the Marn with his chin. "I saw it. Yellow gold. I'm dead maybe, but the bitch there's deader."

"You want anything from this piece of spros, Marn?"

"Nothing I can think up. Lock him up somewhere and send a healer to him. He'll hang tomorrow. We'll leave him dangling to show his brothers what happens if they're tempted by that gold."

* * *

Vedouce watched the guards hustle the captive out, then turned to face the Marn. "Do you want it obvious we're moving?" he said. "Or do we keep preparations under wraps?"

K'vestmilly gripped Heslin's arm and lowered herself onto the chair. She sighed and once more readjusted the Mask; her face seemed to swell unpredictably these days so the weight of the ivory sometimes grew almost unbearable. "We can't move until the ship gets here. No point in alerting the spies in the hills."

Heslin's hands settled on her shoulders, kneading gently at the taut muscles.

She let a breath trickle out, spoke slowly, stopping to think between phrases. "First thing. I want an exact inventory of men, women capable of fighting, supplies and arms. Vedouce, since we've slaughtered and salted down most of the draft animals, we're going to have to find replacements. I'll leave that to you. Locate, be ready to confiscate, but tell your agents to keep their heads down. Panya Valiva, come here, if you will please?"

K'vestmilly scanned the woman's face; now that she knew to look for it, she read intelligence and irony there, a calm acceptance of the world as it was. "Speaker for women, find out how many would choose the Sharr and how many would prefer to come with us. I'd like the numbers within the next day or two, I don't want names. Assure those who chose the Sharr that we'll send them off well before we leave so they can get settled with some chance at peace."

"Two days, O Marn. And the numbers will be firm. No wavering. I'll make that clear."

"Good." She waited until the Panya was seated

again, then turned to Osk. "Pan Osk, if you will have your men get wagons and mounts ready to take baggage, children, those who wouldn't be able to keep up if they walked. Anything that can move, I don't care what it looks like as long as it holds together till we're across the mountains." She rested her arms on the bulge of her child, rubbed one hand back and forth along the wrist of the other as she stared into the shadows at the far end of the room. "We'll start having the dinners again. Osk, your officials, Vedouce, your team. Music ... we'll have Tingajil play for us ... let them hear us making merry ... use the time to plan, get everything ready so we can move the minute the ship unloads. Any questions?"

His anger forgotten for the moment, Osk rubbed at his chin. "How much of this do you want us to tell the Nerodin?"

"Nothing about the timing or the details. Or the ship from the Biserica. But start preparing our people for the move. It will probably help morale if they've got something definite to do and a goal to aim at. Heslin, perhaps we should let the Web know we'll be coming, find out what they can do for us. I leave to you how much you tell Spider One, but I doubt it makes a great deal of difference. Soon as we start moving, the Enemy will be expecting us. No way we can shift this many people secretly." She put out her hand and Heslin helped her to her feet. "I'll leave you to get on with it."

She sat on her bed, watching through the open door as maids trudged past carrying cans of hot water for her bath. Every part of living was harder here, took longer, needed more hands to do it. Water that came from a tap was such a simple thing, but what it did to make life easier was enormous. A millennium ago a Norit sold the idea to the Marnhidda Vos of those days, spent a good part of his life on aqueducts, reservoirs, cisterns and pipes, and when he was finished, life changed in Cadander. *The little Healer said the magic was coming back into the world. I don't think there'll be Nor again, but there'll be something. That little red-headed baby Hus showed me who whistled birds from the trees, she's a sign of things to come. I want a school. Like the Biserica, but in Cadander. I want Serroi there. A nucleus. A draw. Good will from the healing. If she'll do it. If we get through this, both of us alive.*

A tentative knock on the door woke her from her revery. She lifted her head. "Yes?"

"Your bath is ready, O Marn."

"It's Cumura, isn't it?"

"Yes, O Marn." The young girl's voice trembled and her face went red.

"Zdra zdra, thank you, Cumura." K'vestmilly slid off the bed, caught up her towel and went to soak away dried sweat and the troubles that plagued her.

8. Glory in the Ston Gassen

Panting from her long trot through the fields, Tserama dropped to a squat beside the Sacred Way. She wanted to catch her breath before she started an argument with Skyog; the Sem Ris could be nasty when disturbed outside the Reading Round, even if one or more of them had been yelling for her so loudly and continuously she couldn't sleep or concentrate on any of her other responsibilities. She pushed sweaty tendrils of hair from her brow, blinked sweat from her eyes and gulped in air until her body quieted and she was able to pay attention to the Ri across from her.

The silverside grass was shivering erratically, waves of dark and light racing across the patches; small sprays of gravel broke free from the side of the hill and trickled for a while, settled a breath or two, then rattled farther down as the slope twitched again; the air was thick as mucus about the posts and lintels on the summit of the hill and had a purple tinge; at irregular intervals it birthed tiny, crooked lightning wires that snapped at the stone and vanished. She could feel Skyog Itself shifting and pulsing irritably.

She got wearily to her feet, beat her staff against the earth, yelled, "Sem Ri Skyog, talk to me."

Lightning zapped into the grass beside her feet, starting a smoky fire.

Muttering curses on snittish Sem Ris who didn't know their own minds, she stamped the fire out, then banged the staff down again. "Skyog, I am Spirit Reader Tserama. You've been squealing like a pag under a butcher's knife, so talk to me."

The purple aura seemed to hunch down, the grass straightened and stood stiff and the pebbles stopped rolling. There was a sound like a stomach grumble, then the grass turned over and the silver path formed.

The ground nipping her at every step, she climbed to the summit and settled on the stone seat between the uprights; the breath in her nostrils was burnt and sour, a current of *something* she couldn't name ran through her body. It was disconcerting. She'd expected difference but not this much. She lifted her arms, flattened her hands against the upright stones. "Tell me," she said.

> *colors . . . smells . . . jagged passages of light against dark . . . woman's face, the younger of the prisoners, shattering, reforming, shattering again . . . twistiness . . . sense of day folding back on day . . . old woman . . . a root, hard and woody . . . faces melting into faces . . . village tokens writhing and changing one into another . . . darkness . . . horrible sucking darkness . . . sense of helplessness . . . terror . . .*

On and on the babble went, Sem Ri Skyog pouring out Its fear, Its confusion, Its anger until Tserama could take in no more and slapped the uprights to stop the flow.

She squeezed her eyes shut as her Gift reordered

what had been emptied into her, trembling as she began to realize what the Hill Spirit had told her.
When the retransfer of the tale was finished, she said,
"They're taking those women to every Round with
that same warning?"

Thunder rumble, shiver of air.

"The Jeboh? Why?"

Sense of agitation, stinging against her face. A feeling of oppression, then the breath was sucked from
her mouth.

"Compelled? Who?"

Darkness pressed briefly about her head. Even
greater sense of fear.

"The Prudjin?" She rubbed at her eyes. "You
too?"

A sudden stillness, a sense of strangulation, as if
even the air had turned hard and immobile.

She checked the detail in the Prudjin images Skyog
had fed her and found it scant at best. "I know the
song spinners' tales, nothing more. You put her in
your tale before, now you're doing it again. What is
she truly? And what's she got to do with this?"

The hill shook, the air shook, something hit her
between the shoulders and sent her sprawling. The
force invaded her body again, threw her down the
hill, dumping her onto the Sacred Way. Her staff
came bouncing after her, slammed into her and
rolled onto the grass beyond.

She lay a moment, her body a chorus of aches and
bruises, then she forced herself onto her feet, stood
looking down at the staff. "Butj!" With a sigh and
successive winces, she bent and picked up the staff,
then walked away from the Hill and its brooding
Spirit, moving slowly, stiffly, letting the disturbing
things she'd just learned play again across her mind.

The youmbards were hauling the old woman, the younger woman, the boy and the spirit goatboy around all the lake villages in the Ston Gassen, saying what they said in Danoulcha, seeding youmbards like weeds everywhere. The Sem Ris were upset about that, they didn't like change and they had a peculiar proprietary feeling about the people in their rounds. They detested them, tormented them when provoked to it, killed them with plague, dropped houses on them, sent beasts into wild rages to attack them, but to have strangers coming in and claiming what they felt was theirs . . . ah! Skyog wanted it stopped. He wanted it stopped NOW. But what could she do?

The Prudjin. Tserama shivered. She'd got a sense that the Prudjin was licking at the Sem Ris like a child licks at a lollipop, eating away at their unmaterial substance. Skyog REALLY didn't want to talk about that and she didn't blame It. Disturbing thought, because where would the Prudjin stop if she ate the Sem Ris and still her hunger grew?

Hunger and anger and sorrow, in a sad, disturbing mix.

She had only a confused notion what all this meant to the Rounds of the Ston Gassen, what it meant to her children and her friends, and because she didn't understand it, she couldn't see a way to fight what was happening. And Brajid was gone all day, most of the night, gave her glib excuses or slid away when he saw her coming. And Ammeny vanished too, but there was no question about where she was—on her knees in front of the Glory flame, rocking back and forth, mumbling shapeless sounds that no one else could understand. Nor could anyone move her from there until she decided to go, neither the Yubbal nor Tserama when the doyas called her to do something.

A boy yelled, a stone slammed into her shoulder. She whirled, lifted her staff.

More yells. More stones, maize cobs, sticks, clods of dirt.

"Skyog, shield," she cried.

There were a good dozen of the farm boys gathered at the edge of the field, mostly teeners though some were barely toddlings, their faces distorted with hate and a sick, half-fearful gloating because they were attacking an elder with the encouragement of other elders.

"Swarm and sting," she cried.

Beyond the boys, she could see Dustog leaning on a staff, his bren gathered in a ragged arc behind him, all of them watching the stoning with detached, dispassionate approval.

"Fell house and wither maize," she cried, blood trickling from her face, sandy dirt from the broken clods falling from her clothing, the words tumbling from her mouth, building force until she called the Name one last time. "Suck breath, knot gut, Skyog shield, power wield, no quarter yield. Skyog!"

When she walked on, she left maize blackened and rotted, the limp stalks splayed across the ground. Dustog, his bren and their boys were screaming with pain, clutching at their bodies, struggling to breathe, and the farm buildings behind them were torn apart, bits still falling away.

She was grimly satisfied with the outcome, since she'd half expected Skyog to ignore her, Ris were tricksy beings—but they were roily now and ready to strike given the slightest excuse for it. *It's going to be a bad time. Like Maraban's grandmother's tale. Instead of paya and baya attacking, it's boys and bren. Things are*

*wrong and I don't know how to fix them. The Sem Ris
don't know how to fix them. Gan Khora bless and give us
a sign. What do I do, what can anyone do?*

As she left Dustog's Farm, the satisfaction drained
away. She'd left enemies behind, confirmed in their
fear and hate, though she didn't see what else she
could have done. They might have killed her. And if
they attacked with impunity one time, they'd attack
again and again, more deadly with each onslaught.
On the other hand, though the attacks might be slyer
now, shots from shadow and nibbles at her life,
they'd still be coming at her, fueled by a force that
would only grow each time she defended herself. *I
have to do something about Ammeny and Brajid. Get him
into the youmbards? Foul thought, but at least he'd be
safer. Not safe. No one's safe from what's coming. Hm.
Maybe Ammeny, maybe she's already found a way to
make herself a hiding place. Brajid, though . . . I'd better
find out what he's at, he's not stupid so much as heedless
. . . bad part of being separate like I am . . . no one tells
me anything . . . they think it's respect, to which I say
Butj! . . . unless I know, I can't help him, should I want
to help . . . who knows what he's doing? Gan Khora bless,
what am I going to do?*

After she left the outer ring of farms she moved
mostly by night and reached Danoulcha in the gray
light of dawn, limping and exhausted. She stumped
past the house the youmbards had taken as their own;
on the way out she'd circled around it, now she was
too tired to care what the youmbards might see.

A guard stepped out of the shadows and started for
her.

She looked at him, kept walking. Chagu, Piwann's
son. He knew better than to bother her. When she

looked again, he was back in the doorway, staring off into the night, pretending he'd seen nothing.

The slope to her house slowed her to a creep and only the thought of the bed waiting for her kept her moving, but before she was halfway up the hill, she could hear the hibbils quarreling in the thatch and the House Spirit roaring its displeasure. *Gan Khora aid me, what is it now?*

The latch thong was pulled in, the bar was down. *Ammeny, oh Ammeny, you are a trial. Everything's harder with you about.* Tserama swore, leaned her head a moment against the jamb. There wasn't the slightest use calling Menny to open up. Wearily she straightened and hit at the thatch with her staff. "Hibbilkin, open the door."

After a moment's shivering silence, several hibbils came crawling down the wall; they oozed through the latchhole and a moment later the thong came sliding out.

She gave it a yank, heard the bar thumping against the planks, then kicked the door open and stumped inside. "Tsan pyya, what is all this?"

The babble started immediately, coming at her from all directions, from all the spirit dwellers in the house:

> *Menny doesn't feed us . . . Menny brings bad things into the house . . . Menny won't let Brajjy in and he don't feed us too. . . .*

On and on it went, almost as bad as a Sem Ri in full spate. She listened until the litany went into its third repeat, then banged the butt of her staff against the floor. "Enough. I'm tired. I hear you, I'll do something when I've rested. Let me sleep. Gan Khora's gentle arms, let me sleep."

Ammeny was gone by the time Tserama woke.

Ignoring the grumbles of the spirit in the kingpost, she moved through the house, growing angrier by the moment at the changes her daughter had made in the week that she'd been gone. Ammeny hadn't quite dared take over the wallbed, but everywhere else she'd tried to make her own; she'd swept the rooms as bare as new boxes, washed the walls until the smell of bleach was strong enough to choke, removed the tables, chairs, mats, curtains and shoved them out behind the house. The Gan Khora's shrine was gutted, the maize bowl replaced by a lamp of a kind Tserama hadn't seen before, oil with a floating wick in a black glazed bowl, the image that had been there supplanted by the rayed face of the Glory. Tserama's yarns, crystals, mirrors, dried ritsa stalks, oil cruses and all the other things she kept for the little readings she did, the day to day questions people had for her—all these things there jumbled onto a shelf on the pantry, swept away from the rooms in the rest of the house; some of them were older than the house itself, repositories of magic passed from one Reader to another since before the beasts stopped speaking.

As she rescued and rearranged her things, Tserama muttered to herself, "I should have dealt with you years ago, took the easy way, I did, I said that's that way you are, nothing I can do about that, you're my flesh, my blood, I take you the way you come, tsan pyya, that's over, when you did it to yourself, that was one thing, you're pushing at me now, you've gone too far, Menny child, no, that's the problem, you're not a child. If that's how you mean to go from now on, you'll have to do it somewhere else."

She put out maize water for the roof hibbils, polished the kingpost and fixed the House Spirit's meal of oil and maize flour, brought the furniture back into the house and placed her tools and possessions where they'd been before Ammeny got her cleaning fit. There were a lot of things she had to think about, besides trying to decide what her life was going to be in the months to come. Brajid, for one. Where was he? What was he up to? *Who can I ask to tell me what everyone must know? Everyone but me. How much should I try to do for him if he gets in serious trouble?*

So confusing. She had affection for these children who lingered after the others had left, but it was tepid at best. This bothered her because she knew she was supposed to love them and sacrifice herself for them, but she simply didn't feel that way. Ordinarily, custom would help her out, take the place of feeling. But custom was breaking down. All around her the old comfortable ways were eroding. She had nothing to lean on any more and it was hard, thinking out what she should do and why. Passion. She had that, but it was for other things. For the hibbils and the spirits in the houses and byways, the brus and the cuchimi, the unseens who were more her family than any of her blood had ever been.

When she finished restoring the house, she opened the door, started a fire in the brazier and waited for Danoulchers to come and begin her day for her.

Piwann hesitated in the doorway, then came inside, shuffling as if his feet were too heavy to lift. He lowered himself on the stool, looked across the table at her, his mouth moving, going still, moving again;

with all this no words came out. He drooped all over, even his mustache didn't bristle so aggressively as usual.

Tserama waited patiently, watching to see if he needed a gentle prod to get him started. She hoped not; the answers usually went better if the visitor found speech himself, herself.

"Bad times." His voice was low and whispery; his eyes slid warily about. "The daughter's gone?"

"Yes. There's no one else about."

"Chagu came round this morning, early, wanted to see his mother. He's been doing that since they planted him here." The tip of his tongue flicked across his lower lip. "He's not a bad boy, just heedless. You know how it is."

She permitted herself a dry smile. "I know."

"He don't much like what's happening, but him, he's got no say, they say and he does." The tongue tip slid nervously about again. "He said he's got orders, he going to follow 'em, don't push him on that, won't do no good. He said he can look away from a little thing. Here and there. Maybe. If it's just him seeing it and it's not something that leaves tracks, but don't push or he's gonna have to do something he don't want to."

"When he comes by again, tell him the Spirit Reader hears and understands. These are difficult times for all of us."

Piwann laced his fingers together, stared at them. "Something else he said, because he was scared for Karkor, m' youngest, you know, he didn't leave all family feeling when he put on Jeboh's Shirt. He said Karkor's running with Brajid and that lot. He said they thieving. Little things mostly. Barrels of arrag from the Pothouse. A old longgun off the

Headman's rack. Hams from smokehouses, rolls from the baker. Horses, not to keep, just run off their feet in their fool games. They don't pull up, stop their nonsense, the gyaman he's going to have them hauled to the Mita Jri and flogged. Gyaman likes the whip, he said, he going to half kill those boys."

Before she could say anything, he got to his feet, touched his fingers to his brow and hurried out.

She wiped at the sweat on her face, looked at her hand, rubbed it dry against her shirt. *Brajji, oh Brajji, you're such an idiot, just like your father. You want what you want and you won't work for it.*

Footsteps on the path outside.

She lifted her head, folded her hands and waited.

Tarlu, Matsoï's wife, sidled in, a thin drooping woman with a startled-fawn look about the eyes; Tserama found Tarlu's poses irritating, though she knew it could be her annoyance with Matsoï spilling over on the woman.

After edging onto the stool and settling her hands in her lap, Tarlu bit at her lip and looked nervously about; the black lines she painted around her eyes were ragged today and the blush she rubbed onto her cheeks a harsher color than she usually wore.

"Ammeny's not here." Tserama kept her voice low and calm; it was not her business to judge those who came to her, just help them if she could.

Tarlu's mouth twitched briefly into an imitation of a smile, but her eyes kept wandering about when she started to speak, never meeting Tserama's. "It's the well," she whispered, barely moving her lips. "Something's wrong with it, it's not clean. I have to go to the lake to fetch water and he gets mad because it makes me late with everything and the clothes don't get washed like they should and he says the house smells like fish."

"Have you kept the well's cuchimi fed and happy?"

Tarlu's hands twisted against each other. "I try, but he threw the bowls away and he won't let me buy maize flour anymore, he says the bagas I make are burnt and soggy and taste like roof tiles and there's no point wasting money on figments so I can't buy maize flour and have to get bagas from the bakeshop and he gives me just enough coin for the day and counts the bagas to make sure Yigos doesn't cheat me. He can't see them, you know, the cuchimi I mean." At the thought of how Tserama would know that, her mouth pursed, the skin tightened over her cheekbones; she'd let Tserama see often enough that she resented Matsoï's involvement with the Village Wife (Tserama and the ones who came after her), that she blamed the Spirit Reader for Matsoï's habits—the month before his wedding was the time he spent with Tserama and he hadn't changed his ways since. "And what he can't see, he won't believe in. You come and tell him he has to let me set out the offerings. You come and tell him if he wants clean water, I have to do it."

Tserama suppressed a sigh, knowing what it must have cost Tarlu to ask that. "I will go to him and say what must be said. I will go to the well and speak to the cuchimi and explain to them what the trouble is. People tell me your prungs are extra good layers, you could take eggs to Yigos and trade them for a pinch of flour, I'll speak to him and see what he requires. Let me warn you to be very careful with your hibbils. If they grow angry or get jealous of the cuchimi, they'll rot your thatch, spook your prungs and pags and make sure your sleep is fitful at best. Go home and do what you can. I will come this afternoon."

Danoulchans trickled in as the morning passed, most of them women worried about trouble in their houses, disturbed prungs that stopped laying, fretting milkers, pags refusing to eat, plants wilting, wells going sour, a thousand little things and big gone wrong and life made increasingly hard. Only Piwann mentioned Brajid by name, but the others spoke of a band of boys who were causing trouble everywhere, no names, only a sidelong glance at her to let her know what they were talking about.

By the time she shut her door the cold dread had reached bone. She'd been gone only a little more than a week and the change in Danoulcha had been greater than she'd seen in all the years of her life. Flux. Change feeding on change. It frightened her because she could see no end—except blackness at the edges tightening and tightening until there was no light left.

She went into the kitchen, got a rag from the rag-drawer, poured some oil into a saucer and brought them into the main room. Settling herself beside the kingpost, she dipped the rag in the oil and began rubbing at the post, smiling as she felt the House Spirit turn under her hands and heard it start to purr. That, at least, hadn't changed.

Hands on her shoulder, shaking her.
An unsteady whisper filled with desperation.
"Mama, wake up, please wake up. Please will you wake up?"
"Wha . . ."
A hand on her mouth, smothering the word.

"Don't wake Menny, please."

She pushed his hand away, struggled up, whispered, "Brajji? What ... where ..."

"Got to talk to you, Mom. Outside, where Menny can't hear."

Brajid squatted in the shadow of the boiler's chimney, his shoulders hunched, his head drawn down. What little she could see of his face was drawn and fearful.

She lowered herself to the washfloor and waited without speaking.

"It wasn't my fault, Mama."

She sighed. "Never mind that, just tell me."

"We were bored, that's all. That's why we did ... tsan pyya, they told you, didn't they? Anyway, this last time was different. We weren't doing anything bad, least not what you'd call bad, Mom. Brussal, the drayer's son, he's dead. Karkor, the cobbler's son, him too, I think, I heard him yell. Prab and Dabchag got took. Chouse and me, we were ahead of the others, we got away. Youmbards did it, they'll be coming for me soon's they shake my name loose. Chouse, he said he'd be shabbing one of his father's horses and taking off for the Ashtops, so I expect he'll get away. It was the strangers, you know, the ones the youmbards were on about the day they brought those women to the Mita Jri, we were going to help them, the strangers I mean, warn them about staying away from Danoulcha, bring them food, you know. Didn't the hibbils and them tell you they were coming? Sinh, that's Chouse's pet bru ... did you know he could talk to brus? It isn't like he's a Spirit Reader or anything, just he can talk to bits of things nobody takes no notice of. Sinh's a woods bru, it latched onto

Chouse when he was a thumbsucker, it talks to him about things. Anyway, it told him the strangers were coming by, it told him it was a good thing the strangers were at, Gan Khora's work, and he should help them and he told us and we don't like youmbards anyway and it was something to do, so we shabbed food and stuff and went out to meet them and someone must of told on us because the youmbards come . . ." His shoulders were heaving, his voice breaking as he forced it to stay a whisper. "And they start shooting and the strangers shoot back and Karkor and Brussal, they're dead, and we're running and I think the youmbards got the strangers along with Prab and Dabchag and they're going to be coming for me. I don't know what to do, Mama. I don't know where to go. Help me."

She'd been thinking while the words tumbled out of him, now she nodded. "Right. Ytama Round is two lakes west, I've got a brother there, a twin. It's been over thirty years since I've seen him but he'll remember, twins do, Brajji. When I left to be apprenticed, he gave me a token, said to send it anytime I needed him and he'd come. Baragad the Weaver's Son. Hm. Baragad the Weaver by now. You were named for him. Show him the token, tell him who you are. Blood is blood, he'll take you in. I doubt anyone in Danoulcha remembers where I came from, so you should be safe enough." She thought that over. "For a while, at least." She got to her feet. "Wait here, I'll get you some food. Is there anything in the loft that you want?"

She heard a sharp intake of breath, then he said, "Don't wake Ammeny, she'll go running to the youmbards. You'll keep my stuff, won't you? Maybe you can send it to me later."

* * *

She stood on the washfloor watching him trot along the lakeshore until he merged with the night, then, shoulders slumping and a sour churning in her stomach, she eased open the kitchen door and slipped inside, moving silently as she crossed the kitchen and went into the main room.

With an angry exclamation, she flung herself across the room and wrapped her arms about Ammeny before her daughter could get out the door. She hauled the girl inside, pushed her against the ladder to the loft and held her there.

"What do you think you're doing?"

"Let me go."

"No. Tell me where you were going."

"You know."

"I don't want to think you'd betray your own brother."

Ammeny was silent for a moment, her eyelids lowered, her face a mask in the semi-dark, then she lifted her head and Tserama stepped back, frightened.

Eyes glowing butter-yellow, Ammeny smiled. "Who is not of the Glory is no kin of mine."

9. Jail Dance

No answer. Nothing, nothing, nothing. . . . Serroi caught her breath, closed her eyes. The straps of the cage pressed hard against her knees and feet; she could feel their heat through her tattered skirt; her face was tight and burning from the air passing across her skin and she was afraid. Not of dying, but of not-dying— not-dying for hours, for days while her flesh blackened and regrew, blackened and regrew. . . .

Abruptly, all sensation went away. It was the oddest feeling, as if she hung poised somehow in mid-air. As if the world had vanished and she were the only created thing in the void that remained.

She hung in brightness, seeing nothing, feeling nothing, only memories left, memories replaying . . .

A child of seven, stubborn, hurting and afraid . . .

Ser Noris . . . he'd taken her pets and used her gifts to distort and destroy them . . . he taught her fascinating things and loved her more than her father ever had . . . and he used her, twisted her, made her do things she loathed . . .

Ser Noris . . . she remembered being very small and called in to let someone see her . . . she remembered thinking that he was beautiful, snow-pale with finely chiseled lips and a nose straight as a knife slash with a small gold ring passed through the outside of his left nostril, a red stone hanging from the ring that rolled over and glittered when he smiled at her. His hair was black smoke floating around his narrow high-cheeked face. His eyes were the black of the polished jet ornaments her mother wore to the Iangivlan festival at summers-end. He seemed to her more a strange wild animal than a man and because she felt most at home with animals she dared smile back at him. . . .

She remembered . . . the times in his sitting room when, eyes twinkling, he reached down and stroked the tips of his fingers along the side of her head, then across her brow, something no one else had ever done. His fingers would caress the eye-spot and she would feel a flush of warmth, a great rush of love for him. She could have curled up beside him and let him go on petting her forever, content as a chini pup after a long day's play. After a while he'd drop his hand onto his knee. "Go to bed, child. We'll talk again tomorrow." Tomorrow and tomorrow, yes . . .

She remembered . . . Ser Noris coming to find her in the room he'd given her. "Come, Serroi, I need you to help me with something."

Happiness warmed her. Almost dancing, she crossed the room to him and took his hand.

The rock flowed before them, collapsing into stairs as he took her higher in the tower than she'd ever been and opened the door to a room she'd never seen.

As she walked inside, a yearling chini trotted to her, sniffed at her, laid back his ears and crouched whining in front of Ser Noris. Wild or tame, creatures winced away from him. Even the great sicamar crawled on his belly and yowled with fear.

"Look at me, Serroi."

She stroked the chini a last time, then raised her eyes to meet his. They grew larger and larger until she saw nothing but that blackness. She was weeping, she didn't know why, but she could feel the tears dripping from her eyes and trickling down her cheeks while a terrible coldness flowed into her from Ser Noris, stifling all that she'd been feeling, anger and joy, love and despair, chilling her until there was nothing warm left in her, until the tears dried, until her body was stone.

She remembered . . . a gray fog gathered over the chini's body. It hovered a moment then began shaping itself into a likeness of the beast. Red eyes, red tongue lolling over yellow teeth, a great gray body, the demon was a travesty of the living breathing beast yet she sensed that it shared the chini's nature, chini and demon melded into a horrible amalgam that made her stomach churn . . . and that was only the first time, the first of the animals she helped Ser Noris drain and destroy.

She remembered . . . fighting him. Trying to keep from looking through his eyes. She failed. She tried to wall him out of her body. She failed. She tried to push him out once he was inside her. She failed. She exhausted herself struggling against him and lost every time, but she never quit . . . and as she struggled, she felt herself growing stronger; he had to exert more of his power each time he called her to that room . . . finally she shrieked her rage, ran from his towers and refused to go back, prowled about the court ready to claw at anything that moved. . . .

A bad time. A time of refusal, of retreat from horror. . . .

Like this. Like now.

I'm changing again, she thought.

Magic. I've refused it again and again, but it keeps coming at me.

It's changed too. What I remember . . . the old magic doesn't suit this new world.

"I don't . . ." she said aloud, startling herself when her voice faded as the air emptied from her lungs and there was nothing left to make sound. *I'm not breathing.*

As if that croak were all the cue it needed, the haze was gone.

The iron walls glowed red-hot, but iron straps beneath her were painted with frost flowers. At some time when she was *gone* the dolly had burned to ash and let the cage crash to the floor; her knees and feet ached from the jolting the fall had given her. Wincing at the complaint from her muscles, she eased herself around until she was sitting crosslegged instead of kneeling; then she inspected the bruises and ran her hands over them, smiling as the blotches erased beneath her palms.

Around her small flakes of snow crystallized from the air and dropped to sizzle on the glowing floor.

Weird. I suppose I should be grateful to whatever's doing this . . . I'd really rather not perpetually roast . . . I wonder if it's me doing it . . . I can't tell . . . I'm afraid it is . . . Maiden Bless, I don't know which is more disturbing, interference from outside or inside. . . .

She'd been increasingly upset by the changes she'd been recognizing in herself since Kitya woke her from the tree. When she was with people she knew, people she was fond of, she could counterfeit the person she remembered being, even feel some kind of connection with that misborn baby that Ser Noris bought so long ago. When she was alone, though, or with strangers, that counterfeit was wearing increasingly thin. *Something else* was emerging . . . being born from her flesh . . . something she didn't understand or like . . . not at the moment, anyway. . . .

There was a kind of attenuation mixed with a sense of vastness . . . as if she were becoming coterminous with the world itself . . . a feeling of potential without any boundaries she could sense.

Which frightened her.

She'd learned long ago not to trust great power in others. Ser Noris had etched that lesson into her bones. She also distrusted it in herself.

The room cooled; the walls faded from cherry-red to their usual blue-black.

A yell outside the door. Another.

The terror in the sounds knotted her stomach. She swung down from the cage and hurried to the front of the room; straining to hear what was happening, she stood on the non-hinge side of the door where she couldn't be seen through the peephole and wouldn't be hit if the door opened.

More yells. Shots. Other, less identifiable sounds.

She wiped her hands down her shirt, got ready to move the minute she saw a chance of getting out of there.

The door crashed against the wall, the boom echoing down the corridors. A lamia glided in. Her massive head turned slowly. When she saw Serroi, she stared at her a long moment without blinking, eyes green as spring leaves and shiny as stones. She bent her neck in a sketch of a bow. "You will permit, Mother?" Her voice was heavy, husky, with a strong burr on the r's.

Serroi hesitated, then thought, *why not, didn't I*

scream for help? She sucked in air that hurt her lungs, then she was breathing again and could speak. "Yes."

The lamia lifted her and held her cradled like a baby in her powerful arms as she undulated from the iron cell.

Serroi was enveloped in a musky forest odor with an acrid bite to it, strange but not unpleasant. The lamia's skin was faintly mottled and covered with pliant scales, her hair was thick and tangled, a dark bluish green, her features were large, rather coarse, and she moved with an oozing grace in an aura of enormous power.

Serroi started as she heard the clatter of feet overhead, then a crack and a whiiinge as a bullet caromed off the wall near her head. The lamia paid no attention, went on gliding along the hall, relentless as a river in spate.

There were yells of frustration and anger as a flurry of shots all missed—turning aside before they reached the lamia and her burden.

The lamia's body was warm, her breasts soft, her swaying progress as rhythmic and soothing as a rocking cradle. Serroi found her eyes drooping shut, her mind closing down. By the time the serpent woman emerged from the building, she was nearly asleep.

The lamia carried her onto the landing and *called*, her voice sliding up the scale till it passed beyond hearing, though Serroi could feel the vibrations in the breasts she was pressed against. The air itself seemed to shake with fragmented light and that silent sound.

A boat coalesced from a patch of sun-gilded mist and glided toward them, ivory sides and white silk sails, with eyes inlaid on both sides of the bowsprit, outlined in jet with plates of jade for pupils. It nosed up to the landing, extended a boarding ramp and quivered there like a living thing.

The lamia carried Serroi on board, set her on her feet, but when she opened her mouth to speak, the lamia shook her head, commanding silence. She turned, glided down the ramp, slid into the water and vanished beneath the surface of the lake.

The ramp melted, invisible hands shifted the tiller and reset the sails. The ivory boat skimmed away. There were yells behind it, more shooting, oddly muffled and quickly silenced.

Watching the water glitter before her in the sunlight breaking through rifts in the ash pall, Serroi stood with one hand on the mast, feeling it vibrate under her palm as if the boat were humming to her. There was a curious symmetry about this. A very long time ago Magic had come to her on a ship managed by invisible hands with a mage wind in the sails. A journey from one life into another—from sorrow into sorrow . . . and joy, though the joy was more transient than the sorrow. This journey was like that. And though she was so much older, she had nearly as little idea of what the future would hold for her now as she had when she was three.

The trip across the lake was short and swiftly over. The boat slipped up to a deserted landing near a half-dozen houses without roofs that were moldering back to the earth. As soon as she stepped from the ramp onto the rotten planks, the boat melted into the air, its last vestige a faint perfume like old dry lavender.

She shrugged and moved on, back in the world of stenches, splinters and grit. "Ei vai, at least I'm closer to the Ashtops." She walked cautiously along the unstable structure, testing each step before she put her weight down.

With a sigh of relief she reached the shore and jumped from the planks to the ground beyond.

Lightning came searing through her boots, ran up through her body, she was burning . . . then cold, so cold . . . her flesh began to stiffen, to change . . . she felt the tree shape struggling to take her . . . for a moment she was tempted . . . memories of peace and contemplation . . . no needs, no sorrows, only the long slow joys in the dance of the seasons . . . then she remembered why she was here . . . she forced her mouth open, fought for breath, cried, "NAY!"

As suddenly as it started, the attack was over. She was herself again, insofar as she knew herself. The ground was cool under her feet.

She rubbed at her arms, looked hastily about. The lake was empty as far as she could see and the shore around her was deserted. "Ei vai, can't stay here." She wrinkled her nose at the smell of the decomposing buildings, began picking her way carefully over the littered ground between them. The Jeboh and his guards might be frightened for the moment, but they'd come after her again. She had to put distance between herself and the lake, find a horse or a macai to carry her, get resupplied with clothing and food, a thousand things—and the afternoon was already half over. Too much to do to bother with what she was turning into and what all this meant; she turned to immediate things with a relief that unclenched body and mind.

When she rounded a heap of lumber and mud brick, she saw a horse moving toward her, ears flicking, head turned a little, lifted high. He was a dapple

gray with a creamy white mane and tail and slate gray
eyes.

"Ei vai, I know you." She held out her hand, smiling as Horse nuzzled at it. "So what are you doing
here?"

Horse knelt, looked round at her, snorted with impatience and waggled his head as if to say *get on with
it, idiot, you're wasting time.*

Serroi laughed, feeling better than she had in days
as she hauled her skirt up and settled herself strad-
dling the broad back. "A-ric, my friend, easy does it,
it's been a while."

10. Jail Dance (2)

Hedivy glanced at the boy huddled in the corner of the cell, then forced himself onto his feet and crossed to the barred window set high in the outside wall. His head throbbed and his shoulder where he'd been shot felt as if a demon with a bone drill were working on it. After the youmbards had stripped off his blood-soaked shirt, a wincing doya up above had sprinkled a gritty brown powder on the entrance and exit wounds, strapped on pads to stop the bleeding, touching him with a mouth-pursed distaste that made Hedivy want to kick him. They gave him another shirt when the bandaging was finished, a gray-brown castoff with a coarse weave that rasped against his skin. At least it was warm.

Gritting his teeth against the pain, he tucked the hand on the wounded side between two buttons on the shirt, reached into the window opening and wrapped his good hand around one of the bars. He pulled at it, but it was set in solidly, cemented in place with something as strong as the stone. On the far side of the bars the window slanted slightly upward, broke through the thick wall not far from the ground, a stalk of a flowering plant waving past it.

Through the leaves and the clusters of small pale blooms he could see a single star and a sliver of moon; from the size of the moon's curve, it was one of the Dancers, which meant the time was well past midnight. *Lost track while I was out.* Adlayr and Honeydew must have got away, at least they weren't in here with him. If they were out there, they'd be working on a way to pry him loose. *Have to mark this window. Shirt maybe.* He glanced at the boy huddled in the corner. *His, come to it. Zdra, it's whiter than this thing they gave me. Uh-huh.*

He rubbed his foot on the floor. Stone. Stone walls. Door made of planks thick as his hand, with iron strapping and studs. No latch, just a bar on the outside, black iron, heavy, mounted on a swivel whose spike didn't reach through the wood so he couldn't get at it that way. Three iron rods in a hole not big enough for him to get his hand through.

The cell went suddenly gray on him and his knees started to melt. He half-lowered himself, half-fell on the plank cot, ground his teeth and fought back the tides of weariness, pain and fever.

When the haze passed, he looked at the arm dangling from his injured shoulder, lifted it with his other hand and once more pushed his fingers between two buttons; the support eased the throb a little. He hunched forward, inspected the boy. "You." He snapped the thumb of his good hand at him. "What's your name?"

The boy lifted his head, stared at him from black eyes that glimmered in the faint light coming through the window, then went back to gazing at the floor.

Hedivy snorted. "Lumphead, what is this place?"

A muscle moved at the corner of the boy's jaw; he said finally, "GodHouse. Cellars."

"And what've that lot got in mind for tomorrow?"

"I get flogged. Gettin a stake ready for you.'

"Why?"

"Roast you, what else?'

Hedivy eased his hand free and lowered his arm onto his thighs, sweat dotting his face. "Not what I meant. Why jump us in the first place?"

"Jeboh's orders, that's what they said. Chouse's bru, it said you goin at the Prudjin. Are you?"

"Prudjin, don't know Prudjin. One of your mika-muks?"

The boy stared at him again, then let his head fall back against the wall. "What you doin here, then? An't your land."

"My business."

"Him too, that other'n? Where'd he go anyway?"

"You know better'n me, I got that club laid 'cross my head." Hedivy leaned farther forward, eyes nar-rowed, but it was too dark in here to see enough of the boy's face to tell what he was up to. "So?"

"Run off. Left you, din't he?"

"Like your friends." He glanced at the window. The Dancer's crescent had dropped from sight. "Lumphead, give me your shirt."

"Huh?" The boy's eyes popped open, his mouth rounded into a startled O.

"Want me to pry it off you?"

"You? You couldn't crack a bhur worm."

Working on will and rage, Hedivy rose smoothly, took a step toward the boy. "Don't try me, halfling. Might come apart in my hands if I got careless."

"Biiig man, can't even stand straight." The boy came to his feet with a quick, fluid surge and ran to the door. Mouth to the hole, he yelled, "Doya, get me outta here."

As the bar began screeching on its pivot, Hedivy

grabbed at the boy, got hold of a sleeve. Breath hissing between his teeth, the boy wriggled wildly. The sleeve tore free just as the door slammed open and the boy was out and running as Hedivy backed away from the guns pointed at his belly. Four youmbards and the man who'd bandaged him stood in the gloomy corridor outside the cell.

"I see. Yours, was he? Little rat." Hedivy patted at the sweat on his face with the shirt sleeve, threw it in the corner of the cell. "Zdra, what are you going to do now?"

The doya flapped a hand. "Move back. Stand against the wall."

Hedivy glanced at the guns, then at the set of the youmbards' bodies, and did what he was told.

The door slammed shut, the bar chunked into the hooks. He could hear the tromp of the youmbard's boot as they marched off, the doya scolding the boy for bungling his job. Then there was nothing but his own breathing to break the silence.

He retrieved the shirt sleeve. Using his teeth and his good hand, he ripped it into strips, tied the strips into a line. He managed to tie one end of the line around one of the window bars, rolled up the rest and after several tries got the free end to hang out through the window. Then he dropped onto the bench again, sat hunched over, fighting back waves of nausea and dizziness, struggling to keep a grip on awareness so he could be ready to move when the time came.

The attack came subtly, gradually.

A pressure against his mind that was a barely a tickle at first.

When it started he didn't realize what was happening, thought it was just a part of the wound-sickness, but as the pressure became a smothering blackness, the understanding came to him with terrible clarity that he was being Taken.

"Niiiiiik," he howled. "Get oooouuut."

Then he was fighting too hard to make another sound, fighting that pressure . . . that voiceless, wordless DEMAND . . . planting his feet as he would in a fist fight . . . stretching his good arm out to grip the support chain . . . refusing to surrender body or mind . . . DENYING the force with everything in him, with all the resources his life had given him . . . this was what had killed Oram . . . this was what had fouled Cadander . . . this was anathema . . . he was a loyal man, it was how he saw himself, how he needed to see himself . . . and it woke in him his bone deep need to control his own space . . . whenever he'd found others trying to tangle his life his first thought was to kill them, make them not exist . . . if that wasn't politic, he found ways of raising barriers against their interference . . . this tendency had grown stronger in him with every year that passed . . . this *need* for autonomy . . . and he loathed magic in all of its aspects . . . he was afraid of it . . . this attack was magic . . . he pushed it away . . . pushed it away . . . pushed it away . . . despite the confusion from the fever and the weakness of his body, he lashed out at the pressure . . . drove it away from him . . . though it came back . . . though it always came back . . . the Taken appalled him to the heart of his bones . . . surrender his will? Never *never NEVER NEVER* . . . he fought off the pressure . . . pushed it back . . . fought with the feral intensity of a wounded Sicamar . . .

Eventually the encroaching blackness went away, leaving behind a sense of puzzlement and frustration.

He collapsed on the plank of the cot, shivering and only half-conscious.

Trax-Adlayr glided in tight circles above the largest structure in the village, Honeydew clinging to his neck fur. *That's the place where they took him.* He scanned its walls, his raptor's eyesight picking out a whitish flutter. Something was dangling from a small window low down in the wall, half concealed by the stalks of a flowering plant. *You see that, Honey? There, down near the ground.* He dipped lower, stabbed at the corner of the building with the trax's leathery beak.

Honeydew see. Rag waving. Adlee think Hev he did it?

Hev knows we'll be looking. Likely he'd give us a clew if he could. I'll go down, let you off. You crawl in and see if it's him and how he's doing. Then we figure out how to get him out of there.

Honeydew landed in the window, eased herself down the slope and past the bars, the sound of harsh and unsteady breathing in her ears. As she came to the inner edge of the window, she flattened herself on the stone, then peered into the cell beyond.

It was dark in there, she couldn't see much. The breathing came from a long lump on a plank bed supported by wall chains. She bit her lip, launched herself from the stone and fluttered across to the chain nearest the sleeper's head.

It *was* Hedivy, but he didn't sound good. There was a dark stain, probably a bruise down the side of his face, and something white showing in the neck opening of his shirt, bandage, she thought. As she watched, his face clenched, relaxed, his mouth worked but he didn't say anything, his eyes didn't open. She thought he was probably asleep, not unconscious, though she couldn't be sure.

She left the chain and flew to the small aperture in the door, squeezed past the iron rods and dropped onto the bar.

No guards in sight. She could hear someone coughing in one of the other cells, a snore from another. Whoever ran this place, looked like they kept themselves busy with prisoners.

She launched herself from the bar, flew up to the ceiling and moved through the shadows along the wall toward a shadowy flight of stairs.

They led to a gloom-filled corridor lit by candles in black iron holders, the flames shielded by cylinders of glass; the light that crept past the smears of black soot on the sides of those cylinders showed her ranks of doors marching along on both sides. As she flew nearer, she saw that the doors had slides set in them near the top, with most of these slides cracked open so the sleepers could get some air.

Honeydew fluttered to one of them and widened the opening until she could perch on the ledge and look inside.

A man lay wrapped in blankets on a narrow cot. His clothes hung from pegs on the wall, she could just make out the eyeholes of a black hood. Youmbard. Maybe even one of those that attacked their camp on the far side of the lake, enjoying the sleep of a job well done. She snorted, then pressed her hand against her nose and mouth, afraid she'd wake him. A long sputtery snore reassured her and she flew on, stopping at intervals to check the rooms. Some were empty, the rest had more youmbards snoring away.

Footsteps. Bootheels only slightly muffled by the worn drugget that covered the stone floor.

She zoomed for the nearest door, flattened her body on the lintel, pressed her wings against the wall.

A youmbard came marching along the corridor. He banged on a door. "Houp, houp, Jamon, relief time." He called three more, then marched on to another room, one of those she hadn't looked into. She heard water splashing, other noises. *Coming off duty and getting ready for his turn at sleeping.* The doors he'd knocked on were opening, sleepy youmbards emerging, pulling on hoods, buttoning buttons, grumbling about the draw that gave them this watch. By the time they reach the end of the hallway, they were walking in step, not talking anymore.

Honeydew hurried after them, turn and turn again in the labyrinth of narrow corridors that went round the edge of the building, until they emerged into a monstrous echoing chamber with a lot of dust and fragments about, some considerable changes being made on the wall carvings, more work going on about the massive statue of the Maiden standing under the dome. *Was the Maiden's House. Looks like that's changing.* She shuddered. *Gone to Glory.*

Two of the youmbards slapped hands with the guard waiting beside immense double doors fifteen feet tall, carved in deep relief with flowers, leaves and vines; he yawned and went off, while they took up posts there. The other two slapped hands with them, marched off. Honeydew sighed and flew after them. If those two were heading for a back door of some kind, it might be easier to get out that way.

She followed the youmbards through another maze of corridors to the back of the building, saw them relieve the two guards there, then station themselves

beside a much smaller door at the far side of a stone
room with worn benches pushed against the walls. *Ei
vai, I was right*, she thought and did a little air-strut
in honor of her perspicacity, *this looks like it might be
possible. Oy-ay, Honeydew is tired.*

The off duty guards were already snoring by the
time she got back to the sleeping section, the candles
were burnt lower, the shadows thicker and the silence
heavier. As were her wings. Heavier and heavier.

Sweat slick over her tiny body, she struggled back
to the cell, landed on the bar with a small moan of
relief and crouched there, panting, sweat dripping
down her face. When she'd caught her breath, she
squeezed between the bars in the door hole, fluttered
to the window and crawled up it till she could reach
one of the flowers on the stalk that swayed in the
wind in front of the opening. She bit into a petal,
wrinkled her nose at the taste, but ate it, ate the rest
of the flower, found another and ate it.

She rubbed her belly, startled herself with a series
of burps. Honeydew eat too fast. Ei vai, had to do. Honeydew . . . had to do. Poeting again. Adlee, you there?

*What took so long, Honey? I was starting to get wor-
ried.*

Hev is here, Adlee, but he's not so good. He sleeping but
Honeydew didn't try waking him, not yet. Honeydew went
looking to see what's what. . . .

She reported what she'd seen to Adlayr, finished—
Back door's the best way, but it's barred on the inside. Adlee
couldn't get through without lots of fuss. Honeydew think if
Hev isn't too beat up, he can get out that way quietest. All
those youmbards, better they stay sleeping.

Let me think a minute, Honey.

She could feel his mind churning at the problem,

could sense his slow advance and retreat as he circled overhead, riding the wind with his usual skill; he might have trouble getting to ground, but in the air his trax-form delighted her.

Honey, have you figured how to get him out of the cell? Is it like back in the Skafarees, all you have to do is get the key to him?

Oh. Honeydew forget to say. No lock, just a bar, black iron, 'bout as wide as Honeydew is tall. Ei vai, Adlee should get some skinny rope, Honeydew says skinny so Honeydew can lift it, nothing here strong enough to shift that weight, that slimpsy bit of cloth out the window won't do it.

Hm, Honey, I saw some clotheslines over a ways, I'll go fetch one of them. You wake Hev, see if you can get across to him what we're going to do. Question?

Adlee, Hev sleeping hard.

Honey, pinch his earlobe. Hard as you can. Bite it if you have to. That should do it, unless he's really out, too feverish to move. How bad are his wounds, do you know?

Hev is hot, Adlee, big bruise longside his face. Bandage poke his shirt out, leftside shoulder. Breathing hard.

We'll have to see, Honey. I'm going to go for the rope now. Do the best you can.

Honeydew shivered; the lakewind coming through the window was chill and damp and she was frightened now that she had time for fretting. And very tired—though the flowers she'd eaten were beginning to give her back some of her energy. She puffed out her cheeks, whistled a few phrases at the top of her range, notes so high that even chinin couldn't hear them, then with a small grunt she pushed off from the window ledge.

She landed on the plank beside Hedivy's head. Panting and flapping her wings to drive off some of the heat blasting out from him, she caught hold of his earlobe and pinched as hard as she could.

He muttered, the mutters faded into a snore.

Tsah! Using both hands, she squeezed part of the earlobe into a narrow fold, then bit down hard.

"Ayyyah!" Hedivy sat up, shaking his head.

Honeydew was carried part way up, flung off as the shaking grew more violent. She beat hastily at the air, her wings catching hold just before she hit the floor. Her efforts carrying her up past his head, she spiralled away, staying cautiously beyond reach as his face cleared.

"Honey." He brushed at his eyes, ran his fingers through his hair. "Where is he?"

She flew toward the window, perched in the opening. For several frustrating minutes she pointed, gestured, contorted her body as she tried to get him to understand what they wanted him to do.

"Where is he? I can't hear you," he growled. "You know I can't make out what you're saying."

Honeydew sighed and tried some more gestures and signs to get him to understand Adlayr was fetching rope and they'd be moving soon.

He didn't bother looking at her; eyes glazed over, he slumped on the cot and stared at the floor.

A whistle at the window. Honeydew scrambled hastily out of the way as a bundle of rope came flying through the bars. Adlee, Adlee, Hev won't try, won't even look at Honeydew.

Adlayr crouched by the window, his body shutting out much of the light from the stars. *Anyone around to hear us?*

Nay, nay. No guards, just whoever's in other cells.

Where's the rope?

On the floor, Adlee.

Find a place to perch, Honey, leave the rest to me.
Honeydew do, Adlee.

When she was settled in the door aperture, Adlayr called, "Hev, get your head up and listen to me."

Hedivy poked the rope's end through the hole, then fed more and more of it out until he reached the scrap of cloth he'd tied about it to mark the stopping place. A moment later he could hear the mosquito-yammer of the sprite as she flew the end back up to him. Heavy work for her, but she was tougher than she looked; he had respect for the buglet, she did her share.

He pulled the end through, wrapped both lengths about his hand and threw his weight on the loop.

For a moment nothing happened, then the squealing and scraping started as the bar swung on its pivot. He went to his knees, pulling down as fast as he could, feeling the loop start to slip, not wanting to give it time, shoving his good shoulder hard against the planks, ignoring the agony that jagged through his body.

The door opened a thumb's width, then closed again as the rope stopped moving; it held the bar vertical, pressing it against the hole in the door.

Grunting, sweating, eyes blurring, he pulled himself onto his feet, the rope cutting into his palm. *Once I get moving, I'll be all right. Get the mush out of my head. . . .* He straightened his shoulders, squinted at the door and pushed it open.

Hedivy stopped at the top of the stairs, looked along the corridor. It was filled with shadow and a silence broken only by snores of various kinds—whistles, grunts and one odd half-cough, half-gurgle.

Honeydew circled and came back, hovered in front of him, her body all question. He watched her and was pleased that the blurring and double vision had gone away for the moment. "Point me to a room with a youmbard," he muttered and was pleased again when she darted off, heading to the third door on the left.

Hedivy caught hold of the sleeper's head and twisted sharply, smiling a little at the sound of bone breaking. He dropped the head on the pillow, pulled the blankets off the bed and tossed them in a heap on the floor, found a belt and threaded it through the loops on his trousers. The man was about Adlayr's size, so Hedivy pulled his spare clothing off the wall pegs and threw it on the blankets, in case they couldn't locate their gear; the gyes would need something to wear when he shifted back. He took the man's knife from its sheath on the weapon harness, dropped it on the blankets with the clothing, then the harness went over his good shoulder, pulled around so the shortgun in its holster was in easy reach. That put the knife sheath behind his back, but one couldn't have everything.

The room went fuzzy for a moment. He leaned against the wall, closed his eyes. *I will NOT pass out. I will NOT fall down and crawl.* He breathed slowly, carefully until the underwater feeling went away, then eased onto his knees, rolled the blankets into a tight cylinder with the clothing inside, cut a bit off the rope Adlayr had provided and used it to secure the bundle and make a strap for it so he could hang it on his good shoulder and keep his hands free. He looked at the rope a moment, cut another length, tied it into a loop and dropped it about his neck to use as a sling to rest his arm and take the weight of it off his sore shoulder. He slid the weapon harness around, snapped the knife into its sheath, then resettled the holster beneath his hand.

He got to his feet and started to leave the room, went back for the pillow, thinking he could wrap it around the shortgun and use it to muffle the shots if he had to shoot. Maybe. Worth a try. He tucked the pillow under his arm, took a last look round the small room and left.

In the hall, the door pulled shut behind him, he flicked a finger at Honeydew, then followed the sprite as she darted away.

The guards at the postern door were squatting beside a grid chalked on the stone floor, casting dice and arguing in whispers over the results.

Hedivy pressed himself against the wall and watched them for several minutes, the blurring back so he could barely make them out. The gun was useless, he'd probably miss a wall if he shot at it. Honeydew brushed past him, hovered in front of him, quivering and impatient. He saw her as a length of light, her wings faint ripples beside it.

No point in waiting. He dropped the pillow, began walking toward the gambling men, not trying for silence, just the calm, assured sound of someone who belonged where he was. He was almost up to them when one of the guards looked up.

Hedivy lifted the gun, pointed it at the rising blur. "Open your mouth and you're dead." He kept his voice quiet, calm. "That's right. On your feet. Get that door open." His vision cleared enough to see one of the guards starting to look hot. "You want to try me?"

"You shoot that and the whole place'll land on you."

"Maybe so, but you'll be dead. Now get that door open."

One guard looked about to argue, but the other grabbed him, calmed him down. Hedivy was close to spraying as many shots as he could squeeze off at the shifting, blurring images, hoping to hit something and get away before the Godhouse could react; apparently that was visible in his face.

Adlayr was waiting outside.

They left the guards tied, gagged and rolled against the wall, hidden behind the bushes that grew there.

Honeydew perched on his shoulder, clinging to his braid, Adlayr pulled open the door to the small shed near the GodHouse's stables. "I saw them put our gear in here."

Hedivy grunted.

"Youmbards and some men in robes had the stuff, they were arguing over whose it was. I expect they left it here for morning and more argument. There was a padlock on this hasp, but I tickled it open, tossed it in that patch of weeds. Let them hunt for it if they want it." He grinned. "Odd stuff they teach you at the Biserica."

Hedivy stumbled forward, lurched into the wall as he tried to go inside, face flushed, a film of sweat gleaming in the starlight.

"Careful there, Hev." Adlayr caught him by the arm, swore as Hedivy slumped and groaned. "Zhag, I wish Serroi was here. Give me your good hand, let's get you sitting down. That's good, just rest now. I'll saddle the macs, bring them over here. You concentrate on getting your head clear."

Adlayr eased the stable door open, stiffened, started to back away.

"Wait." The woman standing in the shadow stepped forward. "You needn't worry, I'll be going with you."

"What?" He glanced over his shoulder, then past the woman at the faintly gleaming strangenesses that clung to the rafters and walls, eyes like iridescent soap-bubbles staring at him. "Who're you? What're you talking about?"

"My name is Tserama. I am Danoulcha's Spirit Reader. But that doesn't matter. I know things you need to know. I know the Prudjin. I know where she lives."

"So do I. Mount Santak."

"And do you know which peak answers to that name? Don't play the fool, Change-man. This isn't the time for fiddling with words." She moved toward him. "I have saddled your beasts for you. Sunup is in a few hours. We have to be well away by then."

11. Jail Dance (3)

Treshteny moved her arms as inconspicuously as she could; her wrists were rubbed raw by the bindings the youmbards never took off except when they put her and the others in a GodHouse cell for the night. Yela'o leaned against her, his hands wrapped in her skirt. Mama Charody stood like a lump next to her. The old woman had gone silent for the last few days, glowering at the ground and saying nothing when the youmbards prodded her about, staring at the cell walls for hours, neither eating nor drinking, not even talking to Doby.

Treshteny looked out across the crowd gathering in this particular Mita Jri, unfocusing her eyes so she wouldn't see too much. She'd learned not to look. So much pain. So much blood. Hatred. Rage. Even so, she couldn't escape the tree. It rose above the villagers' head, crafted of light and what seemed to her to be souls in torment writhing upwards and out along the branches, the leaves their fluttering hands, their eyes dark emptinesses, their mouths black gapes, endless, soundless screams. At first it was only a faint sketch of a sapling, hardly more than a disturbance in the air, but it grew taller and more solid with every village they visited. She didn't understand what it meant, but it terrified her.

She didn't dare close her eyes. The last time she'd tried it, she was beaten, a leather strap across her shoulders and buttocks. With a worse threat in the eyes of youmbards watching. More than once on this interminable journey she'd heard them speculating about her ... saying she wasn't all that old ... and not bad looking ... her mind shuddered away as they'd discussed her in terms she hadn't known existed ... such a sheltered life she'd led, at home and then at the Clinic ... she had a certain curiosity about men and what they did ... she'd seen things in her visions that gave her a fair notion ... but these words and the way they looked at her chilled her ... it took her days each time to get warm again and not flinch when one of them laid a hand on her ... it was her premoaning fits that had scared them off ... they'd had orders not to touch her, but that wouldn't have stopped them ... nik, it was the fits ... they thought she was crazed and a witch and in that way doubly dangerous to any man who came too close to her.

But she kept her eyes open. Fear was a frail rein, it'd break with the lightest pressure on it.

The gyaman finished his speech. Her guard caught her by the back of her neck and marched her off. She could hear the shuffle of feet as Charody and Doby followed her, the click-clack of Yela'o's hooves, the gathering mutter of the villagers. This was Baimoda Village, the southernmost of the Rounds in the Ston Gassen; like all the Ston folk, the Baimodans were an independent lot, restive and resentful. They didn't like having orders shouted at them, nor did they want youmbards quartered in their village. And that anger

would have its fruit; the stench of blood-to-come almost made her vomit.

Shuffle shuffle, trying to be blind and deaf.

Shuffle shuffle, into the GodHouse like every time
before.

Down a flight of stairs into the punish cells beneath the worship chambers.

The same as before.

The youmbards sliced the ropes off their wrists
and shoved them inside, one of them cupping her
buttock and squeezing, running his hand between her
legs as he shoved her in, Treshteny didn't know who,
didn't dare look around.

The door slammed shut once they were in the narrow room, the bar squealed over and chunked home
in its hooks. There was a table with a jug on it and
a tray covered with a cloth. Two stools. Two plank
cots, their outer edges supported by chains, a thin
blanket on each, folded into a neat square. An empty
bucket in one corner, another bucket filled with
scummy-looking water near the door.

There were scrabbling sounds in the wooden ceiling, eye shimmers looking at them through cracks
and knotholes; another shimmer crouched on the
ledge of the barred window, a ferret knitted from
spun glass. The youmbards called them brus. Yela'o
made an angry sound and jumped at the window, but
the bru wriggled through the iron bars and stood
outside them making faces at the baby faun.

There was a sour smell that seemed to come off
on Treshteny's hands whenever she touched anything, though the cell looked clean enough.

Mama Charody stared at the wall for a moment,
then she smiled, whipped the cloth off the bread,
cheese and bowls of a porridge made from ground

maize that waited for them on the tray. She filled the three mugs with water. "Doby, come you here and eat something. You're not much more than bone, and you'll be needing your strength." She fussed at the boy, used a corner of the cloth dipped in the door-bucket to wash his face and hands, then sat him on one of the stools and cut bread and cheese for him. "Eat, eat."

Doby's tongue moved over dry lips. His eyes were huge in his starved face. "When you do, Mam, I will."

She laughed, rubbed the back of her hand along-side his face. "Bargaining, is it? Zdra zdra, so it's bite for bite, you and me." She drew up a stool, perched on it and cut her own meal.

"The Healer," Treshteny said suddenly. "I see her. Here. Horse is bringing her."

"About time that one did something besides run off." She took a bit of cheese, her dark eyes twinkling as Doby measured the hole her teeth left and bit off exactly the same amount. She chewed, washed the mouthful down with a swallow of water. "Sit down, Timeseer, eat. You'd best have strength for moving fast."

Treshteny blinked, settled herself on a stool and drew one of the porridge bowls toward her. She took up a spoon, inserted it tentatively in the grainy, glutinous mess. Halfway to her mouth, the spoon stopped. She said, "It's only possibles, nothing for sure."

"Kamen say she's coming, that's sure enough for me. Put that stuff in your mouth before it sets on you."

"Ahhh. Kamen. I'd forgot them." Treshteny nodded and obeyed, then dipped up another spoonful. "That's why you didn't talk. You were calling them."

"Close enough."

"Why did it take so long? It didn't take that long before."

"They've been hanging about a while now. Complaining at me. Takes a lot of talking to calm them down. The land's too hot here. They don't like it."

"But they came to the mountain that burned."

"Not that kind of hot, Timeseer."

"Oh."

"Mam, eat."

"Yes, Doby. Bite for bite it still is."

The darkness closed in around them. Mama Charody made Doby lie on one of the cots and tucked the blanket around him; she crouched beside the cot singing softly to him until he drifted into sleep, then went to stand beside the window looking up at the stars.

Treshteny rubbed at her eyes and she spoke the thought that had been troubling her. "How long have the kamen been with us?"

Charody gave a kind of grunting sigh, turned and flattened her broad back against the stone. "Couple weeks now. If you're wondering why I didn't ask them to break us out, it's simple enough. No point in stirring up a fuss, making this lot chase after us when they're taking us where we meant to go all along." She yawned, let herself slide down the wall. "I'm surprised you didn't vision them. Hmp. When the healer comes, they'll break the wall for her."

Treshteny turned her head and watched the door play its changes. "Nik," she said after a moment. "They won't."

Charody yawned again. "Zdra, that's as it will be. There's a while to wait. Get some sleep if you can. It'll help pass the time."

The hum woke Treshteny from heavy, nightmare-ridden sleep. She sat up, letting the blanket fall away, set her hand against the wall. The stone was vibrating with the sound; it felt warm against her palm, disturbingly alive. She looked up. A faint, wavering light shone through the cracks and knotholes of the ceiling. That was it. The spirit people were making the sound. She saw them for the first time as one, not a blur of might-bes; she looked around. The table was one, even Doby was one. She nodded as if she were greeting someone. "Healer."

She crossed to Mama Charody, touched her shoulder, pulled her hand back when she felt the vibration amplified through the body of the old woman. "Charody. It's time."

The old woman was a withered lump, her features sunk in deep wrinkles, her body solid and heavy as a fossilized root. She didn't move.

Forcing herself to ignore the bite of the force running through Charody, Treshteny caught hold of her shoulder and tried to shake her awake. "Charody, get up. Get away from the stone. Listen to me. Get up. Get up."

Behind her she heard the squeal of the iron bar as it swung on its pivot. "Mama, wake up. Please wake up."

A patter of feet behind her, a light hand on her arm. "Let me, Timeseer."

Treshteny sighed and stepped back, her fear soothed by the familiar voice.

Serroi touched the rounded shoulder. "It's time now, Charody."

The old woman's body unfolded and expanded and a moment later Mama Charody was on her feet and moving briskly to Doby. "I hope you've brought more than Horse."

"Oh yes. Macs for riding and supplies. Carry the boy, you can wake him later. I don't know how long this is going to last, you know. I'm not doing it."

"I know." Charody tucked the thin blanket about Doby, making a neat bundle of the boy. She lifted him onto her shoulder and moved quickly for the door.

They walked through the building cradled in the hum, stepped over the bodies of sleeping guards and emerged into the walled court behind the GodHouse where the Yubbal and his doyas kept their riding stock. There were no guards here, nothing but the macain waiting patiently with Horse.

Twenty minutes later they were riding from the village, heading for the Ashtops and whatever waited there.

12. On the March

1

The meie swung from the longboat onto the landing. She was tall and lean with a scarred arm and leg, a mop of coarse hair pale as year-old straw. Out beyond her, in the deeper part of the harbor, the merchanter was swarming with more meien, loading bundles in the ship's other boats and waiting their turn to come ashore. "Heslin." She advanced to meet him, hand out.

"Meie Synggal."

As their voices came small and faint to K'vestmilly Vos standing in the doorway to the Longhouse, she felt a sudden rush of jealousy. These two knew each other very well. And Heslin hadn't mentioned that when he reported what came over the com. Not a word about knowing the meie. Not a word. How many other women in his life, how many would be popping their heads up as time passed? It wasn't something that had occurred to her before, but now it ate at her. He knew too much. How many teachers? She was getting bigger by the breath, her flesh sagged, even with Olmena prodding and scolding her into those tedious exercises, she was going soft as overripe cheese. And anyway he'd never said he cared for her . . . pretended to be jealous of the Poet . . . just an excuse to go off and do what he wanted. What

he wanted? Rule Cadander and take her for it if he
had to. Manipulator supreme, why hadn't she seen it
before. He's too good at it. . . .

She shuddered and pushed the blackness away. It
was the changes in her body doing this to her, that
and the confinement, staring at four walls, watching
them close in on her, couldn't go outside without
someone shooting at her. Dark thoughts, twisty sus-
picions of everyone around her, though they'd
proved their loyalty a thousand times over. And she
couldn't talk about it to anyone, not even Heslin. A
thousand times not Heslin. So it sat in her head and
festered. Olmena, maybe . . . but Olmena was
Osklander, how could she trust her with Osk trying
to . . . Mad's Tits! How could she trust anyone?

Her expression concealed by the Mask . . . *Maiden
Bless the Mask, Mother was right* . . . from the guards
and House women clustered around her, she glow-
ered at Heslin and the meie as they walked up from
the landing, talking intimately as if there weren't another person for a thousand miles, instead of several
hundred men and women gathering from the houses
and sheds where they'd been working on getting
ready to march out of this place. There was a mutter
of voices, shouts from some children, a baby crying,
then another and another, chinin barking and some
distance off the angry honk of a macai as a clawman
filed its talons. As if all that didn't exist . . . her Consort . . . Maiden only knew what he got up to with
the women here while she was shut up like this . . .
couldn't get out and see . . . she should have kept
Hedivy with her . . . he was loyal . . . why did she
agree to let him go off with that lot of no-hopes . . .
Mother had Oram, I need Hedivy . . . the Healer
should have stayed here . . . I need her . . . when the

fighting starts . . . she turned her head restlessly side to side . . . so many of these will be dead before this is over. . . .

Heslin looked up the hill, smiled at her, went back to his conversation with the meie.

She cleared her throat, swallowed the phlegm. Sucked in a breath laden with the stench of dead fish and sweaty bodies. She had to get her voice under control so he wouldn't catch how wretched she felt. He'd soon guess why and she couldn't stand the thought of his pity.

"Meie Synggal, you are most welcome. It's too bad you come just as we're being forced to leave. One tedious trip on top of another." The words came out calm and friendly. K'vestmilly was pleased with herself.

In the watching crowd someone snapped thumb against finger in a welcoming click and the others took it up, a small sound magnified by numbers. They knew the meie meant arms and fighters and supplies like trailfood, tents and blankets—and maybe the edge that could win them back their homes and their old lives.

"So Heslin was telling me. Perhaps it would be best if we packed the supplies directly into your wagons." The meie looked over her shoulder, a quick frown crossing her face as she saw heavily loaded longboats already on their way to the landing.

K'vestmilly glanced from the meie to Heslin who was standing back as he usually did, effacing himself. Not so simple for a man of his size and personality. It occurred to her suddenly that he didn't find this business of being a consort easy or congenial. No time to think about that now. She touched her tongue to her lips, swallowed. "Yes, that's a good idea. Vazdor," she put her hand on the arm of the guard standing beside the door, turned the Mask to him, "Take the meie round where the wagons are waiting, send someone to fetch the Panya Valiva." She turned back to the meie. "Valiva is handling supplies, she'll show you where she wants you to put things. Forgive our momentary lack of hospitality, but time does press. Join us here for the evening meal if it pleases you."

"What's wrong?" Heslin walked across to her, slipped the Mask off and turned her to face him.

K'vestmilly pulled away. "My back hurts, that's all." She walked across the room and lowered herself onto the daybed. She didn't want him here, didn't want anyone in her sitting room, she wanted to brood and be as miserable as she felt like being without having to be polite to anyone. "You've got things to do, go do them."

His face went still. "Of course, Marn," he said and left.

"Hes, I didn't . . ." She whispered the words, wondering what she'd done. Unhappy and ashamed of herself, she let her head fall against the slanted back of the daybed and lay with tears running down her face and wetting the pads.

She needed to see to her own packing, she needed to bundle into an old cloak, argue her guards into letting her out and go talk to people, keep their courage high, reinforce the good the ship's arrival had done, but she could find neither the strength nor the will to pull herself back on her feet until Olmena came bustling in, scolded her through her exercises, into a hot bath, then made her pay attention while

Cumura the Marn Maid packed so she could make sure things she thought she might need wouldn't be shoved to the bottom of the boxes.

K'vestmilly Vos tapped the bent glass straw against the tube glass that held the broth she'd sipped while the others ate their fish and tubers and drank the sour wine from the Sharr.

There was a short bustle as forks and knives were laid down and her guests turned to face the Mask. They expected a speech. Zdra, they wouldn't get it.

"Meie Synggal, we haven't had a chance to talk. Have you and yours got your materiel stowed to your satisfaction?"

"Yes, O Marn. The Panya Valiva was most helpful." She had a voice like the point of a sword, small but crisp and clear.

"You have been informed as to the reasons for the move?"

"Yes, O Marn. And we're ready to leave."

"Ah. Then we will go tomorrow night, as soon as Nijilic TheDom breaks the horizon." She took up her glass of chays juice, turned the Mask from face to face. "I call a toast. May the Maiden bless our journey and guide us home again."

2

Pokad wiped the condensation from the eyepiece of the longglass, set it to his eye again. "Another navsta coming round Uhley Hill, let's see . . . nik, not quite a navsta, I count eighteen men all foot no riders . . . ta ta ta," he sang under his breath as he waited. "And there's a team showing, supply wagon . . . yes, some-

thing piled high under that tarp ... make a note,
Bily, ask Tomal to nose out what was on that wagon,
if he hasn't already, which I expect he will have
done. . . . Spros! there's another. Zdra, I thought so.
Had to be more'n them marching that was kicking up
so much dust. Herd of vul ... mmm ... round two
dozen, four herders on macs ...

Pokad was a long skinny man in Harozh hunting
clothes, his brown hair pulled back and tied in a tail
at the base of his neck. The hand that propped up
the longglass was missing three of the outer fingers
and there was a winding, badly healed scar that
crossed the back and vanished under his sleeve. His
cousin Bily was crouched beside him, taking down
what he was saying in small crabbed glyphs; Bily was
a silent wild youth, a mix of browns that melded him
so thoroughly into the background that even Pokad
had trouble remembering he was there.

Pokad watched the newcomers settle into the enemy camp that had grown up beside the heap of
stone that was all that was left of OskHold—a scatter
of tents, shacks, wagons and rope corrals. It was busy
and noisy as a small city though most of the men
down there were Taken. They were relaxed these
days, not so stiff and mechanical, the discipline of the
march gone for the moment; he watched them wandering in and out of the tent taverns and brothels,
gambling, sleeping, working on their gear, acting
more like everyday folk than they had before, as if
the Enemy had loosed the reins that held them.
Pokad wondered about that. Did it mean the Glory
was busy somewhere else and couldn't spare the time
to see to them? He muttered a comment for Bily to
note down and continued his sweep.

The chovan were still avoiding the Taken. Didn't

even try to steal from them. They stayed in their own filthy camps where they gambled, drank and fought, occasionally butchered each other.

And around the edges swarmed the camp-followers, peddlers and fate-readers, whores, cooks and laundresses, boys off the streets of Dander and Calanda who tended stock, ran errands, worked as shills for the taverners and pimps. Pokad grunted as he saw Tomal sidling around to the section where the newcomers were settling in. He lowered the glass again and glanced at the sun. It was a vibrating yellow-white orb low in the west. "Not much day left. Tomal's sniffin about, you be sure and ask him what he found. If he keeps his hair on, he'll be at the meet soon's it's dark. Bil?"

"Mmh?"

"Tell him be watchin for any sign they gettin ready to move. Marn's marching tonight, Heslin wants to know how soon they get word of it."

"Gotcha."

Pokad's mouth tightened as he saw Lehky Azheva come from one of the brothel tents. She stood there a while, looking around, yawning and stretching, then went back inside. She wasn't Harozh, but she was the widow of a friend of his who'd gone south to work the barges. He hated what she was doing, but gave her grudging respect for doing it. She was Web, one of their best sources about what was going on in Ker's tent. Pan Ker. General Pan Ker. He hawked up a gob, spat.

A dozen or so of the women down there were Web like Lehky, some just treading in place and surviving, waiting for a chance to do whatever damage they could, some actively spying. The rest of them in those tents were women the Glory wars had made widows and childless. Life was hard in Dander and Calanda these days, a lot of the men were killed, had run off, or were Taken, almost all the food and clothing was diverted to the army, not much fish in the river, just corpses of the dead and the scavenger shellworms that lived on carrion. Empty houses were being torn apart for wood to burn for cooking. At least it wasn't cold, not like it should have been. The heat hung motionless over all of Cadander, from the Travasherims in the west to the Merrzachars in the east, from the Harozh in the north to the Bezhval in the south. Plants came up a fingerwidth, then withered and died. But the army was fed and the army was clothed, so those who could bring themselves to do it, they hovered around the edges like dung beetles feeding off the army's leavings.

Zhroudit Pan Ker folded long, thin hands across his stomach and struggled with the anger churning under them. As mildly as he could, picking his words with care to avoid sibilants, he said, "O Marn, would it not be better to return to Dander where you can keep control of what undoubtedly will happen there? The hunger, the agitation, the unconverted, the women without their men; these will mean trouble and you will need to be there to keep it in hand. In addition, O Marn, it will be very uncomfortable for you when we begin to move."

His anger congealed to fear and a sick shame as it always did when the Mask turned on him and those hot yellow eyes swept over him. He saw himself reflected there, if not actually, at least in his mind's eye, as an ineffectual little wisp of a man, a meager creature with a hiss in his speech that made the other Pans titter behind their hands.

"Move. That's a word you don't seem to know, Pan General." Her child's voice was high and light—and more frightening than any basso bluster. "When will you be moving, Pan General? When will you stop dithering and go after that creature?"

"When we complete the training, O Marn. When we have enough material on hand and the road to Dander guarded and clear."

"And do you have a day in mind?"

Behind the canvas that walled Ker's sleeping quarters from the working part of the tent, Lahky Azheva lay without breathing as she listened, silently blessing the chance that sent the False Marn here when Ker was getting ready for his afternoon session of horizontal exercises. Which was what he called pronging her and the others he had. It wasn't so bad, he didn't have much imagination and it didn't take anything fancy to arouse him and this wasn't the first time she or one of her Web companions had heard things she shouldn't.

Probably wouldn't be the last. Ker didn't like women, but he needed them. His orderly would come round to Hanesh's place, whisper the time and be at the back of the Command Tent to slide the woman in through the slit there. And be there again to pay her price and shoo her off when she slid out. And to remind all of them to keep their mouths shut.

"I will have the backroad properly monitored within the week, O Marn. When I have done that, the time will be here to begin our march to obliterate the enemy."

A cough behind him. He swung round, saw it was

the orderly standing just inside the door, the flap in one hand. "What?"

"A messenger from the other side, Pan General. He says it's important."

"Who?"

"Zestat the Chov." The orderly's voice had a tight, disapproving twang, as if he detested the need to say that name.

"Hmmp. I'll be out in a . . ."

The Glory Marn interrupted him. "Nik, Pan General. Have him in now. I would like to hear this."

"You have but to declare it, O Marn. You heard, Orderly Vyborn. Bring the chovan in, remain behind him and watch him. If he blinks wrong, knock him on the head and get him out. You understand?"

"I understand, Pan General."

Ker followed the orderly to the front flap, stepped outside a moment and spoke briefly to him, then came back.

"A moment only, O Marn. You know the chovan, they need a heavy reminder of proper behavior."

Lehky Azheva chewed on her thumb and tried to think what to do. If Ker decided she'd heard too much, likely he'd have her strangled and tossed in the ruins to rot. If she went away now, the guard outside would know when she left, so that would be all right, but she'd miss something that sounded important.

Before she had time to decide what she was going to do, a hand dropped on her shoulder, another clamped over her mouth. "Get out." The orderly's voice, whispering, hot against her ear. "Not a sound or I'll have Hanesh cut your hide off."

She nodded.

He let her get to her feet, stood aside, absently

wiping his hand down his tunic, watching as she collected her clothing and got dressed enough to leave.

Outside, he took her arm, led her away a few steps. "One hour. Be back here then. You'll get your pay when you've done your job. Tell Hanesh that all you know is he wasn't ready for you. If I hear you flapped your mouth about his business, you know what'll happen."

She nodded again and went away, bare feet wincing from the broken stone that littered the byways between the tents, her mind busy with speculation. *A spy from the Stathvoreen with urgent news. That had to be something about the Marn. Hanesh first, smooth him down, then Tomal. If I can find him. He can take word. Spojjin Ker, I could have stayed if he hadn't . . .* She sighed and turned into a narrow lane between two mess tents, moving faster as she got closer to the assemblage of canvas and waste-lumber Hanesh called his House.

3

K'vestmilly Vos swore as the rear left wheel jolted off a rocky lump and sent her stomach bouncing in spite of the mattresses packed into the body of the wagon and the pillows jammed around her. One of her soldiers, a man named Emul Trulha who was a carpenter by profession, had put together a backrest for her, with arms she could hold to keep herself steady. It was a clever bit of work; the whole thing could be folded against the sides when she wanted to stretch out and sleep. The wagon had thick ribs along the sides with rafterpieces overhead and doubled canvas pulled tight over them, a lining inside that to make sure no light could leak through to make her a target

for snipers. Two of the candle lamps bolted to the
side ribs were burning now to give her some relief
from tedium, let her read Heslin's notes or work on
her own journal when the going smoothed out
enough.

"Why did I let them do this to me? I should be out
there riding, not jiggling like a rubber rajja on a
string. And stifling in this hothouse."

"T'k t'k, such a niggle-nuggle." Olmena Oumelic
pulled flat a fold of blouse that had worked between
her back and the front of the wagon. She was sitting
crosslegged on the mattresses, facing K'vestmilly Vos,
but far enough away to give K'vestmilly room to
stretch her legs. "You know very well why you're
here. Weren't for the snipers, you could do whatever
you wanted, you're healthy enough. And I don't
know what I'm saying this for, you've heard it twenty
ways twenty times."

K'vestmilly sniffed. "Doesn't mean I have to like
it." She felt an all too familiar pressure. "I'm going to
have to stop."

"Water?"

"All this shaking, what do you think I'm talking
about?" She pushed at the arms of the rest, drawing
her legs under her. "Tell the driver to hold up a minute. Do you have some kind of screen you can let
down around me? Why didn't I think of this before?
Spros!"

Olmena chuckled. "Going to get worse the bigger
you get. It'll seem like soon's some liquid goes in
your mouth it wants to come out the other end. No
need to stop. When he was doing the rest of this, I
had Emul fix you a chamber pot with a lid and bolt
it in at the back there. Grab hold, Marn." Olmena
pushed up, stood with legs braced and her hand out,

grinning at K'vestmilly. "Once you've been at this a few days you'll be so used to it you won't think twice."

As the wagon bumped and rolled into the night between files of armed riders, followed by other creaking, clumsy wagons filled with supplies, some of the women and the younger children; surrounded by foot soldiers and the rest of the women and their children, with the meies and gyes from the Biserica mounted and riding scout, K'vestmilly Vos tried to ignore the smells from the pot and brooded.

Carefully polite in a way that made her want to kick him, Heslin had brought her his notes of the last call from the Web over the mountains. *We have to talk. Somehow. What if he doesn't come near me? He's got excuse enough. Mad's Tits, there's no way I can go hunting for him. In front of them all, go chasing down my bedman? Zhag, why am I such a blithering fool?* She wrenched her mind from the rut it kept treading, peered at the closely written stack of papers resting on her knees.

Though they had no direct information, indications were that Pan Ker knew about the arrival of the ship and that she and her army were ready to move. No com, Maiden Bless, but relays of messengers—those curséd chovan could make the trip in a few days rather than the month it'd cost the army and the Osklanders. He hadn't made any moves of his own, not yet, but according to her mother's notes in the diary that proggin' Nov stole from her, he was a cautious man and liked to be sure of his footing before he jumped. Her mother had been acidly amused by him, nonetheless had Oram watching him on a regular basis. *I wonder who's got that diary now. If Ker found it, he'd have burned the part about him. Mother cut him to ribbons. Maiden Bless, the things she said.*

Oversexed underbrained wisp was one of the kindest. Not a pain-lover. Saves his viciousness for those he envies. Those who stand in the way of ambitions he won't even admit to himself. *Like Mother. Standing in his way, I mean. He must've celebrated for days when he heard she was dead. May he rot in the lowest Zhagdeep.*

A man of grand ideals who knows what's best for everyone, too bad if they don't agree.

Web says he makes speeches every few days ... to the Chovan, even to the Taken. That's one of his sillier notions. Chovan are bought, what do they care? Taken have no choice, so they need even less convincing. Keeps saying all this blood is only a purging of evil. As soon as the restive element ... me, I suppose, Heslin, for sure, foreigners are a nasty source of corruption ... as soon as we don't threaten to destroy what he builds, Cadander will be a paradise. Hm. Lahky Azheva ... servicing him ... how she can, ungh! ... says Ker talks about Nov sometimes when he's on her ... hates him worse than me, still does though he's dead ... too big and handsome, a leader men followed because they wanted to ... envy ... eats at him. Says he can't stand the Taken either, though he likes the way they jump when he says hop. The Glory's a tool, he says. Once he's got Cadander under his thumb, he's going to clean the Glorymen out before they know what's hit them. Stupid man.

Not so stupid in other ways. He's got the army humming, supplies coming in, training going smooth as a baby's cheek, even the Chovan ... after he hung a few of them. Two thousand men, well armed, well fed, rested. Maiden Bless, they could roll over us without breathing hard. Heslin says no, but I think he's lying.

"Mena!"

Olmena Oumelic jerked, blinked. "What . . . ah! Marn?"

"Do you know Vedouce's plans? When do we stop for a breather?"

"General Pan Pen wanted to make Laza Bay before stopping, I don't know how long that'll be, I don't know what kind of time we're making. Not too good, I think. You want me to call one of the guards over and ask him?"

"Nik." *Where's your head, K'milly? Call a guard over? Chert! That's another thing I didn't think of. I'm letting this get away from me.* "Send the guard to tell Meie Synggal I'd like to talk to her. And before you do . . ." She grimaced, slid the notes into their folder and dropped it beside her. "Help me onto the pot. Spros! You say it's going to get worse?"

"If you'll be seated, Meie Synggal, we can talk."

Synggal's pale blue eyes moved quickly around the interior of the wagon, she bowed and dropped to a squat where Olmena usually sat; the healer was out front beside the driver for the duration of the conference. "Marn," the meie said, waited.

"You were necessarily cautious over the com. I'd like the numbers now."

Synggal nodded, focused her eyes on a spot somewhere behind K'vestmilly's left shoulder. "Had to be volunteers. Prieti Meien is walking delicately over this, couldn't do anything that would mean bringing in the Mijloc Council. Take a year of arguing and then who knows. And there's been agitating to rescind the Biserica's Charter. Don't think they could, but it's trouble she doesn't need." Her gaze shifted momentarily, fixed on the Mask. "Then there's

Heslin. No reports, so the Council's getting antsy, even his enemies don't like the idea someone's messing with their Vorbescar."

Behind the Mask K'vestmilly's mouth tightened. After a minute she said, "A packet of reports are on their way, the messenger left two months ago."

"Good. If . . . when . . . he arrives, that'll take some of the pressure off Nischal Tay. Where was I? Yes. All volunteers. Whoever happened to be in House and willing. Twenty-five gyes, several of them combat instructors, all of them veterans of this 'n that. Forty meien, myself included. Fifteen Dance Instructors." She grinned, pale eyes twinkling. "A traditional title, Marn. Sword dance. Knife dance. Hand dance. Hitting the target dance. You see what I mean. The rest of us are longtimers, been through a lot of Wards, come back with bits missing here and there." She tapped the scar that slashed down her arm.

K'vestmilly Vos smiled with her hands and gave an encouraging nod. It was an odd sensation listening to the woman; Synggal reminded her of Marazheny Treddek Osk. She didn't look much like her, but had the same brisk competence. *I didn't like Marazhney and I don't like this one, but I can work with her. As long as Heslin doesn't . . . nik! I won't go this way again.* "Go on," she murmured.

Synggal dropped her hands on her knees, large and bony hands, well-shaped despite that. "As for materiel, Nischal Tay dipped as deep into the Biserica Reserves as she could justify to herself. We picked up about a half ton of dried fruits and meat in Kelea-alela and Paristo, hit what felt like every gunsmith on the Neck and picked up 500 longguns, two hundred cases of ammunition. We stopped in

Karpan aNor, acquired eight bolts of canvas, six dozen blankets, a hundred fifty sacks of maize on the cob—by the way, the cobs are good for burning once the kernels are off. Plus some other odds and ends I won't bother listing, unless you want them, too."

"If you have a written inventory, I'd like to see it, but that can wait. Can you tell me about Greygen and Sansilly?"

"Ah, yes. When I left, they were settling down nicely. Greygen found a place with the Woodmaster. Sansilly looked about a bit, decided she wanted to know more about the machines we make, got herself into classes and was very pleased with them the last time I saw her. She asked me to see about her sons if I came across them. She sent them to her cousins in the Harozh when it seemed they were in danger from a Purger—you know about them? Good. According to Heslin we'll be passing by AnkHold. I'll see to the boys when we get there."

"Yes." K'vestmilly couldn't manage to inject warmth into the word, winced as she saw the fleeting surprise on the meie's face before it settled into a diplomatic smile. *Fool! You can't antagonize this one. You need her. I need Heslin too. Ahhh Zhag. Get hold of yourself.* She leaned forward. "Is there anything more I should know? From the Prieti Meien or those who aren't spoken of?"

"Yes. I was told to say nothing unless you asked. I don't know why, but that's the Shawar for you. They say this:

> The pivot point advances
> Life with Death dances
> When the stars go out

And TheDom's in rout
The Marn must try her chances.

Make of it what you can."

As the tight knot of men, women, beasts and wagons crept along the coast of the Stathvoreen,
K'vestmilly unhooked the backrest and with
Olmena's help got herself bedded down among the
pillows. She was tired, so she managed to slide into
sleep after a short spate of fretting.

Sleep and nightmare . . . Heslin mocking her and
going off with Valiva and Synggal . . . Serroi dancing
a wild wheeling dance with a huge blackness that
pushed at her and squeezed her until she shrank
smaller and smaller and went out with a pop! . . .

Pop! Chunk! Glass breaking.

They were small sounds, but they reached into the
dream and pulled her awake. "Wha . . ." She started
to sit up.

A hand on her shoulder pressed her down,
Olmena's breath tickled her ear as the healer whispered, "Stay down."

"What's . . ." K'vestmilly felt the wagon lurching
and swaying as the driver snapped his whip round the
ears of the draft vul. She could hear shouts, curses,
hooves tramping, macain hooting, a pair of cracks
from the slopes.

"Sniper. Somebody. Hit a candlelamp, turn your
head, you'll see."

The driver's whip cracked again as if he echoed the
shots from the hills, the vul team blatted, the wagon
began jolting and jumping over the rough ground.
"That fool, he'll break a wheel if he doesn't . . ." She
got her elbow set, began pushing herself up, slapped

Olmena's hand away when the healer tried to push her back. "Nik, that snake'll be running tail-on-fire if the scouts haven't got him already." With some difficulty she crawled over the mattresses to the front, thrust her head through the lapped slit. "Slow down. Now. Before you break the bones that notney missed."

"Marn . . ." The driver's voice squeaked with relief even as he pulled the vul down to their usual amble.

"That's better." *Idiot*, she thought. *Where did he think he was going, or what would happen if he outran the marchers?*

"Marn." Heslin's voice. He rode close to the wagon. "You'd better get back inside. We don't know how many of them there were."

"I want to know what's going on. If I have to come out, I will."

"I'll send Zasya when she's back from the sweep."

She wanted to say *not Zasya but you, Hes*, but she couldn't bring herself to, it was too much like begging. She watched a moment as he moved into the mob of riders, then pulled her head inside. "Olmena . . ."

"Right. I emptied the pot while you were sleeping, figured you'd need it again once you woke. Watch your feet. I think I've got up all the glass, but I can't be sure."

The bullet hole had gone a pale gray by the time Zasya returned. She scratched at the canvas, came inside at K'vestmilly's impatient call.

She glanced at the hole, dropped to a squat beside Olmena Oumelic. "We got one. Hung him. Lost the others in the ravines and rockfalls. Chovan, the one we hung, anyway. At least one Stathvor who knows these hills. And Ildas tells me a Sleykyn was with them. Why he wouldn't do any tracking. He gets very protective sometimes. Sorry."

"I imagine you'll get more chances to take them."

"Hmp. Can't say that it'd go much better if we do, this is rugged country. On the other hand, the General means to travel by daylight after this stretch is done, so an ambush will be easier to spot. In case you're wondering . . ." She flicked a finger at the bullet hole in the canvas. "They were shooting at all the wagons, not just this one. Figure they didn't know for sure which you were in so they spread their fire. That'll change. But if they've got any brains between them, they'll go for the vul next."

"I remember it's what Vedouce did to the Govaritzer army. Didn't stop them."

"Nik, but it slowed them some, gave us time to get ready for them."

"And if we're slowed even more than we are already . . ."

"Not a good idea." Zasya grabbed at the nearest rib as the wagon jolted over a series of ruts, then changed direction. "Looks like we're getting close to the Bay. Anything else, Marn?"

"Nik. Keep me informed when these things happen, I need to know. You can go now."

Olmena followed the meie out. K'vestmilly grimaced as she heard the healer talking about fires and cha waiting for the Marn's arrival. This interminable night was almost over, but the rest wouldn't last long, only a few hours, then they'd go on again. And on and on. Vedouce had estimated twenty days travel before they reached Maznak Pass, the nearest breach in the Merrzachars. A force of Harozh were there already, keeping the road open for them, holding it free of the Majilarn raiders, chovan and other hostiles. She poured herself a mug of water from the skin, sat sipping at it, braced by the backrest, her free hand resting on the lump that was her daughter. *I'm jealous of you, mouselet; they think more of you than they do of me. They'd mourn a little if I was shot, but I'm only me, you're the Hope.*

She hated sewing and was miserable at it. Funny how that was a good thing in its way. Many of the women attached to the army were sewing baby clothes for her; she was grateful for that—and cynical enough to use it to bind these people more closely to her. Her mother's words came back to her as they'd done before—*you'll work like all the demons in Zhagdeep to keep your place, you'll coax and you'll wheedle, you'll bribe and you'll punish, secretly and openly, you'll do the twisty dance the rest of your life.* Ansila Vos was as tricky a politician as Heslin. *As I'm turning out to be*, she told herself, half in pride, half in disgust.

Ignoring the driver's protest, she came through the lapped front curtains and settled herself on the seat beside him—looking about and seeing for the first time in the weary gray light of morning the swarm of people moving with her.

The Biserica force working as scouts were dots on the hillsides, barely visible even to one with longsight. The veterans from the Gritzer war surrounded her, protecting her. Behind them came the other wagons with their loads of supplies with women, old men and children tucked wherever there was room among the sacks and bales. The navstas of footsoldiers from Oskland marched with these. K'vestmilly could hear the tramp of their feet, the growl of their voices in the cool, quiet morning air. Bands of the younger Harozh were riding past, racing, laugh-

ing and joking even now after a hard and dangerous
night, so happy were they to be loosed from their
miserable existence in the village, half the shouted
words so deep in dialect she couldn't understand
them when she could hear them.

A plume of smoke rose some distance ahead, the
fire hidden by an outcrop of rock with a crown of
thick twisted shtekkle brush. She smiled. It'd be good
to get down and walk about a bit in air untainted by
the stink of her own wastes.

13. On the way to the Ashtops

1

BAGKLOUSS

Tserama looked down at her daughter, an ice-knot forming between her breasts; there wasn't much pain in her, mostly anger and disgust, but she didn't let any of it show. Ammeny was knotted into a bundle, ropes wound round her, pinning arms against her body, forcing her legs together, a rag bunched in her mouth as a gag, tied in place by a strip of cloth. "I'll cut you loose in the morning," Tserama said, her voice level. "Then you can do what you want. Just don't come back here and expect me to take you in."

Ammeny stared at her a moment longer, then closed her eyes and turned her head away.

She couldn't think with Ammeny lying there hating her.

She had to think.

She lifted her daughter and carried her to the wallbed. "Pyya, Menny, you wanted my place, you can have it for a while."

She pulled the slide shut and sighed with relief, a weight coming off her shoulders. She crossed the room and put her hand on the kingpost, felt the House Spirit shivering against her palm. "I don't know what to do," she said. "Everything's changing. I don't understanding anything." She set her shoul-

ders against the pole and slid down until she was sitting, staring at the door.

It was late and she was very tired—and afraid. Like
Brajid she saw her life ending. Not death, just a slash
of Fate's knife, cutting her loose from everything
she'd known.

She owned only her clothing and her gift. The
house and everything in it belonged to Danoulcha.
Her children? She hadn't heard from any of them
since they left home, not even Chuskya, her eldest,
though the ties between them had been strongest.
Her children wouldn't take her in if the Danoulcha
Round denied her, they'd go with the others.

What the Sem Ris would do when she didn't Read
and Clear them, she didn't know, didn't like to think
about. It was going to be a bad time.

She rubbed at her knees, straightened her legs out,
drew them up again. *Getting old*, she thought, *the
joints are going. So they caught the strangers. And
Chouse's bru was talking about Gan Khora's work. I wonder* . . . She squeezed her eyes tight, relaxed her face.
"House Spirit, you know anything about Gan
Khora's work? Or these strangers?"

The Prudjin, Reader, SHE is . . .

As if the *name* invoked the *presence*, a dank fog
rolled into the room, rolled over Tserama, freezing
her in mid-thought, withering the voices from the
kingpost and the thatch. It lingered for a long time,
how long Tserama couldn't be sure about when the
thing was gone and her mind stirred again.

Rage. Hunger. Anguish. Fear.

"That . . ."

The spirits twittered till the House Spirit shouted
them down and spoke; *Best not say the name, Reader.*

SHE hears. We didn't know when we said it. We know now.

"It wasn't after me . . . us."

A chorus of voices: *SHE was looking, Reader. We hid you and us. Was the strangers caught HER eye this time. They bore HER gaze and cast it off.*

"Ahh, Gan Khora's work."

In chorus still, the spirits said: *It is so.*

She thought about that a while. "And more to come," she said finally.

It is so.

"Where are they?'

There was silence filled with rustles; they were being stubborn. She waited without speaking, setting her will against theirs.

Finally the House Spirit groaned a word: *God-House.*

"Then I know what to do." She pushed onto hands and knees, then grunted herself back onto her feet. She stood braced against the kingpost while the dizziness drained out of her. The yammer of the little spirits wasn't helping; they didn't want her to leave them, they'd starve, they'd dry up and blow away, the demons would eat them, she couldn't leave them. "Be quiet. I do what I have to do."

Ignoring the rustles and mindwhines that followed her about, she shook out her walking clothes, sighed because she could smell herself on them. No time for washing and she didn't have others sturdy enough to take what she expected to come at her. She fetched in the tsadar she'd left airing on the clothesline behind the house, found a backsack that one of her older sons had left behind when he took up his landgrant, began loading it with food, spell-herbs and her small supply of medicaments.

She stood for several moments frowning at the slide that closed in the wallbed. *Menny, ah my Menny, I can't leave you here tied up like that, who knows how long it'd be before someone came and found you.*

She left the backsack and the tsadar beside the door and went out.

Land brus and wood brus clustered around her when she stepped outside, chattering at her while the hibbils screamed their jealousy from the thatch. She put her hands to her head and *howled* them to silence.

"Tsan pyya!" she said aloud, her eyes moving round the spirit shimmers crouched on the gravel and tuffets of grass outside her door. "Listen you brus, I'm going to do it, I will, but I need your help. Bring me a jennet or a gentle mare. Will you do it?"

Musical murmurs cascaded through her head, then the brus were gone. Tserama closed her eyes and leaned against the door; after a moment she went inside to wait.

The mare was small, gray and gentle, the bru that fetched her riding tangled in her mane. It was a woods bru, long and supple with short legs, round ears and a pushed in face with a mustache of thin whitish hairs that curled out and over its pointy smile. The wild spirit started to wriggle free when Tserama opened the door and looked out.

"No. Wait. Hold the horse steady."

A moment later she was out, carrying Ammeny. She laid her daughter belly down over the mare's back, looked speculatively at the bru.

----!

"Tsan pyya, you know your limits, bru. I'll hold her on when we leave. Let me fetch the rest of my things."

* * *

Tserama's eyes blurred with tears as she pulled the door shut on the house where she'd spent so much of her life. She wouldn't be back for a long time, if at all. She smoothed her hand along the wood as if she patted a favorite milker. Then she squared her shoulders and started down the slope to the village, walking beside the mare, holding Ammeny steady on the horse's back.

A huge black bird flew across the spray of stars, the light from the last of the Dancers touching glimmers of the talons of the wingclaws. It circled round and round above the Godhouse, then plummeted suddenly. Tserama came to the mouth of Brani Lane in time to see it stumble to a clumsy stop in the Lane, shift to a pale manshape and vanish over the back wall of the GodHouse with the ease of a traveling acrobat.

"Stranger, hunh," she murmured.

The bru giggled, sighed as Tserama began leading the mare across the Lane. -----, it said.

"The lock? I'd be pleased to have you open it for me."

------, it said.

"How long will it take them? Will I have time to deal with Ammeny?"

-----, it said.

"That's right, Brajji did say one of them was hurt. And I'll hurry."

She pulled Ammeny off the mare's back, laid her on the paving as close to the wall as she could manage. She hesitated a moment, drew her hand in a gentle caress down the side of her daughter's face. "I'm sorry, Menny, too bad things couldn't be differ-

ent." She shuddered at Ammeny's hot yellow glare,
straightened and led the mare through the postern
gate the bru had unlocked for her.

The naked man was partway visible in the starlight, leaning against the back door into the
GodHouse, taut with expectation. *Shapechanger,* she
thought, *he did that. He'll be coming here. Yes, there's
reason for it, they'll need mounts if they hope to get away.*

The door to the stable was closed by a hasp and
staple, the padlock that had been on it was gone. She
slipped inside, saw saddlebags and blanket rolls piled
in a heap beside the door.

The bru trotted after her, sat on his hind legs pat-
patting at the padlock on a tack box until it sprang
open. Whistling with pride in his prowess, he leaped
atop the box and pranced there until she set her hand
on the lid.

The strangers' weapons were inside, two longguns,
a weaponbelt with a sword and two knives, a holster
with a shortgun held in place with a snap-down flap.

The bru went running up a post and stretched out
on a rafter, gossiping with the roof hibbils, she
mindheard their chatter, but ignored it as she worked
to get saddles on the macain in the stalls before the
strangers came for them. She knew what stock the
Yubbal kept, so it was easy to pick out the stranger's
beasts—two each, mount and remount, from the
marks on them stolen somewhere in the grassland
provinces. She put halters and lead ropes on the
spares and with a grim smile appropriated Yubbal
Paggoh's prize macai for herself.

She was tying the last of the bedroll straps when she
heard the door creak open, then a loud thump against
the wall. She stiffened as she heard a man's voice.

----, the bru said.

He came in, a tall, broad-shouldered man, younger than she'd expected, with hazel eyes, bold cheekbones, a jutting nose, long black hair gathered into a single braid which hung down his back. Naked as he was born, he had a wild air about him, as if walls were not made to hold him. A sprite rode his shoulder, a creature that seemed to her half-real and half-spirit. She hadn't seen such a thing before.

She stepped from the stall.

He stiffened when he saw her, began to back away.

"Wait," she said, smiled when she saw he understood her. "You needn't worry, I'll be going with you."

"What?" His eyes flickered about the stable. "Who're you? What're you talking about?"

"My name is Tserama. I am Danoulcha's Spirit Reader. But that doesn't matter. I know things you need to know." She hesitated a moment. The hibbils and the brus saw she was going to say the *name* and shriveled into their smallest forms. "I know the Prudjin," she whispered. "I know where she lives."

"So do I. Mount Santak."

"And do you know which peak answers to that name? Don't play the fool, Change-man. This isn't the time for fiddling with words." She moved toward him. "I have saddled your beasts for you. Sunup is in a few hours. We have to be well away by then."

The sprite fluttered into the air. The Shapsa talk 'bout spirit readers in the Ston Gassen, Adlee. Honeydew say the reader say truth, talk wastes time. She darted away, circling over the stalls. The macs, the guns, your stuff, they all here. Like S'ramee say.

He stroked the dark stubble on his jaw, producing a soft rasping. "Ei vai, Tserama, my name's Adlayr, him out there is Hedivy and this is Honeydew. If you'll get the macs out, I'll get Hev on his feet and see how he's doing."

Tserama watched as Adlayr finished tying the one he called Hedivy into the saddle; the older man's face was flushed and he kept muttering things she didn't understand. Adlayr did. He was frowning, but he didn't say anything, just kept glancing at the dark bulk of the GodHouse as if he expected it to erupt any moment.

The stillness held.

If his fever didn't break by the time they could stop, she'd better brew some pai-nad root and drodya leaf and get it down him. The Change-man seemed to think they needed him. She shrugged. Adlayr knew about Mount Santak which was something she hadn't expected, so he could be right. Not hers to judge.

"That should hold. You lead, Tserama. We need the quickest way out of this place."

"Aren't you going to put some clothes on?"

"No. Soon as we're clear, I'm taking wing again. That'll give us more warning if they start after us. You can hear Honeydew?"

"Yes."

"Good. Most can't. Let's go."

Ammeny had managed to wriggle away from the wall. She glared up at them as they rode around her, but the gag was still firmly in place so all she could do was grunt. Tserama didn't look back, but she heard the small noises Ammeny made as she worked herself along the lane; the sounds followed them, mixed in with the grinding of the changer's teeth as he ate one trailbar after another with a grim concentration that told her more than any words what it took for him to shift like that.

* * *

At the northern edge of Danoulcha where Subdan's kamba orchard would hide them from observation, Tserama stopped her macai beside Hedivy, touched his skin. "He's burning."

"He's tough and he's been there before." Adlayr slid from the saddle. "I'm going up." When the sprite fluttered over to him, he shook his head. *Honey, you stay here, I know you, and I can hear you farther than the Reader.*

Tserama smiled. He was a cautious creature, this shapechanger. Didn't trust her. She took the lead rein he gave her, and sat watching as he strode away from the macain.

He shifted form, began a lumbering run down the long slope toward the water, powered into the air with only inches left before he'd wet his feet. He flew out across the water in a long slide, using the wind to help him rise.

The sprite gave a tiny sigh, fluttered to Adlayr's saddle. Honeydew and S'ramee need to get going.

Tserama nodded, clucked to her macai and gave an encouraging tug on the leadropes; the wind picking up across the lake meant morning was closer than she'd thought. Tsan pyya, it was better to be armed, supplied and mounted than leaving at a dead run like a scared paglet. *And once we get across the Sacred Way, the Danoulchans will turn back even if the youmbards don't, and that'll cut the danger down.*

She glanced up at the circling patch of black, gasped as a too-familiar chill brushed past her. She brought the rope ends down hard on the mac, yelled the others into a run.

* * *

Adlayr circled off the lake and over the village, the wind filling the stretched skin of his wings, letting him glide without more effort than was needed to ride the gusts. The village was still asleep, no lights visible except the smoky, guttering torches on the front porch of the GodHouse. He dipped lower and saw the dark blotch of the missing guards against the wall where they'd left them. Out in the street the woman the Reader had tied up was lying still, only her head moving. She was trying to rub off the strips of cloth that held the gag in place. He widened his arc as he came round again, went rushing out across the water . . .

And cold came swirling round him, cold that entered into him and brushed his soul.

It wasn't an attack . . . or at least not an attempt to take him over . . . the water called him . . . sweetly at first and then like the throb of his own heart . . . stroked him . . . squeezed him . . . his body changed . . . the broad wings shortened and thickened . . . the fur rebsorbed into him until his skin was thick and shiny . . . he fell toward the lake . . . curved himself . . . turned the fall into a dive . . . split the surface and went deep into the clear, cold water.

Noooooo. . . . Honeydew watched the water settle, clutched the saddle and tried to call Adlayr back to himself as she'd done before, that time in the Forest. Nothing. Nothing at all. An emptiness where her friend had been. She kicked off and darted to Tserama. Do something, she wailed. Help him.

The only thing anyone can do is break the Spell-maker, Honeydew. You and me, we haven't the strength to break the spell.

Serree could. She did before.

Whoever she is, she isn't here. If she's one of you, she'll

be heading the same way we are. That's the best you can
do, little one. We'll find Her I don't dare name and then
we'll see.

2

RAGYAL

His eyes a smoky yellow, Onkyon Bassod of the House
of Bask, Jeboh of Bagklouss, kicked Rodoji off the
couch, rolled onto his feet and began pacing the room,
his silk robe billowing out from his soft, paunchy body.

Rodoji cowered in the cool linen sheets, wanting
desperately to get away; she would have crawled out
and left him to his snit, but she didn't dare. When the
yellows came over him, bad things happened to people
he noticed. Rodoji shivered as she remembered what
happened the day Tygryal was shaving him; he went
into one of those yellow-eye fits and she wasn't fast
enough to get the blade out of the way so she nicked
him. Rodoji was one of those he made clean up the
blood and other stuff after he finished with Tygryal.

He stopped, stood staring out the long window
that led to the balcony; it was a bright sunny day, the
surface of the lake like broken sapphire, but this time
the serene view didn't calm him. He swung round,
came loping round the bed, kicked at Rodoji. She
was careful to roll with the blow so he wouldn't hurt
his foot. "Get the Daggum of the Youmbards here."

As he strolled back toward the balcony, Rodoji
snatched her skonna and ran from the room; when
the door was closed behind her she wrapped the
skonna around her, fingers moving swiftly through
the tucks and folds. She smoothed her hair down as

best she could without a comb, passed her hands across her face to wipe away the lines that fear had written in the skin she'd pampered so assiduously since she was a child. She'd been this long in the Jeboh's Mokan because she'd fought to keep her place there, she wasn't about to let outsiders have any opening to use against her. Serenely self-assured, body moving with the tantalizing sensuality of the Mokan, she crossed the empty waiting room, opened the door and went to find the Daggum.

His voice brittle, the yellow in his eyes bleeding into the air about his body, the Jeboh Onkyon looked down at the man stretched on his belly before him. "You let her get away, that filthy witch. You let her slip through your feeble grip. Do you tell me where she's gone? And these spies, these putrescent foreigners who you should be able to find by smell alone, you catch and let them slip away. And you don't even know how. You with your kyarkyor guards who wouldn't know an idea if it bit them. No. You wait for ME to tell you. The Cave of the Prudjin, that's where you take your men. All of them. I want the foreigners dead, you hear me?"

The recumbent Daggum muttered an agreement into the rugs his face was buried in.

The Jeboh moved impatiently closer to him, set his foot on the Daggum's neck. "I want the foreigners dead. Not captured. Dead. I want that witch, that Green Thing, I want her captured and thrown into the Prudjin's Cave. Not dead. Alive. Stripped and thrown into the Dark. You hear me?" He pressed down, moved his foot back and forth making the Daggum's head roll to one side then the other.

Another mumble, smothered in the standing fibers of the rug.

The Jeboh removed his foot. "Then get out and do it."

3

THE OUTLANDS WEST OF THE STON GASSEN

Serroi lifted her head, grimaced at the stench the wind brought to her. "Another," she said. She turned her macai's head and followed the smell to a farmhouse tucked into the side of a small hill. The roof was caved in, still smoking from the fire that charred the stones, torn bodies were scattered about.

This was border country, wild and dangerous, a place where youmbards seldom came and taxmen never. It was the land of exile and outlaws, with poor soil, little water, a place where people came who couldn't take the constrictions of provincial life. And it was the last stretch they had to cross before they reached the Ashtops.

Serroi slid from her macai, flinched as hot prickles from the earth leaped like lightning through her body. She steadied herself and stood, head turning slowly until she found a thin thread of life among all the death. She walked to a root cellar beside the house, with thick earth walls and a sod roof with charred grass growing from it. The door was partway open, hanging on torn leather hinges. She wrestled it open further, stood in the opening. "It's all right. We won't hurt you."

A whimper came from the darkness, then a scraping

sound. A shadow moved in the shadows, came slowly from behind some broken barrels, turned into a small boy holding a baby clutched against him with one arm; the other hung limp at his side, there was a lump over his left eye and the dark blotch of a bruise. He came to the ladder leading up to the door, stood a minute looking up at her, the whites of his eyes glistening. Her small size seemed to reassure him. Slowly, awkwardly— because he couldn't use his hands—he climbed the ladder. The baby he was squeezing against his chest didn't move, didn't make a sound.

She stepped aside to let him out, using her body to shield him from the worst of the carnage. "My name is Serroi, what's yours?"

"Ramman and this is my sister Berda." He was shivering, and so pale under the smears of dirt that he was almost as green as she was.

She stretched out her hand, but didn't quite touch him. "I'm a healer, Ramman. Let me help you."

He blinked at her, flinched when her fingers touched his brow but didn't pull away.

She closed her eyes. The force grew to a river and flowed through her fingers into the boy. It washed away blood gathering inside the skull, mended cracked ribs and erased internal bruises, popped the dangling arm back into the shoulder socket, smoothed away the hairline fractures in the arm bones, wiped away the bruise and swelling that distorted his face.

Her hand dropped onto the baby, but there was nothing she could do there, death was something no one could heal.

She tapped her fingertips to his face, pulled her hand back.

"There. Isn't that better?"

The boy nodded.

"Ramman, do you know what happened?"

He looked away, nodded after a moment, stood staring at the ground.

"Do you have other kin you could go to?"

"M' ma's sister. Over that way." He still didn't look at her, just nodded his head toward the house. "Couple farms off. If they din't get her too."

She heard the crunch of someone walking on the cinders, looked round. Mama Charody. "Anyone?"

Charody shook her head. "We'd better get on." She smiled at the boy. "You'll be coming with us, then?"

He nodded.

"Good. Best give the little one to the healer, then you come with me. I've got a boy too. He's not that much older. His name's Doby." She held out her strong square hand, smiled again as he sidled round Serroi and took hold of it.

"She's green," he whispered.

"Like a plant. Green things are good, aren't they? You want to give me the baby?"

Once again he didn't seem to hear her. After a glance at Serroi, she led him around the house. Serroi sighed and followed.

The boy didn't look at the dead as Charody led him toward the waiting mounts.

Doby was holding together better than he had the first two times, no more nightmare, no more cold sweats, no emptying out everything in his stomach. He looked at the baby in Ramman's arms, started to say something.

Serroi spoke before he could get any words out. "Doby, where's Teny?"

"She went off that way, ahind those trees there." Doby pointed at some gnarled olive trees, the ripe fruit hanging like black pearls among the gray-green leaves.

Serroi moved up to stand behind Ramman, dropped her hand lightly on his shoulder. She could feel him shiver, then relax as she went on speaking and didn't do anything else. "Fetch her, please. We want to be away from here in the next few minutes."

She brushed her hand across Ramman's eyes, felt him sag, caught him as he fell, taking the dead baby from his loosened grasp. He was profoundly asleep as she lifted him to Mama Charody.

Charody settled him in her lap, his head cradled against her shoulder. "And that?" She nodded at the infant.

"I'll put her back in the root cellar. Her people can bury her."

In the daze between sleep and waking, Ramman groped for the baby, but once his eyes were open he seemed to have forgotten all about her. He lay against Mama Charody and watched Doby arguing with Yela'o who was trotting beside his macai.

". . . and it was so a seven skips, not a six."

He listened.

"Uhuh, Y'el. There was seven plops before it sank, you can't count."

Ramman sighed and pulled away from Charody. "Who he talkin to?"

"The timeseer's boy. You don't see him?"

"M' mam could see spirits, I'm like m' da." He sank his teeth into his lip and sat swaying, his grief so overwhelming he couldn't cry, couldn't talk, couldn't do anything but cling to the saddle ledge in front of him and shake.

"Now, now, now," she murmured and took him back

into her arms. "Now, now, Rammy, lad, you'll be with your own folks in a sniff and a sneeze, it's a bad time, but you're not alone." On and on she went, using her voice as much as her hands and the cushion of her big body to make him warm and secure.

Serroi watched. This was the third hit they'd found and the worst, with so many dead—as if the closer they got to the Ashtops, the stronger and more uncontrolled the raiders got. She healed and healed again, wondering sometimes what she was birthing here, in this land where the magic had never left if what Treshteny said was true.

The Ashtops crept closer.

Serroi fretted because it was taking so long to reach them. The *urgency* grew in her with every step her macai took. She NEEDED to get to the Fetch. She had to touch her. She had to stop this dying, this Taking, this distortion . . . she didn't know what to call it, just the sense that everything she knew was right and good was being twisted and tainted.

Serroi looked at the ground ahead, pulled her eyes away. Dark and light ran in dizzying undulations through the soil, weaving about each other, tearing into each other like wrestling cats all teeth and claws, the dark luminous as the light. The black daggerlines grew thicker and blacker as they came racing at her, ignoring the others. Light flared beneath her macai's feet—then everything was gray and hard, all colors leached of strength as if there were layers and layers of gauze wrapped round her.

The Dark called to her in the Fetch's voice. *MOTHER mother. I SEE you MOTHER. MOTHER I will HAVE you.* And It laughed at her. She clutched at the saddle ledge, willing the Fetch to silence, willing

It to go away. It didn't. Even when there were no words, she could feel the Fetch's breath on her face, the beat of the Fetch's heart thudding in her ears.

The sun was almost down when they reached the farm where Ramman's sister lived. There was a thin thread of smoke from the chimney, and a woman with a child in a sling on her hip scattering cracked maize from a basket to feed the prungs clustering about her feet.

Charody shook the boy awake. "That your aunt, Rammy?"

He rubbed his eyes with his fists, leaned sleepily against her arm. "Yeah-huh."

"It's only a little way. Think you could make it down there by yourself? We don't want to scare your aunt so we're not going to go any closer. So you go down there now and tell your kin what happened. And tell them not to come after us. We mean them no harm, but we have work to do, work that may help stop all this. You got that, Rammy? Tell me what I said."

"You said, I should tell what happened and . . . and that you fixed my arm and my head and brung me here and . . . and they shouldn't follow you."

"That's good enough." She lifted Ramman into Serroi's arms.

Serroi set him down, touched his cheek. "Tsan pyya, Ramman, we'll watch you down, make sure there's nothing bad around." He squirmed a little under her hand. "Yes, I know. Tickles, doesn't it? That's what made the bump go away. Go, go."

She watched him run down the long rocky slope, turned and caught the look on Treshteny's face.

"Don't say it. I don't need to know. I don't want to know."

The boy's voice floated back to them as he called to his aunt. Serroi sighed as she saw the woman drop the basket of feed, snatch the boy into her arms, hugging and rocking him. "Time to go," she said.

4

ON THE RIM OF YTAMA ROUND IN THE STON GASSEN

Her wings glittering like crystal in the light of the morning sun, Honeydew spiraled down, landed on the neck growths of the macai Tserama rode. Youmbards like mogs swarming out a nest somebody kick, going this way, that way. S'rammee know that Brus blowing away the backtrail?

"I know. Any of that swarm coming this way?"

No. Just going round and round. S'ramee, Hev don't look so good.

"We can't stop. Not till we get into the Outlands. If it is his fate to die, he dies. If not, he lives."

Oh. The spirit fluttered to the shapechanger's mount, dropped to the saddle and sat there, legs crossed, shoulders drooping, worrying about her friends.

Tserama pushed the macain as hard as she dared; they were tougher than horses and could go longer without rest or feeding, but there were limits.

Honeydew flew up at intervals to circle above the string of macain and scan the backtrail.

The stillness of the day magnified the pad-scratch of the macain's feet, their hunh-hunh-hunh as they trot-

ted, the creaks, thumps and metallic tinks from the
gear, Hedivy's spasms of muttering as he moved in and
out of delirium. The wind had died down, not a breath
stirred in the maize fields and orchards they moved
past. The brus stared at Tserama from every tree, every
stalk, every clump of grass—more of them than she'd
ever seen before, as if each had divided into a dozen
others. She hadn't seen a single person since the ride
began. That was odd. Not even bren working the
fields. Had the brus chased them off too? So quiet. Eerie. And in that stillness, that silence, the land itself
hummed to her. Rising, falling, changing notes, eerie as
one of Ammeny's stranger self-songs.

Ammeny. She sighed. It hurt more than she thought
it would to see her daughter hating her. She thought
about the other children, the ones she hadn't spoken
to in years. *How many of them will the Glory . . . Glory!
what a name for it. DEATH would be more fitting. The
Prudjin. No, don't think the name. Glory's good enough. I
don't understand this, not any of it. Why is it happening?
Why now?*

S'ramee! They coming. The sprite came darting
down, brushed past Tserama's head, landed once
again in the spongy growths on the neck of the
macai. Three Youmbards, Honeydew don't think they know
where they going, but they coming straight at Honeydew and
S'ramee and Hev.

"How far?"

The sprite's wings fluttered briefly, catching the
light and throwing sparks into Tserama's face. She
looked away, waited for the answer to her question.

Honeydew think maybe an hour behind, Youmbards not
coming fast, just straight.

"Hm." They were moving around Postig's pasture
lands, rough country, lots of small rocky hillocks and

many ravines, clumps of quivering dulmies, their trunks a slick brown with slashes of dark orange, their heartshaped leaves rustling in the slightest excuse for a breeze. A good place to go to ground if the need was there. "Could you guess what direction they are from here and show me?"

Honeydew thought a moment, then jabbed her arm east and a little south.

"And they're moving on a straight line?"

Honeydew watch a while. They don't go right, they don't go left, just straight ahead.

"So if we took a jog south and found some cover . . ."

Honeydew think they go past and know nothing.

Tserama smiled, a tight curve of her mouth. "You want to talk to the brus?"

Honeydew can do. A grin on her small triangular face.

"Tell them to be extra careful about our tracks. With him on our hands," she nodded at Hendivy, who'd settled into a near coma, "we can't call notice down on us."

Honeydew can do.

Tserama turned directly south. Since most of the ravines ran east/west, it was difficult going out here on Ytama's Rim, clambering in and out of ravines, going round those whose sides were too steep to negotiate, circling patches of brush that were too thick and spiny to push through. The sprite went up at intervals to see if the youmbards changed course, but they kept pushing on until they reached the boundary markers of a farm. Postig's Farm, they said.

Honeydew's voice came very tiny into Tserama's mind-ear. Youmbard grab a boy hoeing weeds, shaking boy, yelling at him, Honeydew think. Wanting to know if the boy saw something, that's what Honeydew think. Man coming. Big man with a belly like a melon.

"That's probably Postig himself," Tserama muttered. *What's he doing?*

Postig yelling, waving his arms . . . hah! Youmbard poking Postig with a long, skinny club, pushing pushing pushing, Postig fall over. Youmbards go riding off.

What way?

Same way as before . . . No . . . Youmbards just other side of big house . . . Youmbards stop . . . Talkin, waving arms . . . Honeydew think they arguing about how to go. Postig or Postig's boy didn't tell them nothing .. Didn't see Honeydew or Hev or S'ramee . . . Can't tell Youmbards what Postig don't know . . . Ei vai, Youmbards go on riding . . . Very slow . . . Looking around . . . Talking . . . Honeydew can see mouths moving under those silly mask things . . . Now they going faster . . . Riding straight west.

Any others in view?

Honeydew can see bits of dust and some dark things like bugs crawling . . . All far off and going away farther.

Good. You might's well come on down. Mmm. Tell a bru to find us some water if there's any about.

Honeydew can do.

After Tserama untied the ropes that were holding Hedivy in the saddle, Honeydew teased the macai into kneeling. Tserama got Hedivy stretched out on a bed of brush and grass she'd collected, eased his shirt off, cut away the bandage and shook her head at the sight of the wound. "Too bad your healer friend isn't here, Honeydew, I'm a Spirit Reader, not a magician. Still, we do what we can. . . ."

She went through her pack, took out the roll of bandage and a bottle of Kill-evil. "Tell me about this

healer of yours. Herbmistress? Midwife? Cutter?"
She tore off a bit of cloth, folded it over the mouth
of the bottle, upended the bottle twice so that the
thick purple liquid saturated the cloth. "Hm?"

Honeydew perched on the water-polished stone,
watching anxiously as Tserama worked. Serree? Serree
touches a hurt and wipes it away like it never was. Serree a little person . . .

Tserama smiled, amused by the irony of the sprite
calling someone little.

Honeydew reached up, plucked a leaf from the
bush spreading above her head; it was a duclar bush,
the leaf a dusty olive green. Green almost like this, some
paler though. A magic person. Lots of mmmm fizz in Serree.

"Green? I never heard of that." She scrubbed first
the blade of the lancing knife she kept for boils, then
the skin around the yellow center of the wound.

Serree say she tribe of one. The sprite sighed. Like
Honeydew.

Tserama tore off the scab and jerked back as pus
erupted from the puncture. "It's good he's out of his
head this while. The spirits say you lot are here to do
the Gan Khora's work. To fight Her I don't dare
name." She bent over Hedivy, wiping and pressing,
wiping and pressing until the blood from the wound
ran red instead of yellow.

Honeydew shivered as she watched. Bad things. people killing people. What's doing the bad, Honeydew hear
called glory or mother death, going on at Serree, calling
Serree mama, maybe so, maybe Honeydew's mama too, Serree
heals and things get born, dryads, nixies, ariels, stonemen,
trees that eat people, maybe down here all these brus, all kinds
of things, Serree 'fraid Glory says true, Serree was a tree for
a looooong time, she wake up a while back and this stuff starts

happening, so Serree and Hev and Adlee and Honeydew come here to fix that. Make everything better.

Tserama poured more of the Kill-evil onto the wound and rolled him over to deal with the exit. "I see. And what happened to this Serree that she's not with you?"

A deep contralto voice came suddenly into the half-silent, half-audible conversation. "Youmbards took her, but she's free again."

Tserama stiffened, turned slowly.

A woman stood beside the dulcar bush, a tall woman with long braids the color of ripe grain. She wore a leather skirt dyed russet brown that brushed against boots dyed to match, a leather jacket with long, fine fringes along the sleeves, fringes that swayed as her arms moved.

The sprite darted up to flutter in front of her
Hallee! You went away. How come?

"I had my reasons, Honey. Tserama Spirit Reader, I am Halisan Wanayo, I've come to help you get where you need to go."

14. Marching

1

ON THE SHORE OF THE STATHVOREEN

"Wake up, wake . . ."

Olmena's voice in her ears, the healer's hand on her shoulder gently shaking her, K'vestmilly Vos groaned awake. With Olemena's help she sat up. "What . . . ?"

"Nothing wrong, Marn. You need to eat, that's all. You have to keep up your strength. I've got Cumura waiting outside to fetch your tray soon as you're ready. Now, you just sit there and let me take care of you." She poured some water in a basin, dipped in the corner of a towel and began washing K'vestmilly's face as if she were a baby. "No more baths, Marn, not till we've crossed the mountains. They say water's going to be a problem, too many of us, it'll have to be rationed."

K'vestmilly came gradually awake. It was restful, just for a moment to feel herself back in the nursery, being tended by a young Puzhee with rough but affectionate care. *Puzhee. She drowned herself, they said. Went running through the streets screaming and threw herself in the river. They said it was because she couldn't stand the feel of the Glory in her head.*

K'vestmilly shivered, reached out, touched Olmena's arm when the older woman drew back. "Just something I remembered," she said. "Thank you, Mena." She yawned. "I'm not really hungry."

"But you're going to eat, Marn. Then you're going for a walk and then you come back here and we go through the workout. You don't stop your exercises just because we're travelling."

"I was afraid of that."

"Put this on, Marn. Pull the hood up so the Mask doesn't show." Olmena handed K'vestmilly a heavy dark-brown cloak; it was one of those that the fighters hauled along for cold days, if there were any, and slept in on the march, voluminous as a young tent.

A dozen women waited outside the wagon, all of them wearing similar cloaks, hoods pulled up. K'vestmilly twitched at her hood. "Find the Lady is it? Clever, whoever thought of this. And I do thank you all for coming."

A tall broad-shouldered woman chuckled, a deep warm sound like water bubbling. "Not everyday a woman gets to be a Maybe Marn for some fool up there with his sput on a rock and a glass in his eye."

K'vestmilly answered the laugh with her own, held out her arm. "Walk with me."

They moved briskly along the hard-packed beach, through a gray morning with gray water licking at the sand, the wind coming down off the mountains too warm for the season, teasing up tendrils of fog from the icy water, feeding the clouds that hung low overhead. The women clustered around her, K'vestmilly climbed to the top of a long rock like a flat-iron, the point thrusting out into the receding tide. She stood a moment looking out over the water, then turned her back and glanced from one to the other, bit of chin to side of face; she didn't know them well enough to pick out who was who, something that bothered her as it crossed her mind. It was like growing up in the Pevranamist and knowing nothing about the hundreds of people working there, seeing them as interchangeable shadows, not understanding it until Hedivy jolted her eyes open. So easy to slip back into that tunnel vision. The Mask was suddenly heavy on her face; being the Marnhidda was abruptly like being cased in a tight box. She reached under the hood, stroked the ivory. *Break the box*, she thought, *that's what Hus—ahh, Father, I miss you still—would say. Ask questions and never fully believe the answers you get.*

"The Sharr's across there," she said. "If it were clear today, we could see it. I was told none of the women wanted to go there and wait. After last night, have any changed their minds?"

The tall woman who spoke to her at the wagon set her hands on her hips. "I'm Hosparny Ostat, Marn. Harozh born, married a Osklander who came north with a trading team. Might not be easy, Marn, the walking, I mean, but Harozh both know mountains and hunting as well as any man. Like Vymena. She's near term and the jolting from that wagon she's riding doesn't help, but you never could get her to let Prisking go get killed without her, which she's sure he would be if she wasn't there to scold the Maiden for him. She plans to tuck baby in a sling and indent for a longgun and get herself some Taken."

A shorter dumpier woman pushed up beside Hosparny, slapped her on the arm; when she spoke, her voice was deep, rather hoarse. "Me, I'm Koula Ponor. Was a cook in the Gritz War, my man made it through that with just a thumb shot off, I'm gonna do what I haveta to see we make it home together. Zdra, Marn, some of us aren't Harozh, and some of us are Dander born, never hoed a row or rode a horse, but we can

bind wounds and cook and sew rips and keep camp for
them that do the fighting. You need us near as much.
And we need to take back what's ours."

The woman behind Koula set her hand on the
shorter woman's shoulder. "And I am Setina Bytek,
my man worked up on Steel Point, we lived in the
warren there. It's not just talking, Marn. Me, I'd be
no good with stock or guns, but I can hold household, walls or no. Never had much and my family
was big . . . then . . . but we always ate good and we
always had clothes to our back."

"And I'm Lessie Nepor, I was with Koula being
cook's help. My man was a bargevek and he got
Taken that last bit, you know. Me, Marn, I can't
claim to be much good at cooking or sewing, but
what two hands can do, mine will, hauling or butch-
ering or whatever it takes. What's in the Sharr anyway to keep that filth from coming cross the
Stathvoreen and taking it? And even if IT din't, I
never heard much good of Sharrmen, only one I ever
saw stunk like a stable and used his fist on his
woman. Live or die, here's better nor that."

One by one they all spoke their pieces, strong voices
with no doubt in them to erode the force of their
words. Self-selected for her ward perhaps, or chosen by
a politician who knew her needs. *Ah, Heslin, why don't
you come yourself. Nik, I won't go that road. I WILL not.*
Maybe not representative. On the other hand, all the
women on this march had left their homes to come
with her and the Army, not just this small gathering.
*Hus, Father, I do miss you . . . you knew people like these,
you knew how to talk to then . . . I need people who know
what's real and who won't lie to me. How . . . have to think
on that. . . .* "Ungh! What . . ."

The baby was going bump bump bump, like she

was doing some kind of jig. "Get the healer. She's doing something strange, maybe last night . . ."

The other women crowding round her, Hosparny reached out, didn't quite touch K'vestmilly. "What is it, Marn? I've had three of my own, they get up to things in there you wouldn't believe."

K'vestmilly took the big woman's hand, pressed it against her. "Feel. It's like she's banging her head against me."

After a minute Hosparny chuckled, patted the bulge. "Naught to worry you, Marn. She's got the hiccups, that's all. Probably had 'em before this and you just didn't notice."

"Hiccups! It feels like . . . aaaahhh." Severely embarrassed, K'vestmilly said, "Would some of you mind holding your cloaks out to shield me, I need . . ."

Laughter from the women. They moved away to give her room, held their cloaks out to hide her from prying eyes while Hosparny helped her squat. "We been there, Marn. Little dabays playing kickball with the bladder, catching you short all the worst times . . ."

When they reached her wagon, Hosparny helped her onto the mounting board. She turned to look at them, gave them the Marn's hand smile. "We'll walk again and talk again sometime soon. I thank you for your company."

2

OSKHOLD

Tomal crouched against the side of the guard shelter; dressed in black, with a black rag tied across his face, he was close to invisible as he watched Orderly Vyborn shift from foot to foot behind the Command Tent. His hand tightened around the worn leather sheath of Lehky Azheva's knife when he saw her come round the Officer's Row and walk toward the orderly.

The two guards who circled the tent carefully ignored the orderly and the woman, crossed paths and marched on, backs straight, eyes alert, images of martial readiness that started a giggle deep in Tomal's throat. As soon as they were around the corner, the one he could still see went back to a bored slouch, yawned, scratched at himself and strolled along muttering his annoyance at having pulled this miserable duty. Ker didn't trust the chovan to protect his person and despised the Taken, so his guards were all Bezhvali he'd brought north with him when he joined Nov's conspiracy. They were loyal enough, but they were not much on discipline and mostly bored with all this fiddling about doing nothing. Made things a lot easier for Tomal when he did his slip and slide. The anger in him smiled through his mouth; it was a thing apart, that anger. That's how he felt it, there like a fire burning behind glass.

The orderly crossed to the Officer Row, vanished inside the mess tent. As soon as he was gone, Tomal darted across to Ker's tent, pushed head and shoulders inside and tossed the knife to Lehky. He was out and away with minutes to spare before the ambling guards came back.

Lehky Azheva thrust the knife beneath the mattress on the cot, pulled her working dress over her head, folded it neatly because Ker liked neat and laid it on the floor near the slit. She unbraided her hair, let it fall about her shoulders, dropped the ties on the dress. She could hear the rumble of Ker's voice, the voice of a visitor, but she was too busy to listen and if tonight went right, it wouldn't matter anyway. Bare feet silent on the matting, she padded back to the cot, retrieved the knife and took it from the sheath, kissed the blade, then kicked the sheath under the bed.

It wasn't much, that knife, an ice pick with edges, no more, but she'd used it more than once when she was still down in Calanda. She called it Jasny after the woman who killed the Sleykyn, stuck a pin through his eyes and up into his brain. Jasny the knife was a friend, almost a talisman, and she'd hated giving her up to Tomal, but Hanesh had the women strip-searched before he sent them off with the orderly. She listened a moment. Still talking. Shouldn't last much longer, he ran pretty much to schedule even with his all-night women. She touched Jasny's worn hilt to her lips, then slid her down in the blankets where she could reach her when Ker was well into his pronging. She went to the washstand in the corner, poured water into the basin and washed her feet. He'd ordered her to do that the first time she came here, told her to be clean and ready the next time. No dirt on her. He didn't like dirt.

She wiped her feet carefully, folded the towel and dropped it into the catchbox beside the washstand, crossed to the bed and dropped to her knees beside it, ran her fingers through her hair, pulled it forward over her shoulders. Ker liked long-haired women, that was one of the reasons he'd called her back so often. He liked submissive, flattering women, overwhelmed by his power and importance, hot women set moaning by a touch. He wasn't hard to please.

She sucked in a breath, let it trickle out and tried

to relax. Tension would make him suspicious. She
wanted him relaxed and so caught up in what he was
doing he wouldn't notice her hand sliding among the
blankets, bringing Jasny up and out. *The Marn's on
her way,* she thought. *Tomal brought her the word.
Tomal was a little horror, but he was good at what he
did. The times shape the children. Shape me.*

She'd made the offer through him. *Pan Ker,* she
said. *I'll do him for you,* she told Heslin, *but I don't
want to die. Have someone waiting to get me away
from there.*

Sounds of a chair being pushed back came from
the other part of the tent, bootheels on the grass
matting. They were still talking, voices moving toward the front entrance. *I want to do him clean and
quick. And get away. Hanesh will be waiting for the
money, but he won't make trouble, not till morning anyway, he knows better. I hope. He thinks I'm like his other
women, my soul on rent. You can wait till your toes rot,
whoremaster, I won't be back.* She kept her eyes down,
her body submissive as Pan Ker snapped the flap
aside and came into his bedroom.

She slid through the slit and waited passively as the
orderly patted her down to make sure she hadn't stolen anything. Her hands were clasped behind her
neck, covering the knife tied into her hair.

"I thought he wanted an all-nighter," he said when
he was finished.

"Nik," she murmured; she took her hands down
carefully so she wouldn't dislodge the bit of rag holding the knife in place. "He said tell you he doesn't
want to be disturbed, but you should give him a
wake-up round dawn."

He handed her the money for the visit. "You know the rules," he said. "No gossip."

"I know the rules."

She glanced back as she turned into the track that ran along behind Officer Row. The orderly was walking after her, not watching her, heading for his own quarters. *Good. He bought it. Heslin thought he would. Now if Tomal would show up.* She reached back, pulled the sheath loose from the hair tie. Feeling the hilt in her hand gave her more of a sense she was in control. If they stopped her now, there was a way to run. The knife was quick and easy, she knew just where it should go if that was the only choice she had.

She walked faster, eyes darting left, right, ears straining. The False Marn was gone back to Dander, Maiden Bless. At least there's that. The Taken were loosening up more every day. Something was keeping the Enemy busy somewhere else. If IT felt something wrong, if IT struck at her . . . *Avert! Don't even think of that, woman, you name IT, you call IT on you . . .*

Something struck her leg; she almost screamed, but bit the sound back in time. It was only a pebble, Tomal announcing himself.

He came from the shadows, tossed her a dark cloak and went trotting off. She swung it around her shoulders, pulled the hood over her head and followed him.

Lehky glanced at the star-patterns as she listened to Pokad talking on the com. The Lappet's Ears were just clear of the horizon. *Sunup soon, less than an hour. Then they'll find him.* She shivered and pulled the cloak tighter about her body, pressed her legs together, seeking reassurance from the knife nestling in its sheath, bound once more to her thigh. It was Heslin himself asking the questions. *High folk. Won't be so high when this is over. Nik. That's wrong, fool woman. They'll be just as high and you'll be lower than mud.*

". . . so she did like you said and told the orderly he wanted to be called earlier than usual. We've pulled the Web out just in case things get bloody, most of them anyway. We're at base camp now, waiting. We've got a watcher on the cliff, he says it's still quiet down there. Go."

"Head north for Ankland. There's no point in risking yourselves when the Enemy will be watching everyone. Protect the com. Destroy it if there's any chance it'll fall into Enemy hands. We're moving slower than I'd hoped, but we should still be at Maznak Pass in less than two weeks. Go."

"Some of the Web will want to stay. Go."

"That I will leave to you and them, but the com comes north and they'll be on their own, nothing anyone can do to help them if they get caught. What's the likelihood of the Enemy moving north your side of the mountains? Go."

"None. Not without a long jog west that will take them into the lower Harozh, and then they'd have to fight through Ank's defenses. Can't take wagons and supplies the way we're going to go, and the land is too cut up for riders. Can do it on foot with a few like us. An army, nik. Go."

"Marn and Maiden Bless, Pokad. We'll see you in Ankland. Out."

Pokad thumbed the lock on and slipped the com in the case on his belt. "Lehky, you go see Mama Vys, she'll dig you up some boots and better clothes. Good job, cousin, case I hadn't said it. Zdra, the rest of you, you heard. So go get . . ."

Tomal sidled from the shadow under the trees.

"They found him," he said. "Like a buncha ants running round."

3

K'vestmilly Vos stood on one of the tors by the seashore and looked out across the assembled army, the afternoon sunlight hot on the ivory mask. A chini barked once, then was silent, a child was crying and being hushed by its mother, faces were turned up to her, men and women, some grim, some smiling, eyes fixed on her, Heslin's eyes too, his face unreadable. Vedouce scowled at her, angry that she was making a target of herself—a little of that anger, perhaps, because she'd ignored his reasoned advice. He was a good man, but he had the limits of his class. This was necessary; the people out there, they needed the news she had to give, needed the lift in spirits before they went back to the endless hard slogging that would take them up to the pass.

She gave them Marnhidda Vos's hand smile, a spreading lift that did what her lips could not. "Pan Ker is dead. One of our Web sisters got to him and eased a blade between his ribs. There is confusion and milling about, chovan fighting chovan, panic spreading. It will be a while before the Enemy can come after us, but we can't waste this gift our sister had given us. We must move fast, must increase the distance between us and them. Take Marn's Blessing and Maiden's Blessing and show those notneys what true Cadandri can do."

K'vestmilly Vos insisted on riding as the army formed up and began the long trek to the pass. The road was miserable, a rutted, narrow track used

mostly by traders with packtrains. Getting half a
dozen wagons, two hundred riders, three hundred
foot, along with the able-bodied women and children, onto that road and through the pass into
Ankland was tedious, difficult, but done; they'd sur-
vived a lot already, and she could see the effect the
news of Ker's death had on them, a lightness in the
step, shouted jokes passing in waves across the sea of
folk. They'd quiet down soon enough as the road got
steeper and the going got harder, but she smiled behind the Mask, satisfied with the effect of her speech.

Riding was harder than she expected. And much
more tiring. She'd just about lived in the saddle since
she was two and her tutor put her on a pony, but she
hadn't expected the changes the baby made to her
center of gravity and she hadn't realized how soft her
muscles had grown in the months by the Stathvoreen. It was almost like learning to ride all over
again, and she frightened herself several times by
how close she came to falling off. She didn't let it
show, kept grimly in the saddle despite her growing
weariness, until an all too familiar pressure started
her cursing under her breath. *I can't ask them to stop
so their Marn can pee. And I'm zhagged if I'm going to
wet myself. Vych! Have to hold out a while longer. Vedouce
said he'll order a rest stop sometime round noon. I can't
wait. Nik oh nik oh nik, I've got to . . .*

She dropped back and rode as close as she could to
the wagon. Heslin must have been watching her, because he was beside her before she could try shifting
from the horse to the wagon.

"What is it, Kimi?"

She drew her shoulders up, embarrassed, then she
sighed. "Bladder," she said. "I've got to pee."

He made an irritated hissing sound. "And you

were going to play at acrobatics, were you? Move back a length and wait." A hand signal brought the wagon to a stop, another sweeping signal urged the riders who surrounded the wagon to keep going. He swung onto the mountain board, beckoned her up to him, reached out for her.

She freed her feet from the stirrups, silently blessing Olmena for those exercises she'd hated so much as she clutched at his arms and got her leg over so she was sitting sideways in the saddle. With him almost lifting her (she knew he was stronger than he looked, but in this as in so many other things he surprised her again), she got a foot on the mounting board and left the saddle. Still leaning on him, she climbed over the seat and moved through the slit in the canvas as Heslin tapped the driver on the shoulder and the wagon started on again.

He eased her down, brought the backrest around and locked it in place. "You sure you don't want to sleep a while?"

"Later maybe. It's too hot in here right now. Hes, stay a moment."

He settled with his back against the front wall, sat with his hands on his knees, his face unreadable in the shadows, beads of sweat dropping off his jaw and chin to splat on his tunic. "So?"

"I know I've been bad-tempered and scratchy. Pulling the Mask on you like I did, it was . . . oh, stupid, I suppose . . . I can't even say I didn't mean it, I did at the time . . . five minutes later, I didn't, but at the time I said it, I did . . . Olmena tells me pregnant women get fancies . . . maybe that's part of it . . . but I want to be honest . . . it's how I was raised, Hes . . . it's everything I was taught about who I am . . . I

didn't understand why my father preferred his shop
to the Pevranamist, he said it was because he just
couldn't live there and besides Mother didn't want
him living there . . . I think I see, now. I didn't know
my father long . . . long enough to know he was his
own man and bowed to nobody . . . they stayed together . . . stayed friends . . . only because they lived
apart . . . I don't know if I could stand it if you did
that . . . though I can see . . . you might not be able
to stand it if you didn't . . . I'm younger than my
mother was when she took her consort . . . half her
age . . . I'm jealous of every woman you smile at,
Hes . . . I want to kill you . . . and all the time I know
it's stupid . . . and that doesn't change anything . . .
you smiled at that meie . . . that was why I scratched
so hard . . . I could see you've known her a long time
. . . she's not young or pretty, but you smiled at her
. . . and I wanted to tear her eyes out, rip her lips off
her face . . . nik, don't say anything, just listen . . . this
is hard for me, I don't think I could say it again . . .
Hes, don't go silent on me . . . please . . . don't shut
yourself against me like you did . . . I'll do it again, I
know I will . . . it's in me and I know my temper . . .
it's easy to deal with people I don't care that much
about . . . it'll never be easy to deal with you. . . ."

"Get rid of that zhaggin Mask. Don't talk to me
through it like it's some kind of crutch you need to
lean on."

He's really angry, she thought. *I didn't realize how* . . .
She reached for the Mask, slipped it off. "I'm so used
to it now," she said, "I forget it's on." *It was the truth
and yet . . . he was right, too, it was a crutch.* She watched
him fumble for words; that was the first time she'd
ever seen that and it gave her a twinge of hope.

"Kimi, you can't . . ."

"Uh!" She clutched at herself. "Uh."

"Kimi, what is it?" On hands and knees he lunged at her, caught her by the shoulders. "Are you hurting? What's happening?"

"Nik ... uh ... nik, Hes ... little uh! vixen ... she's hiccuping again. Feel." She caught hold of his hand and spread it over the baby.

When he felt the baby moving against his palm, he got the oddest expression on his face, as if hadn't really believed in her before, or maybe she was only an idea to him. Now he felt how strong his daughter was, how alive, she could see it in his eyes. Abruptly he looked worried. "Is that bad? Will it hurt her? Why's she doing it?"

"Olmeny and the other women, they tell me a lot of babies do that, the healthy ones. She does more exercises than I do, Hes. Punching me and kicking me. She's a lively one." *How stupid she'd been, he'd been so careful with her, then so distant ... he'd seen her letting women touch her, but he'd never felt his daughter kick before. His daughter, not just hers. Mother, you were wrong. I should have known my father all my life, not just at the end of his. Hes needs to know his child. I didn't think he ... ah, I didn't think!*

"Isn't she ever going to stop? That can't be good for her."

"Last time she kept it up a quarter of an hour, maybe a little more. She's fine, Hes."

He took her hand, smoothed it open, kissed the palm, held the hand against his face. "Kimi, I was going to say a lot of things which I probably would have regretted the minute they came out my mouth. We'll find a way. Once this is over, if we're still alive, we'll find a way.

15. In and Out and Roundabout

1

THE OUTLANDS, BAGKLOUSS

Dark swirled through light, light through dark, the earth around Serroi melting until, to her straining eyes, it seemed insubstantial as air, though her macai seemed to have no difficulty walking on it, a tiny pole of stability that helped her deal with the fog. She was aware of the others riding with her—Treshteny as a shimmer of light astride a glow, her strange-son Yela'o (who was oddly far more solid than he'd seemed before) cuddling against her, Horse whose shape was never the same for two consecutive breaths, Charody who was dark and opaque as a stone, Doby who was a dim flicker beside her.

First dark, then light tried to pull her into itself, but a surrender to either would destroy her and have bad consequences for the things and the people she loved; it was something she knew without having to think about it, and it gave a painful edge to her struggle to keep clear of both. It made her even more NEEDFUL. Get at the Fetch. Stop this. STOP IT.

The macai stopped walking.

Hands closed tight enough to hurt about the saddle ledge in front of her, Serroi blinked and shoved at the distortions until she could see more clearly within a bubble that took in the rocky hilltop where they'd stopped in the center of a small grove of stunted twisty khiroda trees whose branches hung low enough to give them a measure of concealment and the land around it for about a half mile out. She made out Treshteny lying on the ground, writhing and twitching, babbling too quickly and erratically for Serroi to catch the words. Doby was using a bit of rag and wiping the sweat from the timeseer's face, Charody was holding her hand and listening intently.

"What's happening?" Even in her own ears Serroi's voice sounded breathy and weak.

They were on the western edge of the Ston Gassen, in hilly lands with patches of brush and grass, a few trees and many dry washes—hardscrabble land with widely scattered farms, houses and barns that were thick-walled small forts. There was one of those a short distance off with a few lower hillocks between the house and their hilltop.

Yela'o leaning into her to help her rise, Treshteny struggled up, sat holding her head in her hands.

Charody patted Doby's shoulder, grunted to her feet and came over to Serroi. "A premoaning fit, Healer," she said. "We have to make a . . ." She broke off at a cry from the boy, turned. "What is it?"

Doby pointed.

Serroi strained harder and saw . . .

A paya at the crest of another hill sat on her haunches, forepaws crossed over the black ruff that marked her as female, turning her blunt-jawed head, looking around. Where there was one, the pack couldn't be far away, six to fifteen of them not counting the infants riding on their mothers' backs. The paya looked back, went fourfoot and shifted a few paces to her left as a rider joined her on the crest, a bearded ragged man more feral than she was, mounted on a lean, fidgety macai.

Charody turned to face Serroi, her face dark with worry. "Do you see that?"

Serroi sighed. "Ashtoppers and payas. Was that what the fit said? Another raid?"

"Some of it. The rest was about all of us dancing with Death. Confused."

Eyes squinting, the effort of trying to see like nails being pounded into her head, Serroi scanned the farmstead below them.

A wisp of smoke twisted against the blue, broke into a tangle of eddies and melted into the air. She followed it down to the stone building sitting in the middle of a carefully denuded strip of ground, tiny windows with heavy shutters, a flat roof with a loop-holed surround made of mud brick. The end facing her had massive doors opening into a small corral. One of the doors was swung back and hitched to the corral poles, several prungs were scratching in the dust, three milkers had their noses in a manger, pushing and shoving as they were wont to do, two draft glans were leaning against the fence, rubbing their heads against a pole, up where the horns started. A short distance off six flimsy bren houses stood in a row, wattle walls and thatch roofs.

Two older bren girls stood on a beaten earth round, scraping hides stretched on frames. Three small boys were pulling weeds in what looked to be a kitchen garden, more children were working in a maize field beyond the bren row, a half-grown boy working the sweep of a well, his companion tipping the leather bail into a flume that took the water to the rows of plants. In the pasture beyond the field two herders were watching over a flock of grazing lugs, while a third had a lug down, its feet tied while he picked large green burs from its tightly curled fleece.

"How bad does Teny say it'll be ... are they all slaughtered?" It was a whisper through stiff lips. Even her teeth were staring to hurt.

"Depends. Worst case, yes." Mama Charody reached out, caught hold of Doby's shoulder, drew him close. "What do you want to do?"

Serroi swayed in the saddle, pressed her palms against her temples. "I can't think," she said. She turned her head. The timeseer was looking pale, but composed, Yela'o curled up in her lap. Treshteny smiled and ran her forefinger along a curly horn.

The dark pulled at her, swirled round her.

The light pulled at her, swirled round her.

Everything blurred except a face—half-child, half-crone, no longer hidden behind the Glory's mask—and a voice: *MOTHER, I know you're THERE. I FEEL you there. COME to me IF you dare. Come TO ME. COME.* The same words as before, grinding into her brain.

Treshteny got to her feet, walked carefully to Serroi and took her hand. Dark and light retreated in angry, angular jabs, the pain muted until it was more a memory than a fact. "Teny, do you know what you're doing?" Again a whisper, but one with tension relaxed.

"A little. You try too hard, Serroi, we're for you. Let go and let us do. Be easy."

Serroi tried a smile and was surprised she could still manage it. "Maybe so, Teny. Trouble is I've always aimed the other way. Ei vai, tell me what's there." She closed her eyes.

"Not I, Serroi. Here."

Serroi felt a coolness against her and looked down;

the faun cuddled against her, his small hooves prick-
ing her leg, one horn a hard curve beneath her
breast. He snuggled and snorted, his breath as cool as
his body. He said something that was only a scritchy
noise in her head, but the noise gave her focus. She
lifted her head and looked, this time without effort,
and minimal pain.

There were two raiders on the crest now, one with
a longglass to his eye. Half a dozen paya had joined
the first, keeping a clear space between them and the
raiders; they were enough at ease to show this wasn't
the first raid they'd worked together. About half an
hour off. *Time enough to reach the farm and warn the
people there about the Ashtoppers, not enough to get away
again. If we circle round, maybe the raiders won't see
us. . . .*

Doby was looking at the children working below,
as he and his brothers and cousins had worked the
day the gritzer army came. As if he heard Serroi's
thoughts, he turned to stare at her then tugged at
Charody's hand. "Mam, we gotta tell them. We gotta
help them. Yela'o, tell her. We gotta. We can't just
walk off."

Once again the faun's voice scratched through
Serroi's head. She couldn't understand his words yet,
didn't know how much Treshteny understood, but by
his shrilling insistence he was making his opinion
quite clear. Then he moved impatiently, pulled free
of her, jumped down and ran to join Doby.

Mama Charody scratched at her chin, glanced at
Serroi then down the slopes to the farm. "They don't
look like they need all that much help, should they
get warned in time." She turned to Serroi again.
"Healer, if that lot come at us . . . zdra, I think there
are reasons to go down there."

As the fog closed back around her, Serroi shivered. Like this she was for anyone's pot. *Lean on Treshteny? She barely survives her own gift. Charody offers nothing but the fact she's here. I don't understand what's happening. It seemed simple once. Now?* She sighed, whispered, "Let's go. If we're going to warn them we haven't time to waste."

Doby kicked his macai into a run and went charging down the last slope; prungs squawking and whirring away from the macai's clawed feet, he reached the bren row and began yelling, "Paya pack comin. Ashtoppers." Over and over he repeated the words as he swooped past the girls at the flensing racks and pulled to a stop in the yard before the house. "Paya. Ashtoppers. They comin."

A tall lean man with a longgun came round the corner of the house. "Who you?"

"Doby. We seen Ashtoppers and a paya pack on hill that way, I come to warn you."

"Why? Whyn't you just go 'bout your business?"

Doby wiped at his face, blinked his eyes. "Rik like that, they kill my kin. I hate 'em. Want 'em dead."

"And your friends?"

"Serroi, she a healer; fix anything, she can. Treshteny, she see things. Horse is Horse. Mama Charody, she my Mam now."

"Tsan pyya, you told us. So go on your way."

A woman stepped through the door, trotted over to him, slid her hand through the crook in his arm. "No, Karul. You can't send them off now." She was round and comfortable, no longer young, but still pretty in her way, with dark lively eyes and smile lines worn deep in velvety brown skin.

"We don't know them, Myrti. Could be Ash-toppers theirselves."

"Buasky, he went up tree with the longglass. He saw a paya come over hill, trottin this way. The boy spoke true. Ayzhal up with gong waitin for word. Give it, Karul. There's no time for fratchetting"

When Treshteny led her inside, ignoring the rest of the farmfolk rushing about, Dark and Light retreated—as if disturbed by the energy and ordinar-iness of the scene—and she had her edges back as she stood in the low-ceiled room filled with comfortable wooden furniture, where daylight was being traded for lamplight as the shutters slammed into place and the iron bracers locked over them.

Men streamed past her, some cursing, some grimly silent, all armed either with longguns or crossbows, with sacs of bullets dangling at their belts or shaftcases full of quarrels. Karul was first up the lad-der. He slid the bar from its hook and shoved, send-ing the trap slamming onto the roof tiles. The rest of the men and older boys followed him onto the roof; she could hear them stumping about overhead as they got ready for the raid.

Women eddied around her. There was a round hearth in the middle of the room with a hooded chimney over it to catch the smoke and lead it out-side. It had a fire burning in it, a heap of coals with new wood added. A woman came from another room with a black iron grate and set it over the stones; two more followed her with a large copper pan. Once they got it in place on the grate, a line of middle-sized girls passed leather buckets hand to hand from the siegewell in the kitchen until the pot was almost full, then they tipped in twisted lengths of something like tarred rope and left the whole thing to boil.

Half an hour later the raid began.

The payas ripped and tore through the livestock, the raiders rode along the bren row, swinging torches at the tindery thatch. When they turned to come at the house, some waving those torches over their heads, others hooting and shaking their longguns, the men on the roof fired into them, the older boys loosed crossbow quarrels, killing several raiders, wounding more, shooting macs from under others. The Ashtoppers scrambled for what cover there was and began shooting back.

Serroi lifted her hand from the bren boy's head, tapped him with her forefinger. "Keep it behind something this time, Gawkin." She watched him dart up the ladder and through the trap, sighed when his body shimmered in spasms of dark and light as he vanished onto the roof. The fog was starting to close in again, swirls of dark and light in the corners of the room, death and blood fetching the Fetch.

Buasky dropped through the trap, blood seeping out from a crease on his left arm. He shied away from Serroi as she reached for him and trotted to his mother, who was binding cloths soaked in pitch and melted butter around the shafts of a pile of arrows. "Mam, Da says are you ready with the burners?"

"Got more to fix, but you can take that lot. In a minute. Now you go let healer do you, Bu. You hear me?"

"Ahhh, Mam. When she do that, an't no scars left."

She gave her warm gurgling laugh. "An't scars that make the man, Bu. You do what I said now."

Hands still twisting the saturated cloth about the arrow shafts, she frowned at Charody who sat hunched over, silent as a boulder come to rest in the middle of the room, then sighed as she watched Serroi pass a hand over her son's arm, wiping away the wound.

The bren women were filling bladders with the infusion from the copper, taking great pains to get none of the liquid on themselves. The bladders were set in individual slings and given to three of the girls, who took them up the ladder and onto the roof. One of these girls giggled as Buasky trotted past her with his load of arrows. He went red, hit her on the arm, then went scrambling ahead of her to the roof. His mother frowned, then went back to work on the arrow shafts.

The room was dimly lit, a twilight crossed by beams of light through cracks in the shutter planks, around the plugs in the loopholes, yellow light dancing with the dust in the air. Light and shadow . . . the hazy glow strengthens . . . swirls around Serroi until she is dizzy with it. Light and dark, pulsing. The bodies of the women working around her moving in and out of the swirls, sometimes glowing pale, sometimes glowing dark, solid forms floating in the striated fog. Voice pulsing in her head. *MOTHER* . . . *mother* . . . *MOTHER* . . . *mother.* . . .

Two nodes. Steady. Root and gracile tree.

Root . . . calling . . . voice low and slow . . . rock groaning . . . calling . . . calling . . .

Tree . . . no . . . spider . . . gracile spider not a tree . . . weaving . . . pale threads . . . threads that spun out and away . . . she can't see the ends of them . . .

Distant . . . voices of the men . . . voices of the women . . . she can hear them . . . she can't shape the sounds into words . . . pops and cracks . . . thunks . . . hot . . . stink of burning cloth . . . what?

Earth fire rose into her head and rolled out of her, glowing, green . . . insinuating between the whorls of dark and light . . . leaping away from her, plunging out through the walls, moving east and east and yet farther east . . . spreading as if it were filling the Ston Gassen. . . .

Mama Charody tucked in her edges and bellowed silently at the earth. I know you are there, earth brothers. Come to me, walk with me. Guard the Mother, shield her. Come here, stop the killing. Stamp the killers into the earth. Come, we need you.

Treshteny saw the images spread before her, the ways that this could go. An idea struck her, something she'd not tried before, hadn't even thought of; she reached out and touched the glass cards with their moving pictures. For a breath she did nothing more, just let the tip of her forefinger rest there, feeling no substance but a coolness, like the idea of glass rather than glass itself. With her fingertip she moved the cards about, watching how the patterns changed, searching for the optimum outcome, then she *chose*.

And in the instant of the choosing, in the hot and smoky room, Serroi's form pulsed, then glowed green.

The sun swelled and changed color until it was green as a lajana plum, ripe, near bursting with juice.

The air thickened about the riders and the killing pack, glowed green in the light of the cold green sun.

A windstorm came suddenly and improbably, blowing in the faces of the riders no matter where they rode, wheeling hungry winds. Winds that carried reeking green-burning fire-arrows at them with a force beyond even the most powerful bow. Even the tarry smoke was green.

The earth opened and stone men emerged behind the paya and the Ashtoppers. Shoulder to shoulder they marched into the wind, trampling into bloody muck the few that tried to stop them, reaching and reducing to mush anything they got hold of.

The paya's alpha female howled to her pack, went racing away, the payas not yet wounded or trampled to bloody mush ran after her, yipping, whimpering, whining in fear.

When the raiders were gone, Charody and Treshteny tied Serroi in the saddle, handling her with caution, even Charody a little frightened by the glow that wouldn't go away. Serroi sat where they put her, eyes wide and blank, gone off somewhere none of them knew about.

Before they could ride away, though, Myrti came to them. The color was gone from her face and she was terrified of touching them, but nonetheless she held up a two-eared crock sealed with wax, moving tentatively toward Serroi, shying away from her to Mama Charody. "This is honey from our hives, Stone Mother. Take it with the blessing of this house. May the Gan Khora guide you where you need to go."

2

LAKE DANU, DANOULCHA ROUND

For several days the Adlayr dolphin played in the crisp clear waters of the lake, tail-dancing on the wind ruffled surface, diving deep and racing through the springs in the deepest part of the lake bed, romping with the convoluted currents and the temperature layers. He was happy that short while, then the growing disturbance in the Spirit Hills of the Danoulcha Round began to make itself felt. The water seemed thicker and sometimes he brushed against currents that burned him.

After one of these brushes he rose to the surface of the lake and drifted there, basking in the cloudy sunlight, diving briefly when he felt too warm, drowsing in comfortable non-thought.

The sun swelled and turned a bright apple-green. The sky darkened to a greenly iridescent purple.

Now a virulent green, the water stung him repeatedly as if it were trying to drive him out.

He squealed protest, but he couldn't hold form.

He shifted and was a black sicamar in water he hated as much as it hated him. Spitting and snarling, he paddled to the bank and began running, the earth burning his feet—running west as if the greenness were a leash pulling him to Serroi.

3

ON THE RIM OF THE YTAMA ROUND

When a shadow fell across the hills Tserama looked up. The sky was a dark purple, the sun was swollen and green like an overripe plum. Beneath her the earth grew suddenly hot. With an exclamation she jumped to her feet and went to join the other Spirit Readers.

One by one they'd come during the past week, while Halisan and Tserama fought to keep Hedivy alive. One by one, drawn by Halisan's harp.

Radanba of Baimoda Round was the first. With Honeydew flittering over her head, she walked into the wash, drank from the spring, then squatted beside the sick man, staring down at him. "My Sem Ris say a hard time's coming. Want a hand with that?"

Tserama gave her the bowl and the rag she used to bathe the man and keep his temperature down a little. She stood, stretched, rubbed at her back. "Thanks. Your Yubbal kissing youmbard feet?"

"Aren't they all?"

Sanonchad of Kyimba Round was the second. She nodded at Tserama, drank from the spring, then began unpacking the heavy load she carried, flour and dried fruit and a jug of kamba brandy. She poured a finger of brandy in three cups, passed two of them to the others and took her own. "The Gan Khora and all her works," she said, and emptied the cup in one long swallow.

* * *

Badaru of Uzaranda Round was the third. She was a tall, gaunt woman with fierce eyes. She nodded at Tserama, drank from the spring, stared a moment at Halisan who was sitting on a boulder, plucking at the strings of her harp, then walked over to stand looking down at the moaning man. "Dead man if I ever saw one."

Tserama shrugged. "Could be, could be not."

And now, under the purpling sky, Padelog of Ytama Round came through the brush. She drank from the spring, glanced at Halisan and went to stand looking down at the dying man.

Tserama dropped the rag in the bowl and got to her feet. "Ytama," she said. "You're the last, though you were the nearest."

"I came when the Call came. I have something for you. In these troubled times it's a pleasure to bear good news for once." She held out her hand, opened it. On the palm was the talisman Tserama had given Brajid. "Your son came to me the second day. Your brother has taken him in and given him work without asking questions or making trouble. He said a bru told him to come to me and tell me this. He said, the bru said I'd be seeing you and to tell you he's learned a lesson or two and as long as he can, he'll stay quiet."

Tserama took the talisman, rubbed her thumb across it, slipped it into her shirt pocket. "Thank you. He's a rogue, that son of mine, but I'm fond of him."

Padelog glanced at the sky. "This I don't know. Do you?"

"No. Probably something to do with them." She pointed at Honeydew who was curled up asleep on the sick man's chest. Hedivy was little more than skin collapsed over big bones; his beard had grown into a red tangle that reached halfway down his chest, the hair near his mouth stained with the infusions Tserama fed him and the meager spoonfuls of soup she managed to get down him. His breathing was labored and noisy, under their thin wrinkled lids, his eyes were sunken, his nose a narrow jut of bone and cartilage.

"We wait here till he dies?"

"If he dies."

Honeydew stirred, yawned, looked around. Her small pointed face lit up. Serree, she cried in her mosquito voice. She waved her hand at the faint green glow rushing at them. Serree, Serree, we here. Hev, look. She pulled repeatedly at his beard, trying to rouse him. Hev, Serree going to fix you. Wake up, Hev.

The Spirit Readers gathered, watched the dying man, who was suddenly no longer dying.

His face flushed a bright red. His skin moved as the flesh plumped beneath it. His eyes stayed closed, but his breathing steadied, grew deeper, slower.

Tserama walked closer. After a minute, she knelt beside the man, lifted his hand, turned it over, bemused by the new muscle. She touched his brow; the flush had faded, it was cool, the skin had a healthy resilience. "I've never seen such a thing," she murmured.

The sprite had settled to the man's chest; she giggled. Serree. It was all she said, as if that name explained everything.

Hedivy's eyes popped open. "Vych." He pushed at the blanket tucked over him, frowned as Honeydew fluttered up and away.

Halisan came forward, gave him her hand to help

him on his feet. "Serroi is moving," she said. "The Last Day comes soon."

He looked round at the circle of women staring at him, shuddered. "Where're my clothes?" He took the garments, looked once more at the staring women and vanished round the other side of the bush. "And where you been?"

"Waiting. And we'll all be waiting a while longer."

"What!" He came back round the bush, tying the laces on his trousers as he moved.

"Look." She pointed.

The green glow was fading, but it was still strong enough to show a translucent wall that closed them in the wash.

He turned, his eyes following the oval. "Spros!" He strode to the nearest section of the barrier, tried to walk through it, cursed again as he bounced back, his beard starting to smolder. He beat the fire out, swung round to glare at Halisan. "The Enemy?"

"Nik. It's Serroi doing this. I don't know why." She took up her harp again, drew her fingers across the strings. "You might as well get something to eat. Looks like we'll be here a while."

16. Into Cadander

1

ON THE ROAD TO MAZNAK PASS

The army laboring up the steep track was a dark mass on the sun-bleached slopes, grimly silent except for whines, whimpers and crying of children packed into the supply wagons. The macain and the horses plodded in and out of the ruts and holes, here and there a macai hooting and threatening to squat as the dust and struggle grew too bad; the vul teams labored in harness, eight instead of four these days, and even then those who rode the supply wagons had to get off and walk on the steeper sections. Sometimes men were called on to work levers set behind the iron-tired wheels while others put their shoulders to the bed. So far they'd got all the wagons over the rough spots, but it was hard, slow work. Women's faces were drawn, layered with the red-and-ocher dust, children walking beside them were quiet, too worn to cry.

The mountains were gaunt and stony, covered with low twisty brush and grass so tough even macain claws didn't tear it loose. And they were dry, many of the streams little more than trickles so that getting water for that many people was a constant worry. Vedouce sent scouts ahead, along with a mounted navsta following, to fill barrels and dig watering holes for the stock, though sometimes digging was not possible, and with the heat sometimes the stream or spring was reduced so much that after the stock was watered, there was very little left for people.

There was a flurry of shots from the brush on a hillside that broke off as a band of meien acting as outriders began converging on the ambush.

The army halted for the moment, surged and howled as the trivuds got order restored and counted the downed. Two dead, one man, one woman. Five wounded, one with a smashed shoulder, one through the knee, one with broken ribs and a creased lung, one with a creased arm, another with a chunk shot out of his thigh. The healers patched up the lightly wounded, got them back on their mounts, the others were taken to the wagon they'd cleared for the seriously wounded. The dead were buried, rock cairns piled over them by their kin and companions.

Two chovan were captured, one died of his wounds, the other was hanged.

And the army moved on.

Day after day. Sniping. More sniping. Weary riders for the scouts.

They picked off one or more of the chovan each time, but never the last, elusive Sleykyn.

Every day bodies were left behind along the trail, buried under cairns, fighters they couldn't afford to lose. Wives, children, husbands, other kin marching grimly on, grief chilling to rage.

The setting sun lurid behind her, K'vestmilly Vos sat on the driver's bench and looked down at Vedouce, who stood close to her knee, scowling out across the camp going up around them.

"Too much rage held in too tight," she said. "It stinks like tar-smoke, General. I hear about fights starting. An Oskland girl was raped, the man's a blood smear and there's talk of going after his brother and uncle. They're Zemyas who've been with us since the Gritz War. We can't afford to lose men like them, but I don't want more women attacked. And I don't want splits opening between Osklanders and Harozh, Zemyas and citymen." She sighed. "Vedouce, I'm going to dump more on your shoulders. Find someone to craft a plan for a police force and cadre of judges. Not military and not just Harozh or Oskland. Or use some of the meien or gyes or both. Maybe that would be best. Less chance of mistakes being made if you use outsiders. Justice must be seen and it has to be the same for all. Heslin spoke about this, but I didn't see the need, I thought ... zdra, I let it slip." She sighed, swayed and caught hold of the seat back, took a deep breath and held it until the dizziness passed for the moment.

"Marn?"

"Nik, General, it's nothing. Can you do it?"

He stroked his beard, his round face closed to her. "I've seen the problem, Marn, and I've thought about it. I had thought we should try to reach the pass before the lid blew, pick up the pieces once we've got a breathing space. In the Mills when I set up a mediator board, the first weeks were ... shall we say, interesting. Until the workers got used to the new way of doing things, all the anger, spite, whatever, everything that the old ways had smothered exploded on me. I had to talk at them till I was hoarse, Marn. Weeks before we were back to past levels of production. We can't afford that kind of disruption, not on this side of the mountains."

K'vestmilly nodded. "I understand. But we also can't afford divisions that weaken us."

He was silent a minute, the fatigue that never left him making his round face almost gaunt. "What I can do is arrange a cadre of guards and authorize them to punish minor transgressions on the spot, take prisoners for later trial. You're right. Has to be either meien or gyes or both. We do need them as scouts, but I'll see about replacing the ones I pull out with Harozh since they're better than the rest with mountains. That's another problem, Marn. I'll get complaints from both sides, that I'm always sending Harozh on the hard jobs, that I'm always favoring Harozh, raising them above the other men. However. We've a week before we reach the pass, I think the guard cadre should hold the lid on until we have time for more. Talk to Heslin about the other, Marn. The Mijloc has this sort of system in place, I used it as a guide for the arbitration board in the Mills. Once he's got something written up, I can go over it, cut and weld till it fits Cadander. While we're in Ankland, we'll have the elbow room to put it in place. It's not something we can craft on the fly, Marn. What we do now will stay in place once we win this. You know Cadandri, we don't like changes, we go with what we have no matter how bad the fit."

She smiled behind the Mask. "You really have been thinking about this, Vedouce."

"It matters, Marn."

"Yes, it matters. I'll do what I can to help smooth things for you. Where's the Poet? I want a song, a marching song. If he and Tingajil can manage it, another *River of Blood*."

Vedouce stroked the beard he'd grown since the retreat from Oskhold. "Tingajil's near her time. Vyzharnos, zdra zdra, you can say he's distracted. A song, Marn?"

"I've seen it work, General. You were off with the army when Vyzharnos and Tingajil came up with *River of Blood*. You didn't see what that did to people, Pan Pen, I did. Bring the Poet to see me—and Tingajil if she's up to it, we'll talk a while. Second thing, I'm going to walk the campfires tonight, talk to people, I'll need one of those cloaks again."

"Marn, nik! It's too dangerous. You'd be an easy target."

"No more dangerous than my tent. Meie Zasya and the Fireborn will be with me." She spread her hands in the Marn's Smile. "As you back your guards, I'll back you. It's necessary, General, you know that as well as I do."

"Marn . . ."

She interrupted quickly. "You're a loyal man, Vedouce, the best I've got. You know that, don't you? And you know there's a time for bluffing and this isn't it. I want it clear to everyone that what you're doing has my blessing, I want it also clear the Marn will not tolerate these cousin quarrels."

"Marn!" The boy jumped up and the others huddled about the fire started to get to their feet.

"Nik," she said, "sit down." She let her hands smile. "Evansal, isn't it?" she said to the man who was the focus of this group (the name whispered to her by Zasya Myers who stood at her right shoulder). When he nodded, a flicker of pleasure quickly suppressed in his pale eyes, she went on, "This is a hard time for us all, harder for some than others. Is there anything you need? I can't do much, but what I can, I will. Speak. Any of you. No one will be punished for the truth."

There was silence a moment, then Evansal passed

a hand across his face. His eyes narrowed. She could almost smell the thoughts scurrying inside his head, the sudden greed; she suppressed a sigh, the same message, close to it anyway, only the players changed.

"Them Harozh, you favorin them over us, Marn. An't fair, them gettin better food and all the ridin stock." His eyes flickered away and his hand covered his mouth again.

"I have heard you, Evansal," she said. "Know that if it is so, it will be changed." She put a light stress on the *so* and saw his eyes flicker again. "Think well what you say, Evansal." She lifted her head. "All of you do likewise. We must fight the Enemy and not each other. The General Pan Pen is gathering a guard to patrol the campfires. I will have no more private vengeance. Those who try it will get what they give." She gave the Marn's blessing and moved on, weary, annoyed at the pettiness of her people, but determined to see that they all got the message—and knew the penalty for disregarding her words.

2

Tingajil grunted and clutched at the lute case. The driver and some of the men marching beside the wagon were singing the new song. That pleased her.

She was riding one of the supply wagons, tucked in among the barrels and bales with other women, some of them pregnant, some of them ill of one thing or another, some of them with children too small to keep up. She was layered with dust, sweating, her hair in braids she hadn't taken down for days now. Breathing was hard because of the ever present dust, grew harder as they got higher into the mountains. She should have been miserable, sometimes she was, but mostly not.

Especially now. *We've done it again*, she thought with pride. *River of Blood wasn't a fluke. Marching to Cadander is going to be as big.*

The pain came again; she began breathing through her mouth; sweat cut runnels through the dust on her face. She wished briefly that Vyzharnos could be with her, then was glad he was not.

Narisa eased Pozhi from her breast, pulled her shirt down, laid the baby across her thighs and began rubbing his back. "Be night soon. Should make camp before your time's on you, and this being your first, might take a while longer'n you think. I'll tell Takovy to put up the tent for you, and don't you worry, Tinga, if the babe hasna come by morning, we'll be staying with you. Tak tells me the Poet's fixed up a horse litter, case the birthing takes longer'n the night. He didn't want to say anything, 'fraid you'd get fussed. Zdra, men don't know, do they." Her chuckle mixed with the baby's gargantuan burp. "That's a good 'un, Pozhiling Pozhee."

Vyzharnos squatted by the fire outside the tent, the red light reflected in the sweat that beaded his face. His hands closed in fists as Tingajil screamed. He shuddered, wiped at his face. This was worse than the war. He knew what to do then. More than that, there were things he *could* do. Now there was nothing but waiting . . . and thinking about Treshteny and her prophecy . . . comforting . . . frightening . . . this fate the timeseer said . . . can't depend on her words . . . so much had changed . . . he remembered . . .

Treshteny walked in, settled on a chair, smiled at the blond young woman who handed her a cup and saucer. "I thank you, Tingajil. You will either die tomorrow or marry twice and have a granddaughter who will be Marn."

"Oh." Tingajil blinked. "You interest me. How am I supposed to die tomorrow?"

"Men will come looking for you. You will hide and be betrayed by your sister. They will slit your throat and throw you into the river. You are dangerous. That song of yours and his . . ." She waved a long thin hand at Vyzharnos. ". . . River of Blood has got too great a hold on Nerodin hearts."

Tingajil blinked, one slim hand coming up to stroke her throat. "And how do I avoid the knife?"

"You leave now, within the hour, and go to Oskland, OskHold. Take only what you can carry yourself and plan for a long stay. You tell no one, not your mother nor your father, and especially not your sister, that you are leaving."

"Treshteny the Mad."

"That is me." She bent down, stroked the soft curls between the little faun's horns. "And . . ." she bent closer, listened, smiled, straightened. "This is Yela'o. He's a faun and just born. We're going to Oskland too."

Tingajil blinked again, glanced at Vyzharnos who was watching the madwoman with intense concentration, then she flung her hand out, impatience in the gesture and in her voice when she spoke. "Why would my sister do such a thing?"

"She has been touched and taken by the Fetch, the Enemy, Mother Death." Treshteny turned to Vyzharnos. "Your father is dead, Poet. They took his head- and showed it to the Marn. It was a present. They're shooting her father right now. You probably thought he was long ago dead, but he wasn't, not till now. They think they've closed their hands tight about the Marn but they haven't."

"What do you read for her?"

"*I may not say that. The words are in my head, but they will not come to my tongue.*"

"*Why did you come here? Why warn us and not others?*"

"*You are the father of the son Tingajil carries in her womb. He will wed the daughter the Marn carries, their child will be Marn if this fate comes to be.*"

"*Tinga!*"

"*I'm not . . . I don't know . . . why do you believe her?*"

"*My fath . . . father and the last Marn did and neither of them w . . . were naive or gullible. Who's this Fetch? Who's Mother Death?*"

"*I may not say that. I know and do not know. There is pain. I do not want to know.*" She got to her feet. "*I must go, the killing will begin soon.*" She stared past them as the wall unfolded before her and she SAW. "*Yes. Yes. Yes.*" Her smile widened. "*It is good. Tingajil will not die now.*"

Tingajil will not die now. He touched his shirt pocket. Or maybe . . . couldn't concentrate . . . notes. He found a stub of pencil and began scribbling fragments he could work with later when his head was right. A celebration of his son's birth. A dark, cloudy night, too warm still for comfort, smelling of sweat, urine and dust, voices around him, sentry calls echoing off the mountain sides, hoots and squeals from macain, horses restless, a sicamar screaming miles away, a wild terrifying sound . . . not more terrifying than the muffled screams of Tingajil . . . bearing his child . . . bearing the future . . . a promise . . .

A hand dropped on his shoulder. He dropped the notebook, sprang to his feet to face Narisa. "Tinga, she all right?"

"No problem, Poet; she did her job like a veteran. You have a son, a fine healthy boy."

He looked down, saw the white flutter of the notebook pages. He scooped it up, tucked it back into his pocket. "I want to see her."

Narisa sniffed. "You wait. I'll see."

She leaned from the tent a moment later, beckoned.

In the flickering light from the single lamp, Tingajil looked tired but happy; her hair was brushed and shiny soft. He touched her cheek, but didn't say anything, all the words he was so free with at other times washed out of his head.

He could feel the women moving about him; the tent was too small to escape from them. A shoulder punched into him. He scowled. His scowl changed as a woman slid a loosely wrapped bundle past him and laid it in Tingajil's arms.

"Your son, Vyzhri." Tingajil's smile glowed up at him, her voice was strong and pure; it made the hairs stand up on the back of his neck. "If you're willing I'd like to call him Zastaros because he's a promise of hope to come."

He looked at the bundle and knew it was supposed to mean something to him. His son, tiny and crumpled, skin like white rose petals and an abundance of hair that looked like dandelion fluff, the future of Cadander if the timeseer's vision held. For the moment, though, all he could think of was Tingajil, and he had to get the way she looked into his poem, that and the awe he felt gazing at her. He touched the baby because he thought she wanted him to, afraid because the skin seemed so delicate a careless stroke would bruise it. His son. An arm moved out of the wrapping, waved aimlessly about until it bumped against him and a tiny hand immediately caught hold of his thumb. He looked at the perfect fingers and felt what he'd tried to force a moment before.

"Zastaros," he said. "It's a good name." Very gently he freed his hand, leaned over and kissed her. "Get some sleep if you can, it's only about an hour till dawn and campbreak."

3

Sunlight flooded in a yellow-gray haze through the gauze dust barrier stretched across the front of the canvas wagon cover in the vain hope that they could get some air inside the shelter without drowning in the billows of dust kicked up by hooves and claws. The smell from the chamber pot and the stale sweat soaking the mattress mixed with the heat and the dust to raise the misery under the canvas.

Stripped to a thin shift, K'vestmilly Vos lay on the mattress, pillows pushed around her to help support her against the jerks and jolts of the wagon. Her breathing was labored, her eyes glazed; she muttered now and then, random words, sometimes sounds without words. Marn Maid Cumura knelt beside her, working the fan over her while Olmena Oumelic bathed her with a rag dipped in a mixture that evaporated quickly and gave her a measure of relief for a few minutes.

A wheel dropped into a rut, the chamber pot sloshed, more stench tainted the air, Cumura dropped the fan as she grabbed at a bracer, Olmena lifted the bowl and held it steady so the mixture wouldn't slop out, grunted as she fought to keep her balance on her knees. The driver's whip snapped and cracked, the vul team pulled the wheel clear and they were moving again. And he was singing that song again. It was bad as *River of Blood*. The words came through the gauze which was too bad, because Ridic had a voice like an ungreased axle. *Marching marching*, he bawled, *sons of Cadander, Glory in our sights. High hills and broad plains, fighting for our rights.*

Olmena shivered. *Dreadful stuff, though her travail hadn't cost Tingajil her gift for tunes. The Poet, now. Poet! Tash, verse-maker. He does have a knack though. Put the two of them together . . . hmp . . . means we won't hear the last of this'n either.* She dropped the rag into the bowl and set them aside, reached behind her for the flask. "Lift her head, Cumi. We'll see if we can get more of the cordial into her. And some water."

Her thin face creased with worry lines, the little maid eased K'vestmilly's shoulders onto her knees and cupped a hand under her head, easing it up so Olmena could hold the glass to the Marn's lips and tilt the thick, golden fluid into her mouth without spilling it.

Cumura watched K'vestmilly's throat work. "My Mam had five babies, she never had trouble like this. Is it . . ." She hesitated, the tip of her tongue fluttered across her lips; as if just saying the words might bring on the evil she named, Cumura said nothing more, just gazed anxiously at Olmena.

"Your mother was mountain-bred, Cumi. The Marn's a lowlander. The babe's not in trouble. Not yet." She took the glass away a moment, used the dampened rag to wipe around K'vestmilly's mouth, brought the glass back. "That's a good girl." She smiled as K'vestmilly swallowed. "Drink it all. If we have to go much higher, though . . ." She sighed. "Zdra, she's healthy. And if the worst happens, there's plenty of time for other babies."

Cumura's lips trembled as she reached for the fan. Her eyes glistened with tears. When she spoke, her

voice was a wavery whisper. "She's going to lose The
Hope?"

Olmena shrugged. "As I said, the Marn's healthy.
Depends on lots of things. If it weren't so hot . . ."
She glanced at the long narrow face of the Marn, the
fringe of black lashes curving against the pale translucent skin. "I suppose she had her reasons, but starting a baby in these times . . ." She tilted the glass
more steeply, watched the last of the cordial slide
into the Marn's mouth. "Good, Marn, you drank it
all, now we'll give you some water to clean the taste
away. Let her head down a minute, Cumi." Over her
shoulder as she worked with the spigot of the barrel,
she said, "All we can do is keep working and wait."

Cumura sighed. "Any natural year, the snow on
the roads would be over our heads by now."

Olmena held the glass to K'vestmilly's lips. "Come,
luv, drink some more, that's good, that'll clear your
mouth out. Hasn't any year been natural since the
Glory showed her face. Ahh, that's good, all gone.
Cumi, have the pan ready, with all this shaking she'll
need to use it soon enough. Ease her down. Zdra,
that's good. Now, luv, let's give you another sponge
down while Cumi fans you, nik, nik, close your eyes,
go to sleep, don't fuss, you're doing fine." Humming
a dronish sleepsong, she poured more of her rub in
the bowl, sopped the rag in it, squeezed out the ex-
cess and began patting at K'vestmilly's face.

Late that afternoon the army reached the pass and
began snaking along the narrow, serpentine dip between the peaks. The wind picked up, blew steadily
in their faces; clouds boiled across the face of the sun
and the day grew measurably cooler.

K'vestmilly Vos opened her eyes. "Mena?"

Olmena moved on her knees toward the Marn, holding onto the wagon's side to keep from lurching onto her. "So you're back with us, are you?"

"Back?" K'vestmilly tried to sit up. "I'm weak as . . ."

"You've had a bad time the past two days. Altitude mixed with heat."

K'vestmilly's hand went to the baby, felt around over the bulge in her middle. "Is she . . . uh!" She lay back, smiling. "Little pest, playing kickball with my innards. Uh! Vych, she's strong. Am I imagining it, or are we finally moving on the level?"

"We reached the pass half an hour ago."

"Help me sit. Where's Cumura?"

Olmena held out her hands, pulled gently as K'vestmilly caught hold of them, helping her ease off her back. "Getting some rest. She was with you all last night. Worried, poor child."

K'vestmilly eased her legs around, rubbed at her back. "Since you can't say it with grace, I will. You told me what could happen and I must say, it did." She took the glass of cordial Olmena handed her, grimaced, but starting sipping at it. "Catch me up on what's happened."

"Tingajil had her baby night before last, a boy, fine child, looks like old Oram more than either of them. Poet's been going round in a daze scribbling at something, useless as a kitten whose eyes haven't opened. Good thing they finished that . . . aaah! that zhag cursed song before her time came. I suppose. Valiva finally talked Osk and Vedouce into letting her arm some of the women, she looked in here, said to tell you sorry she had to wait to do it with you down like that, Marn, but having you out of the way sort of relaxed the men, made it more of a little thing without you there pushing it. She said to tell you she has about fifty women who can hit a target and she's going to set them to teaching the others. She said she'd appreciate it if you didn't mention them once you were up and about again."

K'vestmilly chuckled. Blinked and swayed. Lifted a hand to her head.

"Marn?"

"Nik, I was just dizzy a moment. I mean, I can expect that kind of thing, can't I?"

"After lying flat so long, it's not surprising. Let me know if it keeps up, though. Then we'll have to take a look. Finish your water, you need the liquid."

K'vestmilly grinned at her. "Yes, Momma. What about the Anklanders who are supposed to meet us at the Pass?"

"I haven't heard anything." She shrugged. "Probably the General and the others know, but they're not telling me."

"Soon as we stop for the night, find Heslin. Tell him I'm awake again and want to see him. Zdra, what else? Did General Pan Pen get his guard-force organized?"

"The day you went down he did. Had a couple whippings, two men taken off line, disarmed. Some grumbling, but mostly folks are too tired to get up to much. And since they're all meien, there's not a lot of talk about favoring one or another. And not a lot of challenge either, those are some tough women. Boy fell off a wagon, broke his arm. He's doing as well as you could expect, no way to be comfortable, but it was a clean break, no complications. Talking about breaks, horse broke a leg, Vedouce had it butchered and the meat passed out to the families far as it went. Rider's walking now, they tell me he's complaining every step, but he was acting the fool and did it to himself. Fair lesson to his friends and those like him. Two new men down with that fever, healer Pareshta tells me it's starting to spread faster than she likes, though it's nothing to worry about yet. Since we're close enough to Ankland, the worst won't hit till we've got a place to settle for a while. Probably. Even if you're feeling better, Marn, you're not to go anywhere near them. Matter of fact, I don't want you to leave the wagon, you're too open right now to anything going around. We can't afford anything happening to you."

K'vestmilly finished the water, handed the glass to Olmena. "Pan Osk said it'd be about another ten days march to AnkHold once we're through the mountains. Mena, ah Mena, I yearn for a bath." She grimaced. "And would you give me a hand, please. Same old thing. Spros! I'll proclaim a Celebration the first day I spent without having to pee every second breath."

3

OSKHOLD

Tomal lay in the shelter he'd spent the night scraping together, scanning the camp below with the longglass he'd stolen from an officer's tent. From the beginning he'd had no intention of walking through a bunch of brambles and over a bunch of rocks, just because Pokad said so. Losing the com meant his spying was just for him, but he didn't mind that. It was the way it'd been most of his life till Hus, then Heslin, tied him into their plotting.

The chovan section was breaking up. As he

watched, two bands were quarrelling, someone started shooting and the rest dived for cover.

The unTaken Bezhvali were wild, some of them riding through the tents of the camp followers, throwing torches into the tents, shooting everything that moved, others on foot, pulling men and women out of the shelters, beating them, shooting them, sometimes raping the women first. Tomal squinted ferociously so he couldn't see what the Bezhvali were doing to those women; he knew most of them, they'd made a pet of him. When he moved the glass, he saw Hanesh dangling on a gibbet improvised from a wagon tongue, his tongue protruding from his gargoyle's face. He was still twitching, his feet kicking in a freakish dance. Tomal smiled grimly. He didn't like Hanesh.

The Taken were separating like failed sauce, the Dandri pulling apart from the Calandri, Rodin from Nerodin, Bezhvali from Zemyas, Travisherrs from Merzzes. They weren't doing anything, just moving and moving, the clots getting bigger, the spaces between them wider.

"Yeech! What's that?" He snatched his hand back from the bare stone. Something like cold fire had nipped him. Rubbing the hand, he crouched on the thick bed of withered leaves he'd gathered from the grove of shivering-hevet growing behind the brush patch. When he was sure that force wasn't coming through the leaves, he lifted the glass again and scanned the camp below.

The Taken had stopped moving. They were all standing stiff and silent, faces turned toward Dander.

The chovan had stopped their fighting. They were backing away, careful slow step by careful slow step.

The horses were nervous, some of them huddling together, others biting and kicking at each other, others slamming into the corral fence until they knocked it over. One horse was knocked down and trampled as the others broke through the opening.

The draft vul and the orsks faced west like the Taken and moved into herds joined so tight, shoulder to shoulder, that they seemed more like a single creature with many legs. They didn't spook, they didn't run, they simply started walking, as if lead ropes were pulling them, heading straight for Dander, trampling down tents and corrals and anything that stood in their path.

A *SOUND* vibrated across the valley, like a plucked lute-string, the tone so high it was almost beyond hearing, more felt than heard.

The air went blue—the harsh, bright blue of the bubble that had carried the False Marn here and blown the Hold to rubble. Tomal was in Dander when the Bubble was born, he'd seen it pop through the roof of the Temple and go darting east, growing as it moved. He hugged his arms across his stomach and bit hard on his lips to keep his breakfast down.

The horses stopped their flight, turned west and followed the vul and the orsks. The Taken started walking. The Chovan followed—not Taken, but under compulsion. They struggled like flies in a web, but they were in the trap and couldn't escape. The Bezhvali were the last to succumb, but in the end they too joined the stiff-legged march west, heading fog Dander/Calanda.

In his brushy nest Tomal felt the compulsion like a string around his brain. A string that tugged at him, cut into him until the pain was so great he almost couldn't bear it. But NO was the song of his life. He knew the scent of it, the taste, knew every nuance of it. And now he said his greatest NO—and felt the compulsion slide away from him.

The blue flowed from the valley, and when it was gone he lifted his head.

The valley was empty. Nothing moved down there except dead leaves and other debris stirred by the wind. Not even any birds.

He touched his tongue to his lips, blinked to clear his eyes. Tents. Some of them flattened, some of them abandoned where they stood. The shacks that had served as taverns and brothels and peddlers' stands were mostly torn apart, some of them still smoldering from the fires the Bezhvali had set, others reduced to ash. Hanesh and half a dozen others still hung from wagon tongue gibbets, twisting and swaying in the wind.

"They didn't take nothin." Tomal shivered at the sound of his own voice, a cracking whine, louder than he'd meant to let it get. "All the way to Calanda eatin air for supper." He laughed, and quickly stopped that too.

The blue was gone. The *sound* was gone. He scraped away a section of leaves, hesitated then touched a finger to the ground.

The cold fire was gone.

His stomach growled.

"Zdra," he said, then smiled, the smile broadening until it was a grin that threatened his ears. "All mine. Maybe I gotta walk, but I'll eat good while I'm doing it."

4

MAZNAK PASS

As soon as she saw what was in the meadow, Meie Synggal yelled a warning to the two meien, fell out of the saddle and crouched close to the trunk of one of the larger trees. After a quick glance upward to make sure the tree was untenanted, she straightened, called, "Furrin, circle. See what you can find. Shurib, up the nearest tree and watch my back."

Ten men lay mutilated and dead in the mountain meadow. Some had been sleeping and were wrapped still in blankets. One had fallen face down in a small fire. It was out now, but the smell of roasted flesh clung to the meadow. Two were dead from crossbow bolts and another had his throat cut.

Synggal squatted beside the last body, inspecting the wound. It was a sling slash, the cut so deep only a few tendons held the head in place. "Sleykyn," she muttered. She straightened, moved swiftly back to her mount. "Shurib, see anything? We looking for that murd-spak Sleykyn."

"Nothing, Synggal. There's some trax flying around in the clouds waiting for us to leave. That's all. Who are they, the Harozh who were supposed to meet us?"

"Looks like."

"Why bother?"

Synggal's mouth quirked in a humorless smile. "Because he could. He's twisting a gut because he hasn't been able to get at the Marn. Boast and a warning, Shuri." She hauled herself into the saddle. "And we better see that warning get where it belongs. Hmp. I never could whistle worth a damn. You do it, Shuri. Call Furr in and let's get back."

17. Why the Wind Sighs, Why the River Weeps

1

THE OUTLANDS, BAGKLOUSS

Dark and Light. Tearing at her.

The Dark was stronger, more cohesive, the Light chaotic now, bits and pieces flitting like fireflies, circling round Serroi and the lights that rode with her.

Charody. Old root-woman, warm and strong as the earth. She loomed huge now, the light within that enormous fibrous outline beginning as an eerie black glow, brightening as they rode to a bitter orange that seemed to reach from horizon to horizon. Amber and orange lines of light dropped from her feet and sank to the earth heart, moving with her as her macai paced along in his swinging travel-walk.

Doby was a tiny shine, star in the cradle of a crescent moon. His light was pale at first, almost white, but it changed, darkening to match Charody's glow, a development that gave Serroi a momentary distraction from the forces tugging at her. She smiled, felt the movement of her mouth as something almost apart from herself.

Treshteny was a pure white, cool and restful. Uncomplicated.

Like Doby's, Yela'o's light was changing to match his companion, shifting from the color of newly unfurled leaves to a greenish white luster.

Horse was an opalescent shimmer, pastel ripples

flickering across his form. Strange and wild—nothing Serroi had experienced before came near what she was seeing/feeling, not even those demons conjured/created through her by ser Noris; he was deeply tied to the earth, roots of light striking down from his feet into earth's heart, striding through the earth as he strode across it.

The Dark wailed at Serroi, screamed at her, babbled and pleaded and cursed her—night and day, the *Voice* nibbled at her brain, giving her no rest.

MOTHER mother WHY why LOVE ME I curse you I will swallow you JOIN ME MELD WITH ME why do you deny me you made me MOTHER I hate you YOU MAKE ME RAGE I hurt MOTHER I cry from the wound you gave me ALL THAT YOU LOVE I MAKE MINE mother I reap them and tie them in sheaves they are mine now ALL MINE I'll pluck them all mother leaving not one WHY why MOTHER mother WHY DON'T YOU LOVE ME. . . .

Hands closed about her arms, warm and strong, fingers like fibrous roots. Hands closed about her ankle, cool and trembling a little, fragile. Working together, Charody and Treshteny eased her from the saddle and got her onto her feet.

It was worse than being blind; she could see, but what she saw had little to do with the physical reality around her. Treshteny guided her, talking to her, the words like bubbles of light exploding in her face, but this time Treshteny's touch didn't free her and she couldn't spare time or attention to decipher what the timeseer was saying.

* * *

Serroi sat listening while the others made camp.

Doby and Yela'o giggled, chasing each other as they hunted for down wood and played with the little spirit beasts that lolloped like ferrets through the brush. Big eyes, whiskers and limber forms.

Treshteny sang to herself as she brought water from a spring that bubbled from under a pile of boulders.

Mama Charody chanted under her breath as she arranged stones from the fire, talked to the kaman she'd called up, thanking him for the tubers Serroi heard fall in a series of dull thuds, called to Doby and the faun to hurry with the wood as she moved about the brushy niche among the rocks.

Fire. As Mama Charody's shining shadow moved, Serroi could feel the warmth, she could hear the hissing and popping, the clank of the cookpot, the gush of water, the splashes and thuds as Charody started fixing supper.

A little later, Treshteny put a mug of cha in her hands. "Sip easy, Serroi, it's hot. We'll be having tuber soup again, you'll be smelling it in a bit." She sighed. "The brus, they brought us herbs which may give a new taste to it." Another sigh. "I do miss the Clinic cooks. I wouldn't mind going back when all this is over." She shivered. "When I touched you . . . it was like being in the middle of a thunderstorm at midnight. Is there anything I can do?"

Serroi carefully lifted the cup she couldn't see, missed her mouth the first try, then sipped at the hot liquid, rolling it on her tongue and letting it slide down her parched throat. "Just don't let me fall in a hole." She tried out her smile again and was pleased with the results. "We're getting close, Teny. At least there's that."

"I . . ."

Treshteny broke off as something nearby yowled and hissed; there was an agitation of chittering and screams, then a diminishing flurry of yips. "Payas," she said. "They must've been watching us. Oh! What's that!" The glow that was all Serroi could see of her flickered like a candle flame in a draft.

Serroi rubbed at her useless eyes; when she dropped her hands, she saw a hot, orange fire running low to the ground, circling one way about the camp, coming back, radiating an agitated uncertainty. "Help me to my feet." When she was standing, she called, "Adlayr, I know it's you. Come in, join us. Tell us where the others are."

She heard Treshteny gasp as the black sicamar she could remember but not see stalked into the circle of firelight, rumbled a low growl, then came across to Serroi and flung himself down beside her—though not quite close enough for her to touch him. His glow was like Horse's, though much less complex, smaller and more muted.

He growled at her when she tried to touch him.

"Stuck again, Adlayr? Ei vai, if you won't, you won't."

Treshteny had retreated to stand beside Mama Charody; Serroi could feel her fear. Doby and Yela'o edged closer, nervous but intensely curious, their lights flushing a rose pink with that curiosity.

Serroi reached out, felt the tingle of the lights. "Let him be," she said. "He's more beast than man right now." Her voice echoed in her head as if there were dozens of her speaking, but the boy's lights were steady; apparently they didn't hear anything strange.

Doby dropped to a squat by her knee. "Man, Healer?"

"It's a family thing, Doby, not something to be talked of."

"Like Horse?"

"A little."

"Oh." He stood, walked away, looking back repeatedly over his shoulder—at least, that's what she thought from the way the light twisted. Then Yela'o's white and Doby's orange twisted and turned about each other, moving to the beat of giggles from the boy and chuckling laughter from the faun. They went running in and out of the brush and boulders, taking turns chasing each other, the brus running with them, a herd of wild spirits relishing the wild spirits of the two boys.

The cha in the mug was cold now, but Serroi finished it anyway and went back to fighting off the forces tearing at her and trying to sort some meaning out of what was happening.

2

ON THE RIM OF THE YTAMA ROUND

Honeydew spiralled high above the wash, scanning the country around the camp. *Six more youmbards coming this way . . . ei vai, they look mad at everything, walking like their feet hurt . . . yeek, there's another bunch north of them . . . and let me . . .* She spiralled higher, flew west a short distance. *The Ground's crawling with them, sometimes three in a bunch, sometimes four, sometimes as much as eight. Maybe a third riding, but the rest walking. All coming this way, S'ramee.*

After a brusque acknowledgment from Tserama, Honeydew flattened her wings and let the thermals waft her round and round above the wash. She didn't like the power currents flowing through the ground and everything that grew from it; they made her itchy as if her skin were coming loose and threatening to peel away. The barrier was worse. She couldn't see it anymore, but she knew where it was; it made her hair stand out straight from her head if she got too close to it.

She could have left, of course. There was no place to go if she did, so she just kept gliding in circles, worrying about all the people she loved who were caught up in this thing, fretting because there was nothing she could think of to help them or herself.

The sun and hot, dry wind sucked the moisture from her body, turned her mouth to a desert. She folded her wings and plunged toward the spring, snapping them open at the last minute and swooping across the water to land on a small patch of gravel. Sad because that reminded her of Adlayr, she knelt and scooped up handfuls of water, drinking then splashing it over herself.

The force in the ground made her stomach bump. She fluttered up, flew to one of the browsing macain and landed in the soft, spongy growths on his neck. She wriggled around, got herself settled and started fussing about Hedivy. He was getting stronger fast. Bad-tempered too. He exercised all the time. Stayed as far from the women as he could and did pushups and jumps and all sorts of funny things. In the beginning he looked soft and he lost his breath easier than she remembered, but he was hard now, even if it was only a week ago he started. He could do that exercise stuff for hours. He didn't say anything, and he seemed to think he was hiding what he was feeling, though she had no trouble reading him.

He was purple-faced tooth-grinding mad at everything and everyone and most of all at the Enemy, what Serree called the Fetch. That was a good name, really, because it sure enough was fetching them straight to it. *EEE eee*, she told herself, *bad time comin.*

Hedivy ran in place, his back to the yammering women—what they found to talk about was more than he could guess—his face pinched into a scowl. For the first time he had a moment's sympathy for his father—or at least an understanding of the frustrations that drove Angero Starab to use his fists on people who couldn't escape him or fight back. It was only a flicker in his head, quickly erased. Old habit. He'd a lot of practice in not-thinking about his father.

He stopped running, picked up the elongated rocks he'd found and started curling his arms, up down up down. Sweat ran down his face, stung his eyes, but he went on and on, curl and straighten, curl and straighten, don't think, breathe in breath out, don't think, get the burn, fight for it, don't think don't think. . . .

He dropped the rocks and trotted along the wash toward the ripple in the sand that marked the place where the barrier was. He slammed into it deliberately, hard as he could, bounced back to land on his buttocks.

Skin prickling, beard smoking, he got to his feet

and began running the circuit of the barrier, moving out of the wash, shoving through the prickly brittle brush, climbing over piles of boulders, dipping into the wash again, round and round, cursing everything in Bagklouss as he ran, cursing Serroi, cursing Adlayr, cursing Tserama and the rest of those witches—and most of all, cursing the Prudjin.

The Prudjin was the force behind the Glory.

The Prudjin killed the old Marn.

The Prudjin killed Jestranos Oram. Maybe not with her own hands, but she gave Nov the reason and the means to do it.

The Prudjin had twice come within a hair of killing him.

The Prudjin was the Enemy.

For all of that and all the humiliations he'd suffered, all the hunger and fear and frustration of this journey, he wanted to get at the Prudjin and kill her. He needed to kill her. With his own hands, if he could. She was a wound in him that wouldn't close, that dripped pus and spread corruption through his body.

I've got to get out of here. Vycher magic. I hate magic. Had my way, I'd strangle every brat that showed the signs. I ever get the power, by Zhagdeep and heartbone, I'll do just that.

He passed the spring, saw Halisan sitting beside it, legs drawn up, chin on her crossed arms, eyes fixed on the bubbling water. *She could get out of here if she wanted. Fetch Serroi at a trot and break this prison.* Rage burned through him again; he tucked his chin down and lengthened his stride, running full out, driving through the brush, vaulting the larger boulders and bounding recklessly across the smaller ones. You don't understand, she kept saying, you don't understand. But she wouldn't try to explain.

He ran himself out, trudged down the sandy slope into the wash, dropped onto his blankets and knelt there, chest heaving, head down so the sweat could drip off the points of his face.

Tserama watched the foreign man running and felt a touch of sympathy for his frustration. She left the circle of Readers and walked to the barrier, touched it, felt the burn run along her arms into her body.

The ground throbbed. A force came through her bare feet, flooded her body. Without understanding how, she knew instantly what it was. The Sem Ris were moving. Her Sem Ris were leaving their hills.

Gan Khora! The world's crumbling.

For a moment she couldn't move, then she walked slowly to the other Readers who were standing, all of them, faces blank, eyes huge, voices silenced.

"Did you feel it?" she said.

Badaru hugged her arms tighter against herself. "My Sem Ris, they're coming. Across the whole Ston Gassen, they're coming."

Sanonchad shivered. "And mine. I've never heard of such a thing."

Radonda nodded. "And they're not fighting. With their own Round or the rest. That's the strangest of all. My lot, anyway. They're always arguing and threatening each other."

Padelog managed a smile. "Your lot is nearest the Jeboh, chagga, they always were an itchy bunch. Mine aren't moving yet, they're just stirring in place, like bayas turning round and round before they leave the lair. What's going to happen when they all get to us? And how can we call them Sem Ris when they've left their Ris behind?"

Tserama lifted her eyes to the blue jags of the Ashtop peaks. She shivered again. "It's more than we know," she said, "it's more than just the ONE we mustn't name." She caught hold of Padelog's hand, fumbled on the other side for Radonda's. "It's the Thamyo Juggyal," Tserama said, "The Death of Gods."

They began to chant the ancient warntale, voices in unison.

Halison took up her harp and began playing, supporting the voices.

I speak to the river.
I speak to the wind.
This is what the wind says, this is what the river says.
Blood flows like water, the wells are sour with blood.
The portents pile up.
The sky burns, the stars bolt from a three-tongued flame.
One tongue is white, one is red, the third burns black.
The stars cower in the caves, fear of the black fire chilling their shine.
The Lake is a boiling cauldron.
Waters rise, white hot, towering.
In their fury they lick at the land, they swallow everything they touch.
Lightning strikes the GodHouses though there is no storm.
The GodHouses burn to bare ash.
The wind blows the ash across the face of the sky.

A fisherman's net brings up an ash-colored eel
   with a mirror on its head.
In the mirror a skull stares out.
Day comes no more.
There is no end to darkness.
The three-tongued flame eats at itself.
Gan Khora is one flame, one is Med 'Ah-ne, one
   Arga Chih.
Arga Chih the Elder swallows Med 'Ah-ne the
   Mother, Gan Khora the Maid.
The black swallows all.
There is no end to darkness.
I speak to the river.
I speak to the wind.
This is what the wind sighs, why the river weeps.

18. Marching to Dander

1

ANKHOLD

Pan Ank looked with sullen resentment at Pan Osk, turned his shoulder to the visitor, lowered his eyes and sat chewing on the ends of his mustache. Ank was a long, lean man with sun blasted skin and hair so blond it was almost white. With his white eyebrows and eyelashes, his pale straggly mustache, he had an unfortunate resemblance to the simian snowpiches in his private zoo.

K'vestmilly Vos suppressed a sigh. From the minute the army reached AnkHold, the three Pans had started walking around each other like bull orsks some idiot had corralled together. *The idiot being me,* she thought, *but what else could I do? Mad's Tits, I don't need this.*

Heslin felt her irritation; his hand tightened on her shoulder.

He was standing behind her, effacing himself with that skill he'd practiced altogether too much. *I have to do something about that when we get Cadander back. Talk to him about it, see what it's going to take to deal with this hate/fear of outsiders. Mother left Ank and Osk to themselves too much, I can see why, but that has to change. Zdra zdra, we have to boot the Glorymen out first. So get to work, K'milly, start soothing these rampant males.*

Dance the twisty dance, wheedle and tease. Maiden Bless, I can get very tired of this.

She gathered herself, leaned forward, put a smile in her voice and said, "Come now, Eledilo Pan Ank, sit down. Looking up at you puts a crick in my neck." She waited with tilted Mask and hand slightly raised until he pulled a chair forward and sank into it, his pale pink mouth drooping lower. "Zacadorn Pan Osk and you, General, join us, please. These times are too difficult for stiff formality."

After a shuffling of feet and scraping of chair legs, she turned the Mask from Pan to Pan, lifting and spreading her hands in the Marn's Smile. "You've done well, Eledilo Pan Ank, you've held the Harozh without help or supplies." *And without anything near what we faced, just the Majilarn that you Harozh know so well you can about read their minds.* She lifted a hand in one of the graceful moves Heslin had drilled into her. "And you have been honorably loyal to your Marn. If I could, I would pass through without calling on you for more sacrifice. I can't. If we fail, you will fall because there will be no one to stop the march of the Glory." She paused, drew in a long breath. He was staring at the floor, putting a wall of resistance between him and her; she wanted to kick the stubborn idiot. Couldn't he see the truth in her words? She let the breath out watched him a moment longer. *I think the answer's nik. He doesn't see because he WON'T see.*

"You haven't seen what we've seen, Pan Ank. You haven't seen the Glory roll over a Hold and blow it to rubble in one instant. You haven't seen the Taken march at you. You haven't seen the dead rise to their feet and come at you again and again and you kill them again and again, but the only way you can stop them is chopping them apart." She leaned forward, trying to

drive the words into his head. "You may have to face
that, Eledilo Pan Ank, even here, despite all we can do.
If so, you'll wish you joined us to die fighting and not
as sacrifices in the streets and the Temple."

"We, Marn?" He ran his eyes slowly over her
body, lifted them to Heslin's face, looked at her
again. "In your state, it would be best to stay here. If
I may say this, you will only hamper your men, put
the added burden of your safety on their shoulders."

*Trust him to find a side issue to nitpick. Slip and slide
how you go, Pan Ank, I'll nail you down before I'm done.*
"There is no safety, Eledilo Pan Ank. Not here, not
anywhere."

"You yourself have said it, Marn. Going on is hope-
less. Stay here, behind these walls. At least there'll be a
chance. Marching on the Cities, no chance."

She lifted her hands, let them fall onto the chair
arms. "I do not see it that way, Pan Ank. We have set
something going that may prove a distraction to the
Enemy. And we have loyal servants still in place inside Dander/Calanda. And we have the word brought
by the meie Synggal. A message from the Shawar.
You're a man of books. You know the Silent Ones.
There will be a sign in the sky. When it comes, if
we're ready to strike, there is a good chance we'll win
back what was taken from us. It's only if we do nothing that there is no chance."

"How many men are you claiming, Marn?"

*Shifting ground again, hm? Wherever you go, I'll
follow you.* "We'll work out the numbers. It's your co-
operation I want, Eledilo Pan Ank." There was a
stubborn set to his face and she knew with weary certainty that he would argue every item.

Pan Osk had been silent so far, for which she
blessed him, knowing it was a forlorn hope he'd stay

silent. The legs of his chair grated on the tiles as he
slued around and leaned forward. Before he could
speak, though, Vedouce grabbed Osk's arm, dug his
fingers in. Osk glared at him, but kept his mouth
shut a while longer.

"I want a report of the minimum force you'll need
to defend the Hold; I want everyone else above that
number, male and female both, who owns a longgun
and has the health to stand the march. Eledilo Pan
Ank, it is yours to say whether you will be of more
use leading the defense here or coming south with
us, marching at the head of your men. If you do
come south, you must understand there can be only
one General of this army and he is Vedouce Pan Pen.
That will not change. He won the Gritzer War for us
and, against enormous odds, extracted almost all the
men and supplies from OskHold before it was de-
stroyed. He has my full trust and has from my hands
the authority of the Mask. Pan Osk has shown the
bigness of his mind and accepted this, for which I am
most grateful. I will remember his good sense when
this trouble is done." She stretched out her arms, the
meie Zasya Myers and Heslin helped her to stand. "I
don't require a decision tonight Eledilo Pan Ank.
This you should know, whatever you decide—we will
be marching out in three days, no more."

Cumura came trotting in with an armload of pillows she'd acquired one way or another. Scolding
K'vestmilly in a running whisper for overtiring herself after she'd just been so sick, she tucked the pillows about the Marn, ran to fetch the rubbing lotion,
glaring at Heslin on the way out.

He chuckled. "I'll leave you to your guardian
sicamar," he murmured.

"Wait, Hes. Not yet. Was it all right? Did I get him, or are we going to have more trouble?"

"You made a start, Kimi. He'll be sending his spies around to the army to sniff out the truth of what you told him. The earful they'll give him might flush the grumbles from his belly. With some luck."

She pushed at the sweaty hair straggling across her brow. "I wish it'd scare him into staying here. Maiden Bless, Osk is enough to handle. The two of them . . ."

"I don't know what he'll do, Kimi. He's not stupid, but he's been up here on his own for a long, long time. Logic's no cure for a raging snit."

Cumura came back with a bowl and bathing cloths; she stood, dancing foot to foot in the doorway, waiting with impatience for him to stop talking and go away.

Heslin glanced at her, smiled again. "I'll leave you to rest, hm?" He touched K'vestmilly's cheek, straightened.

"Wait. Ask about the boys, will you? Greygen's pair? Send them up to me. I want to tell them their parents are safe."

"I'll do that."

"And Tingajil. Have her bring the baby up. I haven't seen him yet and I'd like her to sing for me. Nik, that's not right. I need her to sing for me."

"Zdra zdra, I'll do that too." He took her hand, clicked his tongue at the fist it was squeezed into. He teased the fingers open, kissed the palm, his eyes locked to hers. He held the hand a moment longer then left.

2

K'vestmilly Vos smiled at the two boys. Shy and awkward, they stayed close by the door until she called them to her side.

She could see that the Mask was both exciting and intimidating them. The oldest can't be more than nine, she thought, the youngest maybe six? "Tell me your names," she said, reached out and touched the older boy on his shoulder.

"I'm Mel," he said. He set his hand on his brother's shoulder. "That's Noddy, O Marn."

"Mel, Noddy, I called you here to tell you about your mother and father. To let you know that they're safe, though a long way from here. I sent them on a mission to the Biserica and they did it just right. Did you see all the meien and the gyes?"

Noddy blinked huge blue eyes and nodded, too shy still to speak. Mel inclined his head with the courtesy of one a lot older than he looked to be. "Yes, O Marn," he said in his most polite voice.

"Because of your mother and father and the dangers they dared, we have those fighters and many more weapons. If we win this war, and Maiden Grant we do, Greygen and Sansilly Lestar will have played a great part in our victory."

Smiling behind the Mask, she watched them leave. She could see that the younger boy didn't quite understand any of it, but Mel did. His pride in his parents was clear in every line of his body.

That's one good thing I did, she thought. *Hedivy, Serroi, Adlayr, I hope I read the Shawar's message correctly. So many going to die, so much waste, lives and things used up and tossed away. But we have to be in place when the stars go out. We have to be ready. . . .*

She kicked off her shoes and got to her feet, enjoying the touch of the furs, scattered as rugs about the floor, against her bare skin. So long since she'd had any touch of luxury in her life. It was going to be hard to leave here. She was tempted to take Ank's advice and let the Army to on without her, but everything her mother and time had taught her shouted the temptation down. *I am Marnhidda Vos. That's mine! No one's going to take it from me.*

3

ON THE ROAD FROM OSKHOLD

Tomal sneezed as smoke drifted into his face from one of the smoldering hutches. He opened a last corral gate so the horses trapped inside could get out if they had the sense to go instead of standing there and starving to death. He'd caught himself a macai for riding and another for supplies and he let the rest loose. He didn't like people much, but he approved of animals, even rats. They did what they did and didn't go out of their way to think up miseries for other beasts. And mothers tended their get until the young 'uns were ready to go on their own. They didn't get drunk or beat them or tie them up and forget about them. Or sell them . . .

It was stupid, down deep bonehead stupid, but them down here, they'd just turned face and started marching, they didn't take *anything* with them. At least, nothing they weren't already carrying when the blue stuff caught them. Food was left to rot. Ammunition in the storesheds was still sitting there for anyone who wanted it. Guns. Clothes. Grain for the horses and the rest of the stock. Everything it'd taken Pan Ker months to haul up here.

He walked past dangling Hanesh, circling to windward to avoid the smell. The fat old man was a mess of flies and saw-toothed havrans were flying at him, tearing meat from his bone and darting off with it; his eyes were gone and his face mostly vanished. He wouldn't hang there much longer, the tendons of his neck were going fast. Tomal grinned at him, waved and walked on. Lehky Azheva—every time he thought of what she did with one cut of her pet knife, he wanted to dance and sing, turn cartwheels like when he was just a kid.

He rooted through the ammunition boxes, crammed as many bullets and clips as he could into a pair of saddle bags. He didn't bother with the guns, they were too heavy and awkward. Besides, the Web already had guns, it was ammunition they needed.

The sun was not quite overhead when he rode away from the rock pile that had once been OskHold. The pack macai trotted placidly beside him, nose at his knee, as he followed the trampled trail of the marching Taken.

He knew he was getting close to the army when the setting sun began to change color, its red turning purple as it dropped behind the blue haze.

He emerged from a grove of javories and brellim, thick with berryvine and spalleh weed, stopped his macai so he could check the clear space beyond it before he tried to cross it. It was a small meadow with a muddy pond at the northern end, a stream meandering in and out of it, another grove on the far side. The magnified sun had dried the grass to spindly yellow tufts, withered the weeds down low so he could see knobs and lengths of white bone everywhere. After a minute's thought he realized where he was. This was where Pan Pen had wiped out nearly two hundred of the False Marn's reserves. He slid from the saddle and led the macain into the meadow, picking his way cautiously through the leg bones and skulls. The blue haze shimmering above the trees ahead convinced him he'd got as close to the army as he wanted, so he decided to camp for the night. There was plenty of water for the mac and the bones didn't bother him; he was used to the dead and they were a clean lot now, the bugs had seen to that.

It took most of the next day to catch up with the Taken army again. He didn't understand why until he climbed a tree and used the longglass. Even when the sun was gone and he could only see them because of the blue shine, they kept on walking; they must have been going without a stop since they left camp. "You'd think they'd fall down dead," he said aloud. "Why don't they?"

It was that haze, he decided finally. Looked like it took the place of sleep and food and water. He watched for almost an hour, then he climbed down from the tree and set about making camp. The blue visible in the west bothered him, but it kept shrinking and by the time he was ready to eat, the night was more like those he was used to, no strange lights in the sky.

Much later he sat staring into the coals of the small fire, listening to the sounds his macain made as they nibbled at the sun-cured grass and browsed at the brush. There didn't seem to be much real point in trailing the Taken back to Dander/Calanda. He'd seen all he needed to and might as well circle round them, get there first. If he could. Warn the Web and get the news to the Marn. He brooded at the coals for a while longer, then dumped dirt on them and rolled up in his blanket for the collection of night-mares he called sleep.

4

LEAVING ANKHOLD

When the army began its march south, K'vestmilly Vos chose to ride for a short time, preferring the clean air to the fug beneath the canvas of her wagon. Before she passed into the forest around the Hold, she looked back. Pan Ank was standing at the window of his Gatehouse, watching the army march away. She lifted a hand, waved to him. *Bless that kink that scared him out of coming. Agoraphobia, Heslin called it. Maiden's Gift, I say.*

As the mass of men and women poured into the Trees, they started singing. Baby in a sling resting on her hip, Tingajil was riding up near the head of the army, playing her lute, two drummers marching beside her. The song spread out from her, across the army.

> *Marching marching*
> *Sons of Cadander*
> *Glory in our sights*
> *High hills and broad plains*
> *Fighting for our rights. . . .*

The rest had reenergized her people. Sleep, enough food and water, time to make repairs on boots, sandals, clothing, time to do laundry so they started off clean from the skin out. It'd be another twenty days till they could see the chimneys of Steel

Point—if everything went right. But it was all down-hill. Easier on the men, easier on the stock. And the river was close enough there'd always be water.

Marching marching
Sons of Cadander. . . .

The morning was young, the sun still not clear of the peaks, but it was already starting to get hot. By mid-afternoon there wouldn't be any singing. *One blessing, Ank says the Majilarn don't attack when the heat is at its worst. And we can use the river as a moat to the west. Once we get to the river road. Vedouce said, maybe an hour, hour and a half. We'll get some sniping, probably they'll try for the stragglers, cut them off, kill them, loot . . . the meien know the Majilarn, so do our new re-cruits . . . Blesken was almost grinning at the thought of trapping them . . . Mad's Tits, I don't understand them . . . zdra zdra, I don't really need to, not now.*

5

CALANDA

Tomal hid the supplies and turned the macain loose, then crept through the wasteland outside Calanda, slipped into the city as the sun began to slide behind the roofs of Dander across the river.

The streets were empty except for a few hollow-faced men who walked with their heads down, their eyes on the paving as they hurried from one doorway to another. There were no beggars with their rattling cups and their cries of tové tové. No old women with brooms sweeping debris and dirt from the pavement.

No whores. None of the street boys who used to swarm through the market crowds, begging, thieving, wringing payoffs from the merchants so they'd go away. The shops were shut, their windows gray with dust.

Even the crazies were gone.

There used to be lines of flagellants snaking through just about every street, chanting that kazim kazim kazim and swinging their polythonged whips over one shoulder, then the other, the metal bits and broken glass knotted into the thongs drawing blood with each blow.

There used to be scores of ecstatic dancers, men and women gone blind with Glory, whirling round and round, knives in both hands, striking at random.

Belly tight with fear, he slipped through the shadows next the walls, darting across streets and open spaces; he could feel eyes on him, though no one called to him, or tried to stop him.

The warrens felt empty, though a few faint gleams of candlelight struggled out from rooms deep inside. Windows were broken and unrepaired, not even a board nailed over the openings. The paint that used to be washed clean each week and renewed each year by the Marn's Painters was dingy now, peeling and cracking. There were piles of refuse and other debris in the doorways. Except in the Shipper's Quarter, warreners used to have pride in their buildings; it looked like that was gone, too.

Across the river a pall of black smoke hung over Dander, heaviest over the Temple. Tomal's eyes watered and his stomach heaved each time a gust of wind blew traces of that smoke into his face with its reek of rancid fat and roasted meat.

He reached the Mid-Calanda warren, scrambled through one of the broken windows and crouched in the abandoned apartment, gathering his resolution to continue. It was months since he'd been here, anything could have happened to Striza Brodnan who used to be a healer at the Pevranamist Clinic and now was Spider One, director of the Web. He hoped she was all right. He liked her almost as much as he'd liked old Husenkil.

As the sun vanished and the dark thickened, he chewed over his choices. He could spend the night in here, hungry but safe, slip out of the city come morning, head for Ankland on foot or maybe he could steal a boat, he was a river rat and knew enough to get a sail up. Pokad and Lehky Azheva and the rest should be close to AnkHold by now. If the chovan hadn't got them. They could get word to Heslin about what happened to the False Marn's army. He listened for the tramp of the city guard, but all he heard was the furtive scuttle of rats and now and then the rasping call of wood beetles. But they wouldn't know about the blue haze or what happened to that army.

When night was settled over the city, he took his sandals off and slipped from the apartment. He listened a moment, then started climbing the stairs to the third floor, walking next to the wall to avoid creaking boards. It was so quiet in here that the soft pat of his bare feet sounded like drumbeats in his ears.

When he reached the third floor, he counted the doors as he passed them, stopped in front of the fifth. He squeezed his eyes shut, then opened them wide, ground his teeth, knocked gently against the panels, three-one-three.

He started breathing again when he saw Striza Brodnan's long thin face.

She raised her brows, beckoned him inside.

6

MARCHING TO CALANDA

The army spread out as it moved along easier ground, but it kept the pattern Vedouce had drilled into his trivuds' heads. The supply wagons were imbedded in the center of the foot soldiers, along with the women with older children. The mounted navstas were detached islands on both sides, three navstas bringing up the rear to fight off attacks by the Majilarn following them. The women in Valiva's force marched near the rear in three navstas of their own, armed and angry enough to tear apart any Majilarn who got close enough. The mein and gyes rode scout in bands of four, with horns to alert the navstas if they saw threats coming up on the main force.

An hour in the saddle was all K'vestmilly Vos could manage; the heat and strain were making her dizzy so she transferred to her wagon. After she dealt with the pressure in her bladder, she stripped to her shift so Olmena could sponge her to a momentary coolness while Cumura fanned her. There wasn't a trace of a breeze under the heavy canopy of the huge old trees; the coolness that the shadow under the trees had promised turned out to be an illusion.

She lay on the sweat-soaked mattress and let her mind linger over the bathroom in the suite Ank had put at her service, the huge tub with its bright tiles, the taps that brought water at the touch of a finger, hot water and cold, the rose-scented soap, the oils that Cumura had rubbed into her skin until she felt like purring. Clean hair that smelled like herbs instead of sweat and smoke and urine. Hands softened by oil and pinkly clean. Heslin's hand, clean, nails buffed, gentle, knowing. . . . *When this is over,* she thought, *I'm going to build a public bath house. And find a norid or whatever they call themselves now to keep it clean. And clean up the river . . . so much to do. . . .*

Her mind drifted from subject to subject until it wandered into sleep.

They set up the Marn's tent inside a circle of wagons at the heart of the camp.

Dressed in a robe of coarse linen, her hair brushed back from her face and tied with a linen cord, a wall of canvas between her and the people waiting for her, she stood in the bedroom section staring down at the Mask in her hand. She didn't want to go out there but she knew she had to. Osk was there and Vedouce and the meie Synggal, they all wanted to talk to her. Heslin too but he'd be back in the shadows. *Mad's Tits, pulling on me like pups suckling on their dam.* She could hear noises coming muted through the canvas; she shook her head, brushed at her mouth and eyes, settled the Mask in place and went out.

Heslin was sitting on a stool by the folding table. The com was lying on the table; for the first time in days the Web was reporting.

" . . . what Tomal said. The Taken force will be here by tomorrow, probably sometime mid-afternoon. The Enemy is sustaining them now, I don't know what will happen when the haze is taken away. Could be nothing, could be they fall down dead. Go."

"Is Tomal with you now? If so, let me talk to him. Go."

"Tomal here. Go."

"Exactly what happened when you saw the first saw the blue haze? Was what happened different for the chovan and the Bezhvali and the Taken? Go."

K'vestmilly settled onto the cushioned folding chair the Hold carpenters had made for her, waved away the others and listened as Heslin took the boy through an exhaustive description of everything he'd seen and experienced on his journey from OskHold.

"Tomal, good work. Let me talk to Spider One. Go."

"Spider One here. Go."

"You know the Calanda Chitelhall. Would it be out of the question for someone to get into the bell tower, watch the return from there and report what he sees as it's happening?"

"The Chitelhall is shut up, there aren't any chitveks any longer, those that weren't Taken, they've all been sent south to work the farms. The problem is the streets are empty after dark, anyone moving about is game to the Purgers and there are always eyes watching in the daylight, mouths ready to whisper your business to a Gloryman. And anyone who goes up there might get trapped there, end up on a Temple Glory pyre, burning alive so his screams will be a hymn to Glory. I advise against it, Heslin. Very seriously. Go."

"Can you suggest an alternative? Go."

"It's difficult, I ... zdra, Tomal, you can speak. Heslin, the boy insists on offering himself. I want to remind you he hasn't been in Calanda for months. Things have changed. Go."

"Spider One, I'll remember that and weigh it carefully. Tomal, go."

"Heslin, isn't a bad thing I been away. Isn't gonna

be nobody lookin for me, won't be nobody runnin to a Gloryman when I'm not where I'm s'posed to be. Din't have no trouble gettin here, if I leave right now, I could take me some water'n biscuits and get up there and stay till army comes into town. Be safer too with so many new faces hangin in streets, nobody gonna notice me when I come down again. Go."

"Spider One, Tomal's right, he'll actually be safer tucked away like that. Tell you what. We need to know how many men will be coming at us and what shape they'll be in, but it'll be a while yet before we need to use that information. Tomal can get back to you after the Taken are in the city and settled, make his report then. I know what you want to say, Spider One, but the times make men and his years aside, Tomal is very much a man. We've talked long enough. Out."

7

THE BELL TOWER OF THE CHITELHALL

Tomal crouched beside the mouth of the huge bell, rested the longglass on the ledge of one of the tall narrow openings and focused on the front rank of the Taken. They looked like corpses marching, but they weren't gaunt as he'd expected. If anything they seemed plumper, juicier than when they started the long march. He scowled, shifted the viewfield and tried to find one of the chovan to see how they'd fared.

The haze was too thick and they were still too far away for good viewing. He couldn't see past the first few rows of marchers, and they were all Taken.

He watched as the leading edge of the blue bubble that covered them got closer and closer and wondered if it was going to come on into town. He didn't know why, but he didn't expect that.

The shadows were getting long. Out in the river, the nixies were clustering on the west shore making their glubbing, gobbling sounds, rocking, shaking, tearing down the last remnants of the wharves that used to line the west bank where Pan Nov had his warehouses; they were louder than he'd ever heard them. More of them too. Hardly seemed like there was room left for fish.

He blinked.

The blue was gone. Between one breath and the next it had vanished.

No change in the Taken. They kept marching toward Calanda, faces like wooden dolls, legs clicking off the paces with the steadiness of a clock's pendulum.

The chovan were easy to spot with their beards, bad teeth, scars, fingers missing. Wooden dolls like the Taken. Before they'd had a savage individuality; that was gone now, wiped away like the dirt would be wiped away with a wet soapy rag. When Tomal saw that, he pressed his hand against his stomach and swallowed hard.

He kept watching, trying to find some effect from two weeks of marching without food, water or rest.

Nothing. The men might have spent the weeks asleep in bed.

They came flooding into Calanda, packing the streets around the bridge. It took the rest of the afternoon to get them across the river and into Dander, but by nightfall they were camped on the slopes around the Pevranamist; he could see the red of their campfires, flecks of light like the mountain had measles.

He folded the longglass, rolled in his blanket and settled himself to sleep until it was time to creep down from the tower and get back to Spider One with his report.

8

ON THE MARCH TO CALANDA

On the ninth day of the march south the army left the Majilarn behind and moved into an oddly peaceful time as if they walked through dream, not reality. The farm houses they passed were deserted, with an ancient look to them as if they'd been deserted for decades instead of a few months, left to rot back to the earth they'd been built on.

K'vestmilly Vos rode for an hour each day. The macai was very gentle with her, patient, nuzzling at her when she struggled into the saddle, then pacing with an exaggerated smoothness as if it realized how close she was to term. She was in an odd mood also. No fussing, no flashes of anger, just a patient, remote serenity. A waiting.

On the twenty-fifth day of the march south she rode over the summit of a small rocky rise, saw the great gray hulks of the Steel Point mills and felt her first labor pain.

And heard the first shots as navstas of False Marn's army poured into the rolling wasteland and began the attack.

19. The Last Rush Begins

1

THE OUTLANDS, BAGKLOUSS

Dark and light howled round Serroi.

Except for the times that Charody or Treshteny touched her, touches that she felt as if through a dozen layers of blanket, she might have been drifting alone in the middle of a stormy sea at midnight.

She heard things that might have been words aimed at her, but the sounds were too quickly absorbed in the storm whirling round her for her to decipher what was being said. There was one blessing to this—the shouts and whines of the Fetch no longer reached her.

And all this was nothing before the NEED that consumed her. The need to touch. To heal what was wrong with the All.

2

ON THE RIM OF THE YTAMA ROUND

Halison knelt beside Hedivy, shook him awake.

He sat up, looked blearily at her. "What is it?"

"We'll be moving soon. Help me get the macain saddled."

"It's down?" He jumped to his feet, swore as he

saw the fugitive air-ripples that marked the presence of the Barrier. "What are you talking about?"

"I've had a warning. We need to be ready when it's time."

The Spirit Readers were sitting in a circle, faces intent. They weren't saying anything, but he got the feeling they were busy at something he didn't want to know about. The sprite was a shimmer circling overhead. The macain had stopped their grazing and were huddled together, heads bobbing, legs working nervously, extruded claws digging up clods of the hard soil. The dust they threw up hovered briefly, then settled back to earth.

"Them." He used his chin to point at Tserama and the others. "They right about what's coming? Some sort of vychin God battle?"

"Why ask me?"

He scowled at her, willing her to answer.

She shrugged. "A ReUnion, I'd say. Sundered parts coming together."

"What's that mean?"

"A mess." She wrinkled her nose. "Three Pans arguing over where a property line goes."

"Ah. That I know."

Honeydew felt the wind freshen, the air under her wings grow more turbulent. As she fought her way down, meaning to rest on the back of one of the macain, she saw the barrier start to glow, an oval of shining green glass, Serroi's green. *S'ramee, Hallee, something's happening, do you see it, do you?*

The barrier vibrated, began to move, inching across the uneven land, moving through brush as if it didn't exist, leaving it spring-green on the far side as if it healed the wear of winter and dryseason with that pass.

Hedivy swung into the saddle, looked up and held out his hand.

Honeydew swooped down onto it, climbed his arm and settled on his shoulder. She patted his ear to say thanks and mourned once again that he couldn't understand her when she tried to talk to him.

The barrier moved at a brisk walk across the land. There was no stopping, no resting, nor much choice of where macain or Spirit Readers had to walk, though it did avoid the deeper ravines.

When the barrier ceased moving at sundown, by accident or plan, it penned them beside a spring with plenty of graze and browse for the beasts.

Honeydew spiralled upward, slipped off the wind in her surprise as she saw what was around them. She caught herself, darted down to land on Halisan's shoulder. Hallee, Youmbards. Campfires all over the place. Honeydew count five, ten, lots and lots.

"So there are, Honey. Don't worry, they don't know we're here."

"They?" Hedivy looked up from the saddle he was working on, repairing a rip in one of the stirrup leathers. "They who?"

"Youmbards, Hev. Honeydew says there's a small army of them out there."

He stared at her a moment, then went back to what he'd been doing.

Hev is mad again. Honeydew sighed.

"He doesn't like being penned up, you know," Halisan murmured, keeping her voice low so Hedivy wouldn't hear.

Honeydew knows. Hallee knows where Serree is?

"We'll meet when it's time, Honey. We're going to the same place for the same reason."

The muttering from her nine Sem Ris filled Tserama's head and their weight was heavy on her shoulders. Her Sem Ris were getting hotter and tetchier; rubbing up against each other like this was not good for them. Much longer and there'd be a Spirit war as bad, if not worse, than the Thamyo Juggyal. The Juggyal was just gods fighting, if the Sem Ris started trying to eat each other, they'd eat the world first.

Images from all her Sem Ris were pouring into her head, they were sinking their claws into her, demanding she sort them. Sort now. Now. Now. The word was a hammer beating at her. But there was no time for Chastening the Story, there was no garos to give her strength, only walking and a weariness that ate into her bones.

Honeydew slept in fits and starts. Each time she woke, she saw Halisan sitting in the center of a white shimmer as if she'd gathered moonlight into a cloak and drawn it about herself. Hedivy prowled restlessly about the circle, a shadow as massive as Halisan was delicate. The circle of Spirit Readers flickered with touches of what looked like firelight, red and yellow licking shadows from the hollows under their brows, the deeply incised lines about their eyes, the lines running from the prominent noses they all shared to the corners of their different mouths. They swayed in unison, humming a dreary dirge that sounded even more ominous than the prophecy they'd chanted before the moving started.

4

THE OUTLANDS, BAGKLOUSS

Serroi felt her macai stop walking; he shuddered under her, humped his back, fighting the grip on his halter. The bitter orange glow told her it was Charody standing there. She shuddered under her own urge to keep going, the Pull was a torment that never left her; she didn't try fighting it any longer, she wanted this confrontation. She needed it.

"Charody," she said. "I can't stop, I'll take care of the mac, you can camp if you want, come after me later." Her voice came to her ears with so many echoes that she couldn't be sure she was actually saying what she meant. She heard/felt a vibration that might be someone talking at her, shook her head. "Don't say things to me, I can't hear you. There's too much noise in my head."

The macai trembled as the orange light moved away from his head, then resumed his ground shifting long-walk. *Soon*, she thought. *Live or die, this will be finished.*

Treshteny watched the strain dissolve from Serroi's face as Charody stepped aside. She remembered the chaos she'd felt the last time she touched the Healer, a blindness where nothing had shape. Terrifying. The confusion of her own vision was nothing compared to that.

Unlike Serroi, what she saw grew less complex with every day that passed. The blur of past/present/

future was folding into itself; she was being locked into the *now* that everybody saw.

The waning day was bright, the sun still hot, the mountains so close now she could see conifers growing like blue fur across the lower slope, could see the black rock and white snow on the peaks. The air smelled of dust and dead things, withered leaves, herbs, yellow broom and the small, white flowers growing on bushes that hugged the ground, sweet odor, so sweet it was almost unendurable.

Doby and Charody rode in front of her; they were solid and commonplace, an old woman and a child. It was comforting to keep her eyes on them, almost as comforting as the feel of Yela'o curled up against her, sleeping deeply, his breath a warm patch beneath her breast.

Horse, though, was starting to feel strange to her in a way he never had, as if he were finally moving apart from her, even though she sat on his back as she had for so many many days and miles. In his black sicamar form Adlayr loped along beside Horse; the kinship was strong between them. Made her jealous to feel it. She didn't like that, but like didn't change anything.

She glanced over her shoulder at Serroi, looked quickly away. In one sense, the little healer's face hadn't changed, but in another, looking at it was like looking into the sun, not exactly frightening, but hard on the eyes.

She missed the premoaning and the manyness that, despite its terrors and distractions, did give her some notion of events that lay ahead of her and what their roots were in the past. If this was how most people lived their lives, she didn't want it. She wriggled restlessly in the cradle Horse made for her, putting folds in his soft, loose skin and grazing his sides with her heels.

He snorted, curled his neck in an impossibly tight curve and took her leg in his mouth, just above the ankle where the calf began its swell. He bit down hard enough to be felt, but not enough to break the skin, then reassembled himself and went plodding on.

She stayed still after that.

There were ariels overhead, the air was thick with them. As the sun vanished they flushed crimson, delicate crimson flower figures with dangling tendrils—stranger far than the human form up north. Treshteny only called them ariels because they floated like the others and usually were the same glimmering golden color. As the night settled over the riders, the ariels began to release the sunlight they'd collected during the day, turning the night yellow, bright.

The brus kept coming, until they carpeted the ground, small spirit creatures shimmering and glimmering in the light from the ariels. Flocks of shapsas came from the trees and clouds, chattering and darting about, diving at the brus, curvetting around the ariels. There were other spirits more felt than seen. Treshteny caught glimpses of forms that melted into air almost as soon as she saw them. And there things like huge tumbleweeds rolling up behind them— dangerous, hot and angry, with the ozone smell of a thunderstorm as it was setting up.

All night, as they moved deeper and deeper into the foothills, climbing over the roots of the peak ahead of them, a jagged dagger of black and white twice as tall as the other Ashtops, the feeling of danger kept building.

Morning came with no release as the eastern sky went gray then pink, then flared crimson.

Serroi cried out, kicked her mount into a stumbling run though an impossible maze of boulders and lava columns.

On a flat open shelf surrounded by silent conifers, she pulled up, slid from the saddle and stood facing the mouth of a cave.

20. Dance Down the Stars

1

BAGKLOUSS

Perched on Hedivy's shoulder, Honeydew clutched at the wiry red curls of his beard, shivering as the barrier darkened and howled like a storm wind whooooming around them. The air was so heavy she almost couldn't breathe; her wings hurt from the pressure, she was going to be crushed if it didn't let up, whatever this was that was happening.

She rubbed sweat from her eyes, watched Halisan riding up near the front curve of the green oval, guiding her macai with her knees, her hands busy with the harp she balanced on the saddle ledge. Honeydew heard snatches of the music—an eerie, rather frightening music—rippling phrases snatched up and swallowed by the barrier's wail.

Hedivy fought to control his mount; the beast was rolling its eyes, humping its back, snapping its long limber neck against the reins, trying to break them or drag them from his hands.

Whenever he could free his attention from the mac, he looked at the mountain ahead, gazed at it and wanted it, wanted it so badly his body clenched in knots. Mount Santak. He knew by the heat in his bones that they were almost to the cave. That *she* was close. The enemy. The Prudjin. So close he could

SMELL her. He touched the youmbard's knife in the shoulder belt. So close.

Tserama walked behind the riders, shoulders rounded under the weight of the Sem Ris she was pulling along with her. Beside her the other Spirit Readers bent forward, bowed down like her under the same or an even greater burden. "We bind and bear," she chanted with the others, each foot coming down on the stressed word, swinging forward on the others.

We bind and bear	the Sem Kun Zi
Unwind unswear	the nine Sem Ri
So blind and fair	from Hill gone free
The Juggyal dare	that life may be . . .

The barrier vanished.

The noise vanished—except for the spectral sounds from Halisan's harp, sounds that welled up louder and louder until they filled the space under the sky.

Howls. Shots rattling like maize kernels popping in hot oil.

On every side youmbards burst from brush and trees, came riding recklessly down the slopes, whooping as they saw their targets, shooting as they came, racing toward the foreigners—the Jeboh's gold would go to those who got the ears to prove the kills.

The Sem Ris of the Five Rounds growled their rage—a sound that was not a sound, not heard, only felt—a sound that drove the youmbards' horses and macain into terrified flight, that rolled their riders from their saddles and sent them thrashing about on the ground—a sound that twisted and warped the air until currents writhed like mating serpents so even those who were still standing and shooting missed every target they tried for.

The Sem Ris' growl grew louder and angrier.

Hot spots reddened, burst into flame.

Brush caught fire, the flames went rushing away from a calm center where a small woman stood facing a cave.

Tserama and her sisters turned away from the cave, standing in a semicircle at the edge of the storm, hand in hand they stood, chanting, trying to retain a measure of control on the huge and angry spirits, making sure they vented their wrath outward, at the youmbards and the prowling Ashtoppers lured here by the scent of loot and death.

Something came from the cave.

A white light burning brighter than the sun, with a core that seemed solid fire.

The Prudjin in her Power.

"MOTH TH THER." The shout echoed off the mountains, faded into the wind.

Serroi lifted her head. "No," she said. "I am not. I will not accept this."

"It ISSSS!"

"NO."

As she shouted the denial, Serroi felt the enormous power of the Prudjin, felt the Child's mind wielding it, bright and ignorant young girl, with a baby's greeds and needs and no experiences to temper these. "No," she repeated more quietly. "So much pain, so much anger. You destroy. You can't do that." She took a step toward the Light, her hands outstretched, glowing green. Ariels, brus, all the lands spirits came swirling around her, merging into gold light, silver light, maelstrom of light, round and round, plunging into her. Pain. Burning. Her power, that had been as natural to her as breathing, expanded enormously until she wondered if her skin could contain it. She took another step.

Hedivy gave over trying to control the macai, slid from the saddle and began wading toward the cave through the conflicting currents of air. The earth rolled and shifted like water under his feet and the pressure of the outflowing wind was enormous.

Each step was a battle and the slippage underneath his feet meant any gains he made were only inches; more often than not he lost ground. He touched the hilt of the knife and jerked his hand away from the heat that bit at him. Metal. Steel. It was holding him back, he knew that suddenly. Growling like the Sem Ris he ripped off the belt and let it drop. *Don't need steel. Got my hands.*

Bit by bit he stripped off everything he wore and with each discard, he gained more ground. Bit by bit until he was walking naked as Adlayr-sicamar and nearly as dangerous.

Honeydew screamed as the air currents caught her and ripped her from Hedivy's shoulder.

She went tumbling over and over, driven toward one of the fires though she fought the wind, frantically pumping her wings. Then Adlayr-trax was between her and the fire. She banged into him, clutched at his thick black fur and managed to cling to his neck as he fought the winds back toward the cave.

* * *

In the island of peace in the midst of the noise and confusion, Mama Charody turned to Doby. "Wait here," she said. "Don't worry yourself about any of it. It's going to get strange, but you'll be all right." She caught hold of Treshteny's hand and went striding toward Serroi.

Doby didn't believe her, but there was nothing else he knew to do, so he squatted where she left him. A moment later Yela-o came over and crouched against him and he felt a little better. Then Horse came, lay down beside them and made himself into a furry cushion for them to lean against. A moment later the Adlayr-trax plowed beak first into the ground beside them, shifted to sicamar and with Honeydew clinging to his shoulders, threw himself down beside Horse and lay there panting, his sides working like bellows, hot amber-green eyes fixed on Serroi.

Mama Charody grunted, stepped around Serroi, Treshteny walking silent beside her. "Ours, Healer. Stay back a while."

Charody and Treshteny and the Prudjin faced each other in a whirling dance, round and round in a triple spiral that took them closer, closer, closer though they never quite touched.

They grew tall and translucent, till it was a dance of glass giants, stamping, swaying to the music from Halisan's harp.

The sun went out.

Stars shone briefly in the sable sky, then fell like silver rain.

2

BOKIVADA, SHIMZELY

The room went suddenly dark as if clouds too opaque to let any light through had blown across the face of the sun. Chaya set the shuttle down and went outside, stepping through the door in time to see the stars rain down.

The tall thin guard came round the side of the house and stopped beside her. As always he wore metal and worn leather, had his longgun slung by its strap over his shoulder; his gray-streaked black hair was blowing in the sudden wind coming off the bay to tear the leaves about and send grit pinging into the walls. She looked at him a moment, looked back at the sky. "What is it? Do you know?"

His rusty voice almost lost in the whine of the wind, he said, "No, it's not something I've seen before. I've never seen the stars fall."

"I wish Halisan were here. She'd know." She shivered. "I'd better go home. Lavan will be worried."

3

BISERICA

Nine veiled women walked into the inner court of the Biserica Temple.

Nischal Tay bowed, as did Greygen while Sansilly dropped a curtsey, then looked at the Shawar from the corner of her eye.

The sun was directly overhead, its outline shivery silver as it had been for months now.

Nine veiled women walked in a circle, their silent chant louder than a shout in Sansilly's ears. It made her head ache and put ice in her belly as she waited to see why they'd called her and Greygen to the court.

The sun went black in a blackened sky.

The stars came out, shimmered for a moment then fell in a silver rain and there was nothing but darkness left.

4

BAGKLOUSS

"Ah!" Serroi spoke aloud, though her voice was lost in the music. "I see. I understand. Mad Shar the Poet's line, *Maiden, Matron and Crone, severed and severally dangerous.*"

All she had experienced since she wakened coalesced in her and she did understand. "Balance is all. Severally dangerous, but merged, the Whole is complete."

She walked a circle round the dancers and watched them wind into a column of twisted dark and light.

She reached out, put a hand on the dark, put a hand on the light. "Balance is all," she said, and she *healed*. The force she'd absorbed flowed out of her.

The column vanished.

The black sky flipped and was blue again, the sun was shining through the translucent figure of the Maiden who stood, immense and lovely in the form of the images she'd seen all her life. The great face looked down at her and smile, then *changed*.

It blurred, then divided, divided again. Three faces, three bodies melded into one; Maiden, Matron, Crone. One hand held a skull, the other a branch with leaves just sprouting.

Face set, beard smoldering, skin blackening from the Sem Ris' heat, Hedivy fought forward step by step, labored past Horse and the others, reddened eyes fixed on the mutating form of the God.

Charody, dark and root-like, came forth. She moved over to Doby, touched his head, shook hers when he started to speak.

Treshteny came forth, translucent at first as if she were one of the might-be ghosts she'd seen so many times. Trembling a little, she took a step. With each step she was more solid, more mortal. By the third step she was smiling. She held out her arms, Yela'o leaped into them. Cuddling him, she turned and watched the last of the triad emerge.

The Prudjin was a girl not many years past puberty, naked, gaunt and filthy, twigs and dirt in her hair.

She stared up a moment at SHE Who Was Three. She looked down at herself, gazed around at those watching her.

It took several minutes for her to understand she'd lost everything. When she did, she shrieked, leaped at Serroi, fire kindling about her hands.

Hedivy came plunging past Serroi, caught the girl's neck and head in his hands, twisted. . . . He looked at what he held, flung the body away. He squatted, rubbed his hands on the withered grass, then got to his feet. He stared at Serroi a moment, then walked away. After a few strides he started running. In moments he was out of sight.

SHE Who Is Three grew shorter and more solid. SHE spread her hands, leaned forward.

"Go home," SHE called to the youmbards. Her words rang like bronze bells and echoed back from the slopes around her. SHE breathed on the youmbards and they vanished.

"Go home," SHE called to the Sem Ris and the Spirit Readers. Her breath licked over them and they vanished.

"Go home," SHE said to Charody, Treshteny and the others, her voice gentler, silver bells this time. "With Our Blessing for your pain and endurance." Her breath touched them and they were gone.

The Triune God shrank smaller still, reached out a hand, touched Serroi, filling her with the warmth she felt after she healed and Earth returned the energy she'd spent. "Teach the balance," SHE said. "Comfort Our children." SHE bent lower and blew gently in Serroi's face.

21. The Fall and Rise of Cadander

1

***WEB MEETING WAREHOUSE
ON THE DANDER SIDE OF THE RIVER.***

"Even the Chovan?"

Byssa Klidina twisted her hands in the apron she wore cleaning the kitchens in the Pevranamist. The flickering light from the single stubby candle set in a pie tin on the floor deepened the lines of weariness in her long face, making it plainer than ever.

"That's what Tomal said." Striza Brodnan ran her finger through the dust on the broken crate where she sat, inspected the smear on the tip. "Nesmel told me he's seen them. He picked up a few days unloading barges and he's working now, that's why he's not here. He says they're not like the other Taken, they don't talk at all, mostly what they do is sit. They're like wild things put in a cage—you know, the kind that stare and won't eat."

Liskan Pulhodny tapped his fingers on his thigh, stared past the others into the dark between the bales and crates. "And she Took them clear over to OskHold. Which brings up a question. If she can do that, why does she need an army?"

Bakory Comneron stretched, then leaned against the stack of crates behind her. "Yes. Why bother?"

Striza nodded. "When I heard that, I wondered why go on trying." She shrugged. "Nesmel says he thinks she needs a focus. Sun doesn't burn things, he said, but if you hold the right lens at the right angle you can start a fire. He says maybe she needs a lot of Taken around to do what she did at OskHold."

Liskan rubbed at his sandy mustache, nodded. "Sounds right to me. I talked to some bargeveks who saw the Turning of the Taken at the end of the Gritz war. From what they said, nothing much happened until everyone was relaxed, drunk or asleep. Patch that in with Tomal's story, looks like she needs not just some Taken to focus through, but pretty relaxed ones, not men about to get their heads shot off."

"Zdra, maybe so." Striza looked from face to face, pale blurs barely visible in the light of that guttering candlestub. "Plenty of them in the cities these days. Which brings up why I called this meeting. What with the Marn marching at us and Motylla choking down on the chovan, we might just face being Taken and sent out to fight our own. Byssa, what's Motylla like these days? Do you think she might grab everyone soon as the shooting starts?"

Byssa smoothed out the wrinkles in the apron, slipped it off and began folding it, her eyes unfocused. "She's been odder than usual the last few weeks. She had old Domcevek Pato hung from his ankles till his heart burst. Probably irritated her some way, he was a miserable old vych. Another time she set ten of the manservants to digging up the court where Nov had all those people shot and buried where they fell. She made them clean up the skeletons, boil them, then had the bones strung together, skeleton by skeleton, and hung from the ceiling in the Setkan. Her councilors she calls them." She set the small bundle on the floor beside her, shivered, folded her hands in her lap. "She took me in there day before yesterday. She talks to them. And she has this stick, she plays tunes on their ribs and legbones. The way she looked at me sometimes that day . . . a kind of measuring as if she was wondering what *my* bones would look like . . . zdra, it about scared me out of my skin. If she gets to feeling pressed . . . or if she just takes a notion to do it . . . she might decide she wants us all . . . she might not want to take the trouble . . . zdra zdra, there's no way anyone could guess how she's going to jump."

Vynda Angliet, in gentler times a Temple Setra, drew her feet up, patted her hair and said in her precise soft voice, "That is the question, is it not? Would it be best for us to try creeping from the city or to dig a hole and pull the hole in over us? If we stay, perhaps nothing happens, perhaps we are Taken. If we run, perhaps we will manage to reach the Marn's Army, perhaps we will be killed. If we do reach the army, perhaps we will be killed in the fighting. Me, I vote we get the zhag out of here."

"Is it all or none?" Byssa didn't wait for an answer. "I'm staying. Motylla likes me around. If I had to guess, I'd say there are shadows of the child left behind that False Mask, memories of her father wanting me about so he could feel magnanimous and powerful. And there's a chance . . ." she paused, licked her lips, "a remote chance, I must admit, that I could repeat Lehky Azheva's trick and slip a knife where it'll do some good. Even if I missed my hit, I might distract her enough to let the Marn close in."

Liskan leaned forward. "I'm for getting out. Nothing more I can do here, except like Vynda said, dive in a hole. Zachal . . ." He jerked a thumb toward an aisle between the piles of crates where Spider Four stood guard. "He wants out, we've talked things over. He feels like me."

"Nesmel and I did our talking last night. We'd rather be killed clean than run the chance of being Taken." Striza straightened her back, squared her shoulders. "Byssa, you're sure?"

"I'm sure."

"Then you'd best be going now. Do you understand?"

Byssa scooped up the folded apron, got to her feet. "I do. What I don't know, I can't tell should I lose the throw. Maiden Bless you all, it's been a grand run so far."

When she was gone, Striza slid off the crate and knelt beside the candle, beckoning the others to move in closer. "There's this barge Nesmel helped empty day before yesterday, it's being provisioned for a trip back downriver. There's a Taken on board as watchman to keep the rivergangs out of the supplies. Nesmel's been watching him. He comes up, takes a leak off the back of the barge same time every night so far. Liskan, you still got that crossbow? Good. Here's what we've worked out. . . ."

2

WASTELAND NORTH OF STEEL POINT

Tomal's voice came small and tinny through the com. ". . . loading men and horses on barges, three almost ready to go. If the wind holds steady they'll be passing you by nightfall. Five more barges being fixed up. Shot one of the owners when he tried to tell them to get lost. Others got the message, they're tailing out down the Southroad. Calanda-side, I can see a bunch going into the mills, mean to use them as forts or maybe as a staging point. And about ten navstas moving into the waste, heading your way. Way they're moving, they're about three hours off yet. That's it on movements for now. Something else. Go."

Heslin finished his notes, tore the sheet off the pad, handed it to one of the runners, a young girl, nine or ten, no more. He didn't have to say anything, she was out of the wagon and on her way to Vedouce before he'd pulled his hand in.

"Message off, what else, Tomal? Go."

"Me, I'm staying to spot movements for you, but the Web's peeling out tonight. Taking over a barge. Look for it after the Dancers are down. They'll hang a towel over the portside rail, expect a greeting party third landing past Steel Point. The greeters should have white strips tied round the arms. The Word is Spider One's given name, the Response is the family name. Out."

Heslin glanced at the next blinking light to see which scout it was. "Four. Go."

"Six navstas. Horse. Coming from behind the Sheet Mill, circling east, half a stade from the line. Out."

He scribbled, tore off the page, held it out, thumbed the switch. "Seven. Go."

"Majilarn, about twenty, in a bunch of trees next the river. Mounted. Look like they're getting ready to charge. Yes. They're out. Valiva's spotted them, sent reinforcements to the defense levee. Going for the rambuts, looks like. Yes. Front rank's down, about four, five jumping the wounded and coming at the line, rest scrambling for cover. There's one down, two, three. One looks to be wounded, the other two're crouching behind the rambuts, shooting at the line. Ah. Two of them have reached the mound, a woman stands up, gets him round the neck with a whip, three other women're pulling the other off his rambut." A click of the speaker's tongue. "Mad's Tits, he's gone. The two behind the dead rambuts, they went creeping at the mound while the women were busy with the riders. Didn't work. One's dead, other's flopping around, looks pretty bad off. The rest are heading for the woods, looks like about half won't make it. Two dead our side, half a dozen wounded. Valiva's sending down about twenty more from her reserves, they're digging in, piling the dirt higher, setting in some stakes, wicked points those. Quiet now. Out."

The longer note went on its way, Heslin switched bands again, listened and wrote, the runners came and went, on and on without letup as the sniping and feints and skirmishes went on.

3

Concealed by the night and thick leaves in a high crotch of an ancient brellim, the last Sleykyn watched the barge nose into the landing where half a dozen dark figures were waiting, white rags tied about their arms. A short distance off another man waited with a small herd of macain.

A woman's voice came from the boat. "Striza."

A man on the landing answered. "Brodnan." He took the rope tossed to him; with the help of the men with him, he pulled the barge tight against the landing, threw a half-hitch around a bitt and extended a hand to steady the woman stepping from the barge onto the planks beside him. "Majilarn about so we'll make this fast."

The Sleykyn dropped to the ground and moved after the riders; they held the macs to a fast walk, so it wasn't hard to keep up. A shadow merging with the night, he used them to distract while he slid through the sentry lines and went to ground inside the fortifications to wait for his chance at the Marn.

4

Morning light coming gray through the gauze curtains at the front of the wagon pulled up beside the one Helsin was using, K'vestmilly Vos lay on a canvas sheet, sweat rolling into her eyes, down the side of her face; she clamped her teeth on the leather strap and endured. She'd been in labor for the past twelve hours and Olmeny had given up telling her to scream if she had to, that it would be easier if she'd let loose. All she got was a half-mad glare from those green-gray eyes and silence.

When K'vestmilly's jaw loosened, Cumura eased the strap along so a new section was in the Marn's mouth, shivering as she saw the tough leather almost cut in half. She reached for the rag and began bathing the Marn's face and neck, working down her shoulders to her arms. Before she reached the cramped hands, they were once again digging into the canvas and the Marn's teeth were clamped on the leather.

Noon heat. Crackle of longgun fire. Squeals from macain and horses. Curses and shouts from men.

The wail of a newborn broke through the silence in the wagon.

"Give her to me." K'vestmilly's voice was hoarse, hardly more than a whisper.

"In a minute, Marn, let me wash her first."

"Nik. Give her to me now."

"You still have work to do."

"I know. Do what I said."

The baby stopped crying the moment Olmeny laid her over K'vestmilly's heart; she squirmed about a moment then with a small fluttery sigh relaxed all over. K'vestmilly lifted her head and looked at her daughter, a fierce love burning through her laboring body.

She shuddered and the last bit was over.

"Send word," she whispered. "Tell Helsin he has a daughter. Tell Vedouce a Dedach is born."

5

All that day waves of the Taken came at the Army.

There was no plan to the attacks, no leader, nothing but a massed charge of trotting men, navsta on navsta attacking the south and east sides of the earthworks and the unfinished palisades Vedouce had his men working on from the moment the report came that the Taken were leaving Calanda.

They marched, shot, died, row on row of men mowed down; they came on and on, the last Taken on their feet laboring up and over those earth walls, over the stakes, into the lines of the defenders, slashing and shooting until all of them were dead—but not before they thinned the lines of the True Marn's army.

Then the next wave started forward.

And the next.

And each time they came, it was harder to stop them.

And there were always more of them—as if the sack called Cadander were a bottomless hoard of men.

The next day was the same.

And the next.

6

The fourth day of the fighting.

K'vestmilly Vos pulled her blouse down, laid Calander's new Dedach on her thighs and began rubbing the back of the four-day-old Nahera Vos, crooning softly to cover the noise of battle that reached them even here.

Olmena smiled. "She's a strong one, the little Dedach. Greedy for life."

K'vestmilly sighed, smiled. "Why do I suddenly hear my mother's voice, Mena? Saying just you wait, you'll see what I had to put up with."

The baby burped and, like a lamp blown out, the sun was gone; the darkness under the canvas was stygian.

"What? What's happening?"

"Stay where you are, Marn. I'll see." Olmeny rose to her knees, managed to turn round without kicking K'vestmilly; she thrust her head through the curtains blocking off the front of the wagon. Her voice came back, filled with astonishment and fear. "It's not clouds. Stars . . . they're falling!"

"Cumura, take the baby."

"Marn, nik, don't . . ."

"Do it."

* * *

The Mask in place, she crawled through the curtains and used the slats of the seat back to pull herself onto her feet.

It was almost as dark outside as it was under the canvas cover. The wind that touched her left side was colder than she expected, as if the winter that had been put off so long was suddenly dropping over them. She shivered, turned her head, straining to see through the muffling darkness.

On the tor above where Vedouce had his command shelter, a torch flared. It was like a knife slash across the dark and hurt her eyes. And gave her a notion that sent her heart beating furiously. She pulled her eyes away from the red fire-flower. "I know what this is. I think I know. The healer has reached the Enemy. Zasya, where are you?"

"Here, Marn." The meie's voice came from below and a short distance behind her.

"Get to Vedouce. Tell him to move now. Tell him to remember the Shawar's spell."

"I'll see if Helsin has a runner free, Marn."

K'vestmilly Vos listened to the sounds she made moving off, shivered again as the wind cut through the thin shift she was wearing, turned to go back inside.

Something brushed past her. Her skin prickled, she felt a heat that flared and vanished as if someone had thrown a burning stick past her arm.

A man screamed.

She clutched at the seat back, stared.

Ildas was stretched in a burning membrane over the face of a short, stocky man who was clawing at the Fireborn, whining with pain, going round and round in a futile dance.

The meie was there an instant later; a lunge and thrust sent the point of her sword into the man's gaping mouth, the steel going through the Fireborn's body, heated red-hot, burning up into the man's brain. She jerked the sword loose, made the clucking sound she used to call Ildas, cradled him against her as he leaped into her arms. Nose wrinkling from the stench of the charred velater helmet and mask, she looked down at the dead man. "Sleykyn," she said. "That's the last one."

She walked over to the wagon, set Ildas on the driver's seat. He was fading now, the red-gold fire vanishing. In a moment he'd be invisible to most eyes. "Go inside, Marn," she said. "Just in case."

7

IN THE MARN'S TOWER

Motylla Nov stood at a north-facing window in the room at the top of the Marn's Tower. She was alone, the False Mask tossed onto the bed; the light from the descending sun that poured through the windows behind her and filled the room was very unkind to the small scarred face. She'd had the mirrors between the windows removed so she wouldn't see her un-Masked face, even by chance. There were no mirrors anywhere in the Pevranamist.

A twinned longglass was clamped to a tripod set on the windowsill. Legs apart, her belly pressed to the wall, she gazed through the glass at the field of battle; it was a long way off, on the far side of Calanda. But the Pevranamist and this tower were built high enough on Marnhora Mount to give her a clear line of view. She watched the Taken attack and die, attack and die. For four days she'd watched her army crash against the shores of Vedouce's defence, yet nothing had changed. The rebels hung on and there seemed no way she could dislodge them.

And though her people outnumbered them, she was losing so many in those attacks that she began to doubt her ability to close her fist about the invaders and squeeze the life out of them. With Ker's death, she'd lost not only his abilities, such as they were, but the resources of Bezhval. The new Pan Ker expelled all Glorymen and shut the borders against her. No men, no supplies from there. Not any more. Pan Hal had his troubles in the Travasherrims and was ignoring her calls for men and gold while he fought to put down the guerrillas that kept striking at him all along the eastern slopes. The Zemyadel also was on the verge of mutiny; the supplies she'd ordered from Pan Ano were coming in trickles, given grudgingly. Pan Vyk and his household had fled and were in exile in the Skafarees. Pan Sko had retreated to his house and wouldn't open his door to anyone; in any case he was sucked dry, most of his people were already in her army. *I need Power. Now.*

She stepped away from the glass, moved to the broad bed, stood staring down at the white silk coverlet with its elaborate patterns of gold and silver wire, couched in place with gold and silver thread. The Mask lay in the center of a charred spot; these days it didn't try to disguise or contain its heat. Awkwardly, as if her whole body resisted her will, she reached for it and slipped it on.

Though she'd long ago lost any sense of pain, she could feel new bits of her face charring and bubbling as the horrible thing settled home.

She swayed a little, clenched her hands into fists.

"Glory," she shouted. "I'm talking to you. Listen to me."

She waited.

Since the day she'd spent herself calling the Taken home, the Glory had withdrawn from her. Where once it had cuddled and comforted her, it had turned cold and distant. She ached with loneliness and uncertainty; when the essence of the Dancer entered her, she was *changed*; her will was turned to the Glory's will and even now that ruled her, but wisps of what she had been kept brushing across her mind, tormenting her. She needed stroking. She needed the croon that told her she was loved and wanted.

For a long time there was nothing. The sun dropped behind the mountains and all but the peaks were dark—the peaks and this tower. The coverlet on the bed had streaks of red on it, red from the setting sun.

Feeling the Glory's gaze turning on her, she lifted her head, waited. Confident one breath, at the next, uncertain.

It was a cold gaze like the glance of a stranger who didn't know her and perhaps didn't want to.

The words came into her mind slowly, with an absent unconcern. *I'm busy, Dancer, with things more important than you will ever be. Don't bother me.*

Motylla cried out, grief terrible in her girl's voice.

She plucked the Mask from her face, flung it on the bed. It lay there a moment, its surface bubbling and smoking.

A flash. Like lightning striking upward.

Gone. Nothing there but a black charred spot on the bedspread.

She whimpered.

She didn't stop shaking and gasping until the sky went black.

She pulled the tripod down and climbed onto the windowsill, knelt there watching as the stars rained down.

When there was only blackness left, she leaned forward and let herself fall.

8

ON THE COMMAND TOR

K'vestmilly Vos pulled the quilt round her shoulders, but still shivered in the wind that whistled round the three-sided canvas shelter Vedouce had set up. She glanced at Cumura, who was holding the baby, whispering to her, then turned her attention back to the struggle below, leaning forward, trying to penetrate the blackness that hid the Waste and what was happening there.

Behind her she heard the tiny voice coming through the com, Heslin's muttered reports to Vedouce. Before and below her, she heard shots, screams, shouts, grunts, the sounds of men fighting hand to hand, groping for enemies because they couldn't see them.

There was a SOUND.
The sky blinked and was blue again.
Another sound—a rolling scream that ran from horizon to horizon.

She watched what was happening to the Taken and turned her head away, met Heslin's eyes and spread her hands in the Marn's Smile. "She's done it, Hes. She's stopped the Enemy. We've won."

9

INTO CALANDA

K'vestmilly Vos rode beside the wagon driver, the baby in her arms, her Mask in place; as they passed through the rags of the False Marn's army, she covered the baby's head with the blanket one of the women had knitted for her.

Some wandered aimlessly, dazed, not understanding what they were doing here. Some lay where they fell, dead from seizures or heart failure. The minds of some broke completely, though in different ways. There were those who lay like logs, alive but sealed off from the world. There were those who plucked at themselves, ridding themselves of clothes, of hair, peeling their own skin away, then their flesh down to bone. There were those that sat muttering to themselves. There were a hundred different kinds of madness, as if each man found his own way out of reality.

And there were the wounded, lying neglected—shattered arms and legs, great gaping wounds. The smell of blood was everywhere.

And there were the dead. Old, young, men in their prime. Those were hidden now. Invisible beneath hordes of scavenging trax and havrans, many of them staggering from body to body, bellies too full to fly.

She turned her head, tilted it so she could see Olmena. "As of now, Olmena Oumelic, you are chief Healer of Cadander. The Hospital is yours. Whatever resources you need, see me. I can't promise to get you everything you want, but what I can do, I will." She swallowed. "A city of ghosts, even the living are half dead. The waste. The horrible waste."

Holding the Dedach where the people could see her, weary and saddened, K'vestmilly Vos came into Calanda.

Ragged, quiet people filled the streets, coming out from warrens and shops that were as worn and dull as the people. So many of them women and children despite the unending burnings in the Temple court. Which is another thing she'd have to deal with. Some of the Glorymen, the Purgers and the Parsonas served the Enemy freely; the withdrawal wouldn't have hit them like it did the Taken. *I'll need judges,* she thought. *There have to be trials. Soon. Public as possible. Zdra, I need an Inquisitor. Hedivy would do if he were here, but I can't wait. Talk to Heslin? Ah! I know. Spider One. I'll get growls for putting a woman in the job, but she knows better than most what's been done here.* She smiled, pleased with herself. One small difficulty removed. *Step at a time,* she thought. *Keep stepping and it's all done, this generation or the next.*

When she looked down at Nahera Vos, the next generation was crumpling up her face and waving her fists about to demand her next feeding. She laughed, lifted her blouse and set Cadander's future to suck.

EPILOG

1

IN THE MARN'S TOWER

K'vestmilly Vos stood at a window in the Marn's Tower looking out over the city. Heslin stood silent behind her; the baby slept on the bed, pillows on either side of her. The lamps were lit there to give a point of hope in the devastation to the people in Dander and Calanda who were beginning to wake from nightmare. A link to old times, better times.

"I'm so tired, if I let my eyes shut, I couldn't pry them open before Spring comes."

"Mmm."

"It's good to be back." She sighed, a long contented exhalation. "Even better to have money again, hot running water and a bed to sleep in."

"Then the Marn's Hoard was . . ."

"Hidden where the Marn left it. Zdraaaa, Hes, so much to do."

She had to put down the rebellion of the outland Pans, reclaim Zemyadel, the Bezhval and Halland in the Travasherrims, reestablish the rule of law everywhere, and feed her people in the winter that was coming down on them. It should have appalled her, but she found the prospect challenging. She leaned back against Heslin. "I won't be bored."

Heslin chuckled, rubbed his fingers gently on the

back of her neck. After a moment, he said, "Give me a real job."

"I mean to do that. The Pans won't like it. Tough. They're going to have to swallow more than you, love. I thought about making you chief Judge, you'd be better than any of them at that, but I changed my mind. It might get you shot and even if that didn't happen, it'd make bad feelings where I can't afford them. I want you to run the schools. I think the Mijloc has a lot to teach us, and this is as good a time as any to make some changes." She reached up, touched his face. "If you're tempted to get a little too enthusiastic with your people's-rule thing, just remember that your daughter is Dedach and will be Marn. Don't mess with that, my love."

2

JEBOH'S PALACE, RAGYAL, BAGKLOUSS

When the sky clicked from black to blue again, the Jeboh fell down, drooling like a baby, all force and intelligence wiped from him. Rodoji stood looking down at him. "You failed. Whatever it was you were doing, you've failed." She muscled him onto the bed, tore a sheet into strips and bound him so he couldn't move, then forced a gag in his mouth. "Tsan pyya, it's our turn for a while."

She pulled on her robe, brushed her hair and inspected the paint on her mouth and eyes. When she was satisfied, she returned to the bed, lifted one of the Jeboh's eyelids. "Nobody home. Don't worry, Onky, my Mokan sisters and I, we'll run the country for you."

3

BOKIVADA, SHIMZELY

The House of Glory in Bokivada groaned in the darkness; the worshippers inside moaned with the House. Hibayal Bebek stood across the street, enjoying for the moment the pain and nausea passing in waves through his body. He wanted to go inside, but he couldn't deal with that many people; during the past months he'd resigned his place in the Scrivener's Guild, stopped going out of his house, sent his cleaning woman away when she came, spent much of the day soaking in his bathtub, scrubbing at his skin until he rubbed himself raw.

The sky went blue.

The House collapsed in billows of dust and a horrible groan, stone falling from stone, the gilded roof dropping in.

Hibayal Bebek coughed as the dust hit his face. He was alone, suddenly, completely alone, the last touches of the Glory pulled away. As other Bokivadders came running and started tugging at the stones, trying to clear them away so they could get at those trapped beneath them, he walked quietly away.

When he reached his house, he took a bath, then hanged himself in the stairwell.

As Chaya Willish Isaddo-na stood in her garden looking up at the suddenly blue sky, she heard the noise of the collapsing House of Glory, though she didn't know what it was. She listened to the shouts of the wall guards a moment, then started to go inside.

"Chaya."

She swung round. Halisan was standing under the tree, the harpcase slung on her back. It was a shock seeing the Harper; it meant she and Lavan would have to move. "Halisan," she said. "It's over?"

"As much as anything is ever over." She came from under the tree, held out a sheet of parchment rolled into a cylinder.

Chaya took it. The roll felt warm in her hand, as if it'd been left a long time in the sun. She spread it out; it was the deed to the house, complete with all seals and signatures.

"I put it in your name, Chaya, recorded the change with the Scrivener's Guild." She eased the strap, re-settled the harp. "If you need me for anything, look to the Forest."

Chaya stared as the Harper's form went transparent, then vanished. She looked down at the deed, looked at the house, squinted up at the sun. Things might be falling apart around her, but life was going to go on pretty much as it had before. Two or three hours of daylight left and the garden needed work. She went inside to get her tools.

4

BISERICA

When the sky went blue again, the Nine Shawar began a whirling dance that ended with the nine divided into three and three and three.

They turned to face Nischal Tay.

As one, they said, "The Dance is complete. The Maiden is more than Maiden. Changes must be made."

"What do you mean?"

Shawar One said, "We must go apart and consider."

Shawar Four said, "We will Listen."

Shawar Seven said, "The One is Three In One. We will Write what we have Heard and bring these New Things forth."

Sansilly watched the veiled women leave the court. When they were alone, she turned to Nischal Tay. "Does this mean it's over?"

Nischal Tay looked at the sky, then at her hands. She tried a smile. It wasn't a completely successful effort. "Serroi seems to have done it again. I hope she finds some other place to light this time." She puffed her cheeks, expelled the mouthful of air. "Ei vai, I will go see if I can get a com call through to the Marn, or failing her, to Tuku Kul. Then we'll have some concrete facts to plan with."

Greygen tightened his grip on Sansilly's shoulder; she glanced at him, nodded. "Our sons, Nischal Tay. Could you ask about them? And if your people will be coming home, do you think they could bring Mel and Noddy with them?"

"I'll see."

5

WHICH IS THE END.

There was a moment of blackness.

When the blackness receded Serroi looked round.

She was on a mountainside somewhere, with blue-green conifers growing in a tight mass round a meadow with a spring in one corner that sang serenity back at the humming trees. Beside the spring was a small building, its stone walls crumbling, its tile roof broken and half fallen in. Above the door was a crude carving of a woman's face.

Treshteny came through the door, nodded at her. "Healer," she said.

"Where are we?"

"Cadander. If you follow the path through the trees and look south, you'll see the roof of the Marn's Tower."

"And this place?"

Treshteny's smile widened. "I have my manyness back," she said.

"If that's what you want, I'm happy for you."

"Oh yes. As to what this is." She smoothed her hand along the wall. "The stones showed me their history. This was once a Maiden Shrine, but when the Keeper died, folks forgot about it. And this last year it was a place where the Glory danced. But that's done, too. You're going to make a new Biserica, Serroi Healer, did you know that? I saw it and I chose it so now it has to be."

Serroi raised her brows. "Ei vai, I think that's for me to say. And the Marn."

Treshteny smiled her vague smile, reached inside the door and brought out a metal cup. "Come and drink, Serroi. The water's cold and tasty."

Serroi went out into the late afternoon and sat with her face to the sun, drinking in strength from the light and heat. Despite Treshteny's certainty, she did not believe all the timeseer told her. It didn't matter anyway. She was content to wait and let what was to be discover itself.